D1200339

Frances Burney

Literary Lives
General Editor: **Richard Dutton**, Professor of English, Lancaster University

This series offers stimulating accounts of the literary careers of the most admired and influential English-language authors. Volumes follow the outline of the writers' working lives, not in the spirit of traditional biography, but aiming to trace the professional, publishing and social contexts which shaped their writing.

Literary Lives
Series Standing Order ISBN 0–333–71486–5
(*outside North America only*)

You can receive future titles in this series as they are published by placing a standing order. Please contact your bookseller or, in case of difficulty, write to us at the address below with your name and address, the title of the series and the ISBN quoted above.

Customer Services Department, Macmillan Distribution Ltd, Houndmills, Basingstoke, Hampshire RG21 6XS, England

Frances Burney

A Literary Life

Janice Farrar Thaddeus

First published in Great Britain 2000 by
MACMILLAN PRESS LTD
Houndmills, Basingstoke, Hampshire RG21 6XS and London
Companies and representatives throughout the world

A catalogue record for this book is available from the British Library.

ISBN 0–333–60763–5 hardcover
ISBN 0–333–60764–3 paperback

First published in the United States of America 2000 by
ST. MARTIN'S PRESS, INC.,
Scholarly and Reference Division,
175 Fifth Avenue, New York, N.Y. 10010

ISBN 0–312–22981–X

Library of Congress Cataloging-in-Publication Data
Thaddeus, Janice Farrar, 1933–
Frances Burney : a literary life / Janice Farrar Thaddeus.
p.   cm. — (Literary lives)
Includes bibliographical references and index.
ISBN 0–312–22981–X
1. Burney, Fanny, 1752–1840.   2. Authors, English—18th century—Biography.
3. Great Britain—Court and courtiers—Biography.   4. Women and literature–
–England—History—18th century.   I. Title.   II. Literary lives (New York, N.Y.)

PR3316.A4 Z795   1999
823'.6.—dc21
                                                          99–047320

This book is printed on paper suitable for recycling and made from fully managed and sustained
forest sources.

10   9   8   7   6   5   4   3   2   1
09   08   07   06   05   04   03   02   01   00

Printed and bound in Great Britain by
Antony Rowe Ltd, Chippenham, Wiltshire

For Jan Fergus

Contents

Acknowledgements

I began reading Frances Burney in the early 1980s, and this literary life is the culmination of nearly twenty years' acquaintance with her many-sided work. It is also in countless ways a collaboration with other eighteenth-century scholars who generously shared their energy and their knowledge. I can list only a few of them here; some others I have mentioned in the notes, and still others will find their influence throughout these pages. Thank you, all of you, my colleagues and students at Barnard College and Harvard University, and especially the Board of Tutors at History and Literature, who have led me over the years to books I would never otherwise have read and ideas I would never otherwise have discovered.

With Mary Nash, Beth Kowaleski-Wallace, Ruth Perry, and Susan Staves, I read *Camilla* and *The Woman-Hater*, profiting enormously from our warm discussions. When I started working on this literary life, various editions of Burney's work were just about to appear, and their editors freely shared photocopies of their unpublished transcriptions and editorial commentary. Peter Sabor sent Burney's plays on disk; Lars Troide, general editor of the magnificent edition-in-progress of Burney's early diaries, allowed me to see Betty Rizzo's typescript of Volume Four; and Lorna Clark sent me a huge package containing her edition of Sarah Harriet Burney's letters. Sabor's and Clark's editions are now published, so that I have been able to go back and reread their work in its final form, but my book would have progressed much more slowly if they had not been willing to share it sooner. Other colleagues read the entire manuscript in various stages: Patricia Brückmann goaded me on, Betty Rizzo convinced me I was finished, and Peter Sabor read the final draft with superbly intelligent meticulousness. Their gusto kept me going, and their extensive knowledge saved me from many swamps. For help at critical moments along the way, I also wish to thank Doris Alexander, Barbara Darby, Melinda Gray, Anne Fernald, Antonia Forster, Robert Maccubbin, Mitzi Myers, and R.J. Stangherlin. Florian Stuber, even when ill, always inspired me onwards. In the early stages, Naoka Carey was all-too-briefly my research assistant, and Sarah Pershouse was an heroic proofreader. With Joyce Antler and Kathleen Weiler I taught a course in life-writing at the Radcliffe Graduate Consortium in Women's Studies, and their work and our students' work in multiple ways became enmeshed with my own. Balliol College awarded me a sabbatical visitorship, which gave me the opportunity to discuss this literary life with Roger Lonsdale, who was inveterately amused that the person I called 'Burney' was not the person he called 'Burney'. Mary Nash at innumerable lunches discussed Burney's relationship with Hester Lynch Thrale Piozzi, sharing all her research and reveling in our disagreements.

I must thank the staffs of the libraries where I have worked for their speed in retrieving boxes of manuscripts and books, and their cheerful patience: the Berg Collection of English and American Literature, the New York Public Library, the Astor, Lenox and Tilden Foundations; the Bibliothèque Nationale; the Bodleian; the British Library Manuscript Room, the Houghton Library at Harvard University, the Huntington Library, the Morgan Library, and the Beinecke Library Osborn Collection at Yale University. Richard Dutton, General Editor for Literary Lives, tactfully overlooked my many broken deadlines, kept me from including a multitude of extra facts, and when at last I sent the manuscript read it with speed and precision. Charmian Hearne, the publisher, has always cheerfully helped with the multitudinous details.

I owe much to my family: Eva Thaddeus for reading pieces of the manuscript and bringing to my attention certain important passages in *The Wanderer*; Michael Thaddeus for buying me copies of books about Burney whenever he saw them, and for his constant detailed questioning; and Patrick Thaddeus who like M. d'Arblay is 'passionately fond of literature', for living through it all with me and dragging me often to the tennis court. Most of all I must thank Jan Fergus, to whom I have dedicated this book. She set me to it, kept me at it, and read more versions than I can count. She has been, as Burney said of her sister Susanna, 'soul of my soul'.

List of Abbreviations

Berg MS   The Berg Collection of English and American Literature, the New York Public Library, Astor, Lenox and Tilden Foundations.

Camilla   Frances Burney, *Camilla, or, A Picture of Youth* (1796), ed. Edward A. Bloom and Lillian D. Bloom. Oxford: Oxford University Press, 1983.

CB*Letters*   *The Letters of Dr Charles Burney*, 1:1751–1784, ed. Alvaro Ribeiro, SJ. Oxford: Clarendon Press, 1991.

Cecilia   Frances Burney, *Cecilia, or Memoirs of an Heiress*, ed. Peter Sabor and Margaret Anne Doody, with an introduction by Margaret Anne Doody. Oxford: Oxford University Press, 1988.

DL   *Diary and Letters of Madame d'Arblay (1778–1840)*, 1842–6, ed. Charlotte Barrett, with preface and notes by Austin Dobson, 6 vols, London: Macmillan, 1904–5.

Doody   Margaret Anne Doody, *Frances Burney: The Life in the Works*. New Brunswick: Rutgers University Press, 1988.

ED   *The Early Diary of Frances Burney, 1768–1778*, ed. Annie Raine Ellis, 2 vols, London: G. Bell and Sons, 1889, rpt. Freeport, N.Y.: Books for Libraries Press, 1971.

Egerton MS   Egerton Manuscripts, British Library, London (formerly the Barrett Collection).

EJL   *The Early Journals and Letters of Fanny Burney*, eds Lars E. Troide *et al*. Kingston and Montreal: McGill-Queen's University Press, 1988.

Evelina   Frances Burney, *Evelina: or, the History of a Young Lady's Entrance into the World* (1778), ed. Edward A. Bloom with the assistance of Lillian D. Bloom. Oxford: Oxford University Press, 1968 (1982).

Hemlow   Joyce Hemlow, *The History of Fanny Burney*. Oxford: Clarendon Press, 1958.

JL   *The Journals and Letters of Fanny Burney (Madame d'Arblay)*, ed. Joyce Hemlow *et al*. 12 vols, Oxford: Clarendon Press, 1972–84.

Lonsdale Roger Lonsdale, *Dr Charles Burney: A Literary Biography*. 1965. Oxford: Clarendon Press, 1986.

Memoirs *Memoirs of Doctor Burney, arranged from his own manuscripts, from family papers, and from personal recollections*, 3 vols, 'by his daughter', Madame d'Arblay. London: Edward Moxon, 1832.

Plays *The Complete Plays of Frances Burney*, 2 vols, ed. Peter Sabor, contributing eds Stewart Cooke and Geoffrey Sill. Montreal and Kingston: McGill–Queen's, 1995.

Thraliana *The Diary of Mrs. Hester Lynch Thrale (Later Mrs Piozzi) 1776–1809*, ed. Katharine C. Balderston, 2nd edn, 2 vols, (continuously paginated). Oxford: Clarendon Press, 1951.

Wanderer Frances Burney, *The Wanderer; or, Female Difficulties*, eds Margaret Anne Doody, Robert L. Mack, and Peter Sabor, with an introduction by Margaret Anne Doody. Oxford: Oxford University Press, 1991.

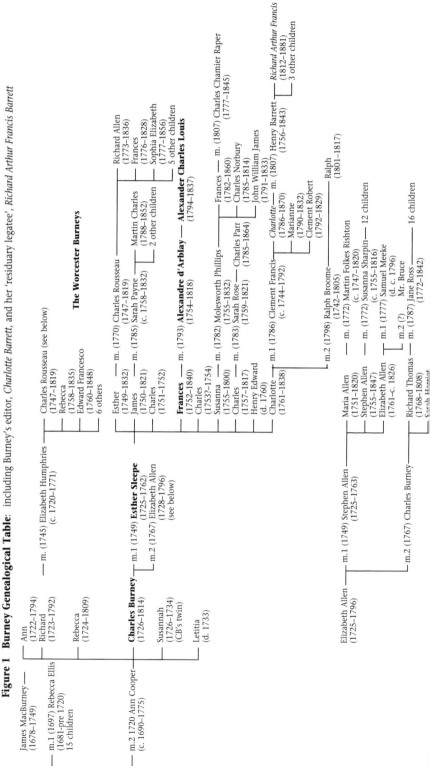

Figure 1 Burney Genealogical Table: including Burney's editor, *Charlotte Barrett*, and her 'residuary legatee', *Richard Arthur Francis Barrett*

1
Writing as Compulsion and the Redefined Audience (1752–78)

> The instances innumerable that rushed upon my memory of the happy effects of courage, & the disastrous ones of timidity, impelled me to resist my affright, & to summon sufficient presence of mind to meet the Eyes of my Antagonist with a look that shewed surprize rather than apprehension at his wrath.
>
> Frances Burney, 1812[1]

A writer's courage: the body and the medley

In August 1812, Frances Burney, Madame d'Arblay,[2] experienced a writer's nightmare. A police officer at Dunkirk nearly confiscated the manuscript of the first three volumes of her novel *The Wanderer, or Female Difficulties*. Burney had been waiting in Dunkirk to return to England with her 17-year-old son Alexander, leaving behind in Paris her husband of 19 years, General Alexandre d'Arblay, who was working at the Ministry of the Interior. They had lived for ten years in post-revolutionary, war-torn France. She was attempting this illegal crossing primarily because she and her husband feared that their son, who in four months would be 18, might be conscripted into the French army. The fiction they had concocted to obtain passports and yet cover this defection was that mother and son were both setting out for a visit to America.[3] Since all correspondence abroad was proscribed, Burney had left behind in her husband's care the manuscript of her current writing project, her fourth novel. The delay, however, seemed endless, and she was frustrated at not being able to work. So she asked d'Arblay to forward the manuscript, and to procure

1

special permission to take it with her if she ever managed to sail. This he had done, accomplishing his task, she says, 'with as much delicacy of care as if every page had been a Bank note' (*JL* 6:716), using every jot of his considerable influence to obtain the permission. What is remarkable in Burney's account is how firmly and calmly she was able to handle a situation which would have driven many writers mad.

Burney's ability to maintain taciturnity appears even more note-worthy when we consider the first sentence of the *Wanderer*:

> During the dire reign of the terrific Robespierre, and in the dead of night, braving the cold, the darkness and the damps of December, some English passengers, in a small vessel, were preparing to glide silently from the coast of France, when a voice of keen distress resounded from the shore, imploring, in the French language, pity and admission.

Burney could assume, of course, that the police officer knew no English, but surely the word Robespierre might have provoked him. Considering the situation, her ability to remain calm was truly remarkable. When she wrote up the incident approximately 13 years later, she gleefully turned the police officer into a personified tantrum:

> When the little portmanteau was produced, & found to be filled with Manuscripts, the police officer who opened it, began a rant of indignation and amazement, at a sight so unexpected & prohib-ited, that made him incapable to enquire, or to hear the meaning of such a freight. He sputtered at the Mouth, & stamped with his feet, so forcibly & vociferously, that no endeavours I could use could palliate the supposed offence sufficiently to induce him to stop his accusations of traiterous designs, till tired of the attempt, I ceased both explanation and entreaty, & stood before him with calm taciturnity.
> (*JL* 6:716)

He seems to mislay his mental capacities. He cannot even 'enquire' or 'hear the meaning'. He loses control of his mouth and his feet. He is a creature unmanned, weak as a woman, a termagant, a body without a mind. Burney renders this nightmare as farce. Though she is a woman, she is primarily a professional writer, controlling a man, a professional officer, both in life and in the text.

In her further development of the story, she emphasizes her own professional accomplishments. It is because she is Frances Burney,

Madame d'Arblay, a writer distinguished and known, that she is allowed unrestrainedly to take out of this chaos a portmanteau full of manuscript pages. She surmises that if Napoleon had been in Paris and not away on his ill-fated Russian campaign, he would never have allowed it. Unmentioned in the account is that under her clothes her body clamps with pain from her recent mastectomy. Reminding the reader of this bodily deficiency is not part of the current action. Instead, Burney tumbles the ranting officer out of his professional status by reinforcing her own, both in the original incident and in the act of writing. She is aware that eighteenth-century conduct-books uniformly instructed women to subordinate themselves. When absolutely necessary she follows their advice, but she is not simply a conduct-book woman.[4] She neither blushes nor compromises in this public space, though eventually she asks a fellow passenger to vouch for her – which he successfully does. *The Wanderer*, book and woman, travel undisturbed to England. The woman is secure in her public position as author, and able to laugh about it.

I begin with this incident, because I wish to stress at the start that Frances Burney at the age of 60 was – at least in some predicaments, and especially in her professional capacity as writer – very strong and confident. Faced with the destruction of years of work, she knew how to handle the situation. This point must be made – and made firmly – because Burney has so often been depicted as self-deprecating, even fearful.[5] Beginning in 1904, with Austin Dobson's edition of the Diaries, Burney was seen chiefly as being genteel, as charming Fanny.[6] Her diaries recorded interesting details about her class and her craft. Published soon after her death, and re-published in various editions and truncations, they stayed in print. Her four published novels were viewed as comedies of manners, 'portraying social correctness and social eccentricities', as Harvard professor George Sherburn put it in 1948.[7] *Evelina* was usually available; the other novels were not. Gradually, the diaries and letters gathered fuller and fuller attention. When Joyce Hemlow's biography (1958) showed clearly that the earlier editions of the diaries and letters were drastically incomplete, Oxford University Press published both Hemlow's biography and – in the fullness of time – her 12-volume edition of the journals and letters. Hemlow dedicated her biography to George Sherburn; he had discussed the draft with her, and her view of her subject was similar to Sherburn's. Their Burney was brilliant, especially as a novelist of manners. Her career as a writer of novels effectively ended after *Evelina* and *Cecilia*; *Camilla* and *The Wanderer* were essentially conduct books – dull, and badly written. Hemlow judges Burney against the realist tradition, and against that tradition Burney suffers. Sherburn notes the slightness of her plots, and if plot is considered all-important, Burney's strengths unfairly diminish. Still, Sherburn admired Burney enough to encourage Hemlow to undertake her mammoth project, and Hemlow inspired others to the gigantic labor of restoring Burney's words.

Hemlow's edition begins in 1791, just after Burney's 39th birthday, the year she finally escaped from service at Court. She did not choose this date because it was significant in Burney's life, but chiefly because it was at this point that Henry Colburn, publisher of Burney's niece Charlotte Barrett's edition of the letters and memoirs, suddenly began to bridle at the project's unconscionable length. It had already reached five volumes. As a result of Colburn's financial resistance, Barrett squashed two-thirds of Burney's life into her final two volumes, with only two pages apiece for her last 20 years. Barrett's 772 pages were to increase six-fold in Hemlow's edition. Slowly and meticulously she and her associates sifted through and reassembled the manuscripts Barrett had cut apart and pasted. The last volume of Hemlow's edition appeared in 1984, 26 years after she finished her biography.

Since then, Burney's career has rapidly gained critical attention. Feminist scholarship has helped. In the 1970s there was only one feminist voice in Burney's camp. Rose Marie Cutting discussed the fact that in each of Burney's novels there is a 'defiant' woman. The plot does not always support her; the heroine may be disgusted by her; but she is there, vivid and riveting. Cutting also wrote an appreciation of Burney's last novel, *The Wanderer*, which every other critic had definitively pronounced a failure.[8] Although Cutting was a lone voice in the 1970s, a chorus of others joined her in the next decade. Burney criticism rapidly moved through three stages.

The first stage portrayed a writer similar to the conduct-book woman in Sherburn and Hemlow, except that these critics took her more seriously as a woman and as a woman writer, and that they added – and stressed – the element of fear. One particularly vivid generalizing statement of Burney's has become part of the current critical literature. When her husband was dying in 1818, Burney thought perhaps she should allow him extreme unction. He was in name a Catholic, and might desire the ceremony – but she was not sure. In this situation she wrote, 'the Fear of doing Wrong has been always the leading principle of my internal guidance' (*JL* 10:878). Burney's niece Charlotte Barrett first focused on this remark as an epitomizing statement in the summation that ends her edition of the *Diaries and Letters*, using it to set duty against the claims of imagination, and to argue that Burney 'employed the best means with which she was acquainted for bringing her feelings into accordance with her judgment'.[9] Among current critics, Patricia Meyer Spacks first pointed out and stressed this statement, applying it both to Burney's autobiographical writings and to her novels, exposing the 'dynamics of fear'. In Spacks the statement takes on many nuances. It enables her to discuss *The Wanderer* seriously, and to show that 'Much more successfully than her female contemporaries, she found ways to manipulate and use her own psychic experience, not simply to avoid it through wishful fantasy or ethical didacticism.'[10]

The second stage portrays a double Burney, and emphasizes the violence that underlies the controlled surface. The fear is not gone, but it is not only the 'Fear of doing Wrong'. It is a fear responding to outside forces that compel fear, and it often functions as a sub-text. Julia Epstein is one of the best critics in this tradition. She defines Burney as having 'a narrative strategy based on indirection and displacement and derived from repressed rage and repressed desire ... In the four published novels, rage and desire are transformed into rhetorical manipulation, madness, carnival: the volcanic spillage produced when female desire is yoked to the service of social propriety.' Kristina Straub depicts a Burney similarly divided, who nonetheless 'unflinchingly expresses the ideological tensions inherent in the lives of eighteenth-century middle-class women – and the strain of writing them into consciousness'.[11]

The third stage in Burney criticism emphasizes her many-sidedness, her wildness, the striking range and rage, as well as the doubleness, the repressed underside. Margaret Anne Doody's biography *Frances Burney: The Life in the Works* (1988) is the chief representative of this view. Doody argues that Burney 'is not content with illustrating comic individual aberration from the norm; she sees in her characters the grotesque and macabre symptoms of society's own perverseness, and of the wildness in the human psyche that leads to the creation of such strange structures as society itself'.[12] Following this vein, Claudia Johnson places Burney – and her contemporaries in the 1790s – in the Revolutionary, Burkean political tradition where emotional excess is the most characteristic expression.[13] Barbara Zonitch attributes Burney's 'powerfully contradictory ambivalence' to the upheaval accompanying the social and economic changes that occurred during her writing life. In her view, Burney uses the form of the novel of manners to imagine 'alternative social forms to replace the ones that were steadily disappearing, most of all the aristocratic patriarchal family and community'.[14] This third-stage Burney in no way denies the other two, but simply encompasses them.

The task now is to bring to Burney's literary life all three Burneys: the one who fears to do wrong, the one who represses her rage, and the one who unleashes her rage. We must accept and attempt to understand the many-headed writer we have at last been able to see. I have stressed Burney's courage when she liberated her manuscript of *The Wanderer* from a meddling official, her confidence in her professional strength. But I do not mean to deny that fearfulness – and much else – was also an essential part of her complex nature as a writer. To illustrate the complexity of that nature, and hence the intricacy and multifariousness of the texts it produced, I will consider next a second incident at Dunkirk. As a kind of companion-piece to the near-loss of her manuscript, Burney told how she narrowly escaped arrest. Even 13 years later, the memory still made her shudder. The way Burney presents the companion-piece reveals more fully the spectrum of temperament that characterized her as a writer in the early 1800s. She tells us that she was unable to work on the newly arrived manuscript of *The Wanderer*. The situation was simply too tense.

To amuse themselves, she and her son Alex had walked the docks, and as they did so they could not help noticing some Spanish prisoners at forced labor. Her near-sighted eyes would not reveal what kind of labor. Surreptitiously, practicing the benevolence that was proper for women of her class and period, she dropped money near them during their rest breaks. Waiting for passage, staring hungrily at the sea, she found solace in those prisoners, impressed by their 'fine dark Eyes, full of meaning' (*JL* 6:718), by their strength and their taciturnity. Their apparent leader, in dignified gratitude for her attention, gives her 'a slight, but expressive Bow' (6:719). The idyll abruptly came to an end, however, when she was caught in the act of fraternizing with these enemies of France.

She was standing alone on the Quay one sultry evening, unmoving, she says, 'as I saw only Men, & did not ambition to be remarked as a Female Wanderer' (6:719). The Spanish prisoners suddenly appeared, unguarded for once, and joyously 'flocked around though not near'(6:720). For the first time she had the 'courage' to talk to them, though of necessity in a bastard mixture of English and French. As often in France, where she knew the language but did not feel eloquent in it, Burney depends here chiefly on a kind of wordless communication that seems to speak volumes. Suddenly the prisoners' leader looked up, startled, and Burney turned to see, standing just behind her, a heavily gold-braided officer of police. Ever ready to assume a mask, she quickly feigned nonchalance:

> To be aware, however, of the peril I had incurred, imbued me instantly with resolution to seek to ward off the threatening blow & the instances innumerable that rushed upon my memory of the happy effects of courage, & the disastrous ones of timidity, impelled me to resist my affright, & to summon sufficient presence of mind to meet the Eyes of my Antagonist with a look that shewed surprize rather than apprehension at his wrath. (6:721)

But this hastily gathered courage was difficult to maintain. The 'tyger' officer insisted that she follow him (6:723). She was afraid of being arrested, of leaving her son alone and unprotected, 'prey to nameless mischiefs', and she found herself in mental chaos, unable to follow, standing in 'motionless & speechless dismay' (6:723). The silence that served her earlier in communicating with the prisoners, now in a more fraught situation becomes a fearful barrier.

This officer is even more farcical than his predecessor. He batters her with questions, and then becomes so enraged as to be unintelligible. His uniform is exaggerated, replete with 'gold trappings', '& his head covered, & half a yard beyond it, with an enormous Gold Laced cocked Hat' (6:721). When Burney realizes that she should follow the officer with a confident air and 'apparent indifference', she manages to speak, and says just the right things. She refers to Alex, just returned from posting one of the daily letters his mother had written to his father, mentions influential friends, and offers the key of her 'Portmanteaux & portfolio', in case she had 'excited any suspicion by merely speaking, from curiosity, to the Spanish Prisoners'. The officer demurs, and lets her go. She tells us how she feels and acts: 'Speechless was my joy, & speechless was the surprise of Alexander, & we walked Home in utter silence.' (6:725) In this case, Burney herself is not taciturn, as she had been a few days earlier when *The Wanderer* was nearly confiscated. The prisoners are taciturn. By contrast she stands briefly in 'motionless & speechless dismay'.

The various and intersecting themes of this passage had been – and would remain – both implicit and explicit throughout her life and work. These Spanish workers are simultaneously superiors, equals, and inferiors. They become Burney's artistic invention. Though she romanticizes the Spanish workers, she also sympathizes. She feels for these actual human beings real compassion, and sauces her compassion with a small monetary contribution to relieve their distress. Communication is often wordless, with speechlessness characterizing friendship, joy, and fear alike. The body, a body controlled to display both genuine and invented information, takes the place of speech. Above all, Burney recreates this corporal experience in words, in extensive detail. She revives the speechlessness, reincarnating it in language carefully set down for herself, for her family, and for posterity. The moods are not set into opposition, as they so often are in eighteenth-century texts. Courage is the primary emotion, but the courage is a mask, covering real apprehension. It jostles with a number of other emotional traits – fellow-feeling, humor (the officer's costume is ludicrous, and he is a tiger), national loyalty, risk, menace, motherhood, homesickness, loneliness, mental exhaustion – and possibly the 'Fear of doing Wrong'. Only hard-won aplomb has enabled her to endure this situation.

I have chosen these incidents to open my account of Frances Burney's literary life, because they illustrate the characteristics of what I call the protean Burney, always shifting from one body to another. Burney always tries to render the body, to imagine it fully. She talks about how characters look, what they wear, how they hold themselves, how they speak through gesture, what masks they assume, and how they change under duress. In addition, she gives us a whole spectrum of different kinds of speech. In her fiction and her diaries we find multiple voices.[15] In all novels – and diaries, for that matter – these competing discourses are more important than plot. But in Burney's novels they are especially so. In Burney, the overarching plot is always girl meets boy, girl eventually gets boy, but in *Evelina* and increasingly in the other three novels, the plot is part of a much larger plan. This whole grand scheme also includes all the other characters and incidents, the assorted people seen and heard along the way. Burney always creates a hub, a strong center, but her greatest power and interest is her talent, her compulsion, to reach out in every direction.

From the start, Burney always tried to be original. She plainly stated this objective in the preface to *Evelina* and reiterated it in letters to advisers and friends throughout her career. Originality is inevitably hard on readers, and Burney's critics have struggled with her variousness. She achieved this uniqueness mainly by changing within the text the shape of her genre, her language, her theme, her mood, and her characters. When she is not fashioning a wheel, she creates a medley. Forty-five years after Burney began her 1768 journal, she wrote across the top that it was a 'strange medley'. The word medley carried two chief connotations in the eighteenth century: a fight and a heterogeneous mixture. Burney's comment on her early journal seems puzzled, not altogether satisfied. But the medley was certainly one of her modes. She tried to include in her writing a variety of incongruous elements, always ultimately controlling them. To borrow and adapt Johnson's phrase on the Metaphysical poets, she yoked the heterogeneous by violence together. I am emphasizing here that Burney's desire to use the body and the voice dates back to the age of 15, but I do not mean to say that she did not change, only that her capaciousness, both early and late, was enormous, a fact that only her contemporaries and some of her most recent critics have noticed and begun to face. Feminist studies, together with the re-examining of the canon, first revived interest in Burney, and in the last decade that interest has increased exponentially.[16]

The writing habit

Some writers choose their profession. Others are chosen by it. From the age of ten, Frances Burney's writing had been a habit, demanding and irresistible. Her need to write, perhaps even greater than the similar compulsion felt by nearly every other member of the Burney family, may have something to do with the fact that she was somewhat backward as a child. She began to talk and read much later than normal. But once she began to talk, she talked inventively. When she saw a play at the age of eight, her father noted, she 'would take the actors off, and compose speeches for their characters; for she could not read them' (*Memoirs* 2:168). Nonetheless, she tells us that two years later she suddenly 'began scribbling, almost incessantly, little works of invention; but always in private; and in scrawling characters, illegible, save to herself.' (*Memoirs* 2:123)

This compulsion to get things down on paper must have been intensified by the fact that Burney's dying mother had enjoined her elder daughter Esther to write letters to her after her death. Burney's mother had never worried about Burney's apparent slowness; evidently she had noticed how observant her daughter was. After her mother's death, Burney was afraid that her incessant writing would make her appear ridiculous. The Burney household had a talent for emphasizing the ridiculous. Burney's older brother James, who according to his father 'in his boyhood had a natural genius for hoaxing, used to pretend to teach her to read; and gave her a book topsy-turvy, which he said she never found out!' (*Memoirs* 2:168). Her father's friends called her 'The Old Lady' (*Memoirs* 2:168). Though often diffident with strangers, she could be strong when the occasion demanded. Once, when she and her sisters were playing with the daughters of the wig-merchant next door, they all donned wigs and were prancing around in them. Cavorting wildly, they managed to drop one of the wigs into a tub of water in the garden. When Burney was 56 years old and away in France, her father wrote up this story. The ten-year-old he evoked said to the fulminating wig-maker: 'What signifies talking so much about an accident? The wig is wet, to be sure; and the wig was a good wig, to be sure; but its [sic] of no use to speak of it any more; because what's done can't be undone.' (*Memoirs* 2:171) This kind of stoicism is quite central to her character. And it seems counter to the diffidence so many observers have stressed.

Similarly, her first grand literary gesture, though private, was as self-approving as it was self-denying. On her 15th birthday, shortly after her father married the loud and to Burney's mind rather vulgar Elizabeth Allen (a woman Burney grew to hate) she burned all her writings, including 'Elegies, Odes, Plays, Songs, Stories, Farces, – nay, Tragedies and Epic Poems' (*Memoirs* 2:124). But the sequel to the novel she had burned, the *History of Caroline Evelyn*, continued to develop in her imagination. Caroline's daughter, Evelina, was 'suspended between the elegant connexions of her mother, and the vulgar ones of her grandmother' (*Memoirs* 2:125–6; an analogue of herself and Elizabeth Allen?). Before Burney had written a word, she claims, she knew by heart the novel that was to become *Evelina*.

Between the manuscript-burning incident and the writing of *Evelina*, Burney had started a journal, one of the few genres she failed to mention in her account of the destroyed hoard. She would keep this journal, whenever she had enough time for it, for the remainder of her life. Frances Burney's later comment on the opening pages of the journal points out the important issues here. 'This strange medley of Thoughts & Facts was written at the age of 15. for my Genuine & most private amusement', an explanation that creeps in ungrammatically after the period. Besides the generic question of the 'medley' the journal functions as the author's 'private amusement'.

Journal-writing raised in Burney's mind the important question of audience, her distinct ambivalence about writing for the public, for any public. Only her sister Susanna was the wholly trustworthy reader; a kind of second self, uncritical though inspiring. But there was no need to write to Susanna. She lived in the same house and they talked constantly. Hence, she had to find another audience – or set of audiences – for her journal. Who? Where? The 15-year-old Burney tells her journal that she wants to write because she wants to keep a record of her life, to be able to read about it in old age, 'when the Hour arrives in which time is more nimble than memory'. The first purpose of the journal is to write to her older self. But she also needs to create a closer figure: 'I must imagion [sic] myself to be talking – talking to the most intimate of friends – to one in whom I should take delight in confiding, & remorse in concealment' – and she decides to call this figure 'Nobody'. Nobody will be an idealizing mirror. Though bodiless, Nobody paradoxically will have a body, a 'Breast' that contains emotions. Nobody will somehow respond and will be delightfully uncritical: 'In your Breast my errors may create pity without exciting contempt; may raise your compassion, without eradicating your love.' The audience she invents she calls 'Nobody', because Nobody will be like Susanna. And yet Nobody will also be no one at all, only herself in the mirror. What happens here, as Burney continues to write, is that the language begins to feed on itself, and the game of words takes on that 'medley' of meanings which the 15-year-old Burney eventually calls 'preambulation'.

Hence, even in this early work, even at the age of 15, Burney's writing becomes diverse, as the discussion of Nobody begins to play over a field as wide as the world: 'my dear, what were this world good for, *were* Nobody a female?' In the medley, the preambulation, Burney has mentioned that Nobody may be the most 'romantick' [sic] and 'tender' character – more so than any real person – 'in as much as imagionation [sic] often exceeds reality.' She then turns to the words that forcibly strike all readers of this piece. Females are Nobody. The world has created this class of people who have no power, who barely exist, and yet who are ineradicably necessary.[17]

After the preambulation, what did Burney say to Nobody during April and May of 1768? What words followed? At some point their author was embarrassed by them and cut them away.[18] They are gone. Nobody is reading them now.

Family and cultural change

Frances Burney lived to be 87, so that her journal beginning with Nobody spans intermittently 72 years. She was born during the reign of George II on 13 June 1752 at King's Lynn, Norfolk, and died five years after Victoria's inauguration, on 6 January 1840. Her life experience simply engulfed that of Jane Austen, who was born 23 years later and died 23 years earlier, and encompassed Sir Walter Scott, nearly 20 years her junior, who died just before she published the *Memoirs*. She lived through revolutions – political, cultural, commercial, and literary. The American Revolution occurred two years before the publication of her first novel and, by marrying an emigré, she experienced the French Revolution with unusual closeness. During her lifetime Great Britain consolidated its empire in India. She was present at the trial of Warren Hastings. When she was born it was possible for people in mixed groups to read aloud in public the racy works of Aphra Behn. By the time she died, this was not only impossible, but shocking.[19] She was at the center of what has been called 'the birth of consumer society'. This drastic change – though many are now emphasizing that it was an evolution rather than a revolution – was persistent and vivid. Some of Burney's most caustic portraits are of acquisitive fops, and some of her saddest ones are of over-spending women.[20] The hilarities and snares of consumerism, the increased availability of personal credit, and the uncertainties of currency are central predicaments in her novels.[21] Money is a necessity and a curse.

The literary profession also changed drastically, especially for women. Burney first began to write in 1762, at the age of ten, and though she burned and excised, she never stopped. In this era, many women wrote merely for their own amusement. They hesitated to publish for fear that they would seem intellectually too forward. Women as capable with words as Burney's friend Mary Delany (1700–88), whose memoirs filled six volumes when published in the nineteenth century, might circulate some of their manuscripts, but never considered publishing them. Delany even hesitated to let George Ballard dedicate to her the second part of his *Memoirs of Several Ladies of Great Britain* (1752), saying, 'I rather wish for shade and shelter than to be exposed *to day's garish eye*'.[22] In the second half of the century, women's attitudes toward publication altered dramatically. According to statistics gathered by Judith Phillips Stanton, the number of women writing in the eighteenth century increased 'around 50 percent *every decade* starting in the 1760s'.[23] Although writing was ill-paid, it was better paid than much of the other work available for middle-class women, such as companion, schoolteacher, or seamstress. Writing was also a comparatively dignified profession, easily practiced in odd hours at home. In 1802, Charlotte Smith, who had supported her large family by what she called her 'literary business', never thought of the term as an oxymoron.[24] Burney was somewhat unusual, if not exceptional, in her ambition to write in every genre of imaginative literature. The manuscripts she burned at the age of 15 included experiments in all sorts of poetry (elegies, odes, epics, songs), drama (plays, tragedies, farces), and fiction (stories and a novel). Stanton has shown that only 54 per cent of the women who wrote novels also wrote in another imaginative form.[25] It is notable that except for journal-writing, Burney chose to avoid non-fiction, possibly because this was her father's bailiwick. She published her one work of non-fiction after her father's death.

The Burney family was a powerful force in Frances Burney's writing life. All families affect children, of course, but the Burney family was more cohesive than most. Whether or not it is true that the ideals of what Lawrence Stone has called 'affective individualism', and the 'companionate marriage' gained strength during the second half of the eighteenth century, the Burney family maintained the kind of close communication and support that characterizes this sort of emotional relationship.[26] Samuel Johnson professed to love all the Burneys he knew, 'and love them because they love each other'.[27] Frances was the fourth of nine children born to her mother Esther Sleepe, three of whom died in infancy. Her surviving three sisters and two brothers grew to adulthood, but to her dismay she outlived them all. Her father's father had been a quite well educated – but feckless – dancer and actor. After his first impecunious wife died and he had married a wealthier woman, his two sons from his first marriage were sent away to a town four miles from the family home in Shrewsbury to be raised by a woman they called 'Nurse Ball'. Although it was not uncommon for eighteenth-century children to be sent off and raised elsewhere, there were usually stronger ostensible reasons than seem apparent here. Dr Burney's biographer Roger Lonsdale finds in this seeming banishment the chief source for Charles Burney's 'desire to compel affection and admiration which would compensate for the inevitable insecurity of his childhood'.[28] His compulsion to inspire affection was in some portions of his life an asset. By his charm he gained access to the homes where he taught music, and by his charm he allured influential people to his house for musical soirées. Money was difficult to come by, and Burney's father descended to activities that later embarrassed his daughter. He worked in a school, for instance, and seems to have owned a coffee house.[29] At the age of 43, however, he took the decisive step of obtaining a doctorate in music from Oxford, which Lonsdale characterizes as 'his last bid for fame, no longer as a "mere musician", but as a scholar and a man of letters'.[30] He is best known today as the writer of a widely researched and highly respected *General History of Music*, published in four volumes from 1776–89, much of which his daughter transcribed for publication. Dr Burney carefully wrote a memoir, including his childhood as well as his adult professional life, but his daughter destroyed most of it, a complicated action I will consider in its place. The important point here is that Dr Burney wrote, and that the act of writing was the central activity in his life, as it was in the life of his daughter Frances.

All of the Burney children were creative people. Esther, known as Hetty (1749–1832), whose mother had wanted her to write to her after death, was an unusual Burney in that she did not become an author, but she was musical, and as a young girl had been one of her father's most able pupils on the harpsichord, often playing in public. Burney's older brother, James (1750–1821), who teased her as a child, chose a career that would suit his high spirits. He accompanied Captain Cook, eventually gaining the rank of Rear-Admiral, and besides his *Essay on Whist*, he published five volumes of *A Chronological History of the Discoveries in the South Sea or Pacific Ocean* (1803–17), followed by histories of other voyages, including the American buccaneers. He contained his wildness only with difficulty, and in 1798 confounded the Burney clan by abandoning his family and setting up a household with Burney's half sister Sarah Harriet, only to return after five years to respectability if not contentment. Her younger brother Charles (1757–1817), who also suffered from untamable spirits, amplified by heavy drinking, was expelled from Cambridge for stealing books, but eventually reclaimed himself. Vicar, LLD, FRS, he founded and ran his own school at Greenwich, became Chaplain to His Majesty George III, and in splendid moral reparation for his earlier peccadillo amassed such a distinguished classical library and British theater collection that when he died intestate the British Museum bought it. Although he wrote mainly scholarly treatises and sermons, his letters reveal irrepressible high spirits, with a style so lively and an imagination so exuberant that he frequently inspired his sister to reply in kind. Burney's younger sister Susanna (1755–1800) was her favorite, such a close companion that they felt edgeless together. The picture of Susanna by her cousin Edward Francesco Burney emphasizes her lively eyes, and she certainly kept her eyes open. Susanna never published any of her writings, but she wrote incessantly, exchanging journals with Burney, upholding her sister's spirits in times of duress. After ten years of an initially happy marriage to Molesworth Phillips, famous for his false claim that he killed Captain Cook's murderer on 14 February 1779 in the Sandwich Islands, her husband's 'wrong-headed & tyrannical spirit' eventually manifested itself.[31] The man who lied about the Cook expedition was counterfeit in other ways. Phillips removed his wife and children to his debt-ridden estate in Ireland, where he separated her from her son, was habitually unfaithful, and freely indulged his 'tyrannical spirit'. Gradually in this plight losing her health, suffering from what may have been tuberculosis compounded by dysentery, Susanna wasted away and died in 1800, shortly after she arrived in England for a visit. Burney never recovered from the bitterness of this loss. Her youngest sister Charlotte (1761–1838) was also an indefatigable and gifted journal-writer, and it was her daughter Charlotte Barrett who became the first editor of her grandmother's journals and letters. She published her edition in 1842–46, as soon as possible after Burney's death.

Burney also had step-siblings and half-siblings. Her father's second wife Elizabeth Allen had five surviving children of her own, three with her first husband and two with Dr Burney. Maria Allen (1751–1820), almost the same age as Burney, felt very close to her acquired step-sister, and in her vivid, hasty style was to write Burney intimate letters about her fluctuating relationship with Martin Folkes Rishton, whom she had impetuously married in Ypres. She eventually discovered that he had carried on a 20-year liaison with her friend Dorothy Tayler (1751–1828). Yet he was also extremely jealous of his wife, and kept her under so tight a rein – allowing no visits and no friends – that she finally left him.[32] Stephen (1755–1847) and Elizabeth (1761–c.1826), called Bessy to distinguish her from her mother, are more vague in the accounts, though Stephen was the most loyal to his mother, requiring Burney to defend her harsh characterization of Elizabeth Allen Burney in the *Memoirs of Doctor Burney* (1832). Bess tarnished the family by eloping in France with a Mr Samuel Meeke, who was evidently evading his debts by living abroad. The marriage unquestionably humiliated her mother and she herself evidently regretted her action, since she was flagrantly unfaithful. Even Susanna's son, five-year-old Norbury Phillips, heard about her sexual escapades and compared her to the 'naughty' Helen of Troy (*JL* 3:4, n. 12). About Richard (1768–1808), first mutual child of Elizabeth Allen and Dr Burney, very little is known. For crimes that were successfully erased from the record, he was shipped off to India at the age of 19, never to return. Once there, he immediately married Jane Ross on her 15th birthday, which might seem unwise, but evidently was not a mistake. Ultimately Richard managed to become Head Master of the Orphan School of Kiddepore. Nonetheless, he was never forgiven by his parents, though Dr Burney did write to him (*JL* 1:203, n. 50). He was possibly an important model for the character of the ungovernable Lionel Tyrold in *Camilla*. The youngest child in the Burney family was James's companion Sarah Harriet (1772–1844), who with Stephen was the only sibling to outlive Frances. Sarah always had a direct, earthy style, such 'fearless open-ness' that Burney often burned her letters (*JL* 1:xxxviii, n. 3), concerned that other people would misunderstand them – or possibly understand them too well. Sarah confronted her unmarried poverty with persistent resilience, making do in the plucky way the Burney upbringing taught all the children but the Allens. Always scrabbling for funds, Sarah Harriet eventually wrote and published fiction, including *Clarentine* (1796), *Geraldine Fauconberg* (1808), *Traits of Nature* (1812), and a number of other collections of shorter works, geared to the nineteenth-century readers' growing desire for brevity that Burney always ignored. Burney in her will left Sarah Harriet a much-needed lifetime annuity of £200.

When Frances Burney was born in King's Lynn, her father was the church organist. When she was seven, they moved to Poland Street in London, so that her musician father could take advantage of the greater opportunities in the city. It was three years later, when Burney was just 11, that her mother died. Her gentle presence must have been a solace to the child their friend Arthur Young teasingly called 'feeling Fanny' (*EJL* 1:6).[33] But her mother had left behind the thought that her children could write to her. The injunction was to Burney's older sister Esther, but it included all her children:

> She told poor Hetty how sweet it would be if she could see her constantly from whence she was going, and begged she would invariably suppose that that would be the case ... she exhorted her to remember how much her example might influence the poor younger ones; and bid her write little letters, and fancies, to her in the other world, to say how they all went on; adding, that she felt as if she should surely know something of them.[34]

Esther wrote less than the other Burneys, but for all the Burneys the act of writing to one another, and possibly to the world at large, was the most insistent human calling.

In her old age Frances Burney recalled not only that she was back-ward, but that she was the 'most backward' of all the children, although it is quite clear that she compensated for this backwardness by learning to listen.[35] Anyone who reads her novels notices that they are written by someone with an uncanny ability to hear and record the swarming individualities of human speech. In an important article on Burney, Dr Kathryn Kris has argued that her early inability to read is related to her strong sense of shame, and her dislike of public display.[36] The sense of shame, which was culturally supported in eighteenth-century women, may have been particularly potent in Burney's early life, and it is this characteristic which has struck those who see as a central theme the 'Fear of doing Wrong'. When Dr Burney insisted on reading to others a poem she wrote when she was 17, or when someone started discussing *Evelina* without knowing she was the author, her nervousness was so uncontrollable that she would run out of the room. On the other hand, her curiosity so effectively would counteract the nervousness that she would stop just within hearing. It seems as if she would then remember every word said. Potent, competing emotions always characterized her. Perhaps she never did lose the sense of shame. Perhaps it was shame that unnerved her in her encounters with the police officers in Dunkirk, while they stamped and preened in the glory of their office. But shame was always only one of a crowd of emotions. Taciturnity may have come only with age, but curiosity and a pervasive consciousness of the grotesque always jostled with the sense of shame, just as Burney's 'Fear of doing Wrong' coexisted with her confidence in her ability to choose among the multiple possibilities that are never exactly right.

2
Publishing Anonymously: the Early Diaries and the Intricacies of the Mask (1773–79)

'I have an exceedingly odd *sensation*, when I consider that it is in the power of *any* & *every* body to read what I so carefully hoarded even from my best Friends, till this last month or two, – & that a Work which was so lately Lodged, in all privacy, in my Bureau, may now be seen by every Butcher & Baker, Cobler & Tinker, throughout the 3 kingdoms, for the small tribute of 3 pence'

Frances Burney (*EJL* 3:5)

In late December of 1776 Frances Burney and her sisters Susanna, Charlotte, and Esther, 'muffled up' her nineteen-year-old brother Charles, disguising him in 'an old great coat, and a large old hat'. In this outlandish rig they sent him off under the alias of Mr King to the Orange Coffee House in the Haymarket. In keeping with a Burney family habit of interleaving play-acting with life, the disguised Charles was delivering the initial volume of *Evelina*. The anonymous author wanted it left for consideration by the bookseller Thomas Lowndes. After a failed attempt to secure the interest of the more illustrious Robert Dodsley, who disdained to deal with an anonymous author, Lowndes was by 'chance' chosen.[1] Burney selected Christmas day to deliver her first inquiring letter. As part of the impersonation scheme, she wrote in an assumed hand, an ugly, uneven, backward-twisted hand. She had drafted at least two versions of the letter, revising it to make it more businesslike. Lowndes replied the same day, writing with a dull pen so fast that he neglected his spelling and punctuation: 'Sir: Ive not the least objection to what you propose & if you favour me with sight of your Ms I'll lay aside other Business to read it & tell you my thoughts of it and at 2 Presses I can soon make

18

it appeare in print for now is the time fore a Novel yr Obedt Servt'.[2] Burney drew back from this precipitous suggestion. She wanted to publish her novel in sections, to test the public, as Richardson had done with *Clarissa*. Besides, she had not finished. Lowndes did not deal in such complications. For the moment, novels published in segments had gone out of style. Lowndes seems immediately to have recognized the quality of the novel that had so mysteriously arrived in his office. But before he would make his final decision, he insisted that Burney finish.

The character of the 24-year-old who wrote *Evelina* was unusual. She was certainly an authoritative writer, the adult who had been the forceful child her father and his friends had dubbed the 'Old Lady', the child who had so decisively put an end to 'the wig is wet' episode. But this was not the whole story. She was also an odd assortment of reticence with a dash of the rowdy. Her sister Susanna described her at 16 as embodying a seemingly incompatible mixture. This included 'sense, sensibility, and bashfulness, and even a degree of prudery'. Burney was confident, even boisterous, with friends and relatives, but in the company of strangers the bashfulness often predominated.[3] Her husband was later to say that she spoke too quietly, and that people mistook the gentleness of her voice for arrogance. But Burney was never quiet with her intimates. A woman she met in France in 1806 remembered: '*you* were so merry, so gay, so droll, & had such imagination in making plays; always something new, some thing of your own contrivance –' (*JL* 6:778). One description more than any other evokes her high spirits. Her friend Samuel Crisp described that at the age of 15: 'You Used to dance Nancy Dawson on the Grass plot, with your Cap on the Ground, & your long hair streaming down your Back, one shoe off, & throwing about your head like a mad thing' (*EJL* 3:238). Letting her long hair stream and throwing off a shoe were not uncharacteristic. One of the most appealing portraits of Burney by her cousin Edward Francesco shows her seated on a bench reading, with her hair escaping its pins, and her naked left foot resting comfortably next to its clog.[4]

Luckily, the year when the seven-year-old Frances Burney moved to Poland Street in London was the height of Dawson's brief career. Burney evidently went to see Dawson perform her hornpipe as one of the 'doxies' in the thieves' dance at the end of Gay's *Beggar's Opera*. Dawson's was the third dance in Gay's flamboyant ballad play. Earlier in the act, the prisoners in *The Beggar's Opera* literally cavorted in their chains. Dawson, by contrast, was unfettered and wild. Three years later, Burney's father was consolidating his success as a music-master, but her mother Esther had died, and Nancy Dawson had retired. The impressionable Burney, however, continued to imitate Dawson, evoking the memorable description from Crisp. Dawson's famous hornpipe, set to a complicated version of 'Here We Go Round the Mulberry Bush', was sexy as well as wild. One contemporary ballad praised 'Her easy mien, her shape so neat', and another stressed 'How easily she trips the stage! / Her heaving breasts all eyes engage / ... O charming Nancy Dawson'.[5] Crisp's description of Burney as Nancy Dawson evokes wildness and energy, but leaves out the center of her body, the sensuality Dawson evidently aroused, a voluptuousness Burney herself must have felt as she danced. In a letter later annotated as 'rapturous, & most innocent happiness during anonymous success', she says that she *'tipt'* Crisp with *'such a touch of the Heroicks*, as he has not seen since the Time when I was so much celebrated for *Dancing Nancy Dawson'*. She 'absolutely longed' to grab his wig and throw it out the window, but knowing that she was associated with a wig caper already, she decided she had better not (*EJL* 3:34).

Although *Evelina* was Burney's first novel, it was not her first sustained effort. Her journal to Nobody had become an extended piece of prose, a way of memorializing her family. With her always handy self-mockery she wrote: 'But for my Pen, all the Adventures of this Noble family might sink to oblivion!' (*EJL* 2:4). The family thus rescued was extensive, including as it did not only the original Burney children, but their stepmother and her progeny.

Also part of the family was the friend Samuel Crisp who described Burney's wild dancing. Crisp was a long-standing bachelor friend of Dr Burney whose career as a playwright had foundered so irrevocably that he retired to a pleasant rooming-house in Surrey. Burney called him 'Daddy', but his true role was an eccentric version of a surrogate mother. He was willing, for instance, to join the children in despising their stepmother, even in her presence. To their delight, the septua-genarian Crisp cavorted behind Elizabeth Allen Burney's back, *'taking her* off! – putting his hands behind him, & kicking his heels about!'[6] For this volatile creature, Burney wrote letters similar to those that her dying mother had requested of Charlotte. More than most children, Burney needed a replacement for her mother. The caretaker who briefly watched over the children when Esther Burney died told Frances in 1775 'that of the Hundred Children she had had the Care of, she never saw such affliction in one before – that you would take no Comfort – & was almost killed with Crying' (*EJL* 2:104).

This bereft child immediately attached herself to Crisp, so intensely that her father called him her '*Flame*' (*EJL* 1:8). Crisp responded with encouragement, mentor-love, and advice. He was not very busy, and he was flattered that this sensible, intelligent child loved him so exclusively. His life centered on hers to a much greater degree than Dr Burney's did. Because he lived in Surrey, she needed to keep in touch with him by writing, and besides her letters began to write a 'journal' to him. He inspired her with his pure delight in her descriptions, and by sending what seemed to be 'incomparably clever' letters in return.[7] Burney rarely wrote about her mother, but the grief remained. She chose to end her 1775 journal with the caretaker's vignette of the 11-year-old child who 'would take no Comfort'.

Unlike Burney's stepmother, Crisp fostered her desire to be an author, and helped ease the transition from private to public writing by sharing with friends the journals she sent him (*EJL* 2:64–5). She was hesitant to give permission for this larger audience, worrying not so much that her own personality would become public property, as that her descriptions of other people might hurt them. For instance, she did not want people reading about Maria Rishton's marriage, her husband's varied humors, her embarrassing habit of sitting on his lap. Indeed, she later crossed out much of the Rishton material.

Contemporary and modern readers of Burney's 1773 Teignmouth journal feel a complicated satisfaction, varied moods in response to diverse material. This is a Burney medley, satiric and diverse. The ubiquitous harassing suitors are here, suitably skewered, one pretending to shelter her from the wind, another claiming that he writes 'Burney' on his heart. Burney mocks the diversions of her class: wrestling, cricket, sailing, watching a soaped-pig race. Mrs Hurrel, whose husband owns a 'pretty' but inadequate boat, 'is an obliging, civil, tiresome Woman'. Burney turns more serious over the fact that Dr John Hawkesworth suffers, is actually ill, because the reviewers of his book on travel have denounced him for his huge copyright fee of £6000. 'It is a terrible alternative, that an Author must either *starve*, & be esteemed, or be vilified, & get money.'[8] She describes the people she encounters with increasing suppleness, and often with particular attention to the body as well as the voice. When she first meets Samuel Johnson at a Thursday morning party at her father's on 20 March 1777, her description of his ungainly body is the most clear-eyed one we have:

He is, indeed, very ill-favored, – he is tall & stout, but stoops terribly, – he is almost bent double. His mouth is almost constantly opening and shutting, as if he was chewing; – he has a strange method of frequently twirling his Fingers, & twisting his Hands; – his Body is in continual agitation, *see sawing* up & down; his Feet are never a moment quiet, – &, in short, his whole person is in perpetual motion.

He was so near-sighted that he 'poured over' the books in the Burney library, 'almost brushing the Backs of them, with his Eye lashes, as he read their Titles'.[9] As we can see here, her judgments on their many visitors are unsparing. At times she can barely quell her violent laughter at their expense.[10] Quite possibly, she was also harshly evaluating the Burney family, but we cannot truly know this, since she later cuts away page after page. For instance, she does not erase the fact that while they were visiting Crisp in 1774, her father made her sleep 'without undressing' in his room for a week to monitor his needs under an attack of rheumatism. She 'began to look so Wretchedly haggard, that all the good folks here grew uneasy for me' (*EJL* 2:47). But all the surrounding materials are gone. Because of all this editing, we feel that we must agree when Garrick says to her 'with a very comical Face' as he leaves one night: '"I like you! – I like you all! I like your looks! – I like your manner! – "' (*EJL* 1:312). The journals to Nobody and the journals sent to Crisp in their present state are sharp and satisfying, but we close the book with an uneasy sense that the medley is no longer complete.

The journals were part of the apprenticeship for *Evelina*, as were the family theatricals. After refusing at the age of 18 to play the 'quite shocking' part of Tag in Garrick's *Miss in her Teens* (1747), Burney nonetheless snatched for herself Miss Biddy Belair's greedy sigh, 'Heigh-Ho', sprinkling it liberally throughout her early journals (*EJL* 1:116, and *passim*). But in public Burney had always simply endured these efforts until 7 April 1777, when the assembled family members put on Arthur Murphy's *The Way to Keep Him*, with a lost extra scene Burney herself may have written. This was followed by a full-dress performance of Henry Fielding's farce *The Tragedy of Tragedies, or the Life and Death of Tom Thumb the Great*. It was in Fielding's piece, with her five-year-old niece playing her minuscule lover Tom Thumb, that Burney as the satirically tragic – and also gigantic – heroine Huncamunca was at last 'forsaken by the Horrors'. This time, she steeled herself with a glass of punch, whose presence the editorial hand of Madame d'Arblay later erased (*EJL* 2:248). In her burlesque tragedy dress, at the beginning of the second act, she wept to her attendant Cleora, 'Give me some Music! – see that it be sad!' While her cousin Rebecca as Cleora sang a rather jolly song, Burney relates, 'I put myself into all sort [sic] of affected attitudes of rapturous attention.' (249) At the time of this Huncamunca occasion, Burney was about to publish *Evelina*, and part of her joy in the public theatrical gesture came from the secret confidence of this accomplishment. Huncamunca, then, marks the moment when Burney first felt her own theatrical powers, experienced the delight of exaggeration, and acted out the tension between sorrow and joy.

Play-acting always had been a part of writing *Evelina*. From the beginning Burney had surrounded her writing with intricate pretense, working in 'odd moments' snatched from her daily labor of transcribing her father's notes on his Italian tour and his German tour, the research for his history of music (*EJL* 2:231). Afraid that a printer would recognize her handwriting, and perhaps also to demarcate the task of creation from that of copyist, she adopted the disguised hand. Although she told Dr Burney that she was up to something, he did not take her seriously. In one part of her mind, she did not take herself seriously. She was simply rounding out a dream. Certainly, money was not her primary concern. The letter Burney seems actually to have sent to Lowndes speaks of 'business', but her earlier draft refers only to the inevitable link between author and bookseller, as if publication were simply an act of osmosis. As might be expected, finishing the book was more difficult than beginning it, and when with intense '*fagging*' (*EJL* 2:232) she reached the end of the second volume, she was dismayed by Lowndes' assumption that she could toss off the third. Still, the duplicity continued. On 15 March 1777, while working on the third volume at Chessington, Burney tells Susanna that she has ostensibly written to her every evening, and 'The folks here often marvel at your ingratitude in sending me so few returns in kind.' (*EJL* 2:221) Enjoying the idea as well as the act of duplicity, she suggests to Susanna that if she is running out of paper, she should steal some, giving in Swift's best directions-to-servants manner a mock conduct-book defense: 'for stealing can never impeach your modesty, – & that, you know, is a female's first recommendation'.[11] For her part, she boasts that 'nobody suspects the brilliancy of the Company I occasionally keep'(*EJL* 2:220). Burney's sisters, her brother Charles, and later her cousin Edward Francesco were confidants, but they had not read the manuscript. Thus far, except for her aunts, who had helped her with her errata, she had written, corrected, and copied out *Evelina* 'having my own way in total secresy & silence to all the World'

(*EJL* 2:234–5). Secrecy and silence had always been her habit, but behind the mask there was a riot of voices.

By the time Burney did finish the third volume, nearly a year later, Lowndes was somewhat more lackadaisical about replying, and when he did accept the book, he offered a mere twenty guineas for the full three volumes. This sum actually was not low pay by Lowndes' practice, nor even by general practice.[12] Even so, Burney briefly complained, ineffectually protesting that she thought her novel was worth at the very least ten guineas per volume. A novice at negotiation, she gave Lowndes an easy out: 'if, however, you think it's [sic] value inadequate to this sum, I would by no means press an unreasonable Demand' (*EJL* 2:288). Quite probably Lowndes printed an edition of 500 copies. He charged 7s 6d, sewed.[13] This means that he would have grossed approximately £187. How much money did he make on this first edition? When in 1797 the publishers Hookham and Carpenter printed for subscription Emily Clark's two-volume *Ianthé*, the costs for paper, printing, corrections, and advertisements came to approximately £90.[14] A three-volume work would then have cost £135. If Lowndes bore similar expenses for *Evelina*, his profit on the first edition would have been approximately £32.[15] This would have increased to £52 for the second edition and twice that amount for the third. This is a considerable profit, though not as large as many Burney commentators have implied. Certainly Lowndes was being tight-fisted when he delayed sending Burney the few authors' copies she requested. The ten guineas he finally sent to Burney's father as additional copyright money for the third edition was certainly too little and too late. Burney never considered publishing with Lowndes again. However, it is important to note that through the third edition, at any rate, Lowndes probably had not yet made a profit of £250, which was the amount Burney and her father negotiated with Payne and Cadell for *Cecilia*. But that was far in the future.

Many eighteenth-century authors published anonymously, but few remained anonymous to their publishers. By insisting on doing this, Burney limited her options. Of the four ways an eighteenth-century author could publish – copyright, subscription, profit sharing, and commission – only the first was available to an author who wanted to remain strictly unknown.[16] In some ways copyright was the most debatable choice. Limited copyright had been available for only four years, and practice concerning it was far from fixed. Booksellers who published books generally kept their copyright offers low, for fear that they might lose money by overestimating the market. The other publication methods were safer for them. Later in her career, Burney would use her reputation as a successful author to negotiate with her publishers, and at that time she would drive a particularly hard bargain. However, she never tried commission, which her father had used for his Italian and German musical tours, and which could be the most lucrative method of publication. Eventually, she made the other, less hazardous, methods work for her. In 1776, attempting to publish her first novel, she saw herself primarily as an idealized immaterial genius, pure Author.[17] She allowed herself only a brief flurry over the price offered. The most important thing was to be printed, to be an author, to reach the public. She had not even seriously considered what it would be like to have readers. Beginning authors rarely do. Nor had she really thought through what it would be like to be a woman and an author.

At approximately the same time, Laetitia-Matilda Hawkins (1759–1835), a younger contemporary whose career closely paralleled Burney's in a number of ways, was also publishing her first novel. An analysis of their markedly similar adventures refines our understanding of the nuances of Burney's experience. Like Burney, Hawkins published anonymously and was rejected on this ground by her first-choice publisher. She needed to change from Cadell to Hookham and Carpenter. Like Burney's father, Sir John Hawkins was the author of a history of music (which appeared in the same year as Dr Burney's first volume), and like Burney, Hawkins worked at copying her father's manuscripts, snatching only a few odd hours for her own writing.[18]

Within this matrix of similarity, the differences are instructive. Hawkins feared that her handwriting would be recognized, but she never thought of adopting a disguised hand. She lacked Burney's desire to create her life as if it were a dramatic script. Nor did Hawkins romanticize the profession. At this point, she tells us, she was writing primarily for money, turning out what she viewed as a potboiler about experiences she barely understood. Hawkins' father, unlike Burney's, had married a fortune and was quite comfortably off, but instead of cementing his family's relationships, this money evidently increased their distance from one another. The son of a carpenter, Hawkins senior responded to his wealth by such penuriousness that he even irritated the other eight members of Johnson's club. For this and his general 'tendency to savageness' Johnson memorably dubbed him 'a most *unclubable* man', an apt, coined word that Burney enjoyed. We owe our knowledge of Johnson's opinion to Burney's 1778 journal (*EJL* 3:76). The Burneys themselves frequently claimed that Hawkins, in his position as magistrate, 'sent a man to prison for calling him a Codger'.[19] In the 'unclubable' intellectual atmosphere of the Hawkins household, where the children were not allowed to speak unless spoken to, money was always lacking, always desired. Hawkins says in her memoirs that she needed 'a sum of money for a whim of girlish patronage, and having no *honest* means of raising it, I wrote a down-right novel'.[20] Either Hawkins wished to deny her father's penuriousness by dispensing cash to someone else, or she was deluding her readers away from the assumption that she simply wanted money to line her own pocket. The ironies about the worth of writing are even stronger here than in Burney's self-descriptions, in part because Hawkins' father condemned novels much more severely than Burney's. Burney's father condescended, but he did not overtly repress. Dr Burney was sometimes distant, sometimes distracted, but no one would have called him 'unclubable'. He laughed when his daughter told him she planned to publish a work of fiction, but he did not forbid it. Hawkins' father may never have deliberately prevented his daughter from publishing, but the family atmosphere was such that Hawkins never showed her anonymous works to anyone, and published in her own right only after her father's death.

Anonymity meant Burney's publishing venture was theoretically safe. If the book were to fail, Burney could remain totally anonymous, as Hawkins did. Did she expect to fail?[21] Her view of herself as author is so tightly encased in self-deprecation and irony, together with the erasures of hindsight, that we cannot be sure. Perhaps she was not sure herself. She wrote to her friend Catherine Coussmaker that she thought Evelina's 'only admirers wd be among school girls, & destined her to no nobler habitation than a Circulating Library' (*EJL* 3:180–1). This remark must be set against her journal entry in March 1778:

> This Year was ushered in by a grand & most important Event, – for, at the latter end of January, the Literary World was favoured with the first publication of the ingenious, learned, & most profound Fanny Burney! – I doubt not but this memorable affair will, in future Times, mark the period whence chronologers will date the Zenith of the polite arts in this Island!   (*EJL* 3:1)

By calling herself 'Fanny' in this pronouncement, the author has maintained her family self even as she ironically describes her compli-mentary literary historians. Since it is clearly impossible that she can be seen as the best writer in the island's history, she links the child and the dream in such a way as to save face should the dream fail to materialize. In fact, perhaps in part because she was very ill, she began this journal only after she received her first review.

Undoubtedly, Burney had been combing the reviews ever since the publication of *Evelina*. She did not have to wait long for this first notice, by William Kenrick, which appeared in the *London Review* for February. It was disappointingly brief, but bracingly positive. *Evelina* was described as: 'The history of a young lady exposed to very critical situations. There is much more merit, as well respecting stile [sic], character and incident, than is usually to be met with among our modern novels.'[22] To a twentieth-century reader this may seem faint praise, but for an anonymous novel, this review was exceptionally supportive.[23] The *London Review* specialized in irony at the expense of authors, saying that they 'doomed to perpetual celibacy' or immediate marriage (whichever would be worse) the author of an inadequate book on marriage; judging the material in a published commonplace book as 'common-place stuff indeed!'; and quashing a novel called *The Mutabilitie of Human Life* by saying that though some readers might like this kind of amusement, 'we are not among those, however, who are so much "given to change"'.[24] Threatened by the possibility of put-downs like these, Burney must have felt relief and anticipation. She could hazard her own irony about reaching the 'Zenith of polite arts', only thinly veiling in her archness her hope that she would triumph, that she would be toasted and touted as a first-rate author. She caps her initial description of her family's readings of *Evelina* by copying Kenrick's review into her journal.

Living as Burney had in her father's house, always competing to be accepted by the best company, she was concerned about other matters beyond reviews, apprehensive at the thought that she had absolutely no control over who would now be able to read her.[25] While hovering in Bell's circulating library at 132 the Strand, listening to her cousin Edward inquiring about *Evelina* (the 'shop man' knew about the book, but it was out on circulation), she suddenly realized that 'it is in the power of *any* & *every* body to read what I so carefully hoarded even from my best Friends'. The book 'may now be seen by every Butcher & Baker, Cobbler & Tinker, throughout the 3 kingdoms, for the small tribute of 3 pence' (*EJL* 3:5). The people she squeamishly refers to as her three-penny readers – the butchers, bakers, cobblers, and tinkers – would have been almost exclusively male. One gets the distinct impression that Burney would prefer if she could to prevent the humble working-class men she names from reading her book. This distaste for humble men would erode somewhat as Burney grew older and wrote more. Her own experiences of powerlessness sensitized her to a greater sympathy with shopkeepers. She always carefully polished her own status, but her identification with the sufferings of women gradually in time alerted her to the inequities of class. Within *Evelina* itself, questions of class are more fully and sympathetically considered than this statement would seem to predict. Evelina is experiencing the shudders both of class and gender when she bursts out to the ever-kind Lord Orville, 'O my Lord ... it is from you alone that I meet with any respect – all others treat me with impertinence or contempt!' (p. 314)[26]

In 1778, however, the shock of publication was new, and – at least as regards her own social position as author – Burney's sheltered snobbery was largely intact. She saw herself as a mogul forced to accept 'tribute' (*EJL* 3:5) from everybody and anybody, and especially from lower-class men, a sudden translation into a world that – though theoretically desirable – was strange and unnerving. No author, writing a first book, can truly anticipate the difference between sitting alone assembling words on pieces of paper and entering a crowded room where every stranger in some sense can claim to know you. When the book is a success, the difference is drastic. And *Evelina* was a sensational success. At first Burney was able to control the situation. She conceived of the publication of *Evelina* as comedy, with secrecy and gradual discovery the central device. The plan worked very neatly for months, although it would finally spiral dizzyingly out of control. At the time of the book's publication on Thursday, 29 January 1778, no one knew about it but her confidants and her aunts Ann and Rebecca. In February, there was the review. In March, Edward bought a copy of the book and brought it home to Brompton with him, where his aunt began to read it aloud to the assembled company. At this juncture, Burney wrote in her diary, 'I was quite sick from my apprehensions.' This nervousness she allowed to stay in the record, but she later expunged her next thought: '& seriously regretted that I had ever entrusted any body with my secret' (*EJL* 3:5–6). She could erase the regret because the situation did in the end unfold as comedy, and all the ironies and chance encounters resolved themselves in the novel's success and the author's prestige.

The publicity would have been painful for most women born in the latter half of the eighteenth century, raised to be delicate and proper. For Burney, whose verbal development had been slow, whose family was exceptionally careful about public opinion, the evolution – even of comedy – was at times nothing short of excruciating. Hence she briefly regretted admitting to her authorship – and hence with hindsight she later erased this regret. Burney's cousin Betsy, Edward Francesco's sister, immediately guessed the author, an eventuality Burney called 'abominable!'. Burney sent her two letters, an *'angry denial, abusing the Book'*, and another, presumably owning up. Betsy had in any case promised silence. Hence, the drama and tease of anonymity could continue (*EJL* 3:17, 23). She herself read *Evelina* to her mother-figure, 'Daddy' Crisp, a choice she regretted. The task required that she combine a dramatic rendering with narrowly observing the response, always being careful not to reveal her authoritative views about the text. After finding that she could not dramatize her own text as well as she could a stranger's, and following this unsatisfactory course for the first two volumes, she pretended that her copy was suddenly unavailable, and eventually Esther read the last volume to Crisp, who was gratifyingly impatient to continue.

Dr Burney, the family member who most cared about what other people thought, read notices before he saw the actual book. When Susan tipped him off, he grabbed the *Monthly* and was so pleased at what he read there that he immediately asked Charlotte to copy both the *Monthly* and the *London* reviews for him and sent a servant to buy the book. He wept over the dedicatory poem, and then began to read the novel to Lady Mary Hales and Miss Catherine Coussmaker, relishing this complicated situation as his daughter had been unable to do when she read to Crisp. Seeing himself at the center of a drama appealed to him more than it did to Burney. At the scene where Evelina's long-lost father recognizes her, Dr Burney was so moved that he could not continue. 'I never read anything higher wrought than it is', he commented (*ED* 2:245). Like himself, Sir John Belmont loved an emotional scene, and Dr Burney's daughter had rendered the scene with a passion quite different from comparable moments in Fielding. The emotions surrounding fatherhood in *Evelina* were gratifying, although Belmont had by no stretch of the imagination been a decent father to his child. Dr Burney then read *Evelina* to his wife, privately behind closed doors morning and night, in bed. Charlotte and Susanna listened through the door and transmitted every comment, every laugh, to their sister. To Burney's surprise her father soon asked if he could, as she puts it in an unnervingly sexual way, 'break the seal' of her anonymity (*EJL* 3:52). Her response indicates that a large part of the anonymity was for her father's sake, perhaps to be sure that the family did not suffer any damage to its carefully wrought and precarious social position. She knew that his life was a continual struggle, both social and financial, and she sympathized with his plight.

In March of 1778, after Burney's sister Susan told her that Miss Coussmaker's reading was going well, she ventured to join the group, and while she listened to the reading and the comments it generated she could scarcely prevent herself from nodding her head monarchically and 'saying "*You are very good!*"' (*EJL* 3:6). Her flirtatious cousin Richard, whose persistent attentions to her she later discreetly erased from her journal, could not understand why Evelina was so confused when Lord Orville spoke to her, and Burney could barely refrain from explaining.[27] Richard admired Orville so much that they all 'fancied he meant to make him his *model*, as far as his situation would allow' (*EJL* 3:9).

Of all the people who early became interested in *Evelina* the one Burney cared about most was Hester Thrale – 'She, she is the Goddess of my Idolatry.'[28] Eleven years older than Burney, married in 1763 to a wealthy Southwark brewer, she was in public Burney's opposite: brilliant, talkative, and outgoing. Her faults she described to herself in 1788 as 'Confidence Loquacity & foolish Sensibility'.[29] Sensibility and confidence she shared with Burney, but her loquacity – and the foolishness of her sensibility – measured the difference between them. To the Thrales' elegant home at Streatham, about six miles north of London, Thrale began in the 1770s to gather the intellectuals of the day, especially Samuel Johnson. Dr Burney by his sheer affability had made himself a place in this society, and the Thrales hired him not only to give their daughter Queeney a weekly piano lesson, but also to stay for the evening and the night, for which he received £100 per annum (Lonsdale, p. 234). In 1778 Thrale had just bought a new harpsichord for Queeney and Dr Burney. The unsuspecting Thrale had actually recommended *Evelina* to the author's father, and when she found out the truth, generously invited Frances Burney to stay with her at Streatham, thus beginning one of Burney's most important and most uneven friendships.

Burney was so flattered and uplifted by Thrale's attentions that she seems not to have realized at what cost the woman whom she knew at Streatham maintained her gaiety. Thrale's husband had impregnated her often enough to produce 12 living children, of whom only four survived, but though she tried to secure his love, he was phlegmatic and philandering. Burney had noticed that he seemed unhappy. He was now mismanaging the brewery, and he was in love with Sophia Streatfeild, whose chief accomplishments were that she knew Greek, liked to make married men fall in love with her, and could weep on demand, a single tear if she wished. Thrale rejoiced that her bit of property was entailed. Her last line in her *Family Book*, in December 1778, promised the Lord Jesus that 'I will not fret about this Rival this S.S. no I won't' (Hyde, p. 218). As collateral she pleaded that she might never have to bury another child. Her wish was not granted, but she lost to death only one more of her offspring. Her youngest, Henrietta Sophia, died of whooping cough at the age of four while Thrale was in the throes of deciding whether or not to marry the children's singing teacher, Gabriel Piozzi.

In addition, though Thrale enjoyed and needed Burney's company, she was irritated by Burney's egregious need to be an equal. Burney's father was on salary, but she emphatically was not. This meant that Burney's definition of friendship was narrower than it would have been for someone with a more relaxed sense of class. Thrale could not ask her to do the simplest friendly errands, complaining that she 'dare not ask her to buy me a Ribbon, dare not desire her to touch the Bell, lest She should think herself injured' (*Thraliana*, p. 400). And, though Thrale certainly did admire *Evelina*, referred often to the characters in it, and knew many bits by heart, she originally noted that she thought it was 'flimzy' (*Thraliana*, p. 329). Given this fact, Burney's self-importance grated the more.[30] But the women were indispensable to one another. Though at this time Thrale prided herself on being immune to the twittering of romantic love, she was impulsively affectionate and emotionally deprived. Thrale had not yet managed to fill the void left by her mother's death three years before. She needed Burney, and Burney needed her. Burney's sisters provided the company of women, but there was no older woman, no one like Evelina's strong, middle-aged mentor, Mrs Selwyn. Burney thrived on advice that was less guarded than that she received from her daddies. The two women, always with reservations, cherished their friendship, and supported one another's ambitions as writers. In 1778–79 the new-minted author of *Evelina* flourished at the Thrales'. She left the safe precincts of anonymity behind her and precipitately became a famous author.

3

Evelina: the 'Male' Author and her Boisterous Book (1778–79)

'She was amazed that so delicate a Girl could write so *Boisterous* a book.'

Hester Thrale quoting Elizabeth Montagu

In 1778, Burney was basking in Thrale's support, and *Evelina* was gradually becoming one of the most important literary events of the season. *Evelina*'s success was extraordinary. It was certainly one of the most talked-about books of 1779, and it was steadily reprinted. Why did this simple story of an orphan girl, a seeming nobody who marries a lord, elevate its author so quickly and effectively? In what way did it differ from its fellows? Both contemporary and modern readers have assessed *Evelina* in a variety of ways, and those who insist that it is pure comedy of manners, a gem, simply deny the critics who see it as permeated with fear. This is not surprising, because the book successfully contains both interpretations – and many others. Although Elizabeth Montagu did not particularly like *Evelina*, she nonetheless remarked that 'She was amazed that so delicate a Girl could write so *Boisterous* a book.'[1] Boisterous is a strong word, which in the eighteenth century meant: rough, violent, tempestuous, with superabundant energy. The important thing is to allow all of these interpretations, to see that they are not mutually exclusive. Burney did not confine herself to one restricted genre. The book is many-faceted.[2]

Margaret R. Hunt has discussed the sources that lead to this kind of energy. She argues that historians must recognize the persistent tension and conflict between commerce, gender, and family relations. Writing about the 'middling sort' from 1680–1780, she concentrates on people Burney mainly satirizes in this novel, where the idealized characters are aristocratic or religious.[3] Yet when reading *Evelina*, we must recall that Burney's father gave music lessons and for fifteen years appears to have been 'proprietor of Gregg's Coffee House' (*EJL* 3:457–9). When we think of the Burneys, we remember first that the family mingled chiefly with people higher on the social scale, but Burney was acutely aware of that scale, in all its permutations and its more cruel distinctions. In *Evelina* comedy may be the mode, idealism and charity the template, but betrayal, suffering, callousness, and pain reside in the past and always lurk as a possibility in the present and the future. There are also many intermediate conditions, like boredom and pretense.

The superabundant energy is connected to Burney's recognition that the influx of new money has untied the social hierarchy, which now runs uninhibited in strange directions. To Burney we might apply the observations of Peter Stallybrass and Allon White, who emphasize in *The Politics and Poetics of Transgression* that there is a 'correlation of the mixing of genres with the subversion of social hierarchy'.[4] In her boisterousness, Burney was reinventing the novel, which by her lights was no longer what Fielding designated as a 'Comic Epic Poem in Prose', but rather what Burney called in her subtitle the 'history of a young lady's entrance into the world', a world that was financially heaving and insecurely moored. The result in Burney's case is what Catherine Gallagher has called a '"wild space," unmapped and unarticulated',[5] what one might call the comic narrative of satire and sensibility, though that definition is somewhat too bland as a description of the eruptions in this narrative.

With new money came a plethora of new things to be bought with the money. The influx was so rapid and so various that traditionalists of all stripes were disturbed. Swift's Gulliver remarked in 1726 to his Houyhnhnm master that the world had to be circumnavigated three times before an English female Yahoo could 'get her Breakfast, or a Cup to put it in'.[6] Even those who celebrated the benefits of capitalistic culture were at times taken aback. Adam Smith himself at the end of *The Wealth of Nations* (1776) voiced concern that people who bought 'baubles and trinkets' deceived themselves into the belief that they could purchase happiness.[7] Burney would have been reading reviews of Smith when she was writing *Evelina*. We certainly find acquisitiveness, vulgarity, and the transgression of class relationships. Dr Johnson recognized the derisive rendition of the new economic situation, and particularly liked the satiric portraits. Burney tells us: 'his greatest favourite is The Holborn Beau, as he calls Mr Smith. Such a fine varnish, he says, of low politeness! ... and, above all, such profound devotion to the ladies, – while openly declaring his distaste to matrimony! ... at last, he got into such high spirits, that he set about personating Mr Smith himself!' (*Memoirs* 2:155) Johnson sees the humor, but it is humor writ large, a wicked ironic portrait, where Burney and Johnson join in condescension toward the 'varnish' of 'low politeness'.

In her preface to *Evelina*, Burney immediately counteracts the reader's expectations for 'the fantastic regions of Romance' (p. 8). While not denying economic transgression, this novel centers on modern family life, showing this disrupted institution as a center of misused power. At the start of this epistolary novel, the author conveys Evelina's sad family history for three previous generations. Evelina's grandfather, raised decorously by a clergyman in Dorsetshire, transgressed the boundaries of class by marrying in a moment of folly a French 'waiting-girl at a tavern' (p. 13). She turned out to be vain, stupid, and manipulative. On his deathbed, Mr Evelyn left instructions that his infant daughter Caroline should not be raised by her mother, but by his own surrogate father the Reverend Arthur Villars. Burney here invokes the legal power by which fathers could take children away from their mothers. This power often lacerated capable and loving eighteenth-century women. In this case, Burney in no way questions the father's action or his right. His wife deserved to lose her child. Almost immediately, however, the parental right to coerce children comes into play and is questioned. This inadequate mother (now Mme Duval), is a strong patriarchal parent. When her daughter Caroline came of age, she insisted that she come to France, and attempted to force her to marry M. Duval's nephew. In desperation, this innocent and sweet young woman ran away with Sir John Belmont and married him without witnesses. Predictably, her patriarchal mother disowned her, and Sir John in a fury tore up the marriage certificate. The strain on Caroline, bereft of her legal proof of marriage, thus instantly reduced to whoredom, was untenable. 'Her sufferings were too acute for her tender frame' (p. 15), and she died in childbirth. She had fled to Villars, who now raises the third generation of Evelyns, Caroline's daughter, whom he calls by an anagrammatic twist Evelina Anville, a mixture – one might call it a marriage – of her mother's name and his own. Meanwhile, Sir John Belmont continues to defy legality and degrade the family by becoming involved in another sexual escapade which produces a bastard son, Mr Macartney. For most of the book, neither father nor son is aware of the relationship, because Belmont simply deserted Macartney's mother, and she was packed off to Scotland by her family, who were, Macartney judges, 'justly incensed' (p. 228). Adding the soupçon of incest that appeared so frequently in novels of the time, Burney allows Macartney to fall in love with the woman whom Sir John Belmont has been raising in the belief that she is Caroline Evelyn's daughter. If she were his daughter, it would certainly be illegal if not immoral for Macartney to marry her. Mme Duval asserts her own legal rights just at the moment when Evelina at the age of 17 becomes a marriageable property. Mme Duval wishes to reassert her grandmotherly rights not only to meet her granddaughter, but also to convey her to France and, by implication, to marry her to some wealthy and unworthy man. Evelina has gone to London for the first time, to visit friends, but she will also meet Mme Duval. At the start of this epistolary novel, the world that Evelina enters is full of menace.

The sense of pervasive danger persists, a near neighbor to Burney's interest in the immoral and the illegal. One of Evelina's bravest acts in this novel subtitled 'the history of a young lady's entrance into the world', is to prevent a stranger from committing suicide. He intended robbery, not suicide, but her kindness rescues him from this criminal intent. He turns out to be Mr Macartney, her half-brother. When Evelina at last meets her father, Burney abandons the legal for the ideal world, though she does not adequately reconcile them. Evelina is reunited with Sir John Belmont in a scene where Burney does not attenuate Evelina's sudden, passionate attachment, in spite of her father's past conduct. The reader carries this knowledge and applies it, since Villars has explicitly mentioned that she 'has reason to abhor' her father's character (p. 19). Presumably he had the decency to raise his daughter, though he unluckily allowed a servant to hoodwink him into believing that her child was his own. But this belated attempt at reparation is not enough to erase a word like 'abhor'.

As if the family were not destructive enough, Burney shows the rest of the world in some of its most fearful guises, especially in matters of sex. She uses the lens of a 17-year-old, as the world 'appears' to her.[8] Besides the threat of being carried off to France, Evelina is prey to marauding males, who think that her poverty and her retiring character are license for their sexual advances. The middle-class characters are confused. As William C. Dowling points out, Burney depicts in *Evelina* 'a new kind of social obtuseness brought into being along with a new world of urban mobility and fluid class distinctions' (p. 210).

The unpleasant Mr Smith, a silversmith who lodges with Evelina's cousin, thinks she would be lucky to get him as a husband – if he were the marrying kind. Sir Clement Willoughby believes his title precludes his marrying her, but he considers her fair game for a mistress, and harasses and deceives her cruelly. But since the mode is comic, Burney supplies for Evelina a gentle and understanding aristocrat, Lord Orville, who sees her worth and appears to respect her. Toward the end of the novel, when he asks her to marry him, Burney sees to it that he declares himself while he still believes Evelina to be a nameless orphan. As regards family, however, Burney finishes her novel ambiguously. Evelina recognizes her father ('wilt thou ... own for thy father the destroyer of thy mother?' he says, humiliated (p. 385)), and marries the man who has been caring for her as if he were her brother ('All is over', Evelina writes (p. 406)). But these men do not have the last word, for the just-married Evelina is hastening 'to the arms of the best of men', her mentor, Reverend Villars (p. 406).

From the beginning, readers tended to respond to the novel differently, depending on the part they most identified with. They reacted to the many shapes that characterized what I have designated as Burney's protean style. More than other novelists, Burney had been able to include in *Evelina* something for everyone – or at least for everyone who was a member of her own class. Certainly every Londoner could enjoy the descriptions of its shows and pleasure-gardens. Evelina visits or at least mentions the Opera House, Ranelagh, the Pantheon, Buckingham Palace, Kensington Gardens, Vauxhall, Marylebone gardens, Cox's Museum, Bedlam Hospital, Hampstead, Salter's Coffee House, Sadler's Wells, the Tower of London, the Monument, St Paul's, and the Little Theatre in the Haymarket, together with several more working-class gathering places. Nearly all the descriptions are laced with irony or ambiguity.

When writing *Evelina*, Burney always kept her audience in mind.[9] This audience was not only the schoolgirls she disingenuously mentioned to her friend Catherine Coussmaker, or the miscellaneous people who could borrow the novel for three-pence, but it included them. Evelina herself says that she cannot bring herself to write down Captain Mirvan's actual language, bowdlerizing it even for her mentor Reverend Villars.[10] This was a sensible reticence, and the reviewers took notice and approved. As the review in the *Gentleman's Magazine* put it, 'these volumes will afford a pleasing, innocent amusement'.[11] Like many other novels – and certainly more so than Smollett, Fielding, Sterne, or even Richardson – *Evelina* was decorous enough to be read by anyone, and especially by any woman. Gina Campbell has pointed out that Burney's dedication 'To the Authors of the Monthly and Critical Reviews', her hedge against fate, quite deliberately instructs them on how to respond to her work, requesting their 'annotations', and rather cringing at the last. She actually writes to her future critics that 'not to despise' *Evelina* 'may, alas! be out of your power' (p. 3). Campbell says that because of Burney's 'pact with the critics ... she agrees that in the expectation of being read by gentlemen, she writes like a lady'.[12]

By emphasizing Burney as daughter and female author, Campbell ignores the fact that Burney introduced *Evelina* in three ways, and that in all three the stance is masculine. First there is the poem to the author's father, the 'author of my being' (p. 1), and it is followed by the dedication to the reviewers, and finally the 'Preface'. The preface is written in so clearly a male tradition that readers not in the know uniformly attributed *Evelina* to a man. Yet Campbell is right that in her preface Burney is claiming to write like a lady. She has assumed a canny transvestism in order to control and extend her audience. Burney in her preface evoked the male novel-writing tradition, mentioning Johnson, Rousseau, Fielding, and Smollett at least partly to convince reviewers that the anonymous author was male. Though mentioning them, she also denied their influence, saying that they were 'barren', that they had left nothing for an imitator to cull (p. 9). Burney deliberately avoided mentioning any of the women writers whom, as we can see in her journals, she read and admired. Disingenuously, then, the transvestite author claimed no originality even as she asserted originality.

Burney is most directly professional in her dedication to reviewers. Reviews were a relatively new enterprise in this era. Some critics took their task very seriously. They feared that the wrong sort of book might actually corrupt its readers. The twentieth-century public assumes with at least half its mind that stories do not change people. How otherwise could we countenance the violent fictions that daily assail us? Eighteenth-century readers assumed otherwise. Didactic works were popular, because they were thought to be effective, and because human beings were seen as imperfect, but teachable. Hence, when the *Critical Review* in 1784 reviewed the anonymous *Dangerous Connections; or, Letters collected in a Society and published for the Instruction of other Societies*, by M.C **** De L***[13], the judgment of the reviewer was that though well written this book would gradually do nothing less than destroy its readers. The theory was that: 'An improper story, or the insinuations of a depraved heart, infuse a slow and secret poison, whose effects are more fatal as the approach is more delusive and secret. ... The author may allege, that the work which reveals these artifices, is the most essential instructor; but we fear, and indeed have much reason for our fears, that where one is guarded from the villany [sic], ten will more completely learn the mysteries of seduction.' (p. 473) There is poetic justice in the book under review, but that is not sufficient. The *Critical Review* wishes the author well, and yet simultaneously shudders at the effect of the work.

When the review of *Evelina* was published in the *Monthly Review* in April 1778, the brief notice mentioned no didactic purpose in the novel, but found it 'extremely interesting'. The review in the September *Critical Review* commended *Evelina* both 'in a moral' and 'literary light'. Here, *Evelina* is recommended as a book for the ideal family, an interestingly selective reading of this book that in so many ways subverts the family:

> This performance deserves no common praise, whether we consider it in a moral or literary light. It would have disgraced neither the head nor the heart of Richardson. – The father of a family, observing the knowledge of the world and the lessons of experience which it contains, will recommend it to his daughters; they will weep and (what is not so commonly the effect of novels) will laugh, and grow wiser, as they read; the experienced mother will derive pleasure and happiness from being present at its reading; even the sons of the family will forego the diversions of the town or the field to pursue the entertainment of Evelina's acquaintance, who will imperceptibly lead them, as well as their sisters, to improvement and to virtue.   (pp. 202–3)

What is worth noting here is that mothers evidently seem to be listening to the novel read aloud. The idea is that the family will join together for this amusement – and instruction – like the Burney cousins at Worcester. The book is praised for its subtlety, since it 'will imperceptibly' change the sons, just as it now seemed to be changing Richard Burney, who aspired to imitate Lord Orville. The daughters are more likely to weep, though evidently the *Critical* reviewer thinks that it is their laughter that will increase their wisdom. How, then could they become more virtuous? The *Critical* reviewer assumes that the answer is implicit in the book. There is a model for a man, but Burney makes clear that a woman needs more than laughter to grow wise.

The *Critical* addresses one more important issue. The review notes with approval the anonymous author's dedicatory poem to 'his' father, the 'author of my being'. 'To the well written performance now before us is prefixed this poetical and affectionate dedication', the *Critical* reviewer intones, quoting the poem in full, assuming that it is a dignified outpouring by a son to his parent. Burney's actual relationship to Dr Burney is one of the most important components of her literary life, and it needs to be kept in mind throughout this literary life. Margaret Doody sees the father–daughter relationship as central to Burney's life, and argues that in this dedicatory poem 'primary authorship, authority in all senses, is yielded to him' (p. 32), maintaining as well that 'Even as an adult she had to reiterate protestations of placatory humility' (Doody, p. 31). I would read Burney as being throughout her life much more ambivalent toward her father. He was certainly a father to notice and admire. Dr Burney's children were all smitten by his appealing gestures. He charmed them with his many stories, knew how to rouse their insecurities, and how to win them over by hugging them at charged moments. They admired and profited from the fact that Dr Burney was so deft at pleasing that he gained entrée into circles far above his own rank. Noting this, Thrale thought that 'if he has any Fault it is too much Obsequiousness' (*Thraliana*, p. 368). The reason Thrale did not dare to ask Burney to do her small favors was that Burney was particularly afraid of being obsequious. She also attached herself to many others besides her father, such as her sister Susanna, Samuel Crisp, and, of course, d'Arblay and their son Alexander. She liked to please Dr Burney, and she certainly loved him, but even as a young woman, she knew where her edges were. The habits of emotional dependence always vied with intellectual resistance. The situation was complicated by the fact that they were both writers, but they did write different sorts of books, and found security in their separate genres. Though Dr Burney was affable, he was also self-absorbed, with an emotional absence so great that he was to be destructively unaware of how inappropriate it was to convince his daughter Frances to accept a position at court. Burney's memory of her mother as inspirer was particularly vivid. Viewing herself as a lover of silence, a listener, a nobody with big ears, she remembered in old age as she wrote her own memories into the *Memoirs* of her father, her dead mother's 'encouraging accents' (*Memoirs* 2:124). But her mother was lost, and in her family only her father, who had unaccountably married a woman whose literary instincts were misdirected and crass, remained as muse.

One of the reasons that Dr Burney was so powerful as muse was Burney's employment as his amanuensis. For four years at least, she had been copying his manuscripts.[14] To copy someone else's prose is one of the most sure ways to begin to feel as if you are that person. If, page after page, you see in your own handwriting words you have copied and re-copied; if, like Frances Burney, you tend to retain what you have read, you cannot but recognize that your greatest influence is the book you have laboriously rendered plain. Not long before she wrote her own dedication, Burney would have copied from her father's draft: 'it may, with utmost truth be said, that it was composed in moments stolen from sleep, from reflection, and from an occupation which required all my attention, during more than twelve hours a day, for a great part of the year'.[15] Continuing, after this hedge against criticism, Dr Charles Burney stated his purpose: 'talking in common language of what has hitherto worn the face of gloom and mystery, and been too much "sicklied o'er with the pale cast of thought"' (1:19). In her own dedication archly and more specifically addressed to those powerful fellows, the *Monthly* and *Critical* reviewers, Burney calls her novel 'the trifling production of a few idle hours' (p. 3), asks for mercy, and like her father sweetens the prose with Shakespeare. In her case the quotation is from the *Merchant of Venice*, more germane than her father's rather far-fetched importation from *Hamlet*. Then, because Burney, though imbued with her father's prose and his mental habits, is also irrepressibly independent, she also quotes from Pope and Buckingham, putting herself even more squarely in the company of men, to add a moustache to her mask. She talks to the reviewers where they feel most: 'Remember, Gentlemen, you were all young writers once', as the writer is young (p. 4). They are now 'Magistrates' and 'Censors', (p. 3) people who dispense justice. But all of us need mercy, and all of us were young writers once.

Burney's story of *Evelina* bears no further clear resemblance to her father's work. The subject and the form do not allow imitation. But that act of being so close to her father's work, the fact that writing – and publishing – were so central to her father's aspirations and fears, must have felt unavoidable for her. Her pleasant father was so busy that the best kind of intimacy she could share with him was the hours of copying his words. During these hours, she was continuously reminded both that he was an author and that by fathering her he had authored her. Hence, one night at four in the morning, in a large and evidently hasty hand, she wrote the words that the *Critical Review* quoted and referred to as 'this poetical and affectionate dedication'. In *Evelina*, this poem appeared as follows:

> To – - – - – -
>
> O author of my being! – far more dear
>   To me than light, than nourishment, or rest,
> Hygieia's blessings, Rapture's burning tear,
>   Or the life blood that mantles in my breast!
>
> If in my heart the love of Virtue glows,
>   'Twas planted there by an unerring rule;
> From thy example the pure flame arose,
>   Thy life, my precept – thy good works, my school.
>
> Could my weak pow'rs thy num'rous virtues trace,
>   By filial love each fear should be repress'd;
> The blush of Incapacity I'd chace,
>   And stand, recorder of thy worth, confess'd:
>
> But since my niggard stars that gift refuse,
>   Concealment is the only boon I claim;
> Obscure be still the unsuccessful Muse,
>   Who cannot raise, but would not sink, your fame.
>
> Oh! of my life at once the source and joy!
>   If e'er thy eyes these feeble lines survey,
> Let not their folly their intent destroy;
>   Accept the tribute – but forget the lay.

In the first draft, one beginning referred only to 'Friend of my Soul, & Parent of my Heart', but in the same draft, in the phrase that stayed, Burney compared her father to the muse, to God: 'author of my being'. Generally, here, Burney maintains a position of weakness and self-abnegation – a tone not out of place in dedicatory poems, but here because of the filial connection seeming unusually strong.[16] She changed very few of her original words, but by those few changes the depicted father becomes more distant. In addition to the 'author of my being' revision, 'you' in line 18 becomes 'thy'. 'Planted' in line six was originally 'kindled', which fulfills the metaphor much more aptly but also more predictably. The flame appears later in the poem, but the tree blooms in silence. The freedom of the tree, as compared to the appropriately vestal flame, is an important indicator of an unadmitted power. Similarly, in the next-to-last line, 'intent' eventually replaces 'the attempt', with the result that the author gains much more agency. Though Burney here admits to a general parental influence, the implication – and the fact – is that she wrote *Evelina* in complete isolation, seeking no advice whatsoever.

Burney must have been aware that her father had received considerable help in his enterprise. Throughout the writing of the history of music her father had leaned heavily on the gadfly advice and support of the Reverend Thomas Twining. Twining in fact dampened his own personal ambitions, handing over his research to Dr Burney. Dr Burney tried to be as unbuttoned as he could when he wrote to Twining: 'Let us slap down our Thoughts as they come, without the Trouble of seeking or arranging them. ... – so I seem *inside-out* with you, & inclined to tell you every secret of my *Life*.'[17] And Twining though always jocular was thorough in his criticism, avoiding himself the 'bloated bladderosity of the Johnsonian school', and warning Dr Burney to avoid this temptation as well.[18] He also discussed questions of audience with Dr Burney, such as how he was to appeal to the 'Masters & Misses' who were his pupils, and yet to reach scholars, and, indeed, the general reader. Although Frances Burney's father was dependent on this kind of advice, she rarely sought help. When it came to her unasked, she did consider it, but she infrequently acted upon it in detail. Though often blushing and apologetic, Burney was her own woman, striving to keep to the lonely way of originality. This poem to her father does not deny that originality. It is the kind of outcry a child produces when the father is rather distantly admired, and the child wants to do something to command attention. Once Burney had made her artistic decisions and acted on them, she was happy to bask in approval, but she never confused approval with advice.

Intellectual daughters were rare in the eighteenth century, when daughters seldom managed to catch a serious education. Hence, in their relationships with their fathers they had few models to follow. Maria Edgeworth and her father achieved what seems to have been an exceptionally effective working relationship. Others were not so successful. Laetitia-Matilda Hawkins was one among many. Playwright-manager Colley Cibber's (1671–1757) daughter Charlotte Charke (1713–60) made desperate attempts to secure her father's attention. Although Charke in 1755 dedicated her *Narrative* of her life to herself, by the 11th page she made it clear that her main purpose was to explain herself to her estranged father and procure his blessing.[19] This was a particularly difficult task, since she was addressing a parent whose dislike for her was long-standing and deep. One of Cibber's most striking pronouncements about her occurred when she was five. With characteristic intrepidity, Charlotte had decided to ride bareback a donkey foal 'about the height of a sizeable greyhound'. When Cibber saw this feat through his window, he remarked: 'Gad demme! An ass upon an ass.'[20] There is no evidence that Cibber regarded Charke's *Narrative* as anything more than an asinine offspring's extra bray.

Unlike Cibber, Dr Burney did respond, with tears, to the poem his daughter wrote to him. Once she had revealed herself as an author, he also tried to influence her career. Though he was to be one of the most important positive influences on her literary life, his conscious attempts to guide her were on the whole destructive. The relationship of parents and children is always tangled. Although there are brutal and destructive parents, there is no such thing as a perfect parent. In this poem, Dr Burney is seen as perfect. In life, he half created and half destroyed his daughter, and in both enterprises the effect was more intense than most parents would have achieved. He encouraged her to write, but hindered her more subversive creativity. He urged her to incarcerate herself at Court. The strength of her father's effect on her, however, had as much to do with Burney's personality as with her father's. She idealized the literary life he represented. When she was young and untried, she saw him as her 'light', Urania, her muse. Later, she would come to believe that in many ways she was more powerful as a literary figure than he. When, 54 years after *Evelina*, Burney published the life of her father, her version of his *Memoirs*, once again she published this poem to the 'author' of her 'being', with revisions. In 1778, Dr Burney still seemed irreproachable.

The father in the dedicatory poem is distant, unapproachable, and yet nonetheless admirable. The father in the text is much more mixed. One of the Coussmakers, probably Catherine, responded mainly to the darker side of the family depicted in the novel, elements that reviewers and many subsequent critics have until recently condescended to as sentimental, passed over, or denied. She claimed that the scene where Evelina discovers herself to her father 'is so tragical that I declare it worked me as much as the death of Desdemona or Belvidera though the subject is totally different'.[21]

Burney actually divides her recognition scene into two parts, and in both Evelina's father rejects his daughter even while he accepts her, stressing that he loves the memory of her mother, whom she uncannily resembles. 'Tell her I would at this moment plunge a dagger in my heart to serve her', he assures Mrs Selwyn, 'but she has set my brain on fire, and I can see her no more' (p. 373). This is not really very helpful behavior for an orphan who is longing to find her parent, and to be loved. The second scene is similar. Evelina's father is more involved in his own guilt than in affection for his child. She abases herself before him, pleading for him at least to bless her before banishing her forever. Every eighteenth-century daughter whose father was a distant and difficult figure could identify with this situation. Coussmaker is aware of the art in here. The scene 'worked me'. The artists she chooses for comparison – Shakespeare and Otway – are distinguished: so much so that one discounts as mere flattery the extravagance of the comparison. Coussmaker is, after all, writing directly to the author. However, if we give this response the benefit of the doubt, it seems that Coussmaker was terrified and really moved by this encounter.[22] Both women she mentions inhabit a violent and terrifying world – Othello kills his innocent wife, and Belvidera, who in the attempt to save her father from death has sacrificed her husband and his associates, goes mad. Poor Coussmaker complains that she knows 'so many Sir C. Willoughbys' and 'hardly any Lord Orvilles or Evelinas'. Since Burney's hero and heroine are idealized – with Evelina containing 'Eve' and Lord Orville a city of gold – it is not surprising that Coussmaker did not know very many. Indeed, it is surprising that she knew anyone she might compare to Burney's unusually strong and sensitive creations. However, Coussmaker deserves sympathy, since anyone who has to put up with 'many' Sir Clement Willoughbys must live in real and present fear. Even if not assaulted or kidnapped, she is without any recourse mercilessly chivvied about. Evelina encounters aggressive sexuality; she experiences pervasive sexual fear.[23]

Though no one is actually raped in *Evelina*, and no one is actually murdered, violence of a different sort erupts continually in the text, where greediness and other desires clash and explode. This is the most important thing for a twentieth-century reader to understand about *Evelina*. The words 'violent' and 'violence' punctuate the text.[24] A twentieth-century reader would find more of what we call violence in Fielding and Smollett, where even the gentle Parson Adams frequently brandishes his crabstick, and in *Humphry Clinker* a fire, a horsepond, or a brace of pistols is always just in the offing. To say that Fielding and Smollett are violent and that Burney is not is to ignore eighteenth-century usage, where a 'violent passion' can erupt in terrifying ways.[25]

In Burney, 'rage' and 'fury' often flank 'violence', and 'cruelty' is a frequent motive and result. Mme Duval is a violent person, and so is Captain Mirvan. Mme Duval suffers from 'violence of temper' and twice delivers a 'violent' slap to someone's face (pp. 141, 88, 147). The 'insatiable Captain' (p. 152) loves to torment people. He cruelly molests Mme Duval. Anger is his dominant condition.

Violence in its twentieth-century meaning also reverberates throughout *Evelina*, though this novel has so often mistakenly been called, in Sherburn's phrase, 'coolly decorous and elegant'.[26] Catherine Coussmaker was distressed by the fact that Evelina's father by his cruelty and rejection hastened his wife's death.[27] The other most striking incidents of destructive behavior connected to class transgressions and servitude include Mme Duval's adventure in the mud, the 80-year-old women who are forced to race one another, and the monkey who quite understandably slashes Mr Lovel's ear. Writing in her spare hours, the young woman who listened to every voice threw her imagination into the angers of the world she knew.

Violence in Burney is rampant, but it is violence ultimately allied to comedy. Mme Duval's accident is most remarkable because it is presented as farce. When we first hear of Evelina's grandmother, she might easily stand as an analogue for any cruel and venal parent forcing a child to submit. When she arrives in England to seek her granddaughter, she adds to her moral and emotional blindness character faults that both Evelina and the reader reject. She is addicted to her possessions, wailing over the muddy fate of her 'Lyon's silk' (p. 67). For reasons she cannot possibly understand – 'for I'm no such great weight' – her companion M. du Bois has slipped and dropped her (p. 65). She is a great weight, but we also learn that Captain Mirvan gave M. du Bois 'a violent push' (p. 76). Mme Duval miscalls Evelina's natural behavior *'bumpkinish'* (p. 67), and she ungratefully refers to Villars as 'that meddling old parson' (p. 68). Evelina is her granddaughter, but this relationship for Evelina is the source of embarrassment rather than joy. By marrying the genteel grandfather of Evelina, this bar-maid Mme Duval escaped her class, but she has not been able to erase these origins. Vulgar and unpleasant, Mme Duval does not elicit sympathy, though in the kindly Evelina she does occasionally compel compassion. Burney is at times in *Evelina* sympathetic to those who have suffered because of their class, but she makes Mme Duval suffer for her callousness and hypocrisy. Captain Mirvan despises Mme Duval because she is French, but also because she is so affectedly French. By a mock-robbery Mirvan thrusts her for a second time in the mud:

> Her head-dress had fallen off; her linen was torn; her negligee had not a pin left in it; her petticoats she was obliged to hold on; and her shoes were perpetually slipping off. She was covered with dirt, weeds, and filth, and her face was really horrible, for the pomatum and powder from her head, and the dust from the road, were quite *pasted* on her skin by her tears, which, with her *rouge*, made so frightful a mixture, that she hardly looked human.   (p. 148)

Burney does not here give us what Susan Staves has called the 'comedy of attempted rape', a staple in Fielding's novels.[28] Unlike the bovine Slipslop in *Joseph Andrews*, Mme Duval does not fear sexual assault. She is quite sure that she is being robbed. Yet the picture of a woman raped is what Burney has nonetheless represented: all of Mme Duval's clothes – linen, negligee, petticoats, shoes – are torn, falling away from her body. Besides her linen underclothes, her negligee (loose upper gown), and her petticoats (upper and under), what else can she be wearing? The narrative modulates, however, into a description of someone who has been tarred and feathered, with the difference that the tar is Madame's own makeup and the feathers are the weedy filth from the ditch. Mme Duval must look as if Birnam wood has come to Dunsinane. The distinction between 'dirt' and 'filth' from the ditch also implies that she is covered with garbage – or even sewage – as well as mud. Her attempt to be fashionable is totally undermined. All the items she has bought and applied with such care have turned from allurements to disgusting filth. As a result, she has nearly lost her humanity.

In addition, she has also slipped from her precarious hold on the class she married into, and this is a source of comedy both for the reader and for the other characters. Evelina tells us more than once that 'the servants were ready to die with laughter' (p. 148). This class slippage is metaphorically made quite explicit when Madame Duval says that her cloak 'looks like a dish-clout', an appropriate condition and metaphor for a former bar-maid (p. 154). Her acquisitiveness also emerges. Her cap is ruined, and she says to Evelina, 'Now you must know this was the becomingest cap I had in the world.' (p. 154) She was especially fond of its pink ribbon, which she had bought particularly in order to please her devotee M. du Bois. Evelina is not sympathetic to her aged vanity. She remarks that, 'had I not been present, I should have thought it impossible for a woman at her time of life to be so very difficult in regard to dress' (p. 155). Indeed, at this time of life a woman becomes something not-quite-female. Mme

Duval in her rages is quite masculine, losing her sense of bodily decorum to such an extent that 'with frightful violence, she actually beat the ground with her hands' (p. 147). Illustrators John Hamilton Mortimer and James Walker embodied this masculine quality in the frontispiece to Volume 2 of the third edition, where Mme Duval's face, framed wigless with muddy wisps of hair, is much too coarse to seem female.[29] In a comic recasting of Burney's childhood wig caper, Mme Duval's wig is wet beyond redemption. In addition, her predicament is decorously moderated. Though the illustrators have drawn an unpinned negligee, their petticoats modestly cling unassisted to their owner's body. Hogarth or Rowlandson would have drawn Mme Duval with her regalia fully demolished. Burney dares the words, which will unsettle her genteel readers, but her verbal description is too excessive for visual representation within her own genre.

Another important incident where class attitudes slide and collide occurs in Volume 3, when Lord Merton and Mr Coverley wager on a race between two women who are over 80. The two men had wanted to hazard £1000 – in order to show, no doubt, that they could conspicuously consume – but Lord Orville has talked them down to £100. For some, this scene is pure comedy. Dr and Mrs Burney, as overheard by Susanna, roared with laughter (*ED* 2:241). Earl R. Anderson wrote in 1980, 'One of the most delightful incidents in Fanny Burney's *Evelina* is the foot-race.'[30] The elements Burney has combined, as Anderson points out, are literary backgrounds (such as the footraces in the *Iliad*, the games in the *Dunciad*, and possibly a scene in Smollett), the laws against gambling on athletic events, and the popularity of running as a sport (Anderson calls it 'pedestrianism'). Lord Merton and Mr Coverley are such unfeeling people that it is fitting that they should ignore the Queen Anne statute of 1711 forbidding betting on athletic activity beyond £10. Races – whether wagered upon or not – were in vogue in the 1770s, largely because of the activities of Foster Powell, who attracted large crowds for his popular running exhibitions, such as a seven-hour 50-mile run up the Bath Road, and a 402–mile run from London to York and back. 'Freak' races had been a lower-class activity for a century at least. Anderson gives an instance of a 1660 footrace between two wooden-legged men (pp. 66–7). A callous attitude toward betting on human objects was not above even Burney's dear friend David Garrick. At some point in the 1770s, Garrick invited a clutch of his best friends to dinner at Hampton, and in order to distract them from their negative response to some 'verses' Garrick insisted on reading (where he characterized some of those present), he commanded them to the garden. 'When there', a contemporary account tells us, 'the whole amusement consisted in an old man and a young one running backwards and forwards between two baskets filled with stones, and whoever emptied his basket first was to be the victor. Garrick expected that his guests would have been interested and have betted on the runners', but they were irritated and did not rise to the bait.[31] The contest here is between old and young, and it is a kind of nasty egg-race – with stones instead of eggs – so that the whole enterprise seems not only pointless but also exhausting.

Garrick's real race shares with Burney's fictional one a total disregard for the feelings of the participants. In Burney, Lord Merton has already shown that he believes old women are beyond the pale, remarking, 'I don't know what the devil a woman lives for after thirty: she is only in other folks way.' (p. 275) Hence, when Burney introduces the wager-race, she heightens the situation: her old women are by design over 80, and they are with 'difficulty' persuaded to practice. During the actual race, since they are, after all, over 80, they naturally stumble and fall; they hurt themselves. Indeed, the race ends when one of them is so badly injured that she cannot continue. Doody argues that this is Burney's 'version of the fall of woman, of woman's well-known tendency to make a slip', but that Burney deliberately denies her readers the lubriciousness they enjoy when a Rowlandson or Fielding woman falls and exposes her backside (p. 56). Like the prostitutes Evelina met earlier at Marylebone, these women have no individuality: no specific clothes, no faces, no names, no voices. Like animals, they belong to their trainers: 'to the inexpressible diversion of the company, they stumbled and tottered: and the confused hallowing of "*Now Coverley!*" "*Now Merton!*" rung from side to side during the whole affair.' (p. 312) In this case, however, as was not true of the Marylebone prostitutes, their depiction as nobodies elicits sympathy. Evelina refers to them often as 'poor women', and 'poor' carries a triple sense: old, lower class, and unfortunate. Even though Evelina – and possibly Burney – sympathizes with them, she does not restore them to their humanity. The difficulty of accomplishing that feat within the context is underlined by the fact that when one of the women slips, and she falls 'with great force', Lord Merton prevents Evelina from helping the woman, 'calling out "No foul play! no foul play!"' (p. 312) Other characters also react in varying ways to this activity, so that Burney provides a spectrum of responses to compare to the callousness of the perpetrators. Mrs Selwyn, in her strong and forthright manner, simply refuses to bet; Lord Orville is 'grave', and earlier he has objected altogether to the wager; but Evelina is faintly miffed that she is not considered important enough to be asked to put in her bid. In depicting this scene, Burney has combined the Hogarthian mode of bitter satire with a conflux of other attitudes. Comedy is the ultimate result. If the women had been more individualized, comedy would have been if not impossible, at least more fraught. This is the protean Burney, who gives us unlimited ways to respond to a scene. Only someone who oversimplifies it can respond to the comedy alone and dub the race 'delightful'.

Perhaps Burney's most thorough mixture of violence and farce in *Evelina* is the incident right at the end of the novel where Captain Mirvan the arch-practical-joker introduces an overdressed monkey to the self-centered fop Mr Lovel, claiming that he assumed the monkey must be Lovel's brother, and fulfilling in actuality his earlier claim that men of fashion 'are no better than monkeys' (p. 113). This was the scene that was chosen to illustrate the third volume in the fourth edition. It was also the only scene that Burney's father actively objected to. When Burney copied into her journal her sister Susanna's rendition of Dr Burney's remarks, she included his criticism that 'Mirvan's trick upon Lovel is, I think, carried too far, there is something even disgusting in it'.[32] But she omitted her father's further, more detailed statement: 'I don't hate that young man enough, ridiculous as he is, to be pleased or diverted at his having his ear torn by a monkey.' (*EJL* 3:29, n. 77) Did she erase this observation merely because she was over-sensitive, or was she embarrassed that her father seemed to miss the point? Dr Burney was not 'pleased or diverted', but to please or divert was not his daughter's intention. The monkey scene is so prominently juxtaposed with the Reverend Villars' fervent consent to Evelina's marriage with Lord Orville that it asserts the unruliness of things,[33] recalls the fact that laughter and pain are always right in the room with us, and that human dignity is achieved only momentarily and with effort. Furthermore, the monkey is definitely within his rights, since Lovel deals him a totally unprovoked 'furious blow' (p. 401). Evelina is too busy to sympathize. But the reader gets the point, or at least some readers do. The mixture of feelings in this scene is much more various than Dr Burney was willing to accept. In some eighteenth-century satires, such as Hogarth's *Marriage à la Mode*, the pain is unmediated by laughter. Dr Burney wanted his laughter unmediated by pain. His daughter was unwilling to give him this simple fare.

Though *Evelina* is the most ungarnished of Burney's books, it shares with her early letters and diaries a deliberate tendency to slide from laughter through violence to pain. Captain Mirvan, Mme Duval, and Sir Clement Willoughby are always on the verge of fury, on the margin of control. Humor and terror mingle in nearly every scene. Evelina is thrust into situations too complicated to explain. Silence presses against speech. When Sir Clement Willoughby is caught in a lie, the Branghtons can only laugh, unrestrainedly, unendurably (p. 211). Sir Clement's articulateness is no match for their brutal mirth. The apparently suicidal Mr Macartney can communicate to her only through writing. The medley is strange, but the mixture is artistically satisfying.

A writer's first book is both the hardest and the easiest. It is the hardest because it is the first. All those unfamiliar thresholds must be crossed. It is the easiest, because there are no outside expectations to meet. Once published and public, an eighteenth-century woman in her closet was no longer alone. No matter how prettily furnished and airy her dressing-room study might be, it was no longer a sanctuary. Burney had sneaked away quietly to write and copy *Evelina*. In a house full of enigmas, this was one of the best-kept secrets. If *Evelina* had been a failure, or even a moderate success, the adjustments would have been different. Hester Thrale in her direct way told her nervous, hesitating friend that she could not escape: 'If you *will* be an Author & Wit, – you must take the Consequence!' (*EJL* 3:116) For all writers at all times, one of the most difficult experiences to handle is the kind of pressure created by an overweeningly successful first book. The approving public is always poised, ready to pounce, minds churning with questions. What will she do now? Perhaps she will merely repeat herself? If she chooses a different genre or theme, will she succeed? Can she do it again? Now Burney's friends and relatives in the name of support applied pressure, invaded her plans. She had lost the freedom to be nobody, the joy of being alone and the power of choosing alone.

Given the fact that all writers undergo some version of these experiences, modern scholars have over-emphasized both the pleasure and the pain Burney associated with the response to *Evelina*. I would hazard that no other writer – not even Samuel Richardson – has supplied in such detail the aftermath of a publication. Burney tells us how her family reacts, including cousins. She quotes family friends on the subject of *Evelina*, both when they know the author and when they do not. When she takes up residence with Hester Thrale and meets Johnson, Burke, and Reynolds, she quotes what these influential men have to say. She goes to the circulating library, eavesdrops, then writes in detail about her visit. *Evelina*'s fate is the subject of letter after letter, journal entry after journal entry. We also find out about Burney's writing plans, who encourages her to write drama, and who does not. We can see every joy and every hesitation, minutiae that are lost for other writers. Because Burney wrote it all down, she appears more self-centered than most, and also for some readers more hesitant, more insecure. By comparison, George Eliot, who does not give us this kind of detail about the aftermath of publication, seems to have needed much more encouragement than Burney ever required. Her companion George Henry Lewes protected her from reviews, muffled every unfriendly voice. Eliot may have been particularly uncomfortable because she was living with Lewes, unmarried. Her family refused to speak to her, and this kind of rejection may have made her more vulnerable. Still, whatever the reasons, Eliot was quite unable to accept adverse commentary.[34] It is important, then, to emphasize here that being criticized by strangers, and often anonymous strangers, is delicate and difficult for everyone. Burney told us so much about it that we mistakenly think of her as an exception. One of the reasons we have inherited all this material about the reception of *Evelina* is that Burney was writing to her sister Susanna. She loved Susanna totally, unreservedly, as the one person in the world who understood her and shared her tastes. The sisters dreamed of an unchanged relationship, and had planned a 'little snug Garret scheme', where they would live together always, '& end our Lives 2 loving Maiden Cats'.[35] With Susanna she had the habit of sharing every frisson. When Susanna was not present, she had to write out the conversations they had once verbally shared. Burney dramatized her *Evelina* encounters to keep her sister's interest. On the spectrum of authors' sensitivity to criticism, Burney's position was by no means the most extreme.

4
Open Authorship: *The Witlings,*
Cecilia, and the Unruly Text
(1779–84)

> Wyndham & Johnson were talking of Miss Burney's new
> Novel – 'Tis far superior to Fielding's, says Mr. Johnson; her
> Characters are nicer discriminated, and less prominent,
> Fielding could describe a Horse or an Ass, but he never
> reached a Mule'.
>
> Hester Thrale in *Thraliana* (p. 555)

Burney's first post-*Evelina* project was a play, *The Witlings,* an enterprise that called on different recesses of her personality from *Evelina.*
Although the young Burney was known for a kind of quietness that
would have pleased the conduct-book writer Hester Chapone, she was
always listening. In her journals she would often '*Theatricalise*' her
dialogues (*EJ* 3:146), so that the journals frequently read like a series
of dramatic scenes. The Irish General Mr Blakeney inveighs against
apothecaries; 'my feet swelled as big as two Horses Heads! – I vow to
God I'll never consult one of those Dr. Gallipots while I live again! –
lost me, Sir, 4 years of the happiness of my life!' (*EJL* 3:427). Mrs
Cholmondeley pounces when Burney calls her 'Ma'am': 'Don't be
formal with *me*! – if you are, – I shan't like you!' (*EJL* 3:227)[1]
Throughout her life, Burney was always trying to catch humanity in
the act.

She also noted down particular types. Among her unused characters appear an assortment of serviceable human variations: Miss
Embellish, Mr Downer, Mrs Teizer, Mr Fastidio, Mr Jocoso, Mr Dry,
Mr Laconic.[2] Inveterately, she jotted down bits of dialogue, listed
character types with their distinctive speech, littered her manuscript
caches with scraps of paper containing bits of plays. The interest was
there. In all, Burney wrote eight completed (or nearly completed)

plays – four tragedies and four comedies – but only one of them was produced, and none was published. She worked on her plays during her entire writing life, timing them for production even as late as the 1830s. She obviously treasured these drafts of plays, leaving carefully copied versions of nearly all of them to be discovered by posterity. The question of why they were not produced is complicated, and will never be entirely understood. Burney's father certainly disapproved of her theatrical ambitions, and in her 20s she deferred to his authority and experience. But as the years passed, and she gained more authority, she increasingly resisted his opposition. As Burney came to know herself better, she recognized that her imagination was happiest when unleashed – from social pressures for conformity, from her father's opinions, and from her audience's expectations. She valued her father's opinions, but her talents were more varied than he could acknowledge, her wit more subversive than he could sanction. She learned to resist him, but even so, unforeseen events consistently and effectively scuttled her attempts to stage her plays and even to publish them.

Undoubtedly, besides having a splendid ear, Burney must have been drawn to dramatic writing because the financial returns were more likely higher than for novel writing. *Evelina* had earned her £21 (plus £10). In 1783, only five years later, John O'Keeffe received £368 18s. 6d. for the copyright of his play *The Castle of Andalusia*. This fee was paid by the proprietor of the theater, and the playwright was not allowed to publish until the 14 years of the original copyright period were past. Since the standard fee for publication was only £200,[3] this loss of the power to publish was sweetened by additional funds. Besides the copyright fee, the playwright was also given a cut of the receipts. Up to the 1790s, this meant the third, sixth, and ninth nights, and afterwards was more likely to be a stated fee of £300 for the first nine nights, and another £100 for each of the 20th and 40th nights.[4] Dr Burney, whose Rousseau-like farce *The Cunning Man* had run for 14 nights, had made, according to *The London Stage*, at least £92 2s. 0d., much less than was possible for a full-length play, but much more than a young novelist could likely hope for. Frances Burney was never a rich woman; the amount of money she earned was always important. In 1778, at the beginning of her career, her friend Hester Thrale emphasized that a play 'is the Road both to Honour & Profit' (*EJL* 3: 133).

Dramatic writing is arguably the most public of all genres. Novelists can send off their books anonymously and wait for the responses, but playwrights who want to retain the power of authorship have always needed to work with actors and directors. In the 1770s Burney first needed to convince one of the managers of the two Patent Theatres to accept her work, then she had to revise it to his liking, read the play to the assembled company in the Green Room, help to choose the cast, attend rehearsals to make further changes and suggestions for stage business, and within two weeks of production send it with the manager's imprimatur to John Larpent the Examiner to be licensed as fit for production. She needed to find someone to write the prologue and someone else to write the epilogue. In addition, at the performance itself, the plays were normally enhanced for the audience by quite irrelevant but popular dances or pantomimes between the acts, perhaps something like the hornpipe Nancy Dawson performed in *The Beggar's Opera*. All of this represented a great deal of public exposure for a woman who in her 20s was trying to fulfill the period's widely published strictures on female delicacy.[5] Some authors managed to remain anonymous by allowing Garrick to carry their plays through to production, but in such cases they lost control over the revisions and sometimes even the casting. Since Burney's name was her greatest drawing-card, this route was not practical for her.

Nonetheless, in the late 1770s, all her friends urged her toward drama. In 1778, Thrale repeatedly advised that Burney should write a play, emphasizing as Burney put it, how 'I so naturally run into conversations' (*EJL* 3:64). Thrale and Johnson archly indicated that if they were satirized in such a play, they would persevere as friends. Burney had started a play even before Thrale and Johnson had urged her to it. They anticipated one of her themes: they knew that she viewed literary hangers-on with a judgmental eye. Others had noticed this as well. Miss Theophila Palmer, niece of Sir Joshua Reynolds, believed that 'there was no escaping' the author of *Evelina* 'with safety', and she said that her uncle and her friend Mrs Mary Cholmondeley shared her opinion (*EJL* 3:141). Burney knew that part of *Evelina*'s strength was that she had consulted no one in the writing of it, 'except Esther & Mr Burney' (*EJL* 3:51). She knew perfectly well that crude people like the Branghtons were necessary to the book, but she was also afraid that her readers would 'conclude I must have an *innate vulgarity of ideas* to assist me with such coarse colouring for the objects of my Imagination'.[6] Johnson urged Burney to speak (and write) aggressively and aim high. When Mrs Montagu was about to arrive at Streatham, 'Dr Johnson began to see-saw, with a Countenance strongly expressive of *inward fun*, – &, after enjoying it some Time in silence, he suddenly, & with great animation, turned to me, & cried *"Down* with her, Burney – *down* with her! – spare her not! attack her, fight her, & *down* with her at once! *You* are a *rising* Wit, – *she* is at the *Top*, – & when *I* was beginning the World, & was nothing & nobody, the Joy of my Life was to fire at all the established Wits! – & then, every body loved to hallow me on".' (*EJL* 3:150–1) This was not to say that Johnson disparaged Montagu, but only that he thought this kind of sparring was expected among writers.

All commentators agree that Burney's first play, *The Witlings*, was never produced because both her father and her extra father Samuel Crisp objected, and she acceded to their wishes. She was 27. Her mentors feared both notoriety and failure. Although they saved her from notoriety, they plunged her into her first experience of failure. They themselves informed her that her play was inferior. Not everyone has agreed. Doody argues that, 'If *The Witlings* had been staged, we would now remember Frances Burney as a predecessor of Pinero or Ayckbourn.' (p. 98)

The subject matter of *The Witlings* is predicted by the title: the witlings, both male and female, are writers and their hangers-on, all of whom aspire to be members of Lady Smatter's Esprit Party, a blue-stocking mutual-admiration literary group. The central plot in *The Witlings*, as opposed to the subject matter, is romantic. Cecilia Stanley is already having her trousseau made for her marriage to Lady Smatter's nephew and heir Beaufort, but she loses her fortune, and Lady Smatter is only with difficulty and after many impeding scenes brought to agree once more to support the match. The actual substance of the play – beyond plot and subject matter – concerns competing kinds of authority, intellectual, financial, and familial. The medium in which authority acts is often clotted, and people are hampered by delay. Working-class women figure largely in this play, and they are sympathetically as well as satirically presented.

One of the chief sources of humor in *The Witlings* is the viscous medium that causes delay, especially the encumbered anticipation an audience feels when a character is announced and fails to arrive. Hence, the first scene, which takes place in a milliner's shop, Doody encapsulates as 'Waiting for Cecilia' (p. 79). Similarly, because Censor has prevented Beaufort from rushing to reassure his suddenly impoverished fiancée, three of her later scenes may be called 'Waiting for Beaufort'. The need to wait is linked through Cecilia to women's powerlessness and loneliness. Cecilia at her nadir considers working as a companion, a toadeater – a job where she will experience what her lover Beaufort calls 'corroding servility' (3.214; *Plays*, 1:42). She is so isolated that she fears she will go mad. Although the mood often veers toward darkness, the play is persistently comic. Insanity is seen as an ironic threat as well as a real one. Censor tells Beaufort he is crazy to try to argue with Lady Smatter, and Lady Smatter herself is fit only for a satirical Bedlam. Burney repeatedly mocks her ultra-serious hero and heroine. On the title page the author designates herself as 'A Sister of the Order', and all the issues Burney herself struggled with – the issues of diffidence and self-promotion – are playfully strewn among the characters.

Although Burney's play is primarily contained within her own class – professionals and the middle gentry – she reaches gingerly beyond the teapot tempests of fortunes made and lost to the working-class sorority among the needlewomen. Mrs Wheedle, the milliner, is depicted as being somewhat venial and sycophantish, but it is clear as well that she must carefully watch her expenditures and collect her bills. Her friend Mrs Voluble out of financial necessity rents a room to Dabler and maintains the connections with other women by which she locates lodgings and a possible job for Cecilia. Other kinds of class differences reverberate in other scenes in the play. For instance, when Mrs Sapient, fearing that she will be discovered prying into Lady Smatter's affairs and seeking out information about her adored Dabler, hides in Mrs Voluble's closet, the resulting imitation of Sheridan's screen scene from *The School for Scandal* turns not on whether or not the hiding female is a 'little milliner', but on whether or not she is the cat among the cutlery, and Burney the author was aware that her audience would notice this difference and speculate about it. In this play no one is preying sexually on the little milliners, though their financial condition remains unstable. The chief tension here is Mrs Sapient's fear that she will be discovered slumming and Mrs Voluble's concern that she can retain both her boarder's rent and a richer woman's influence. Burney mingles Mrs Voluble's fatuousness with her financial need.

The Witlings, although including among the satirized witlings the self-absorbed poet Dabler and the overly hesitant critic Codger, most flamboyantly depicts three flawed women who aspire to literary power. These women are types. Mrs Voluble is as empty as her name suggests, covering with babble her prying sycophancy. Mrs Sapient chants her received opinions on every subject, only to disagree with herself. She states that 'a proper degree of Courage is preferable to a superfluous excess of modesty', and then blandly affirms 'How much more amiable in *my* Eyes is Genius when joined with Diffidence, than with conceit!' (2.255–6; 288–9; *Plays*, 1:27) The most vivid portrait is that of Lady Smatter, who indeed in some respects resembles Montagu. A partiality to Shakespeare might be seen as a general addiction, as is a desire to form a literary salon, but having a dependent nephew likely to be your heir was more unusual, and Beaufort's relationship with Lady Smatter resembles the position of Matthew Robinson Montagu (Hemlow, pp. 133–4). Lady Smatter affects literary knowledge, but she is chronically vague. Another character defines her exactly when he explains why he wants to avoid her: 'will she not ... stun me with the names of Authors she has never read? – and pester me with flimsy Sentences which she has the assurance to call Quotations?' (3.165–8; *Plays*, 1:41) The number of interrupted speeches in *The Witlings* is exceptionally high. Amid the babble, none of the Witlings, male or female, reveals any redeeming characteristics. Toward intellectuals, as not toward milliners, the young Burney is quite pitiless.

When the play was finished, all appearances boded well. The playwright Arthur Murphy effervesced over the first two acts. Sheridan, egged on by Reynolds, had told Burney that he would take any play of hers for Drury Lane sight unseen, at which point 'my many & encreasing scruples *all* give way to encouragement so warm from so experienced a Judge' (*EJL* 3:236). Her sister Susanna wrote that at Chessington, where her father read the play aloud to the Crisp household and to herself and Charlotte, the event seemed to go well, except for a slight flagging in the fourth act. 'It's *funny* – it's *funny* indeed', Mr Crisp cried out at the end of the first act. At one point 'Charlotte laugh'd till she was almost black in the face', while Susanna herself was moved by the sentimental sections and cried 'in 2 or 3 places' (Doody, p. 92). Both she and Dr Burney wanted Burney to amplify the sentimental plot somewhat, a desire puzzling to twentieth-century tastes, but quite understandable in the current market. The heroine in her penniless state is much like Juliet Granville, the 'wanderer' of Burney's 1814 novel, thrust into a predicament that eighteenth-century women thoroughly identified with and understood. Being homeless and despised, planning to take a job as a toadeater, a groveling humble companion – this was the fate of many a portionless daughter.[7] Burney recoiled from this fate, though her own years of groveling at court were still to come. She already enacted in her relationship with Thrale the companion fearful of being thought to be inferior.

Why, then, did Burney's mentors trash her play? Mrs Thrale said pleasantly to Murphy, 'I believe this Rogue means *me* for Lady Smatter' (*EJL* 3:279), but she later noted in her diary that the play was quashed because it was feared that Mrs Montagu would take umbrage, and noted as well that she was 'pleased' that Burney had decided to abandon her play, 'for fear it may bear hard upon some Respectable Characters' (*Thraliana*, p. 401). Doody speculates that in addition Burney's father might have identified with the self-important yet sycophantic poet Dabler, and that he might also have 'been dimly aware that the unkindly treated Lady Smatter bore a slight resemblance to his wife, as well as to Mrs Montagu' (p. 96). Doody's speculations about Lady Smatter are exactly right. Since the publication of Doody's book, the editors of the *Early Journal and Letters* have printed a letter from Burney's stepmother to 'Madam Fanny', annotated by Madame d'Arblay as 'in the style of a certain Lady – ', where the 'Lady' writes, 'as Dean Swift says there's nobody's work so well done as those who do it themselves' (*EJL* 2:292;293). One of the Burney children's confidential sobriquets for their stepmother was 'the Lady', but surely the reference to a 'certain Lady' in Burney's later annotation must also be to Lady Smatter, since Elizabeth Allen Burney has attributed a banality to Swift exactly in Lady Smatter's manner. Readers notoriously fail to recognize themselves in satiric portraits, but even if Burney's father overlooked Dabler, he quite likely noticed the resemblance of Lady Smatter's flimsy sentences to his wife's daily patter. Troide argues that in the attack on *The Witlings* Crisp's voice was strongest, that he convinced Burney's father that 'the enmity of the Blues could threaten CB's career as well as the reputation of his daughter',[8] and in contrast Doody writes of Dr Burney that 'It is hard not to feel that he used Crisp' (p. 95) to corroborate his own uneasiness. The difference in tone between Burney's letters to Crisp and to Dr Burney supports Doody's reading of this situation, as does the fact that Burney's satire touched her stepmother so nearly. In addition, Dr Burney wrote to his daughter discouraging her from writing a play while the country was at war, and Crisp for his part suggested enthusiastically that she write a play about 'the reciprocal Follies of Parents & Children' (*EJL* 3:353), evidently not noticing that this was already one of the strongest themes in *The Witlings*, nor noticing that this is one of the ways one might describe the way Burney's two fathers responded to her play.

Burney herself, writing to her father, regretted most (she said) that item which is the true gold coin of the writer: the loss of '*Time*, –

which I with difficulty stole, & which I have Buried in the mere trouble of *writing*' (*EJL* 3:347). She went on with a complicated argument that needs quoting in full:

> What my Daddy Crisp says, 'that it would be the best *policy*, but for pecuniary advantages, for me to write no more' – is exactly what I have always thought since Evelina was published; – but I will not *now* talk of putting it in practice, – for the best way I can take of shewing that I have a true & just sense of the *spirit* of your condemnation, is not to sink, sulky & dejected, under it, but to exert myself to the utmost of my power in endeavours to produce something less reprehensible. And this shall be the way I will pursue, as soon as my mind is more at ease about Hetty & Mrs. Thrale, – & as soon as I have *read* myself into a forgetfulness of my old Dramatis persona, – lest I should produce something else as *Witless* as the last.
>
> Adieu, my dearest, kindest, truest, best *Friend*, – I will never proceed so *far* again without your counsel, & then I shall not only save *myself* so much useless trouble, but *you*, who so reluctantly blame, the kind pain which I am sure must attend your disapprobation. The World will not always go well, as Mrs. Sap. might say, & I am sure I have long thought I have had more than my share of success already. (*EJL* 3:347–8)

This letter is remarkably dutiful, considering how harsh the 'catcalling epistle' evidently had been, and yet it also contains alternate currents, evidence of the later figure I have called the protean Burney. The statement begins by saying that Burney agrees with Crisp that she should write nothing more, 'but for pecuniary advantages'. For a woman just turned 27, this was crushing advice, especially so since her only pecuniary gain thus far had been £21 plus the additional £10 her father had requested. Burney agrees, but the co-operation immediately changes into revolt. She redefines Crisp and her father into the 'spirit' of their words, and refuses to be a mere child ('sulky') or a convinced adult ('dejected'), but rather to take action, to 'exert ... power'. She gives her daddies no choice, telling them that this is her plan, only reassuring them that this time she will consult with them along the way. Her altruism is there, in her concern for her sister Hetty who has suffered from a persistent fever requiring quinine, and for Thrale, whose finances were suddenly precarious, and who had just miscarried a perfect boy (*Thraliana*, p. 400), and indeed for her father's misery over the need to write the catcalling epistle. Yet Burney's play is still so much a part of her that she refers to it twice, identifying herself as a witless witling (allowing her parental advisers to escape the identity they had failed to acknowledge), and yet quoting Mrs Sap., not Lady Smatter, even though all readers of the play know that Mrs Sapient tends to say the opposite of what she means. Finally, if Burney has had more than her share of success, the fact is that her success has far overshadowed both her father and Crisp. In this sense, she has certainly had more than her share. The letter is full of double meanings and ancillary meanings, some probably half-realized, some undoubtedly subconscious. One effect of the suppression of *The Witlings* was that Burney did not try to write anything at all for months. Her confidence, pride, and eagerness had vanished, and she felt 'more Fear than hope, & Anxiety than pleasure in thinking at all of the Theatre' (*EJL* 4, forthcoming).

The play did not die easily. Five months later, in January 1780, Sheridan worked so hard on Charles Burney that he promised to send *The Witlings* immediately. Sheridan emphasized that he preferred to see unfinished and hence malleable plays; in addition, Murphy wheedled and coaxed. This time, Burney wrote to Crisp, saying that she herself did not want to send the play forward: 'I had taken a sort of disgust to it.' (*EJL* 4, forthcoming) She was so 'fidgetted' that she rewrote the fourth act,[9] and she planned to remove the Esprit club, cut down the parts of Smatter and Dabler, and expunge the nephew–Smatter relationship – 'in order to obviate the unlucky resemblance the *adopted Nephew* bears to our *Female Pride of Literature*' (*EJL* 4, forthcoming). In addition, she planned to excise the offer Beaufort's friend Censor makes to Cecilia, and to provide a friend for Cecilia to rescue her from the catastrophe. Of course these changes would have left an empty shell of a play, and as Troide and Sabor emphasize, Crisp dealt the final blow to this modified version of *The Witlings*, meanwhile stressing that even the original would not hold an audience. What is most interesting about these changes is that Burney was going to take out Dabler as well as Smatter. Who recognized himself as Dabler if not Charles Burney himself? Crisp held out one slim hope, that they might send the play to Sheridan secretly, so that if he turned it down no one would know, a suggestion couched so disturbingly that Madame d'Arblay later erased a third of the words.

This fear of a flop was something of a canard, as was Crisp's insistence that women who wanted to retain their reputations as prudes could not write interesting plays. Crisp, like Charles Burney, had experienced failure in the theatre. The disappointing history of his play *Virginia* had discouraged him, and like Charles Burney he had never tried again. But many other playwrights, including women, had slid out of troughs back to the top of the wave. And a woman did not have to abandon her reputation. Not everyone was as notorious as Aphra Behn and Delarivière Manley. Susanna Centlivre (1669–1723), who as wife of Queen Anne's yeoman of the mouth (chief cook) was of course more déclassée than Burney, began her eminently successful career as a playwright with three failures, and her new plays continued intermittently to run into difficulties, in spite of the spectacular success of *The Busy Body* (1709), *The Wonder: A Woman Keeps a Secret* (1714) and *A Bold Stroke for a Wife* (1718). Although *The Busy Body* was her most successful play, a stock comedy in the 1770s, the actor Robert Wilks had during a rehearsal 'in great Dudgeon flung his Part into the Pitt for damn'd Stuff, before the Lady's Face that wrote it', and 'before it came out ... those who had heard of it, were told it was a silly thing wrote by a Woman', so that the first-night audience was drastically thin.[10] Yet it survived for 13 nights, and remained a repertory item well into the nineteenth century. Mary Pix (1666–1709), a minister's daughter, had produced 12 plays, both tragedies and comedies, with varying critical success, retaining throughout the process her unblemished character as a woman. In the long run she was certainly a successful author, although by Burney's time her plays had fallen into oblivion. But Centlivre's plays were continually revived, an indication that a woman could succeed as a playwright, and become a classic. Joanna Baillie (1762–1851), just ten years younger than Burney, whose father was a clergyman and professor of divinity, achieved with her plays on the passions the kind of reputation Burney might have hoped for, though even she was attacked so vigorously in mid-career by Francis Jeffrey that she turned chiefly to other genres. Still, even this attack did not keep her from both writing and publishing plays through her 70s. There was a nearer example in 1775 with Hannah Cowley's (1743–1809) *The Runaway*, which included a woman whose notions of her own intellect were significantly inflated. This play had had a respectable run, and it was produced again in subsequent seasons. Cowley was the daughter of a bookseller, and her respectability was a good model. Burney was in London when *The Runaway* was produced in 1778, and she might have found discouraging the fact that it was acted only once that season. Cowley's play, like Sheridan's *The Rivals* (1775), treated women in ways similar to Burney's Esprit club attack, but both plays were placed in a safer matrix. Indeed, *The Witlings* could be read as a conflation of Sheridan's *The Rivals* and *The School for Scandal* (1777), with a tripled Mrs Malaprop heading a 'School for Intellectuals'. Cowley's *Runaway*, the model both by a woman and satirical of women (how was Burney to know that Sheridan had borrowed Mrs Malaprop from a draft-play by his mother?), once again was revised for a commendable run of five nights, but by then Burney had irremediably suppressed her own play.

The suppression of *The Witlings* was a turning-point in Burney's writing life. One can only speculate on the difference to her career the experience of having a successful play would have made. The money, the notice, the inevitable stride toward independence – what changes would these have accomplished in her heart and mind? But would *The Witlings* have succeeded? Is Katharine Rogers right to say of Mrs Montagu's presumed response that: 'Had the play been produced, her justified fury would have destroyed Burney's precarious social position' (*Plays by Women*, pp. 290–1)? Was the play good enough to succeed? Joyce Hemlow says that the characters remain in an 'embryonic stage', functioning only as 'aggregates of foibles, failings, humours, or pretensions, somewhat inadequately clothed with human flesh and spirit' (Hemlow, 'Fanny Burney: Playwright', p. 172). Even if true, does this matter? Doody emphasizes the play's originality, and concludes with the accolade quoted previously, that 'If *The Witlings* had been staged, we would now remember Frances Burney as a predecessor of Pinero or Ayckbourn.' (p. 98) *The Witlings* was first produced in 1994 (*Plays* 1:5), and may well become a well-known drama from the period, but we will never know quite what it would have been like if Burney had worked through it with professionals. What turn might Burney's career have taken if she had not been so brutally crushed at this juncture? If the play had been sent to Sheridan, would he have cared about Montagu's response? Would he have helped Burney to mold the play in such a way that Montagu could have gracefully ignored it? Johnson clearly approved wholeheartedly. He wanted Burney to topple the reigning wits just as he had done. Except for Hannah Cowley, women had not traditionally attacked their fellow-writers. Though Thrale had been supportive at first, she was ultimately glad that Burney desisted. Perhaps Thrale thought Burney might undermine her career, or scuttle her chances for a good marriage. Before actually writing *The Witlings*, Burney herself wrote to Crisp, in a statement emphasized by Spacks and others, 'I would a thousand times rather forfeit my character as a *Writer* than risk ridicule or censure as a *Female*' (Spacks, p. 165; *EJL* 3:212).

These are strong words, but the unyielding dichotomy they present is by no means the whole story. In context, Burney is replying to Crisp's warning that she cannot be known as the writer of salty language or even of slightly off-color incidents she could freely laugh at in the theater. Crisp says that plays without such language and incidents are simply boring, and that 'Comedies Larmoyantes' are worse (EJL 3:188). Young and unmarried, Burney wanted to retain the kind of character the men she desired would see as marriageable. When she wrote these words to Crisp she was smarting under the publication of a poem referring to her condescendingly as 'dear little Burney'.[11] She was having to face the sudden realization that she could not protect herself against public statements about her. And yet she did not really want to 'forfeit' writing. Although content to repress sexuality in her writing, Burney wanted power. In a period when, as Foucault has emphasized, there was a shift from the desire for respect to a desire for power, Burney wanted the dichotomy.[12] The only kind of acceptable rebellion for a woman who wanted to keep her reputation for fitting prudery was underhanded rebellion. Burney often mentions in her diary Colman and Garrick's *The Clandestine Marriage*, where the heroine, aptly called Fanny, secretly marries the man she loves and is finally rewarded for her quiet disobedience. The subject of Burney's play, which Katharine Rogers attributes to 'strange perversity' (*Plays by Women*, p. 290), was also a bid for power. Rightly or not, Burney felt superior to the people she called witlings, including Montagu and her circle. In page after page of her journal she exposed these witlings for the delectation of her sister Susanna. It was entirely natural that these creatures should be the subject matter of her play. When her father and her surrogate father marshalled all their concerted power to discourage her, she crumpled. She was not afraid of failure, but she was afraid of the unknown, the as yet scarcely imagined things strangers could say (and publish) about her. If Burney's *Witlings* had reached the stage, if in her 20s Burney had continued writing drama, she might have found a way to include the imperious Huncamunca attitudes, the wild Nancy Dawson body, and even the eruptions of clandestine passion. No play in the last decades of the eighteenth century managed this feat. As it was, Burney did not return to dramatic writing for eight years.

In effect, the success of *Evelina* was immediately followed by a problematical failure. Burney's father and surrogate father insisted that she abandon her play, flattering her general abilities but brutally criticizing this particular project. She was young and untried in this new genre. Her 'fathers' also warned her that in theatrical work she could lose her character as well as some of her professional luster. The conflict between her public character as woman and as author was always with her, and she faced daily and excruciating dilemmas. After a brief fight with her two fathers about trying her hand at play writing, she returned to fiction.

In the spring of 1780, two and a half years into her life as a professional author, she accompanied the Thrales to Bath, where she met all the best people and experienced the kinds of pseudo-witty, and possibly some truly witty, evenings that in eighteenth-century society were designated as 'flash' and 'ton'. Samuel Crisp was ecstatic that his beloved protegée had broken into this kind of society. He had heard from her parents that there was a plan to go abroad, and he wrote in May:

> of a delightful Tour You are to make this Autumn on the other Side of the Water with! – M^r & Mrs Thrale, Dr Johnson, Mr Murphy &c! – Where will You find such another Set! Oh Fanny! – set this down as the happiest Period of your Life! & when You come to be Old, & sick, & health & spirits are Fled – (for that time may come) – then live upon this remembrance, & think that You have had your Share of the good Things of this World, & say, for what I *have* receiv'd, the Lord make me thankful!   (*EJL* 4, forthcoming)

This passage is a good example of the hindered joy Burney's mentors allowed. Crisp loves her and is thrilled to see her succeed. He idealizes the people she is living with; they are the best that the intellectual life can offer. He himself, however, is old and increasingly infirm, and he cannot resist imagining her in the same situation, so instead of letting her simply enjoy the present, he insists on visualizing the time when her body will fail her, and memory will be her one solace. Perhaps one of the reasons that Burney could identify so easily with old women was that her friend Crisp would talk to her about her own old age. Meanwhile, with her greater sense of irony, certainly far greater than Crisp could ever muster, Burney was describing in her journal how people invited Montagu and Thrale and sat around and listened to them talk. At one evening, where Thrale was supposed to be conversing with a Bishop, and neither one found an appropriate way to begin the conversation, Montagu leapt delightedly into the gap: 'Mrs. Montagu cared not a fig, as long as she spoke *herself*, & so she Harangued away' (*EJL* 4, forthcoming).

Burney discovered that people used her presence and her authorship as an ice-breaker in conversations. Once, having just left the Pump Room, she returned to fetch something forgotten only to overhear one woman saying to another, 'Have you read *Evelina*?' She did not stay for the answer. Sometimes the people who praised her to her face were so fulsome that she fantasized about throwing herself out of the window to change the subject. People would come in waves, egging one another on to say outrageously complimentary things, and she would desperately beat a retreat. One little girl insisted on being told what all Burney's characters were doing now, and suggested that Burney should think about that and write it all down, since there would then be more of *Evelina*.

She was being watched: total strangers thought of her as their intimate friend. One night at *The Merchant of Venice* she and Thrale criticized the play, and though they were surrounded by strangers, no less than four people were quoted the next day as having heard that they were very severe on the actors. Burney's response to this sort of experience is matter-of-fact, but also extreme; the situation seems familiar to her, since the gossiping reminds her of her own home town:

> But Bath is as Tittle Tattle a Town as Lynn, & people make as many reports, & spread as many idle nothings abroad as in any common little Town in the Kingdom: & I am perpetually discovering that I am well known here by people that I am unconscious of having ever seen, & quite certain I have never spoken to. I shall be more guarded in future in my Criticisms, though I am sure I never thought myself less observed. (*EJL* 4, forthcoming)

The lesson Burney learns here is to be more 'guarded', to protect herself as a 'female', even while she despises those who have nothing else to talk about than about what Miss Burney thinks of a performance. None of these lessons is easy, and none is without its dilemmas.

She finds herself flung into instant intimacy with people she has never met before, though sometimes that intimacy is unnervingly displaced. She meets a 'Miss White', who tells her that men are '*all bad, – all*, in one word, & without exception, *sensualists*'. And, Miss White continues, 'the reason the men are happier than us, is because they are more sensual'. She looks for a man or woman worthy of her own passion, but never hopes to find one. God will not help, since Miss White has been reading Hume and has given Him over. If she should find, and then lose, her lover, she will simply kill herself. Burney expostulates, suggests reading material, worries that such a girl is particularly vulnerable and that she will be preyed upon. What is most strange in this situation is that it is clear that Miss White thinks Burney is the author of *The Sylph*, a novel where the heroine is married to a libertine and is watched over by an anonymous earlier admirer who calls himself 'the sylph'.[13] Hence, as Betty Rizzo points out, the whole conversation is skewed (*EJL* 4, forthcoming). Though few books could be more different than *Evelina* and *The Sylph*, this confusion is understandable. Miss White made this connection because Lowndes had disingenuously advertised *Evelina* and *The Sylph* together, in an effort to increase his sales by making people think they were by the same author. Dr Burney wrote a complaining letter to Lowndes, but there was no other recourse.[14] Life is difficult enough for authors cornered by people who have read their books carefully, but it is worse when they are harangued by those who only vaguely remember their books, or as in this case have totally mistaken them for someone else. In such situations, everybody's ego turns soggy in the fog.

One of the chief characters in *Evelina* who had been criticized – by the *Critical Review* and by Burney's father – was Captain Mirvan, a brutal portrait of a man rendered angry and insensitive by his life at sea. In Bath, whenever Burney met a Captain, she was the butt of pointed remarks. The effect of these remarks was not to raise a sense of shame or of regret, but to reinforce her initial decision:

> the more I see of sea Captains, the less reason I have to be ashamed of Captain Mirvan: for they have all so irresistable [sic] a propensity to wanton mischief, to *roasting* Beaus, & detesting old women, that I quite rejoice that I shewed the Book to no one ere printed, lest I should have been prevailed upon to soften his Character.
>
> (*EJL* 4, forthcoming)

Burney gives herself a double message here – that when she shows people her writing she can be harried to change it, and that she should resist this.

Though staying with the Thrales in Bath was certainly interesting, it was depleting as well. Whether consciously or unconsciously, Burney had failed to notice the strains in the Thrale marriage, but now it was impossible to ignore the effect of Mr Thrale's stroke, especially his manic and unreasonable behavior. The need to circulate through Bath society was much more tedious than Samuel Crisp thought. Burney thought of going home to St Martin's Street, Leicester Square. To escape her meddling stepmother, she might incarcerate herself in the cupola, once Newton's observatory, where the rest of the family had watched with trepidation the fires during the Gordon Riots. This would be an inspiring place to write. Eventually, she and her father escaped to Samuel Crisp's at Chessington, where they could both work without interruption. Since Frances Burney was now an author in her own right, she could no longer be employed to copy the *History of Music*. Burney's sister Charlotte came for that task, leaving Susanna to take care of her stepmother. After a while, Charlotte and Susanna changed places. When Burney went to Chessington on 22 August 1780, she allowed Crisp to read the beginning of her new novel. He supplied the support every novelist needs at the start. He came to her room and said only, 'It will do! It will do!' Shortly after *Cecilia* was published Burney recalled this moment in a letter to Crisp: 'From the moment I heard those welcome Words, from the severest of all my Judges, I took inward courage.' (*EJL* 4, forthcoming) Crisp had been a strong voice against her play *The Witlings*, so that his support here buoyed her all the more.

Writing and actually finishing a novel, revising it, copying it, correcting it, was always particularly exhausting for Burney, who stayed on at Chessington after her father left, working unceasingly. Lowndes had asked her to finish her third volume of *Evelina* as if it were the work of a minute, and she had complained bitterly about his thoughtlessness. Now she saw her father as the chief slave-driver. 'I am *afraid* of seeing my father', she wrote in January to Susanna. Her father had an amanuensis, but she did not, and her book was more than twice as long.[15] Burney's father applied pressure and a sense of urgency. His motive was professional. He thought, rightly, as it turned out, that if he were to publish his second volume of the *History of Music* in the year when she published her second novel, both books would gain by the association. And he was planning to finish in 1781. Burney felt the strain, complaining eloquently to Susanna:

> Think of a whole Volume not yet *settled*, not yet begun! – & that so important a one as the last! – O that I could defer the publication, & relieve my Mind from this vile solicitude which does but shackle it, & disturbs my rest so abominably, that I cannot sleep half the Night for planning what to write next Day, – & then next Day am half dead for want of rest! (*EJL* 4, forthcoming)

At the same period, her father was brought with difficulty to reconcile himself to her brother Charles, whose wild spendthrift habits had meant that the Bishop of London refused to ordain him. In addition, she was worried that Susanna's plan to marry Molesworth Phillips would result in mutual penury, not to speak of the fact that she would be losing her alter ego, her best friend.

The situations in her life are clearly reflected in her novel – not being able to control your own destiny, not being able to help those who are about to make mistakes. These personal difficulties may in part account for her tiredness. She was soon to come down with a fever, requiring rest, a recurrent health problem that pursued her throughout her exceedingly long and essentially healthy life. So far, in February 1781, she had finished only the first volume. It is clear that Burney was being pushed, but it is not really unusual that a writer should write herself into illness, and groan: 'I cannot sleep half the night for planning what to write next Day, & then next day am half dead for want of rest!' (Hemlow, p. 143) Her sister Susanna noted in her journal that Burney never had much physical energy, and that any 'anxiety or distress of mind' always 'touched' her (Hemlow, p. 145). There were many emotions that Burney felt as excess, beyond her frame, but rather than avoiding them, she deliberately chose to write about them.

These excessive emotions in *Cecilia* have disturbed readers, who have tended to discount them as unrealistic. Terry Castle, for instance, in her perceptive discussion of *Cecilia*, complains that 'the novel often lapses into bizarre and hectic melodrama', and suffers from a 'discontinuous, confused narrative structure'.[16] This, I would argue, is to take two of Burney's most distinctive qualities and re-define them as defects. Samuel Johnson commended Burney for her 'mule' characters. These mules and these bizarre episodes are essential to the many-faceted achievement Burney deliberately sought. *Cecilia*'s abundant characters and scenes are painstakingly planned so that the many incidents resonate meaningfully with one another.

Evelina had been 'boisterous', said Mrs Montagu. *Cecilia* was even more so – more rough, more violent, more tempestuous. Complaining every step of the way, writing as fast as she possibly could, Burney spent another year finishing the first draft of her second novel. Part of the problem was that the conception of *Cecilia* required that it be much longer than *Evelina*: 'the work will be a long one, & I cannot without ruining it make it otherwise' (*EJL* 4, forthcoming). Its length was part of the superabundant energy that one would find in a 'boisterous' writer. In December 1781, Burney finished the first draft. She attended her sister's wedding in January, enjoying Susanna's happiness, but as she had written earlier: 'there is something to me in the thought of being so near parting with you as the Inmate of the same House – Room – Bed – confidence & life, that is not very *merrifying*' (*EJL* 4, forthcoming). She had achieved with Susanna a kind of intimacy few people ever know.

Under an extremely tight deadline, Burney recopied her work for the press. By March 1782 she had finished copying the first volume. It was already in press while she was transcribing the later volumes. Indeed, in some cases she simply transferred her first draft into the final version without recopying. The fact that *Cecilia* is approximately twice as long as *Evelina* marks an important transition in Burney's work. After *Evelina*, like nearly all her contemporaries, she wrote expansive and inclusive novels. In order to incorporate all of the themes she wanted to address, all of the characters she needed to develop, she required approximately 400 000 words.

Evelina, though replete with fathers, is the story of a woman who is effectively an orphan. In *Cecilia*, Burney dispensed with her heroine's entire family. Mother, father, siblings, all are gone. What is left is the typical orphan virgin whom Johnson ridiculed in *Rasselas* as the center of his hero's dreams.[17] Cecilia Beverley is an orphan, but she is a lucky orphan. She possesses an elegant form, a beautiful face, a liberal heart, intelligence, understanding, sensibility, and fortitude. And she is rich. Besides a fortune of £10 000, she has an income of £3000 a year. Even with all these advantages, Cecilia suffers, agonizingly, from the strictures imposed on women who lack families. She has three guardians, all either fools or knaves. Evelina's guardian Mr Villars is sometimes wrong, but always well-meaning. Cecilia's three guardians are all monsters. Mr Harrel is a consumer and gambler whose chief interest is *ton*, how to attain it and keep it. Mr Briggs is a sordid miser, whose money comes from trade. He combines fanatic avarice with a jolliness and friendliness that is nearly as unnerving as his covetousness. Mr Delvile, an aristocrat, is always too busy to be human: his pride chills everyone who has dealings with him. Besides the three guardians, there is Mr Monckton, an old family friend who hopes his aged wife will die soon enough for him to marry Cecilia. The only apparent hindrance on Cecilia is the stricture (fairly common in the eighteenth century) that when she marries, if she wishes to collect her income of £3000 per annum, her husband must take her name. It is her misfortune to fall in love with Mortimer Delvile, whose name his father and mother take seriously. Naming – actual names, nicknames, and sobriquets – was part of the masking behavior so popular in the Burney household and indeed in the households of many of their friends and neighbors. Burney's father called her 'Fan', and she loved to play with her brother Charles's name, dubbing him Carlos or Carlucci. Mary Delany when married to Pendarves signed herself 'Pen', and gave all her friends nicknames and sobriquets; Samuel Johnson referred to Sherry-Derry, Bozzy, and Goldy. When, at the end of the novel, Cecilia's suffering becomes so acute that she loses her mind, she clings to her husband's name. In her madness, the name becomes a talisman, a specter, and a child, all at once: 'three times I called upon it in the dead of night . . . and when I was abandoned and left alone, I repeated it and sung to it' (p. 907). Cecilia goes mad because she is completely alone. Her father-in-law has refused her admittance to the family home. She fears that her headstrong husband will fight a duel. At last she sees him, and runs after his just-vanished form. Passersby fleece her pockets. Soon she is lost, moneyless, agonizingly isolated.[18] Her only comfort is the memory of a name, a memory which seems to be all there is left. What's in a name? Burney gives us joy mixed with suffering, but no final answers.

Joyce Hemlow regrets that Burney did not have the opportunity to revise and cut, and nearly every contemporary review wished the novel shorter. It is true that many of the characters talk at length. Some of this particular repetition could have been cut out, but such cuts would not have excised very much. Even though many reviewers were frustrated at the length, the *Critical Review* said in December 1782 that *Cecilia* 'draws us on insensibly from page to page, and keeps up our constant attention from beginning to end' (54:414). Gibbon read it in a day, and Burke found this claim unbelievable, because he read it in three days, and he 'never parted with it from the time I first opened it' (*DL* 2:141). Among the most avid readers of *Cecilia* were the schoolboys at Rugby, nine of whom borrowed the novel as soon as it arrived at the local lending library. The youngest reader was only ten.[19] *Cecilia* is a page-turner, and page-turners resist being fiddled with. What it might have gained through pruning, it might have lost in power.[20]

On 19 December 1782, just as Burney finished her first draft of *Cecilia*, she and her father signed an agreement for publication. She had abandoned Thomas Lowndes, whose skimpy original offer and tardy addition of a mere £10 extra were not sufficient to inspire loyalty. No longer hampered by anonymity, she had gone to a family friend, her brother James's father-in-law, Thomas Payne. From the start, Payne was interested. In a practice common at the time, he decided to share the capital costs with fellow-bookseller Thomas Cadell.[21]

When Lowndes realized that he had lost that valuable property, Burney's second novel, he wrote to her father, enviously suggesting that Cadell had 'circumvented you with unbecoming Art', although depicting Payne as 'a worthy honest Man'.[22] Lowndes was clearly smarting. Calling forth his best financial hyperbole, he says, 'If your Copy had been worth £10 000 I could have raised it as soon as any Man in the Trade, and my Character is as fair as any Merchant's of *London*. At a Meeting of Booksellers this Day, I was asked, Why I had not *Cecilia*? I answered, I did not know, but I would tell them soon. – I beg you'll tell me the Reason.' It is astounding to a twentieth-century reader that Lowndes wrote to the author's father rather than to the author. He said at the beginning of his letter that he had stopped by to purchase the second volume of Dr Burney's history of music, and to talk about *Cecilia*. Hence he was writing to the author of *The History of Music*. Lowndes' desire to negotiate with the most powerful male in the picture is not atypical. It is also just barely possible that he thought the father more malleable. Unmentioned in this exchange was the flap over Lowndes' advertisement of *The Sylph*, but this action, by linking Frances Burney with a quite equivocal if not steamy production, may still have rankled with both father and daughter. Though Lowndes wrote to the father, the reply he received, dated from Surrey, 16 September 1782, comes from the daughter. It is crisp and unremittingly professional, with no apologies and no details.

> The Author of *Evelina* is much surprised that Mr *Lowndes* should trouble himself to enquire any Reason why he did not publish *Cecilia*. She is certainly neither under Engagement or Obligation to *any* Bookseller whatever, and is to no one, therefore, responsible for chusing, and changing as she pleases.   (DL 2:482)

Burney may have received help in composing this letter, which took about nine days to write. Did she in fact write it? If her father had written it, the style would have been more politic. In its directness and imperturbability it sounds more like the woman who would later face down the gendarme threatening to confiscate the manuscript of *The Wanderer* at Dunkirk in 1812.

Burney and her father appear to have done most of the negotiating. The terms they settled for were, as with *Evelina*, a simple agreement for copyright. The publishers between them would pay her £200 for the first edition and £50 if there should be a second.[23] Although in choosing Payne the Burneys had assumed that the family connection would assure fairness and honesty, they nonetheless suffered from sharp practices. Burney had to apply pressure even to receive her initial payment, due upon publication. Her sister Susanna's husband Molesworth Phillips had to dun Payne for this £100, which did not arrive until 14 July 1782, two days after publication. Burney used some of the money to visit her sister Susanna, with the express purpose of reading *Cecilia* to her. Cadell took even longer. It was a full month later that Payne collected his partner's £100 and brought it to Burney. At the signing of the contract, Dr Burney had not stipulated the size of the first edition, expecting that it would be a mere 500 copies, like *Evelina*. When Burney was at last paid her second £100, she discovered that instead of 500 copies, Payne and Cadell had printed 2000, calling this enormous cache of books the first edition. Burney wrote to Susanna of her annoyance about the egregious size of the first edition: 'This was not fair, as the £50 was *jockeyed* out of me by surprise, *after* the Bargain had been settled with my Father, & as Evelina had at first, only 500.'[24] Presumably the figure Dr Burney settled on was £250. Payne and Cadell evidently then asked Burney to accept £200 for the first edition, with the extra £50 to be paid for the second edition. This would have been reasonable if the edition had consisted of 500 copies, which the Burneys had every right to assume. Payne and Cadell also invidiously delayed paying even the £50, holding it up until December, even though the bloated first edition had sold out in October. Dr Burney was irritated: the publishers were 'mean *Cretters*'. Dr Johnson calculated that the booksellers had made a whopping £500 from their 2000-copy first edition.[25] Eventually, it seems, Payne and Cadell paid Burney another £50, bringing the whole sum to £300. This is quite paltry, considering the number of copies sold. Although envy may have been the chief source for Lowndes' criticism of Cadell, he certainly hit the mark. Samuel Crisp, on the other hand, wrote to his sister Sophia Gast that this was 'a pretty Spill (£300) for a young girl in a few months to get by sitting still in her Chamber by a good Fire!' He also mentions that they planned to give her in addition 'a handsome pair of Gloves'.[26] Crisp's condescending, bland satisfaction entirely ignores the fact that *Evelina* had been published four years before. The comfortable girl had made only £75 per year (and a cash bonus worth a pair of gloves), which is hardly munificent, especially since she had also been felled by a fever presumably brought on by overwork. The next time Burney published a novel, her dear, condescending Mr Crisp was dead. She did not allow her father to supervise the negotiations for *Camilla*.

The reception of *Cecilia* was extremely satisfying. Not only did the public race to buy the huge first edition, but also the subsequent editions continued to sell out. By the time of Burney's death there were at least 27 of them, almost as many as of *Evelina*.[27] Burney would have been happier, of course, if she had been receiving some of the money earned by the continued popularity of her book, but being a popular author was extremely satisfying. Anna Laetitia Barbauld asserted that 'next to the balloon', Burney was 'the object of public curiosity'.[28] The reviews for this second novel were very supportive, though they included some critical comments, partly perhaps because they were on the whole much longer. For the second edition, Burney made some changes. These were minor, but they indicated that she carefully considered details. She re-distributed her material so that the five volumes were more nearly equal in size, and altered approximately a hundred words and phrases. Many of the verbal shifts were in the direction of greater linguistic simplicity.[29]

In the *Critical Review* the notice of *Cecilia* immediately followed the review of her father's second volume of *The History of Music*. As Dr Burney had hoped, the two reinforced one another. *Evelina*, because anonymous, went to the monthlies unaided, but Dr Burney liked to control the responses to his work, and he carefully monitored the reviewing process. Dr Burney's review in the *Critical* might well have been written by his friend and mentor Thomas Twining.[30]

Although the *Monthly Review* published its notice of *Cecilia* before it actually reviewed her father's book, an entirely laudatory notice by William Bewley on *The History of Music* appeared later in 1782. Lonsdale says of the dual publication that although Twining wrote Burney a letter speculating about who would read the *History* if *Cecilia* was going to sell at such a rate, Dr Burney was never jealous: 'he genuinely cared less for his own fame than for that of the family, as a whole, of which he was the head' (p. 270). According to Twining, then, Dr Burney's egotism as a patriarch was as great as his desire for fame as an author, a likely equivalence in the eighteenth century, but actually not true in Dr Burney's case. It is true that Dr Burney was perennially concerned that the members of his family should be equal to its public image, an image necessary for their always somewhat tenuous social situation. He was so busy maintaining this image that he worked when riding on horseback. Dr Burney was undoubtedly proud when Edmund Burke wrote to his daughter 'on the great honour acquired to his family' by *Cecilia* (*DL* 2:94). The family was certainly important. But *The History of Music* was the center of Dr Burney's life. When Arthur Murphy in 1778 said 'what a sad man is Dr Burney for running away so!', Thrale gave a harsh but just assessment when she replied, 'I often say Dr Burney is the most of a male coquet of any man I know; for he only gives one enough of his company to excite a desire for more.' (*DL*, 1:203) This was the busy, distant father who had insisted that his daughter rush through the writing of her novel so that they could publish together. Thrale remarked that Dr Charles Burney was the most beloved father she had ever seen, but later on, when Burney published her version of her father's *Memoirs*, she understated the contiguity of publication between *Cecilia* and *The History of Music*. She discussed the reception of her father's book before even mentioning the composition of her own. The year is 1782, but the two books are never mentioned in the same context. Love and envy are not so incompatible as we sometimes like to believe.[31]

Burney had said in her strong introduction to *Evelina* that she would not follow the paths used and made barren by her famous male predecessors. In many ways in *Cecilia* she also resisted influence. She wrote as many pages as she needed, even though her father wanted her to finish quickly. Because it suited her purposes, she retained the plot in which a young woman marries into the aristocracy, even though the *Critical Review* had eloquently objected to this plot in *Evelina*. This review argued that the plot was unnatural and that the romantic dreams it fostered 'embittered' readers' lives.[32]

Various ranks do collide in *Evelina*, but Lord Orville is certainly the most idealized character in the novel, and he is a Lord. To marry a Lord was not a condition which Burney's readers could reasonably hope to achieve. In *Cecilia*, a pretty working-class woman named Henrietta Belfield aspires after Delvile, who will someday inherit a title, but her desires are depicted as completely misplaced. Though eventually she does marry up, she does not marry into the aristocracy. Her brother, who searches everywhere for the independent life, finds that though every other field seems greener and more beautiful, none of them brings true independence. Belfield at last contentedly enters the army, hardly a sentimental solution for a quixotic young man who has tried writing, day-laboring, and manifold other possibilities. Choderlos de Laclos, author of *Les liaisons dangereuses*, particularly liked the characterization of Belfield. The older Delvile, who from the height of his lofty pedigree despises everyone, even writers, is the chief representative here of aristocracy. What drives him is not pride, but rather 'self-sufficiency', a word Burney inserted to replace 'pride' in her page proofs (5:263). Of writers he warns: 'Let me counsel you to remember that a lady ... should never degrade herself by being put on a level with writers, and such sort of people.' (p. 186) These characters are examples of one of the most important qualities of *Cecilia*. Doody emphasizes that 'Burney is one of the first novelists to see that each person is the bearer or representative of what Marxist critics have taught us to call an "ideology".' (p. 118) Burney notices this in life; we see this kind of portrait in the diary. But she also has a literary source in the philosophical tale, including Voltaire and Johnson. Burney's characters are different from those in a philosophical tale in that they are much more mixed. They carry their ideology, but the ideology is at times incompatible with their personalities, or they suddenly shift to a different ideology or discourse, as real people will do.

For the middle class, whom the *Critical* designated as the chief audience for novels, Burney created Mr Hobson, a shopkeeper drawn from the 'temperate zone of middle life', whose unflappable directness and pleasant self-centeredness derive from his statement: 'Let every man speak to be understood, ... that's my notion of things.' (p. 409) As for what the *Critical* called 'the chilling climate of low life' where happiness is difficult to find (p. 204), Cecilia is aware of the need to recognize that some people are happier with their peers. She directs that the children of a pew-opener whom she supports should 'be coarsely brought up, having no intention to provide for them but by helping them to common employments' (p. 791).

The author who made these choices also wrote the 'Advertisement' which she placed right after the title-page of *Cecilia*. This touts the successes of *Evelina*, denies vanity, and is addressed not to the reviewers but to the public, which responded to the novel even more positively than the reviewers. The tone of this brief welcome is quite different from the longer, canceled preface which still exists in the Egerton Manuscripts.[33] Burney was right to drop this preface, which was too large a bundle for such a rich book. But this canceled preface is an important key to Burney-as-author. There the author depicts three kinds of writers: those who think they have genius, those who are more addicted to vanity, and those who might be called the 'Quakers of Litterature' [sic]. The last are both fearful of public response and passionately inspired. Burney was like this herself. At one point she eloquently evokes the kind of complexity I have been recreating in this literary life. Her motives for writing, she says, 'are so minute & complex, as to baffle all the power of Language', and that to express them, to characterize the 'Mind of Man', she needs to quote Addison on the 'Ways of Heaven', 'Dark & Intricate, / Filled with wild Mazes, & perplexed with *Error*' (p. 945). This quotation represents her own mind, and the minds of her characters. The work of Frances Burney is 'filled with wild mazes'. When we read her we must always be aware that there is nothing we can with full confidence call the truth.

The *Critical* piece on *Cecilia* is positive, but the review is not really intelligent. The reviewer quotes pages from a love scene, with the implication that women readers will enjoy 'the interesting and pathetic', and complains that some of Burney's middle-class characters 'interrupt more interesting business' (pp. 416, 420). More energetically, *The London Magazine* speaks of the author's 'vigorous and capacious' mind, a phrase worth remembering when we consider how often Burney has been called inhibited, even timorous.[34] *Town and Country Magazine*, indulging in the kind of condescension Burney was trying to avoid when she masqueraded as a man in the preface to *Evelina*, calls the style 'classical', 'though written by a lady'.[35] *The Monthly Review* does mention some of the characters included in this vigorous and capacious book. Albany, for instance, catches their attention. They are themselves driven to torment by one tormenting scene, a scene whose characters are so irritating that the reviewers wish the author had omitted the incident altogether.

Having abandoned the epistolarity of *Evelina* for the freer style of third-person narrative, Burney had found a more limpid medium. Her third-person narrative stays close to the center, and as Doody has pointed out, she often uses *style indirect libre*, or free indirect discourse, where a character within the third-person narrative can from time to time become the intellectual center of that narrative without any need for the author to pass judgment.[36] Hence, the characters seem extremely life-like, puppets who have escaped their strings. Burney's friend Thrale claimed that Burney had written a novel not for all time, but for the age, calling *Cecilia*:

> the Picture of Life such as the Author sees it: while therefore this Mode of Life lasts, her Book will be of value, as the Representation is astonishingly perfect: but as nothing in the Book is derived from Study, so it can have no Principle of Duration – Burney's Cecilia is to Richardson's Clarissa – what a Camera Obscura in the Window of a London Parlour, – is to a view of Venice by the clear Pencil of Cannaletti.[37]

This insistence on the accuracy of *Cecilia*, and its lack of 'study', is remarkable, because twentieth-century readers have almost entirely lost the ability to see the book as a slice of life, although they have become increasingly aware of how much 'study' went into it.[38] What is obvious to us is completely different from what was obvious to Thrale, and what is obvious to us is changing as we reconsider the eighteenth century through heightened understanding of feminism, and experience increasingly the violent uncertainties of the present-day world.[39]

Burney rendered these qualities with her 'camera obscura' and with all the art she could milk from her male and female predecessors, and especially, as someone who had been smitten with Garrick's performances, from Shakespeare. In this book the body, as always in Burney, is both passion's center and the site of intimate cruelty. But more omnipresent than this intimate cruelty is the sense that there is a character who, like Hamlet or Lear, is out of control, who manipulates other people in ways that drive them wild. In these scenes, as often in Shakespeare – even in eighteenth-century adaptations of Shakespeare – comedy and tragedy are promiscuously mingled. These episodes take place at the edges of experience where few would dare to venture.

Stymied in her efforts to stage a play, Burney had turned her dramatic interests and techniques to the novel. All the action of her novel takes place in 1779, when she was working on her play and carefully assessing the theatrical scene. Although her third-person narrative brings her much closer than she was in *Evelina* to Fielding's style of comic epic, and actually uses his division of his novels into books with separate chapters, Burney divides *Cecilia* into five volumes, which serve as acts. Cecilia meets her mysterious hero Delvile dressed as a domino at a masquerade in Volume I; her relationships with her guardians and suitors are developed in Volume II; the climax occurs when her guardian Mr Harrel commits suicide in Volume III; in spite of their interrupted wedding, she reaches an understanding with her lover Delvile in Volume IV; and after a torment of impediments she finally marries him at the end of Volume V. Rather than including a first-person author–persona, which is Fielding's and Sterne's technique, or interposing an interlocutor, as Sarah Scott does in *Millenium Hall* (1762), Burney chooses instead to provide a half-mad commentator, who serves as an embedded chorus. This 'crazy old moralist' was her father's favorite character. This pleased her, since no one else, before the *Monthly Review*, had even mentioned him. His name is Albany, after the 'milk-livered' husband to Lear's evil daughter Goneril in *King Lear*. The hero Delvile was originally called

Albany. He was to be alter ego to the purely white Albina, Cecilia's original name in earlier drafts of the novel. Burney might have found the name Albina in Hannah Cowley's play of that name (1779), and throughout the novel there is evidence that she was affected by her reading of other women dramatists.[40] Eventually, Burney chose the name Delvile for her hero, giving him the 'ville' of *Evelina*'s admirable characters, but changing it radically by removing one of the final l's, so that it veers to 'vile', and extremely close to 'devil'. The surname becomes even more questionable when the young man's first name, after being 'Egerton' and 'Randolph', becomes the more deathly 'Mortimer'. In keeping with Burney mixed characters, however, Delvile would also be the 'noble Mortimer' referred to briefly in Shakespeare's *Henry IV, Part 1* (1.1.38). Burney transferred Cecilia as the heroine's first name from her quashed play *The Witlings*. She uses the connections between Cecilia and Saint Cecilia as patron of music subtly, and not often, linking her through music to Albany when both of them listen 'enraptured' to Pacchierotti, the Italian castrato whose music Burney had heard in her own home and whose sexually ambiguous sweetness appealed to her (p. 65). By including Albany, Burney has unsettled the simple oppositions of her original names and thereby expanded her meanings.

The fact that Albany and Mortimer appear in Shakespeare is important. Rather than reflecting Homer and Cervantes, as Fielding did, or establishing layers of allusion similar to those Charlotte Lennox produced in *The Female Quixote* (1752), Burney decided on the original and ambitious course of creating in her novel a tissue of references to Shakespeare. She had to do this without being heavy-handed or obvious about it, or neglecting what Thrale calls the camera obscura. Sarah Fielding had also gone to Shakespeare for inspiration, but either deviated into philosophical dialogue, as in *The Cry* (1754), or stayed very close to the text, recasting Shakespeare's characters into her own dialogues in *Octavia and Cleopatra* (1757). Burney's method is quite different. In *Evelina* she mentioned that her heroine attends a performance of *King Lear*, leaving it entirely to the reader to make the parallels to the rejecting father and the worthy daughter. Here, she borrows lightly throughout Shakespeare's works, trying in particular to create characters who cannot easily be type-cast.

The plot of *Cecilia* is a remake of *Romeo and Juliet*, set squarely in 1779.[41] 'What's in a name?' is the central question. *Evelina* was a nobody, a woman without a name. 'Anville' was only an anagram of Evelina. Her real family name of Belmont, though always privately known, arrives publicly only at the end. In *Cecilia* the heroine's name and its significance are at the center of the plot. The Delvile family will not allow their son to change his name to Beverley, as Cecilia's uncle's will requires.[42] As in *Romeo and Juliet*, then, family pride – or family self-sufficiency – cripples the lovers' plans. In addition, besides the fact that the heroine meets the hero at the masquerade in the first volume, two duels are fought, and whenever there is a quarrel a duel always threatens. There are many rivals who are analogues for Paris; the lovers secretly marry, with disastrous though in this case remediable effects; and there are three characters who act the pandering part of the nurse. Burney makes this comparison to *Romeo and Juliet* unmistakably explicit when an irrepressible meddler named Lady Honoraria suggests that the departing Delvile should look up at Cecilia's window:

> for if he will play Romeo, you, I dare say, will play Juliet, and this old castle is quite the thing for the musty family of the Capulets: I dare say Shakespear thought of it when he wrote of them. (p. 503)

A few pages later, Delvile connects himself to Romeo, when he tells Cecilia how much he loves her, prefacing his declaration by saying, *'he jests at scars who never felt a wound'*.[43] *Romeo and Juliet* was acted in London 20 times during the 1776–80 seasons.[44] Burney knew that her audience was familiar with the play. According to a contemporary actor, Garrick's most thrilling line was: 'Parents have flinty hearts, and children must be wretched.'[45] Burney was struggling to write in the midst of her father's pressure to finish, family quarrels with her brother Charles, her sister's struggle to convince their father that her fiancé could support her in marriage, and her own illness. For Burney Romeo's lines must have rung particularly true.

Castle discusses Burney's use of *Romeo and Juliet*, emphasizing that she makes her plot much more 'sentimental'. Burney allows her protagonists to live and marry, just as Nahum Tate had revised *King Lear* into a love story between Cordelia and Edgar. Compared to Fielding, Burney is a sentimental writer. For one thing, her language is much more genteel. But people do not go insane in Fielding, and they do not kill themselves. The characters tend to be single rather than multiple, horses and asses rather than Shakespearean or Burneyan mules. Johnson had been so moved by *King Lear* that he had never been able to re-read it until he was forced to do so as an editor. Reading Shakespeare he would look up, startled to find himself alone. He hated the endings in Shakespeare, because there was no poetic justice. Sensibility in the eighteenth century, as recent scholarship has shown, is more pervasive than has been thought. Syndy Conger argues that even though Wollstonecraft rejected sensibility in her *Vindication of the Rights of Woman*, she did so only as an intellectual necessity, renouncing its public but not its private forms. A person who embodied sensibility could be irrational, idealistic, intellectually passionate, suicidal, or a combination of all these. The extremes could be terrifying, the transformations sudden, but the emotions themselves were the stuff of eighteenth-century life.[46]

Burney did not confine *Cecilia* to *Romeo and Juliet*. In addition to the *Romeo and Juliet* frame, Burney also quotes and imitates other Shakespearean plays including *Hamlet, Macbeth, Henry the Fourth, Part One,* and *King Lear*. She and Mrs Thrale had attended *The Merchant of Venice* in Bath. This play provides perhaps the most important of the other Shakespearean resonances in *Cecilia*. Allusions to *The Merchant of Venice* turn the novel from tragedy to comedy, amplify the importance of a 'bond', and remind the reader that one of the main subjects of this novel is money. Doody calls Cecilia 'an impeded Portia', whose choices are obstructed by the strictures on her inheritance (p. 111). There are at least three references to *The Merchant of Venice* in the novel.[47] But *Romeo and Juliet* pervades the text.

Romeo and Juliet is a good model for Burney's purposes for a number of reasons. The subject matter of family pride and the arbitrariness of naming are central elements. The heroine is isolated, and must rely on advice from people who are not sufficiently trustworthy or not sufficiently informed, like Juliet's nurse and Friar Laurence. In *Cecilia* the heroine has difficulty making herself understood. Lovers and strangers are equally dense. Straub emphasizes that *Cecilia* 'marks a shift in Burney's fiction from a romance plot that points to its source in female creative desire – signalling its own generic limits – to a plot that emphasizes far more painfully the tenuousness of female creative control over audience' (p. 171). There is also a wildness of genre in *Romeo and Juliet* that is similar to the combinations of fear, violence, love, and humor in *Evelina*. Though *Romeo and Juliet* is a tragedy, the comic elements nearly overwhelm it. In the famous 1750 contest between Covent Garden and Drury Lane, when both houses competed by playing *Romeo and Juliet*, Mercutio at Covent Garden was played as slapstick. *Cecilia* is a much more ambitious novel than *Evelina*, longer, more involved, entering into a wider world. *Evelina* mixed violence with comedy, but there were no deaths. Although suicide seemed a possibility, it was redefined. In *Evelina*, though evil was not denied, it was expressed chiefly in excessive behavior. In *Cecilia*, suicide happens, and evil people inhabit the center of the plot. Although Burney allows a happy ending, her novel is both darker and funnier than Shakespeare's play, closer to the edges where emotions turn wild.

Though Burney borrowed wholesale from Shakespeare, she retained careful control of her text. Her chapter headings, for instance, were not printed separately in the first edition. When put together, as they are in the World's Classics edition, they demonstrate that Burney was thinking of one central effect in each chapter. All of the chapter-headings are general, most of them consisting of the article 'A' and a single word, such as: 'A Supplication', 'An Evasion', 'A Man of the Ton', 'A Disturbance', 'A Calm', 'A Shock', 'A Prating', and 'A Termination'. One of the most striking is 'A Torment', the chapter that ends Book VII. Cecilia is journeying to meet Delvile in order to marry him, and the Harrels' flock of *ton* friends impede her: 'her total inability of resistance obliged her to submit, and compelled her to go, stop, or turn, according to their own motions' (p. 608). According to the *Monthly Review*, some of these 'ton' friends were 'intolerable, and almost as intolerable in fiction as they would be in reality. We are always sorry to meet with them, and glad to get rid of them.' The *Monthly* reviewer's 'dislike of such insignificants rose into indignation ... when Cecilia met with such a provoking interruption on her journey to London' (p. 450). This objection raises the interesting question of whether the reader of any novel should ever be made to suffer as much as the protagonist. Are the 'insignificants' sufficiently comic to warrant their presence in the book? For one eighteenth-century reader, some kinds of suffering were evidently acceptable. This kind of torment was not.

Since the contemporary objection was so specific, this scene requires consideration. What did the *Monthly* find so intolerable? Does the scene strike a modern reader as equally insupportable? The characters the reviewer protested against appear at the start of the novel, and keep reappearing. In this scene they are (besides two pleasant and unremarkable elderly women, Mrs Mears and Mrs Charlton) Mr Morrice (a young lawyer so supple in his disposition that he is 'rising in his profession' because he makes no enemies and proves useful to so many people that he can call them his friends (p. 11)); Mr Aresby, ('a captain in the militia' who throws French words into nearly every sentence and makes it his business to adore the ladies, 'whom he held himself equipped to conquer'(p. 11)); Miss Larolles (whose volubility and self-regard are irrepressible); Mr Meadows (so careless of other people that attempting to gain his attention exhausts all but the most assiduous); and Mr Gosport (an elderly gentleman who talks rather like a conduct book and interferes repeatedly in other people's affairs; he divides the 'TON misses' into 'the SUPERCILIOUS, and the VOLUBLE' (p. 40)).

In the offending chapter, Cecilia (with her old friend Mrs Charlton) is on her way in a chaise from Bury in Suffolk to London, where she plans secretly to marry the hero Mortimer Delvile. They happen to pass an overturned chaise. When they hear such a torrent of words that they realize that Miss Larolles is one of the passengers, they attempt to escape the inevitable time-consuming commiserations. But Morrice, who is on horseback and has recognized them earlier, engineers the situation in such a way that Cecilia must walk to the next inn so that the two elderly women in the group can ride in her reliable chaise. We later learn that Morrice has been sent by Cecilia's perfidious adviser Monckton. At this point he seems merely to be egregiously officious. Delvile, meanwhile, rides by to check on her safety, and is recognized by Gosport. Cecilia is in torment because of Gosport's pointed questions, and because the Captain and Morrice at one point gallop off to try to unmask the muffled stranger who is Delvile. The torment is all mental. The only creature who suffers physically is Miss Larolles' unnamed lap dog. Though she loves it better than anything in the world, she forgets it from time to time, and then when she needs to carry it because its leg is broken, she discovers that it is rather heavy, and entrusts it to the Captain on his horse. He is so eager to catch the mysterious muffled rider that he drops the dog and breaks its other leg. This inability to take care of other creatures encapsulates one of the central human inadequacies in this novel. The dog's misfortune replicates in the body what the other characters have been enacting in the mind. The monkey in *Evelina* serves a similar purpose.

Burney easily could have omitted this chapter. If she had, what would have been lost? Up to this time, the *ton* characters have been an irritant, cause for fun, something to be avoided. They have been the vehicle for commentary by the author on pretension, sententiousness, insipidity, and a galaxy of other characteristics to be met with in *nouveau riche* society. Now they become not an irritant but a 'torment'. Miss Larolles chatters on: 'How is Mrs. Harrel? I was never so sorry for any body in my life. I quite forgot to ask after her.' (p. 599) No one bothers to answer her. She can be ignored, but Gosport has been questioning Cecilia closely. He develops a metaphor implying that she is like Delvile castle, impregnable from the outside, but inside perhaps entirely changed, 'while within, some lurking evil, some latent injury, has secretly worked its way in the very *heart* of the edifice'. The subtextual implications of this metaphor are so clearly tied to loss of virginity and accidental pregnancy that even the most innocent reader would be slightly shaken. 'Do you not know', says Gosport, 'that the place to which I allude may receive a mischief in as many minutes which double the number of years cannot rectify?' (p. 598) Meanwhile, Morrice tries to goad Meadows into remembering the night of Harrel's death, and Miss Larolles blurts out that Harrel's friends are furious because he had promised them that they could repair their fortunes by marrying Miss Beverley. Morrice escalates the fear and embarrassment of this situation by saying that old Delvile 'took her off into the country, on purpose to marry her to his own son' (p. 601). In the midst of this insinuating patter, Cecilia's fear of discovery becomes almost unbearable.

Burney has added another disturbing element by emphasizing Miss Larolles' injured dog. The fact that it has no name allows the reader to think about Delvile's dog Fidel. Unlike Evelina, who recognizes as inappropriate her guardian's advice that she act coolly toward Lord Orville, Cecilia had been following the stricture that a woman must not reveal her love to a man. Her secret was betrayed when Delvile overheard her telling his dog about the true state of her affections. Though she suffered excruciatingly at being thus found out, she was unable to retract her statements. Now another dog is being broken because the Captain is chasing Delvile. The dog is a terrible analogue for what may happen to their love. All this would be lost if Burney had cut the scene. Like the masquerade scene discussed below, like *Cecilia* itself, it is a tissue of allusion and realistic action. Unlike the *Monthly* reviewer, Choderlos de Laclos said that 'this scene of tiresome people would perhaps not have been disavowed by Molière'.[48]

Intolerable suffering in Burney is often connected to money. In all her novels, especially in the last three, she dwells on the effects of access to a wider variety of objects to buy. One of the chief reasons why *Cecilia* seemed so realistic to Burney's contemporaries (others also saw Thrale's camera obscura effect) is that, as Julia Epstein writes, Burney's 'merciless concern with financial detail ... marks this as a novel that broke new ground in the eighteenth century' (p. 160). This is a novel about money. As in *Evelina*, different classes accost one another, and stake out their positions in the hierarchy. In this novel the lower and the oppressed classes, especially the women, are allowed to speak. Though they are sympathetically presented, they are not idealized or sentimentalized. Mrs Hill, for instance, whose carpenter husband is dying, comes to collect the money owed her by Harrel. She is affecting, patient, informative, and kind, but also irritating. She never stops haranguing Cecilia about her dead son Billy. Even so, Cecilia takes pity on the family, and, when it appears that Harrel will never pay what he owes, pays the bill herself and helps the family to regain its economic foothold.

In *Cecilia*, more significantly than in *Evelina*, there are climactic, violent scenes, especially the masquerade where *Cecilia* first meets her lover; the scene where Harrel kills himself; and Cecilia's temporary insanity. These episodes take place at the edges of experience where few would dare to venture. Each scene is a nexus for the multiple emotions Burney would cluster at one event, as she had assembled them in *Evelina*. Such occasions in *Evelina* as Mme Duval's adventure in the ditch, the old women's race, and the angry monkey's rampage were opportunities to test characters in extreme conditions. In Burney's second novel the entire conception of the book is so much more complicated that the gathered many-voiced encounters are whipped up to a condition nothing short of frenzy. Perhaps the majority of readers have either ignored or rejected these wild emotions. Terry Castle condemns the final scenes: 'The plotting in the last volume of *Cecilia* is garish and hysterical, and comes more and more to resemble sheer paranoid fantasy.' (p. 281) I would argue that Burney's world – the one she actually lived in, as compared to the one she created in her fiction – was certainly at times garish and hysterical, and that she was rendering these qualities with her 'camera obscura' and also with all the art she could milk from her predecessors. The masquerade where Cecilia meets Delvile offers a good example.

The masquerade, which flourished in England most flamboyantly in the eighteenth century, has been brilliantly analyzed by Terry Castle. Castle shows that the masquerade was a place where both men and women, but especially women, could escape into a world where it was possible to talk to strangers and indulge without consequence in forbidden sexual innuendo. Public masquerades were more hazardous than private ones. There were tales of wives who thought they were going off with their husbands and were instead raped by strangers, but such events were not likely, although they added to the myth of danger. Catherine Craft-Fairchild sees the other side of the masquerade. Women in eighteenth-century fictions become as the century passes increasingly 'thwarted, balked, and frustrated', and the need to take part in an actual or metaphorical masquerade is an emblem of their restriction (p. 14).[49] *Cecilia* can contain both of these interpretations.

Burney's masquerade is both private and public. It begins in a private house, but eventually the crowd migrates to the Pantheon, a gigantic hall built in imitation of the original Pantheon at the corner of Oxford and Burney's old street, Poland Street.[50] Cecilia's guardian Mr Harrel, wishing to show the world that he has not suffered financial reverses, has decorated his home with a gallery to house an orchestra, and an awning with cut glass and lamps over the dessert table. He plans to invite masqueraders to gather in this splendid setting before the public event. If he were a careful person, his private masquerade would have had a guest list and an arrangement for everyone to unmask at a particular moment. Harrel and his wife ignore all these safety measures. Their one adoption of private practice is that they and Cecilia, as hosts, attend their own masquerade without costumes. This throws Cecilia into a world where everyone knows her, but she knows no one. She should be frightened. Instead, she is frustrated and confused.

The Harrels' masquerade is realistically presented, reflecting accurately the popular entertainment Burney herself experienced. It is also a usefully complex literary trope. Castle points out that as early as the first decade of the century masquerades had become in the literature of the period 'a familiar popular topos, a modern emblem, carrying multiple, indeed protean, metaphoric possibilities' (p. 4). Castle stresses that the masquerade is meant to show the 'profound financial theme of Burney's fiction' (p. 261). She also emphasizes that this scene is full of literary echoes. Besides the *Romeo and Juliet* references, there are a plethora of literary costumes, often sitting ironically on their wearers. Minerva is the air-headed Miss Larolles, Mentor cackles, and Shylock makes rapturous love. Others are exactly suited to their costumes. The idealistic and unwittingly destructive Belfield appears as Don Quixote, Briggs is a smelly, sooty chimney-sweeper (the costume costs him nothing), the callous and fortune-hunting Baronet Sir Robert Floyer is a Turk, and the devious Monckton is quite in character as a black devil, so heavily swathed that no one knows him. Monckton thought that in this costume he could keep Cecilia from making dangerous acquaintances, but his situation becomes wonderfully ludicrous, because he has growled so balefully at all her friends and admirers that he cannot unmask himself without revealing his duplicity. He attempts throughout to imprison her, to drive away all likely prospects, but in the end he imprisons only himself.

Meanwhile, as at the ball in *Romeo and Juliet*, a seeming stranger has managed to talk to her. He is dressed as a white domino, the entirely neutral costume, and he seems to know her other two guardians. He is in fact Delvile's son, and has crashed this party merely to meet her. He has fallen in love with her. As in Shakespeare, this is love at first sight, which we may think of as sentimental, but it happens. Throughout the evening people thrash one another as if in fun, especially when they are around Monckton in his devil costume. But none of the violence gets out of hand, and in spite of the ominous possibilities, the evening ends in farce. Morrice as Harlequin attempts to jump over the dessert table, and brings down the awning on the company.

Many disasters and 36 chapters later, there is another lunatic public scene. Cecilia has handed over to Harrel her £10 000 in ready money, borrowed from a Jew since she is not yet of age and Briggs wisely will not advance any sums small or large. With this sum in hand, Harrel is about to leave for the Continent. His houses will be seized by his creditors. There is nothing else to do. In a chapter coolly entitled 'A Man of Business', he insists on taking his wife and Cecilia to Vauxhall (the pleasure garden where classes mingled most freely) for one last fling before he departs. There he meets his creditors, Hobson and Simkins, and invites them to dinner with his rattling acquaintance Morrice, and sundry others. His wife objects along class lines to this horse, ass, and mule dinner party: 'Are you mad, Mr Harrel, are you mad! ... I am sure I shall die with shame.' (p. 402) Like Hamlet, he replies, 'Mad! ... no, not mad but merry.' (p. 402) But mad and merry in this situation are the same. Though Harrel is supposed to be apologizing to his wife, he is not really capable of true kindness, and he does not try to hide the fact that he is really more interested in Cecilia. He wishes, for instance, that he had met Cecilia before he had the habit of gambling. Her 'bright pattern of all goodness' (p. 399) might have been a model for him. Here though Harrel nearly quotes the mad King Lear on being a 'pattern of all patience' (3.2.37), he is also like Lovelace in Richardson's novel *Clarissa*, who briefly wishes that he had met Clarissa before he had depraved himself. If anything, Burney increases the irony, because Harrel is Cecilia's guardian, not her husband; her presumed mentor, not her inferior. Secretly, Burney must have often thought that children were morally superior to fathers. Harrel bristles with literary connections, but he is also realistic, a man trying just before he kills himself to make some kinds of amends, but too weak, too late, and too innately cruel. This is yet another example of Burney's skill at depicting intimate cruelty. Harrel's last act is to demand more company. He sees some pretty girls and despite Cecilia and Mrs Harrel's pleas and cries, he insists, drawing on an eighteenth-century husband's wide prerogative, 'I will teach you to welcome them.' Mrs Harrel names this plan accurately: 'This is cruel indeed', adding 'did you bring me here only to insult me?' 'No', he cries out dramatically, 'by this parting kiss' (p. 413). Then he stands on his bench, leaps over the table and the side of the box, and disappears into the crowd. They soon hear a pistol shot: Harrel has committed suicide. He is so drunk that he almost botches the job, but he does die after briefly lingering, lingering long enough so that Burney can show that Cecilia is sufficiently brave to try to help him, though she arrives too late. All she sees is blood covering the waiter who first reached him. Sir Robert Floyer, characteristically, has refused to comfort Harrel in his last agonies.

The most violent scenes in *Evelina* are in counterpoint with Evelina's meeting with her father. In *Cecilia* the comparable scene is the one where Delvile defies his mother, insisting that he will marry Cecilia. Instead of relenting, she cries 'My brain is on fire', and runs into the room next door, where she collapses, 'her face, hands and neck all covered with blood' (p. 680). She is unable to speak, but she is still imperious, and she will survive. This defiance by the dutiful child of the powerful parent is the antithesis of the scene in the earlier novel, where Evelina dutifully adores the father who has by his cruel neglect killed her mother. Crisp objected to the Mrs Delvile scene, but Burney refused to change it, explaining how carefully she had prepared for her mixed character of pride and kindness. This kind of mixture was unfamiliar to eighteenth-century readers, and required careful preparation. In the page proofs Burney made alterations that actually intensified the inconsistencies in Mrs Delvile's character. Burney was pleased to have her father's approbation for *Cecilia*, but it does not appear that she changed anything in order to indulge him or 'Daddy' Crisp.

Blood is a central memory in the episode where Cecilia loses her mind. Sir Robert Floyer and Belfield have already fought a duel over her. She fears that Delvile, who is as rash as Romeo, will become embroiled in the same situation. Belfield, 'whose size and figure exactly resembled' Delvile's, has become through a series of misunderstandings the target of Delvile's misplaced jealousy.[51] Eventually, Delvile will fight a duel, though it will be with Mr Monckton rather than with Belfield. Cecilia is right to worry. When she runs down the street after the vanished Delvile, all the events of the novel become confused in her mind. She believes that she, not Harrel, must go to France, because her husband has fought a duel and must sneak away, covered with blood. In all three scenes the classes are mixed, metaphorically in the first, and actually in the other two. The insane Cecilia stumbles into a pawn shop, where the owners lock her in a room without food or water, believing that they are giving her the proper treatment for a mad person. They think about finding her some straw to sleep on, since the stereotypical mad person was always lying like an animal on straw. Just as at the masquerade she could not escape the imprisoning devil, so here she cannot make herself understood. She is literally locked in. At times her madness is gentle. She is the victim who can only repeat her hero's name, with accents like Ophelia's. At other times she is more like a character out of *Lear*. She feels that the secret wedding she has at last contracted with Delvile is itself by its very nature evil. No longer recognizing her husband, she cries out to him:

> I am married, and no one will listen to me! ill were the auspices under which I gave my hand! Oh it was a work of darkness, unacceptable and offensive! it has been sealed, therefore, with blood, and to-morrow it will be signed with murder!   (p. 903)

Burney knows that when a woman is married she loses not merely her name but her legal powers. Hence, for Cecilia to say that she is married, and that therefore no one listens to her, is exactly just, though Cecilia does not know it. Like the mad Lear and the disguised poor Tom, her metaphor is 'darkness'. Here, Burney's text resonates again with itself, with the Harrel masquerade, where there was also a poor Tom, who sweated too much. Now Cecilia has turned tripartite: a grimly isolated Juliet, Lear and poor Tom wrapped in darkness, and Ophelia singing to figments, bleakly alone. But she is also a very realistically presented mad person, much stronger and more stubborn than when she is sane, tossing her head wildly back and forth, afraid that they will 'bury her alive' (p. 908). Is this madness simply a plot device gone wild as Castle says? I would argue that it might be the fate of any young woman who has been blocked at every turn, with every prop knocked away.

Cecilia is alone and friendless in an unruly city. She becomes feverish, and instead of being given the liquid needed to bring down a fever, she is denied food of any sort. This is the kind of material that Thrale thought of as so realistic, so timely that future generations would fail to understand it. To some degree this has been true. This phantasmagoria has seemed forced. Readers have for two centuries fled to the saner world of Jane Austen. Only now are we able to understand how genuine these scenes are. Only now, recognizing how justly Burney is depicting a woman's situation, can we reach beyond her realism and appreciate the way the various shapes collide and change in these three scenes. Belfield looks just like Delvile, and their names cross. Although there is minimal physical resemblance, Cecilia thinks briefly in her madness that Delvile is Mr Monckton, a connection so apparently unlikely that we must ponder it. Like Monckton, Delvile has desired her and made her suffer for his desire. It is not by chance that Monckton either acts or is compared to the devil. The Delviles are close to being devils themselves, in their name as in everything else. Nearly all of Burney's characters are mixed, speaking in several voices, shifting to disparate shapes. To show how difficult the world is for women, she created this scene. She did not see it as beyond the sensibilities of her times. We as readers need to listen to her message.

Cecilia ends in a way Samuel Crisp also objected to, and Burney again refused to change. The last chapter is called merely 'A Termination'. At the very end Cecilia's happiness is called 'imperfect', because human (p. 941). Cecilia regrets that she has had to give up her fortune for what the good family doctor, Dr Lyster, one of the most kindly and rational characters in the book, calls mere 'PRIDE and PREJUDICE'.[52] But she compares herself to others and realizes that her miseries are minor compared with the rest of humanity. She bears 'partial evil with chearfullest resignation' (p. 941). This ending was unusual for the period. Like Crisp, Burke objected: 'in a work of imagination ... there is no medium' (*DL*, 2:139). Burney did not quite possess the conversational ease to lock horns with Burke, but she had refused to change the ending to please Crisp. She thought *Cecilia*'s conclusion 'somewhat original', different from the 'hack Italian operas, with a jolly chorus that makes all parties good and all parties happy!' If she were to change it, she said, 'my whole plan is rendered abortive, and the last page of any novel in Mr Noble's circulating library may serve for the last page of mine, since a marriage, a reconciliation, and some sudden expedient for great riches, concludes them all alike' (*DL* 2:80–1). Actually, Burney did allow Cecilia to inherit money from Delvile's aunt, but even so Cecilia 'knew that, at times, the whole family must murmur at her loss of fortune, and at times she murmured to herself to be thus portionless, tho' an HEIRESS' (p. 941).

Regarding this ending, Burney's language to Crisp is exceptionally strong: 'my whole plan is rendered abortive'. In *Cecilia* Burney brought to her work all her literary experience, and especially her literary experience in Shakespeare's world. She depicted extremes of every sort, violent emotions and violent responses to them. But she also embedded this work in life as it is, in what Burney's imitator and parodic reviewer Godwin would later call 'things as they are'.[53] Cecilia experienced the extremes, but people do not live always at the extremes. Having given up her money and accepted the gentle yet headstrong Delvile, Cecilia does not live out her days in uninter-rupted, unalloyed joy. Every day there will be moments when having the fortune she had given up to marry Delvile would have enabled her to exercise the benevolence so central to her well being. Every day her husband will need special patience because he is so easily irritated, so quick to misunderstand. The work of the imagination, as Burney saw it, did allow the medium as well as the extremes. The template Burke and Crisp were imposing on her work was more patriarchal than comprehending. Certainly it was more rigid. It could not satisfy a protean writer like Burney.

5
Sufferer, Tragedian, and Witness (1784–92)

Taught with elaborate glare to hide each feeling
Frances Burney, *Edwy and Elgiva* (1.11.19; *Plays* 2:24)

In the years between 1783 and 1786 Burney lost three of her most important props. Samuel Crisp and Samuel Johnson died, and Hester Thrale ceased to be her friend. Her favorite sister Susanna was 20 miles away in Mickleham, Surrey. In spite of her fame as an author, her future was insecure. *Cecilia* reached its fifth edition, and there were serialized abridgments in magazines, five editions in French, and a German translation, not to speak of a couple of pirated Irish editions.[1] All of this brought increased fame, but no money. Choderlos de Laclos, the celebrated writer of *Les liaisons dangereuses*, in April and May of 1784 published the 7000–word review in which he placed Burney's *Cecilia* at the top of its genre, with the exception only of three other novels: *Clarissa*, with the most genius, *Tom Jones*, the most perfect, and *La Nouvelle Héloïse*, the most beautiful. In France, Burney had won both popularity and fame.

But she was not married. At least partly by her own choice, she had by 1783 passed the age of 30 unattached, and hence had become by most people's reckoning an old maid. She had anticipated old-maidenhood from a very early age. Just short of 23, she wrote to Daddy Crisp: 'I have [long – later erased] accustomed myself to the idea of being an old maid – & the Title has lost all its terrors in my Ears. I feel no repugnance to the expectation of being ranked among the Number' (*EJL* 2:125). A few days later, she was arguing even more positively: 'Liberty is not without its value.' (*EJL* 2:129)

Burney's hesitations about marriage were well founded. For eighteenth-century English women, marriage could be stifling. By simply saying 'I do', they gave up all their legal rights and nearly all their personal freedom. Yet marriage was a middle-class woman's chief career, the way to make one's fortune, the key to becoming independent of father and brothers. Although the imaginative literature of the period increasingly emphasizes romantic love, the overflow of powerful feelings not to be denied, actual life often determined otherwise. In 1735 Sarah Chapone drew on a particularly flagrant case in her anonymous pamphlet, *The Hardships of the English Laws in Relation to Wives with an Explanation of the Original Curse of Subjection Passed upon the Woman. In an Humble Address to the Legislature.* While emphasizing that women are slaves to men in all marriages, Chapone noted one instance:

> the Case of Mr *Veezey*, tryed at the *Old Bailey*, where it was proved that he confined his Wife for some Years in a Garret, without Fire, proper Cloathing, or any of the Comforts of Life; that he had frequently Horse-whipt her; that her Sufferings were so great and intolerable, that she destroyed her wretched Life by flinging herself out at the Window.[2]

The case itself was shocking, but the decision in court was even more so: 'But as there was Bread found in the Room, which, though hard and mouldy, was supposed sufficient to sustain Life; and as it was not thought that he pushed her out of the Window himself, he was acquitted' (pp. 10–11). Evidently no kind of abuse was actionable, short of murder.

Because marriage was an irreversible step, and husbands were legally so powerful, a woman's choice of a spouse was particularly crucial. Unfortunately, many young women, immured in daily family life, could meet few eligible men. Public entertainments such as balls and ridottos were ways of multiplying encounters, although such passing acquaintances often created problems. As Samuel Johnson put it in the marriage segment of *Rasselas*, 'A youth and maiden, meeting by chance, or brought together by artifice, exchange glances, reciprocate civilities, go home, and dream of one another. Having little to divert attention, or diversify thought, they find themselves uneasy when they are apart, and therefore conclude that they shall be happy together.' (p. 107) The vicissitudes of Burney's thinking on this subject are painstakingly displayed in the diaries and letters.

Burney had no independent money. She needed to make a good marriage. Because her father supported the family by his music-teaching, and hence by cultivating those with wealth, taste, and power, she met a wide range of people. This persistent social activity was somewhat deceiving, however, since Burney was clearly lower on the social scale than most of her acquaintance. When she published *Evelina*, she became notorious, but no more acceptable – possibly less so. As it was, Burney had at least three important relationships with men, all of which reverberate in her diaries and novels.

Since talking was always laborious for her, she found especially difficult the chitchat of early acquaintance and the slant combination of double meaning and avoidance that accompanied developing love. Her first encounter with an offer of marriage was, however, quite different. She did not love the short (but handsome) Thomas Barlow, and because her affections were not involved, she was totally in control. She begins her account of this affair by writing in her journal in May of 1775, just short of her 23rd birthday: 'This month is Called a *tender* one – It has proved so *to* me – but not *in* me.' (*EJL* 2:115) A person whose tenderness is not '*in* me' enjoys marvelous freedoms. Since Barlow exists for us not only in Burney's untender phrasing but also in the examples she includes of his own prose, posterity has approved of Burney's decision. No one can read the marriage proposal that Barlow wrote after one evening's acquaintance and wish that he had married Frances Burney. Nearly 20 years later in the *Vindication of the Rights of Woman* Mary Wollstonecraft emphasized that most men did not sufficiently care about their wives' minds. Barlow is one of that ilk; he talks about Burney's merit, but her merit seems to reside chiefly in her 'Affability, Sweetness, & Sensibility' (*EJL* 2:118). Readers of Burney know that she was all of these things, but that she was also demanding, ironic, and intellectual. In *Rasselas*, couples who have briefly met act on their dreams. 'They marry, and discover what nothing but voluntary blindness had before concealed; they wear out life in altercations, and charge nature with cruelty.' (p. 100) Perhaps Burney's affability would have prevented such an outcome, but she knew from the start that she was not uneasy apart from Barlow. She did not share his romantic dream. She faulted him at least partly for failings she herself shared, especially that he was tense in company.

But his letter was a declaration, and she followed the forms. She told her father, and he agreed that she should not accept, suggesting that she not even write a reply. But pressures began to build. Her aunts cheerfully – and also somewhat pitifully – suggested that she avoid their unmarried state. Crisp pushed harder, so hard that when in the nineteenth-century Burney blotted out phrases and pages in her papers, she diminished his rage by cutting out: 'god damn my blood but You make me mad! – '(*EJL* 2:121). Crisp invoked the unmarried aunts, and then in more wheedling tones, argued, 'Suppose You to lose y^r Father – take in all Chances. Consider the situation of an unprotected, unprovided Woman –' (*EJL* 2:123). As usual, Crisp played on fear, old age, and weakness, possibly because he felt them himself. Soon, Dr Burney had second thoughts, and urged his daughter to reconsider, pulling her heart-strings: 'Thee shalt live with me for ever, if Thee wilt!' he burst out, weeping, and yet he also added, '– only – do not be too hasty!' (*EJL* 2:147).[3] After this exchange, Burney spent what she characterizes as the most painful night of her life, imagining herself irrevocably shackled to this dull young man. The imagined marriage felt as ghastly as her mother's death.

Dr Burney's decision that his daughter should not write back to Barlow proved to be a mistake. She was always more confrontational than her father, and she knew that only direct rejection would discourage her suitor. When Barlow continued to call, she pretended that her not-quite-written rejection letter had been held up at the post office (a lie later erased), and made it clear that the letter was such that it needed no reply. In spite of Burney's habitual reticence, she describes herself as quite forceful in this scene. She deliberately played it as comedy: 'He seemed to be quite overset; having, therefore so freely explained myself, I then asked him to sit down, & began to talk of the Weather.' (*EJL* 2:142) Only slightly fazed, Barlow persisted – and persisted – an extravagant example of a man who thinks that 'no' means only 'I want to be persuaded'. Eventually, Burney had to stifle even the common civilities. At the end of their final interview, with a maneuver that embarrassed her sufficiently so that she later erased it, she waited till she heard 'the street Door opened'. Then making herself barely visible 'in the Passage', she called out to him (and this she did not erase) to wish him 'a good Walk'. Even after all her cold-ness this minimal gesture encouraged him sufficiently so that he seemed to be about to return, but she withdrew so quickly that at last he comprehended the finality of her message (*EJL* 2:152). As is so often true in Burney's novels (and in life – any life?), this experience was a medley of comedy, sensibility, and pain.[4]

The pain associated with Mr Barlow was the fear that somehow she would find herself married to him, imprisoned in body and mind. Her next important brush with the possibility of marriage entailed a different kind of wound, an intolerable dilemma that was a fairly typical experience for an eighteenth-century woman. She fell in love with the Reverend George Owen Cambridge, who for whatever reason did not want to marry her.[5] Over the three years from 1782–85, Burney noted down every look, gesture, and word of this man whom she described as 'sensible, rational, and highly cultivated'. She was impressed with his tact, and his attachment to his father. The elder Cambridge was very like her own father. When he and Dr Burney talked they 'not only talked enough for us all, but so well and so pleasantly that no person present had even a wish to speak for himself. ... Our sweet father kept up the ball with him admirably, whether in anecdotes, serious disquisitions, philosophy, or fun.' One of Burney's reasons for admiring Cambridge was 'observing that he quite adores his father. He attended to all his stories with a face that never told he had heard them before; and, though he spoke but little himself, he seemed as well entertained as if he had been the leading person in the company –' (*DL* 2:158–9). She could certainly identify with this. In addition, Cambridge recognized that such fathers were so self-absorbed that they did not notice other people's discomfort. When Soame Jenyns launched into such a high-flown panegyric on *Cecilia* that Burney could not comprehend, much less reply to it, Cambridge commiserated with her the next day. They both had noticed that Dr Burney had not even observed her discomfiture (*DL* 2:186–91).

Most important was the fact that the inarticulate Burney felt released in George Cambridge's presence. When their fathers were not around, they could laugh uproariously together. She mentions evenings of 'almost riotous gaiety' at Mrs Montagu's, and gives instances of the kind of wicked humor they shared, like laughing when Mrs Vesey lamented that it is 'disagreeable' to have someone die when one has just met them '& likes them'. Burney was laughing so hard she had to pretend to be 'filliping off the crumbs of the macaroon cake from my muff' (*DL* 2:234). Another evening, Cambridge and she talked, even though Mrs Hester Chapone[6] tried to control the conversation. Cambridge, Burney says, 'braved all difficulties to talk with me, & stood facing me, & chatting all the night, & though Mrs Chapone frequently offered to join in the discourse, we were both in too high spirits for her *seriousity*, & rattled away without minding her'.[7] Except with Cambridge, Burney was still diffident in public. Though she was thoroughly confident of her abilities and her achievements, she was careful not to overstep her maiden modesty.

In the spring of 1783, when John Bogle had done an appealing miniature of Burney, someone suggested that an engraving might be made to be sold in booksellers' shops. When Burney wrote nervously to Thrale about this possibility, her friend replied:

> Why will you resolve against letting the people have your picture?
> The Form and Face of *a very great Writer* would then have been
> remembered. The Modesty of a *delicate Maiden* will *not* be remem-
> bered. There are *delicate Maidens* enough.[8]

This flattering, memorable, and forthright advice did not convince
Burney. The thought of strangers possessing her face was too
disrupting for her sense of decorum. The miniature remained
uncopied. As the years passed, the still-unmarried Burney wanted to
keep her options open, and having her face in hundreds of households would not, after all, increase her stature as a writer, and might
decrease her stature as a marriageable maiden. Doody suggests that
possibly the chief reason Burney did not immediately begin another
novel after publishing *Cecilia* was her desire to appear proper enough
to be George Cambridge's wife.

But George Cambridge, although his animation in her presence
convinced her and everyone else that he loved her, never declared
himself, and she prided herself throughout their relationship on never
revealing her feelings. She was a great writer, but she played the delicate maiden. Though Burney derided conduct-books, she knew also
that in some situations their advice was law. Cambridge 'would be the
first, I am certain, to detect the smallest impropriety, & to pay it with
its due contempt', she wrote in April of 1783 to her sister Susanna,
adding that she still preferred being single. But the woman who
insisted that she preferred the single life did not let John Bogle's
miniature enter the shops. Meanwhile, the relationship with George
Cambridge, whatever it was, alternately glowed and sputtered for
nearly seven years. Burney's astute ability to read gesture and tone –
so useful when she wrote her novels – tortured her in this actual and
ambiguous situation. In her enforced passivity, the fires of her affection burned hotter because banked. During 1783 and 1784 she wrote
to Susanna full accounts and analyses of her frequent encounters with
'Mr G: C'. Infuriated that he had the power merely by his address to
spark rumors of their approaching marriage, she could regain power
only by refusing to speak to him. Having found someone she truly
hungered to converse with, she was forced to deny herself that exhilaration. She could not hate George Cambridge, who had the 'power of
electrifying her by the tone of his voice'[9] But she could not love him
either, without his permission.[10]

Meanwhile, her friend Hester Thrale was being tortured in a
different way. During the writing of *Cecilia*, which Thrale read in

manuscript, they shared a unique intensity. Knowing that Burney's sister Susanna was her 'Heart's earliest darling', Thrale wove her own hair with Susanna's in a locket that Burney kept by her for the rest of her life (*JL* 11:206). But their friendship did not survive Thrale's marriage to Piozzi. In January of 1783, when Thrale was struggling over the decision of whether or not to link her fate indissolubly with a man considered socially unsuitable, Burney, who was trying to convince herself that she really enjoyed the single life, became the advice-giver. She was not prepared for this role, which represented a shift. Previously the advice had always flowed the other way. Burney was 30 and in many ways inexperienced. In the throes of a completely different situation, longing for a man who would not commit himself to her, she was unable to imagine Thrale's dilemma. Though Burney was a narrow observer of humanity, no one as young and green as she could have truly understood the feelings of a woman who had borne 12 children to a philandering and distant husband. Burney could see only what Thrale was likely to lose – 'children', 'religion', 'friends', 'country', 'character'.[11] Having regretfully watched her sister Susanna marry, she still felt a year later that more was lost than gained. She extrapolated her sense of loss to her friend. She also assumed that Piozzi was not to be depended on, equating him with the fence-sitting George Cambridge, mistakenly applying her limited experience to Thrale's quite different case.[12] While Thrale was repaying her debts, in preparation for marrying Piozzi, Burney put herself into the untenable position of being friends both with Thrale and with her imperious 18-year-old daughter Hester, nicknamed Queeney. In age Burney was just halfway between them, and even though she loved the mother, she also identified with the daughter. She mused that if only she could have combined them into one person, she would have found the perfect friend. Ultimately, Thrale blamed Burney for alienating Queeney, though Queeney's affections had been long gone, and this was merely Thrale's excuse for her daughter's innate coldness. Still, the fact that Burney had entered into a secret correspondence with Queeney, and abetted Queeney's granitic refusal to remain with her mother after her marriage was quite simply unforgivable. Though the women eventually met again with seeming cordiality more than 30 years later in Bath, Thrale never trusted Burney again. And Burney, for her part, never really understood why her friend had insisted on marrying, even though her own eventual marriage to General d'Arblay was comparable. She too was to become a woman of 40 who fell passionately in love with a man who also was a Catholic and in many other ways inappropriate. Yet Burney never thawed toward Gabriel Piozzi. How did he differ from d'Arblay? A singing teacher was not in the same class as an emigré General. Besides, Piozzi's English was rather quaint. Burney thought that Piozzi was not Thrale's intellectual equal, though Thrale felt that he was in every way suited to be her partner. By Burney's lights, Thrale had married beneath her, always a fraught choice for an eighteenth-century woman. Long after Thrale's death, Burney compared her intellectually to Mme de Staël, but added unkindly that, like Mme de Staël, Thrale 'took out a licence to desert her maternal duties for a similar indulgence of passion' (*JL* 11:209, n. 13). At the end, then, Burney admits that Hester Thrale did not 'desert' religion, friends, country, or character – only her children. Even this was unfair. Thrale wanted her children to live with her after her marriage, and they refused. She located a good caretaker for them. But even so Burney would not exonerate her friend. Burney's own affections were directed mainly to her family – to her father, her siblings, and eventually to her husband and son. Loyalty to one's children needed to transcend romantic love, she thought, perhaps influenced by the knowledge that her father had married a woman who became such an egregious stepmother.

Beyond Burney's family circle there were important friends, and she was careful not to rupture friendships. Thrale was an exception, an exception she rued. This woman at one of the most important junctures of her life had been simply indispensable. Doody argues that 'it can be suggested that the one lasting gift Burney gave to the woman who was once her dearest friend was the model of a writing career' (p. 107), though by the time Thrale was actually publishing, the friendship had broken. Perhaps the best way to summarize their relationship is the comment Burney put at the top of one of Thrale's letters, remembering how in February 1781, her friend had once driven over wintry roads to Chessington because she had heard Burney was very ill. 'Ah', Burney wrote, 'how I loved her!'[13] The friendship, which was never quite what she thought it was (what friendship is?), eventually shattered. But among the final words, long after Hester Thrale Piozzi's death, full of longing and regret, was, 'Ah, how I loved her!'

Although in 1785 Burney was proud of her autonomy and urged it on her friend, she needed to marry. Her novel-writing would not support her, and her father could not promise her enough to live on. When George Cambridge did not speak, Burney accepted another offer, a reluctant decision she came to regret. Her friendship with the lively and well-connected 85-year-old widow Mary Delany had introduced her to the Royal Family. In due time, Queen Charlotte offered her a position at Court as 'Second Keeper of the Robes'. This meant perhaps influence by which she could help her brothers. It meant that she would have a home and a small salary. Dr Burney was so flattered at the offer that he pressed her to consent. Not seeing any other alternative, she complied, although she 'always and uniformly had a horror of a life of attendance and dependence' (*DL* 2:366). She had clutched at her independence even in Mrs Thrale's house, where the threat was slight. In *The Witlings* her heroine Cecilia views with dread the prospect of being a companion to a rich woman. But by comparison to these positions, the Court was a prison.

Burney had always rebelled against the restraint of the body, and the Court, with its requirement that people stand in the monarch's presence and its complicated bodily protocol was particularly galling. The repressed body is a more important theme in *A Busy Day* than in Burney's earlier works, but she had always subversively complained about this particular set of strictures. In 1774, at the age of 22, she referred often to her fanciful nine-volume mock conduct book, '*Treatise upon politeness*', playfully advising her friends never to cough, and certainly not to smile, sneeze, laugh or blow the nose. It is polite, she says, to pick one's teeth if you have a 'little *Glass* to look in before you' (*EJL* 2:48–51). At court, this satirical diversion turned disturbingly actual, and in a letter to her sister Esther, Burney imagined a bodily repression so extreme that it required self-cannibalization. You must not cough, sneeze, or show that a black pin is sticking into your head:

> If, however, the agony is very great, you may, privately, bite the inside of your cheek, or of your lips, for a little relief; taking care, meanwhile, to do it so cautiously as to make no apparent dent outwardly. And, with that precaution, if you even gnaw a piece out, it will not be minded, only be sure either to swallow it, or commit it to a corner of the inside of your mouth till they are gone – for you must not spit.   (*DL* 2:353)

Burney's awareness of her own body was increased by her nearsightedness. At Court she suffered from the fact that strangers would suddenly approach, and that she could not recognize them until they were very near. Burney held the position as Court attendant for five years, 1786–91, and she became so frail with misery that she nearly died.

Macaulay, who assumes that Burney reaped £2000 for *Cecilia*, finds this interlude incomprehensible. He blames it on Dr Burney's repellent worship of all things monarchical. He notes that Dr Burney was 'transported out of himself with delight' (p. 570), and never stopped to consider that this kind of work would bring his daughter's writing to a halt. Betty Rizzo surmises that Burney's father would not have urged her to accept the position if he had realized how grueling and constricting it would be; some posts at court allowed the holders to come and go almost at will, but Burney's required her constant presence. She was only rarely authorized to visit the father she ambivalently worshiped; their first really long talk together occurred after she had been at court four years. She lived like an orphan, as if she had no family left: 'My time was devoted to official duties; and all that in life was dearest to me – my friends, my chosen society, my best affections – lived now in my mind only by recollection, and rested upon that with nothing but bitter regret.' (*DL* 4:392) Up at 6 and not released until after midnight, forced for nearly six hours every day to amuse – not the Queen, but the aggressively unpleasant Keeper of the Robes, Elizabeth Juliana Schwellenberg – called to her duties like any school girl by a bell, seven days a week, she was often condemned to Picquet. 'Life hardly hangs on earth during its compulsion', she said of this card game, 'in these months succeeding months, and years creeping, crawling, after years' (*DL* 4:469–70). Shortly after she arrived she realized that Mrs Schwellenberg expected her to be 'her humble companion, at her own command!' (*DL* 3:9). She thought immediately of resigning her position but she told Susanna that she could not do this, because of her father, and 'the honours he conceived awaiting my so unsolicited appointment'. She dared not 'thwart his hopes' (*DL* 3:10). At last, more than four years later, she described to her father what her life was like. And yet, who could complain effectively about such a gilded prison? Burney's father, who had been so busy he barely missed her, only realized how peculiar the situation was when the Comtesse de Boufflers, who had asked Dr Burney if she could meet his daughter, and was told she could not, remonstrated, 'Mais, monsieur, est-ce possible! Mademoiselle votre fille n'a-t-elle point de vacance?' (*DL* 4:391). Burney's father, suddenly recognizing the cramped vacationless life into which he had condemned his daughter, suggested that she resign, but then he lacked the courage to support his resolve. The situation dragged on until it was clear that her health was failing. She had a pain in her side, and felt an uncontrollable lassitude. At last she asked to be relieved of her duties. At first she was granted only a leave of absence to recover her health, and when she refused that offer, was reluctantly given permission to leave. It took her nearly six more months finally to extricate herself. The Queen promised her a lifetime annuity of half her salary, £100 per year.

How did this interlude at Court affect Burney's literary life? Since George Cambridge had never spoken, not even when he knew that she was about to incarcerate herself, Burney was thrown back on her talents. Though at court she could seize only about two hours a day for her writing, after a period of depression she went back to an earlier habit, and wrote a semi-public journal to her sister Susanna and her dear friend Frederica Locke. Susanna kept up her own end of what she called their 'pen and ink conversation'.[14] She replied, commiserated, inspired. Frequently, she flattered Burney on the quality of her journal, reminding her sister that she was a writer, and an able one. She kept Burney in touch with normal life by depicting her own family, especially her delightful son, Norbury, who made up stories, including one about a country where the Queen gave people extra right arms, an addition Burney certainly could have used. Susanna judged her own writing harshly, marking her 1789 notebook as: 'Provision for the Convent ... Bad fare, but plenty of it.' Inspired by Susanna, whose 'fare' was never as bad as she thought, Burney in her 'convent' wrote about what she saw. Her journals and letters from this period, the public thoughts and the private ones that will be easily available only when the Troide edition is published, are important to historians. For life at Court, Burney was an incomparable witness.

In 1788, she saw the beginnings of the Warren Hastings impeachment trial. From the start, the tone of the proceedings struck her as inappropriate. She firmly told one of the prosecutors, William Windham, that she knew Hastings, and that he had told her about India, 'the people, the customs, habits, cities and whatever I could name' (*DL* 3:432). It had been clear to Burney that Hastings cared deeply about the country where he had been Governor General of Bengal. She saw him as a victim. When, after a trial of seven years, Hastings was acquitted, the court reflected Burney's view. Twentieth-century historians, with qualms, place him among the more enlightened administrators in a time of imperial exploitation.[15] In 1788, Burney abandoned her habitual reticence, as she often did, and outspokenly shook Windham's confidence that everyone agreed with him, restoring in Windham's mind the humanity of the man on trial.

She watched the king slip in and out of the frenzy she did not call madness. He was polite, in spite of the weirdness of it all, sewing his fingers with Burney's needle so as to have a remembrance of her, he said, often unable to sleep, and talking, talking unceasingly. He changed from his habitual 'What? What?' to a repetitive, unstoppable outpouring. His condition varied so unexpectedly that they were all on the edge of hysteria and panic. The Queen, whose position Burney admired, but whose person she drew as sweet, careless, and cold, had no sister Susan or friend Fredy to support her. Burney pitied the Queen's 'solitary anguish' (*DL* 4:125).

She depicted the insufferable pettiness of her companion Mrs Schwellenberg, 'Cerbera' as she called her, a female version of the three-headed dog at the gates of hell, 'gloomy, dark, suspicious, rude, reproachful', an exact copy of her stepmother.[16] Other animated individuals appear here. The lax and lively Colonel Digby, the Queen's vice-chamberlain, whom she dubbed 'Mr Fairly', insouciantly insisted on coming up to her room to talk to her and read poetry while she did her sewing. When he suddenly became engaged to someone else she was reminded once more that men are careless and cannot be trusted. Colonel Greville, whom she archly designated as 'Colonel Welbred', unnerved her by telling her that he watched her so closely at a performance of James Cobb's *The Humourist* that he was able to tell her exactly which lines she had liked. Charles de Guiffardière, 'Mr Turbulent', liked to suggest that the women of the court were reading naughty books, or countenancing fallen women, and toyed with their embarrassment. In spite of the insufferable dullness of the place, Burney found ways to make it interesting, to laugh over its pettiness and pretension. Her court journal has been one of her most popular books, even when Burney's personal sufferings are largely erased, as they are in Charlotte Barrett's version.

But laughter was only part of Burney's response. At Court she was, as always, the protean Burney. She filled the rest of her time by writing tragedies. In October of 1788, two years and three months after she had withdrawn from the world to live in the palace, 'in mere desperation for employment', she began to write in this dark vein because 'my mind would bend to nothing less sad, even in fiction' (*DL* 4:118). Her tragedy saved her from the combination of boredom and hysteria the king's illness induced, although when his condition worsened she was altogether unable to write, lived tragedy canceling out invented woe. Eventually, the gloom at court inspired her to continue writing tragedies. Lonely, wanting to love but always needing to hide her feelings, she also wrote her personal condition into these plays. Just before she began to write her first tragedy, in a passage excised by Charlotte Barrett, she writes about how Colonel Digby and she had talked alone together so naturally and effortlessly that they did not answer a knock at the door. Burney's presence in the room quite surprised Lady 'Courtown', come to fetch Digby to the Queen. At the same time, she refused a trip to Twickenham, for fear of meeting George Cambridge. She writes to Susanna and Fredy Locke that all 'surmizes' in that direction are 'finally eradicated'. But we can see that if they have died, they have not died easily. Burney adds with a thick, dull pen at the bottom of this entry, 'Will he never marry? – I often wonder at that –.'[17]

A few days later she writes: 'Had not this composition fit seized me, *societyless*, and *Bookless*, and *viewless* as I am, I know not how I could have wiled [sic] away my being; but my tragedy goes on, and fills up all vacancies.'[18] Her friend and solace Mrs Delany had died at the age of 88 seven months before. Now, she affixes to her wall Mrs Delany's copy of Vandyke's Saccharissa, 'This, like the tragedy I have set about, suits the turn of things in this habitation.' (*DL* 4:119) Surrounding this statement are more pages detailing the arid relationship with Digby. There is also a frustrating rumor that Burney will leave court soon, in order to marry George Cambridge. All love, all companionship seem to be gone. Eventually, in 1790, she finishes her first tragedy, writing in her journal about this achievement in the third person, lightheartedly, and yet as if she were already dead. She is not sure that the tragedy is well written, but 'Nevertheless, whether well or ill, she is pleased to have done something at last, she had so long lived in all ways as nothing.' (*DL* 4:413) Burney rarely referred to herself in the third person; this objectification of her writing self gives her tragedies a unique place in her work. They were wrested from her by a kind of automatic writing, something she could not hinder. Usually, when she wrote something, she would regard it professionally, and would begin to polish it. In this case, locking her first tragedy in her strong-box, she immediately started on a second. At the age of 15, she had begun archly, writing her journal to Miss Nobody; now, incarcerated at Court, she was 'nothing', only a pen, writing about pain. By the time Burney left the Queen's service, she had written four tragedies into various stages of completion.

Burney was thoroughly versed in theatrical history and current play-writing practice. She and Susanna were also particularly fond of opera. When she wrote tragedy, the plot she turned to was the dilemma of conflicting loyalties, especially between family and nation, a standard plot that also reflected her personal situation.[19] Popular plays she was familiar with included Garrick's version of Thomas Southerne's *The Fatal Marriage, or the Innocent Adultery*, where the blameless Isabella, believing herself a widow, marries a second husband only to have the first one return. In the often-produced Thomas Otway play *Venice Preserved*, Garrick excelled as both Pierre and Jaffeir, men caught in agonizing choices between friendship, patriotism, and love. Jaffeir's wife Belvidera must betray either her father or her husband. There is no alternative. But life's dilemmas were equally instructive. There was Mr Barlow or no one, lifelong penury or the Court. A charismatic father could simply forget his daughter. Burney's ways to depict these implacable alternatives often veered into the Gothic. There are Gothic overtones in all of Burney's plays. Like many of her contemporaries she knew that the Gothic in many ways replicated women's lives, with its emphasis on stifling confinement, meaningless violence, and the mingling of sex and fear. Burney also drew on history. From the age of 16, she had set herself projects in the reading of history, especially classical narratives. She mentions John Dryden's *Plutarch*, Conyers Middleton's *Cicero*, Nathaniel Hook's *Roman History*, and Temple Stanyan's *Grecian History* (though this last she may not have finished) (*EJL* 1:23, 167, 58). At the same time she embarked on Hume's *History of England* (*EJL* 1:40). While at Court, she continued to read history and to embroider on its stratagems. Many other writers simply borrowed their plots from other plays. Burney wrote stories that were either entirely original, or based on historical narratives drawn from her extensive reading. Although no one has argued that Burney's tragedies are among her best works, and they are not likely to be staged today, they are nonetheless vivid and original. Contemporary tragedies did not depict so fiercely women who, in Darby's words, 'suffer *because* they are women' (p. 45). The kind of suffering Burney depicts here, domestic woe so extreme that it reaches an intensity, an unbearable pathos no catharsis can mitigate, was more fully understood by eighteenth-century audiences than it is today. Similar calamities still undermine people's lives, but a theater audience will not stay to hear about them. In the novels, one of Burney's most important strands was intimate violence, the way people inflict verbal or bodily suffering on their own companions and relatives. In these tragedies, society is the perpetrator.

Society is increasingly at fault, but the characters here, even more intensely than in the two novels, dramatize the hodge-podge of inconsistent characteristics that Burney thought was typical of human nature. She often recalled her mercurial friend Mrs Thrale, knowing that her disapproval of Thrale's marriage to Gabriel Piozzi had damaged their friendship irremediably. Thrale's 'Wild, entertaining, flighty, inconsistent, and clever' book of travels[20] appealed to her so much that although she read it with the Queen in 1789, she read it again in 1790, and found it 'just like herself, abounding in sallies of genius' (*DL*, 4:364). The characters in her tragedies were often, like General Coelric in *Elberta*, an almost oxymoronic collection of attributes, 'made of contrariety'. Hubert de Vere is a 'Thing of Storms! / Blown by conflicting Passions', and King Edwy is not dependable, hiding his true emotions under 'elaborate glare'. 'Elaborate glare' is a fitting description for Burney's forced gaiety at Court.[21]

There are political and religious dimensions in these four tragedies, but chiefly Burney has depicted women who suffer, as she herself was suffering in unrequited love and loneliness, torn between duty and family.[22] In *Edwy and Elgiva*, the tenth-century English King Edwy, as depicted in Hume, foolishly marries his cousin Elgiva before he has been crowned king, in spite of a Church prohibition against marrying close relations. Seeing a weakness, Edwy's ambitious enemies brand Elgiva as a courtesan, hamstring her, release her to wander, and eventually stab her to death.[23] Burney's version emphasizes what she calls the 'Gothic' setting, and Elgiva's strength in misfortune. The hamstringing is downplayed, but not denied. The stage directions describe Elgiva as 'tottering', a word that evokes the historical Elgiva's shocking fate.[24] In this bleak play, both protagonists die at the end. Personal affections do not survive in this public world.

In August 1790, with the unpolished *Edwy and Elgiva* resting in her strong-box, 'imagination seized upon another subject for another tragedy'. She explored the new plot: 'I well know correction may always be summoned, imagination never will come but by choice.' (*DL* 4:413) Unrequited love was her subject as it was her condition. In *Hubert de Vere*, which takes place in the twelfth century on the Isle of Wight, Cerulia, a young, unprotected, Ophelia-like girl placed as an unwitting decoy for the exiled Hubert, falls in love with the man she is supposed to lure. De Vere was exiled for treason, but the guilty party is Cerulia's father de Mowbray. To protect himself, de Mowbray hopes to destroy de Vere, with his (unacknowledged) daughter as pawn. But Cerulia is destroyed instead. Hence, a daughter dies in this play, because her father has placed her in an untenable situation and essentially forgotten her. This situation poignantly mirrors Burney's.[25] When Cerulia discovers that de Vere loves another woman, three specters visit her in 'sulphurous sparks of fire' (5.98; *Plays* 2:150) and point her way to death. She bares her breast and covers it with mold, as if she were already a statue on her own grave. Her mind breaks, and she dies. The way de Mowbray uses his daughter in this play is truly shocking, a savage comment on the way politics ravages families.

Meanwhile, yet another tragedy occasionally pulled her away from *Hubert de Vere*, and she allowed herself to follow her imagination, working 'capriciously' wherever inspiration led her.[26] In *The Siege of Pevensey* an eleventh-century civil war shows how private affections are destroyed by the public battle. Here, although Burney has taken her names from historical sources, she has invented the central plot (Darby, p. 219, n. 22). While the sons of William I are fighting over the throne, Burney's heroine Adela finds herself in the untenable situation of loving one man, but needing to release her father from prison by marrying another. No slouch at negotiation, she offers to immure herself in a convent, so as not to sell herself in marriage. The scenes where she proves her daughterly fidelity to her father are unusually sensual: 'O let me cling to Thee' Adela says, 'till I regain / My lost felicity' (4.5.128–9; *Plays* 2:210). It seems that when writing her tragedies, Burney must have felt her sensuality countered by her constricted life. The plays are openly sensual. Elgiva asks her husband to possess her one last time. When Elberta invites her husband Arnulph to stay with her, he says, 'Think of the danger.' She says, 'No! – think of the joy!' (1.12.28–9; *Plays* 2:250). The women's free-floating sensuality in these plays occasionally lands on the father, where it evidently felt more acceptable than if enacted by an unmarried woman with a lover. Burney was so careful of her reputation that at this point in her life she had never allowed her own sensuality to shift away from her father, though these plays certainly indicate other dreams. *The Siege of Pevensey* unlike the other plays ends, as Burney's husband Alexandre d'Arblay later skeptically pointed out, without a drop of blood being shed. It is a dream of control, where a woman seizes her own fate, the opposite of Burney's actual condition at Court. The ending is too pat, not supported by the cultural conditions in which Adela finds herself. It is not clear when Burney finished *Pevensey*. She never tried to rewrite it.[27]

Burney was just about to leave her position at Court in June 1791, when she began her fourth tragedy. The Queen asked her to stay just two more weeks, and she feared that she would not survive them. Her first three tragedies were unfinished, but she could no longer work concertedly. 'I could only suggest and invent.' In this condition, 'I began – almost whether I would or not – another tragedy.' (*DL* 4:478) She could write only fragments of this new tragedy, called after its heroine *Elberta*, while she was still at Court, and it remained in fragments. Not until 1995 did anyone realize that most of the draft of the play exists in these fragments. Stewart J. Cooke has definitively squeezed this text out of the extant bits and pieces, and *Elberta* appears in the Sabor edition of Burney's tragedies. This tragedy like all the others is about conflicting loyalties, and a broken family. Elberta's outcry could be Burney's own. Elberta, too, is 'a Daughter' who is a prisoner, 'Reft of her Father in sad banishment / Sever'd from every tie of human fondness' (1.10.4–7; *Plays* 2:246). Her suffering is especially poignant because she is separated both from her husband and her children, whom she was struggling to protect. The play takes place in eighth-century Mercia, and derives as did *Edwy and Elgiva* from Hume. Elberta is secretly married to Arnulph, who is commander of King Offa's forces, but King Offa killed Elberta's father, and understandably mistrusts his daughter. Arnulph is his heir-designate, and he wishes to destroy the children born of this disloyal marriage. Elberta hides away with her children, and Burney evokes them tenderly. Elberta, like Elgiva, is a strong woman. Although the children are successfully abducted, they survive, and it is Arnulph who dies. Though Elberta typically wishes to join her husband in death, his last injunction is 'live', and she feels she must persevere for the sake of the children. Her final lines are striking: 'I'm marvellous glad he's dead – for now I'm calm – / 'Tis marvellous how I'm changed! I grieve at nothing' (5.8.17–18; *Plays* 2:302). Whenever Burney wrote these lines, she knew the strength that mourning can bring. Burney worked on *Elberta* as late as 1814, writing on pages torn from a calendar of that year. Perhaps she wrote the passages about children when she herself had a child; certainly some of them are on the 1814 calendar. As late as 1836, perhaps influenced by her son Alex, she timed readings of *Hubert de Vere*, *The Siege of Pevensey*, and her comedy *Love and Fashion*. Alex knew how important it was to keep his octogenarian mother working in a medium she loved perhaps more than any other.[28]

All of Burney's plays, in part because they were unproduced, continually worked in her mind. Their themes played and replayed, with variations, in her notes and in her novels. Among the notes for *Elberta*, for instance, was a fragment that did not finally become the plot of the play:

A Female is mentioned, who wild and unknown is seen roaming about – no one is informed whence she comes – woe is in her voice, terror in her aspect, – she never weeps, yet frequently wails, tho in

terms unintelligible from their wildness –
    Her interesting appearance –
    Some she affrights – others is derided by –
    Her fierce harangues, though wild when offended –
    Her gentle supplications to shadows.
    Her inattention to pursuit –
    Her stated calls on.
    Stated visits to.[29]

This mad woman bears some resemblance to Cecilia at the end of her novel, and though she does not appear in *Camilla* or *The Wanderer*, the possibility of madness always lurks in those books. Camilla remains steady, even when her father is sent to jail. No one is informed whence Burney's Wanderer comes. She frightens some and is derided by others. But she keeps her sanity, as Burney heroines tend to do, in spite of conditions that would drive many other people mad. These are strong women. In 1788, talking one day with Digby, Burney noted that he had transformed his sad history into a 'melancholy pleasure', adding of herself: 'Tis never but *perforce I* am of that number! – My mind, when left to itself, falls naturally into gayer retrospections. –' (Berg, MS Diary and Letters, p. 3318). For Burney there was always, as Yeats said about Shakespeare, 'Gaiety transfiguring all that dread'.[30] Burney found darkness at Court, in the Hastings trial, in the King's madness, and in the recesses of her own despair. Her tragedies contain various and variegated characters, but no humor. Eventually she overcame that darkness, transfigured it with gaiety, but it never left her.

6
Camilla and the Family (1792–1802)

> The perverseness of spirit which grafts desire on what is denied.
>
> Frances Burney, *Camilla* (p. 7)

Throughout the negotiations for *Cecilia*, Burney's chief worry was the aesthetic judgment of her peers. Money was not the principal or even an important object. She had allowed her father to act for her, and had accepted the terms he negotiated. *Camilla* was another story. Burney was aware that in the cases of *Evelina* and *Cecilia* she had enriched the booksellers far beyond her intentions or their dreams. When in July 1795 the time came to negotiate for *Camilla*, her father and her brother James were pushing the claims of James's father-in-law Thomas Payne, who had published *Cecilia*, and his son, who had now taken over the business. But Burney thought, rightly, that Payne had not treated her well enough. Given the terms by which *Cecilia* had been published, it was also perfectly clear that neither Dr Burney nor Burney's volatile elder brother James was a hard-headed enough negotiator. By this time, Frances Burney was married to the gallant but impecunious French emigré, General Alexandre-Jean-Baptiste Piochard d'Arblay, and they had a baby son. Their son was an excuse for strenuous negotiating. When unmarried, Burney had worried about maintaining her image as a passive, marriageable female. Now she could assume the role of mother foraging for her offspring. She wrote to her friend Georgiana Waddington that she and d'Arblay were attempting to realize as much money as they could from the book, so that 'it may be a little portion to our Bambino' (*JL* 3:124).

In marriage the author of *Camilla* had found both personal and professional freedom – the opposite of the usual effect of marriage for a woman at this period. Burney's choice of a marriage partner was one of the most powerful and sure decisions of her life.

She left the record of their courtship in her diary. Readers can never trust a diary. No writer can and no writer wants to tell the whole truth. As readers we must always read slantwise, accounting for the silences that differ for each era, catching individuals in their lies and self-deceptions. Burney liked to write about her own attachments, and for her period she is remarkably honest, but even so her approach differs for each experience. The Barlow passage is an achieved piece of writing, an interlude largely comic. The George Cambridge episode, more protracted and ambiguous, is scattered semi-suppressed through diaries and letters. But the mutual courtship with General Alexandre d'Arblay, concentrated and definitive, evokes all the emotions of romance fiction at its most convincing best. Edited only lightly by the widowed Madame d'Arblay, with an occasional erasure by her niece Charlotte Barrett, this courtship has survived in unusual detail. We have many of the 'Thèmes' Burney and d'Arblay exchanged in an initial and mutual study of language, the letters they sent to one another, and a journal Burney kept for her sister Susanna. Both d'Arblay and Burney were adept communicators. They seem almost instantly to have fallen in love: three months after they met d'Arblay proposed marriage. The next four months were the period of courtship, the interim when these true minds studied, before full commitment, the impediments to their marriage. These impediments were many. He was French, Catholic, liberal, and unemployed. She was impoverished and nearly two years older. Burney firmly believed that a man as charming as General d'Arblay could easily land a younger woman with a much larger income. She was immediately sure that she would be happy with him, but she was not so sure about his side of the bargain. He loved her, certainly. But if he married her, might he later regret his decision?

It was not until January 1793 that Burney met General Alexandre d'Arblay. Thrale, whose marriage to Piozzi Burney had disapproved of, would have applauded the fact that this handsome and passionate general treated Burney not as a delicate maiden, but as a great author. Often during their first acquaintance he even called her 'Cecilia', as if to encompass the character, the work, and the woman. Burney had first heard about d'Arblay from her sister Susanna, who described the emigrés from France renting Juniper Hall, Surrey, near Norbury Park, the luxurious home of Burney's dear friends Frederica and William Locke. Burney had received Susanna's letters on this subject in

Aylsham, Norfolk, where she was comforting her sister Charlotte, whose husband had suddenly died, leaving Charlotte with two daughters and a 16-day-old son. In this sad moment Burney learned from Susanna that d'Arblay, the newest arrival at Juniper Hall, was warm and full of '*gaieté de coeur*' (DL 5:139). The former Adjutant-General to Lafayette had been on guard at the Tuileries when the King escaped to Varennes, and was arrested. Though he was ultimately freed, he had lost all his property, '*Et me voilà, madame, réduit à rien.*' (Hemlow, p. 229) Though for a moment when the king was executed he was to regret that he had cried out for liberty, he had been and remained a constitutionalist.

When Burney first met d'Arblay she mentioned to her father that he was 'a very elegant Poet' (JL 2:19). He had actually published a volume of poetry six years before. Possibly d'Arblay did not show Burney this volume, or at any rate did not show it to her immediately. Certainly it did not appear among her papers at her death. D'Arblay's book, *Opuscules de Chevalier d'Anceny en vers recueillies et publiées par M. d'A****, was too steamy to introduce at the start of a serious relationship. Taking as his pseudonym the name of Choderlos de Laclos' romantic lover in *Les liaisons dangereuses*, d'Arblay had written poems in something like Danceny's voice, with an amused introduction describing his pieces as *jeux d'esprit*, 'bagatelles'. Even if he did show these poems to Burney, however, though they would certainly have embarrassed her, they would not have worried her. D'Arblay's poems recall Danceny in that they address women whom he admires, but differ markedly in tone from the mixture Laclos has assembled for Danceny, a mixture of gullibility, idealization, and free-floating desire. The longest and most striking poem in the collection is the last, 'Les doigts, à Rosine'. To my knowledge, no one has discussed this poem, either in its own right or as it might relate to Burney. This neglect is unfortunate, because 'Les doigts' is an indispensable key to their relationship.

D'Arblay's 'Les doigts, à Rosine' is as unexpected as it is riveting. It is a frank, sensual, and hilarious paean to the joys of masturbation, especially mutual masturbation. Referring at the beginning to a poem by 'm. de Bussy' that boasts, 'j'aurai pour elle un doigt de plus', d'Arblay rejoins, 'mais Rosine a trouvé que *ce doigt de plus*, seroit un doigt de trop, et il n'en a plus été question'. D'Arblay's extra 'finger', his penis, unlike de Bussy's, was for Rosine not an object she desired, but simply one finger too many. Literal fingers, however, *were* desirable. In occasionally rhyming, slightly rough tetrameter lines, d'Arblay-as-'Danceny' mentions Hortense, who in her convent, 'au DOIGT mouillé jouant souvant / sait gaîment faire pénitence', commenting that he likes these innocent games, and that he thinks that for a young woman to use her wet finger is preferable both to abstinence and to sexual intercourse. Further on in the poem, when he is embracing Rosine, the implication is that his fingers excite her. Meanwhile, 'Rosine, sur mon instrument, / promène ses DOIGTS lentement', until 'Tout fut d'accord et bien ensemble'.[1] The chief writers on masturbation, with finger and dildo, concentrate on the fact that it provokes rather than satiates desire. Hence Samuel Tissot emphasized its dangers in *L'Onanisme, ou dissertation physique sur les maladies produites par la manstupration*, and Ménuret de Chambaud and Denis Diderot carefully tempered their most positive articles.[2] Robert Darnton shows that masturbation as a safe activity for a couple is positively, even 'deliciously' presented in the anonymous *Thérèse Philosophe* (1748), where sex and philosophy combine to titillate and instruct.[3] What is remarkable in d'Arblay's poem is the combination of excitement and innocence, the mutuality of the experience, how good-humoredly the speaker lets Rosine's fingers follow their own candid voluptuousness on his 'instrument', how concerned he is that he and Rosine should be in agreement, and that she should be experiencing her satisfaction together with his. This lover retains his partner's delicacy even as he arouses her pleasure.

Burney's family was puzzled by her instant attraction to General d'Arblay. When her stepsister Maria Allen Rishton heard about the marriage, she compared the couple to Othello and Desdemona, and wanted to know what sort of a man had like Pope's Abelard 'raised "these Tumults in a Vestal's Veins"'.[4] Fittingly, the epigraph of 'Les doigts' is from Eloise's letters to Abelard. Probably no one ever showed 'Les doigts' to Rishton, and perhaps d'Arblay in his haste to leave France had not even been able to carry a copy with him, but if Rishton had read d'Arblay's poem, she would have instantly understood. A vestal Burney may have been, but she had never been someone to deny the body. She welcomed tumult.

The rejected Mr Barlow's 'Language' had been 'stiff, studied, & even affected' (*EJL* 2:126). D'Arblay, in language as well as body, was precisely the opposite, and Burney praised him to her father 'for openness, probity, intellectual knowledge, & unhackneyed manners' (*JL* 2:11). George Cambridge had monopolized her to such a degree that onlookers assumed they were engaged. When d'Arblay hitched a ride in her coach he staged complicated evasions so that only the footman noticed. Once in the coach, having already written her a delicately worded declaration of marriage, he flung himself on his knees. Burney gently ignored this gesture and managed after many evasive conversational moves to assure d'Arblay that it was for his sake that she would not listen. She wanted d'Arblay to think through more thoroughly what he was saying and doing. She did not say – I have no money, no position, no power, I am nearly two years older than you are, possibly past child-bearing – and I fear that these privations will deplete our relationship together. She said only, to his 'why':

> C'est – qu'il faut que vous songez plus à ce que vous faites! – oh oui! pensez! pensez! – Songez, songez! – à ce que vous faites! – à ce que vous dîtes! –
>
> (JL 2:72–3)

Think about what you are doing! This is truly wise advice, from a woman who has seen in many venues, especially in the relationship between her father and her stepmother, the differences between the moonlit joys of high romance and the inexorable dailiness of marriage. Burney is in love, but she is wary of marriage. She knows that if d'Arblay does not share her wariness, her willingness to economize and compromise, they will not be happy. Her sister declares that d'Arblay would happily marry a woman even ten years older than he. Clearly, one of the reasons he loves her is that she is mature, that she has an independent mind, that she is the author of *Cecilia*. But he needs to think through all the attendant disadvantages she explicitly names for him, so that he will not regret them later. 'Pensez', she insists, 'Songez!' Only those who have thought about their dreams, imagined the future realities, will be comfortable together. Her widowed father married a pretty woman who disliked music, whose sensibilities were by Burney standards rough-hewn. They had all suffered from this unlucky decision. D'Arblay needed to consider, and consider again.

Their relationship had been smooth from the start. At her sister Susanna's house, two weeks after their first meeting, d'Arblay had suggested that he should be Burney's 'Master of the Language', and they agreed on writing themes for one another, to be corrected and returned. In addition, they read books aloud to one another. 'Pray expect wonderful improvements', Burney wrote to her father (JL 2:19). Burney saved many of these themes for her grandchildren, nephews, or nieces 'to obviate their being Dupes of false accounts' (JL 2:188). One important subject in these early themes was Mme de

Staël. As both a literary woman and a friend of d'Arblay's, she was coin they could exchange. When Dr Burney sounded alarms over de Staël's moral life, claiming she was mistress of de Narbonne, another of the emigrés, Burney and d'Arblay exchanged views on this subject, and thus they were able safely to fathom one another's opinions on married love and faithfulness. D'Arblay claimed to believe that Mme de Staël was innocent of the charges. These protestations, whether ill-informed or politic, revealed that he would be a committed spouse, not a stereotypical flirting Frenchman. Burney, for her part, showed that she valued Mme de Staël sufficiently to deplore the British strictures, but also to feel constrained by them herself. 'I wish the World would take more care of itself, and less of its neighbours', she wrote later to Frederica Locke. 'I should have been *very safe*, I trust, without such flights, & distances, & breaches!' (*JL* 2:123).[5] In the meantime, both Burney and d'Arblay were learning their mutual languages extremely fast. Within three weeks their exchange evolved from clumps of halting sentences to complex discussions of the state of Europe. Soon d'Arblay refused to return the themes written by the woman he called his 'master in gown' (*JL* 2:28). He kept them in a 'little pacquet, folded in silver paper', safe in a pocket he had specially made in the bosom of his coat (*JL* 2:71). He sent her a rose bush. He insisted on meeting her father, and remained charming even in the face of Dr Burney's rejecting manner and immovable political conservatism. He sent her a pen he had owned for 21 years. What she responded to most was his frankness and his unguardedness. To Susanna she described his letter of declaration: 'plain, noble, upright, simple – yet containing from time to time a stroke – a touch – that makes its way to the inmost soul' (*JL* 2:42).[6] Eventually Burney told him even more directly that she wished to find for him someone 'plus riche, plus belle, plus jeune, plus – plus – plus toute chose de bien' (*JL* 2:82) – richer, prettier, younger, with more of everything good. But this was not what d'Arblay wanted. He was content if she was, he said, to live 'à l'abri du besoin' (*JL* 2:82). She listed her exact income, which would indeed just barely shelter them from need: think, reflect, meditate, deliberate, she told him. Meanwhile, she made him small loans, a fact which she later attempted to erase (*JL* 2:106). He planned and dreamed. He would learn English so fast and so well that he would secure a job in England. He was studying English six hours every day. Meanwhile, possibly the political situation in France would stabilize itself and he would secure his pension. Burney listened to these plans with apprehension. She thought that they were ill-founded. She worried that even her own £100 might be with-drawn. But d'Arblay did not want a richer, younger, prettier wife. He wanted the author of *Cecilia*.[7]

He described to her as her only fault the fact that she occasionally did not speak loudly enough, and that others construed this habit as self-centered. Since they were to spend the rest of their lives together, he listed his faults – to see the dark side of things, to lose his temper (briefly) from time to time, to be brusque, to be overly vivacious (*JL* 2:103–4). He noticed that she was worried about the anger, so he immediately reassured her that he was also gentle.

Seven months after their first meeting, Frances Burney and Alexandre d'Arblay were married – twice – first on Sunday, 28 January 1793 at the parish church in Mickleham and then to assure that Burney would share in any restitution of the General's property in France, in a Catholic ceremony two days later at the Sardinian Chapel in London.[8] Burney's father did not attend either wedding. He reluc-tantly gave his consent, but would not approve a marriage attended with all the difficulties this one presaged. Burney's siblings were much more supportive, trusting that their sister was making a deliberate and correct choice. They were impressed that one of Burney's chief reasons for wanting to marry d'Arblay was their mutual desire to share their literary lives. To her friend Mrs Waddington, the just-married Madame d'Arblay wrote: 'M. d'Arblay has a taste for literature, & a passion for reading & writing as marked as my own; this is a simpathy [sic] to rob retirement of all superfluous leisure, & ensure to us both occupation constantly edifying or entertaining. He has seen so much of life, & has suffered so severely from its disappointments, that retreat, with a chosen Companion, is become his final desire.' (*JL* 2:179) She misread him slightly, but not disastrously. If he had been content merely to stay retired their marriage would have been more comfortable. Even so, as marriages go, theirs was one of the best history has to offer.

In the early years, as Burney had warned her suitor, they certainly needed money, and of necessity Burney was the breadwinner. '*Print, print, print!*' her sister Susanna urged her. 'Here is a ressource [sic] – a certainty of removing present difficulties.' (*JL* 2:148) During her courtship and marriage, Burney had indeed been working on her plays. Although both her father and Crisp had failed as playwrights, Crisp's negative influence ended with his death and Burney became increasingly independent of Dr Burney. Just 23 days before her marriage, John Philip Kemble accepted *Hubert de Vere* for production at Drury Lane. When Susanna vigorously encouraged her sister to 'print, print, print', in order to support the d'Arblay household, Burney followed her advice. Four months after the marriage, Burney published her first work as Mme d'Arblay, combining her interest in women and French emigrés by addressing to 'FEMALE BENEFICENCE' a plea that it might support this charitable cause (p. 4). Her current publisher Thomas Cadell issued the *Brief Reflections Relative to the Emigrant French Clergy: Earnestly Submitted to the Humane Consideration of the Ladies of Great Britain*, indicating on the title page that it was 'By the Author of *Evelina* and *Cecilia*'. Buyers could be sure that they were getting a work by a famous author. Her aim was to create a political role for women, but unfortunately the reviewers misunderstood her. The *British Critic* used Burney to criticize Wollstonecraft, who was too 'gentleman-like', and thought by contrast that this essay suggested a way that women could act in a public cause and yet retain their delicacy.[9] Burney does differ from Wollstonecraft in that she distinguishes between the socialization of men and women. Women, she argues, can be more charitable than men, since they have not endured 'the heart-hardening effects of general worldly commerce' (p. iv). But women whose hearts are not hardened are not necessarily weak women. This work was an important step toward Burney's increasing support of strong women, her investigation of the boundaries between private and public life.[10]

In April of 1794, within a year of her marriage, even though she was nearly 42, she became pregnant. Her pregnancy did not slow her down. She revised *Edwy and Elgiva* and submitted it to Drury Lane in place of *Hubert de Vere*. Almost simultaneously with the birth of her son Alexander on 18 December, she heard that *Edwy and Elgiva* was to be produced. She nursed her baby, but he developed a thrush infection which he transmitted to her. Her right breast became infected. Sadly, she had to wean Alex. Meanwhile, the first reading of her tragedy took place without her on 5 January 1795, and the reaction was ominous. Hester Thrale Piozzi recorded in *Thraliana* that while Charles Burney read his sister's play, 'the Actors dropt silently off, one by one and left him *all alone*' (p. 916). The first rehearsal did not take place until two months later, and in between the play seems not to have been revised.[11] All during this period, Burney was suffering from the abscess in her breast, and that, in combination with the plain fact that she was a mother and enjoying her new role, seems to have distracted her from working on her tragedy. Another distraction, of course, was that motherhood in the eighteenth century always unleashed fear. Three of Burney's brothers had died as infants, one when she was eight years old. Every day was precious. In all, there were nine scheduled rehearsals of *Edwy and Elgiva*, one of which was dismissed.[12] With Kemble himself as Edwy and Sarah Siddons as Elgiva, the play opened on 21 March and was immediately withdrawn. At least 25 reviews appeared in newspapers and magazines, and the tone was overwhelmingly – though not exclusively – abrasive. (*Plays* 1:xiv–xv and n.'s) In a letter quite admiring of Burney's fortitude in this situation, Sarah Siddons nonetheless commented to Hester Thrale Piozzi that 'The Audience were quite angelic and only laughed when it was *impossible* to avoid it.'[13] The scenery was incongruous, the acting uneven, and the play itself badly in need of revision. When Edwy called out, 'Bring in the Bishop', for instance, the audience was hilariously reminded of hot wine and roasted oranges *(Plays* 2:20 n.). 'Bishop' was actually one of Johnson's favorite drinks. John Palmer, who had a large part, did not know his lines, and others evidently made up their lines along the way. This fiasco hurt Burney and it upset her father. But she was too busy to be devastated. She was quite ill with her infection, enervated after childbirth, and enchanted with her husband and her baby. She and d'Arblay tinkered with *Edwy and Elgiva*, considered publishing it, and ultimately let the matter rest.[14]

After the failed attempt to realize a profit on her dramatic writing, Burney turned back to fiction. In spite of her reverses in the theater, *Camilla* was the book that ultimately came easiest for Burney, though it was an interrupted book. She had made notes on it during the five-year period when she was employed as Queen Charlotte's Second Keeper of the Robes, so that it had been in her mind for eight years when she took it up again in August of 1794, a year after her marriage to d'Arblay. The need for money was an effective spur, and she actually enjoyed the extra incentive. Besides, d'Arblay was encouraging and interested. The book was long and capacious, but her interest never flagged, not even when she neared the end: '– it is so delicious to stride on, when *en verf*', she wrote to d'Arblay in February of 1796 *(JL* 3:157).

She was ebulliently happy with her husband and son, and she wrote about her family with the joy in details of gesture and word that characterized her novels. When Alexander was 14 months old, in the same letter where she spoke about how 'delicious' it was to work on her novel, she wrote to her briefly absent husband:

The Mother & The Bambino are already leagued in the most intelligent sympathy; 'Where, I cry, is Papa? – He jumps, & points with his little Finger to the Window, – I carry him thither, & his quick Eye traverses *our Grounds*, – he sees no one, – & disappointment takes place of vivacity, & he draws in, with a sorrowful little shake of the head, & an inquisitive glance at me, that says mais où, où est il donc, mon Papa? Then we go up & down stairs, – &, at every entrance into a room, he springs almost out of my arms, exclaiming At! At! At! – but no At is there! – Dearest At! – come back to us on Friday, – J'ai beau vantée mon hermitage, – it won't do without my Hermit! –   *JL* 3:156

She had written fourteen and a half pages the night before, she proudly boasted, striding on '*en verf!*' Her family life and her working life were inextricably blended, and she immediately added: 'Yet we played a full Hour at Where's My Baby? Where's My Baby? – ' (*JL* 3:157). One of the reasons Burney enjoyed writing this book more fully than the others was that at last she had secured the services of an amanuensis. D'Arblay wrote out the fair copy. To top it all off, the Queen allowed Burney to dedicate *Camilla* to her.

The heroines of Burney's first two novels are orphaned and isolated. By contrast, Camilla Tyrold is surrounded by parents and siblings. This complex yet unified story grew so slowly in Burney's mind that she described it to George III as 'a little baby'. (*JL* 3:176). This is a family book. The members of Camilla's family do not save her from isolation, but they are abundantly alive. Her sententious clergyman father inconsistently but realistically combines a rather distant air with occasional kindness and thoughtfulness. Camilla's mother is so fully attuned to her children's joys and doubts that in order to allow the plot to lacerate her offspring, she must be sent off to Lisbon to attend to a sick brother (p. 216). The three Tyrold sisters are all initially beautiful, but their childish uncle Sir Hugh foolishly allows the delicate and uninoculated Eugenia to be exposed to smallpox. In addition, while accompanying her on the upswing of a makeshift seesaw, he accidentally drops her. A child himself, Sir Hugh often joins the children's games. As a result of this fall, Eugenia's body is as misshapen as her face is ugly – a more unusual situation in fiction than in life, and one Burney had been thinking about for 13 years or more. Sir Hugh adds education to injury by allowing the solipsistic tutor Dr Orkborne to 'teach her just like a man' (p. 48). The maimed and unduly educated Eugenia is the youngest sister. The eldest, Lavinia, is the foil. Dutiful and pleasant, luckily possessing 'internal serenity' (p. 223), she emerges unscathed. The girls' brother

Lionel is a medley, a protean character, one of the most vivid rendi-tions of a decent, gleeful person who is particularly cruel to those closest to him. He does not through nonchalant behavior kill those he loves, as Evelina's father killed her mother, but merely ignores their claims to happiness. He is like *Evelina's* Captain Mirvan, but Mirvan is vengeful and Lionel is manipulative, a practical joker. He is, as he describes himself, 'a light, airy spark' (p. 241). For the sake of a good laugh he will sacrifice anyone who comes his way. He is sorry, but only after the fact.[15]

The family here is extended rather than nuclear. Camilla's cousin and Sir Hugh's ward Indiana Lynmere, the orphaned daughter of her deceased aunt, is another foil for Eugenia and for Camilla. She is perfectly and vapidly beautiful, with a mind as vacant as her looks. Her brother Clermont is similarly self-centered and petty. Intended for Eugenia, he refuses her not only because of her looks, but also, 'recov-ering from a long yawning fit', because, 'what have I to do with marrying a girl like a boy?' (p. 592). He fears that Eugenia's knowledge of the classics will inhibit her in the kitchen.[16]

In shaping *Camilla*, Burney appears to have been influenced by the opinion of her husband's friend Laclos, the most famous and most laudatory critic of *Cecilia*, who included among his few complaints that the novel was somewhat too 'épisodique' (p. 453). Burney was proud of the structure of *Camilla*. It is an expanded, vast novel, many-peopled and many-voiced. When her father worried that it was a series of 'detached stories', she replied, 'it *is* of the same species as Evelina & Cecilia: new *modified*, in being more multifarious in the Characters it brings into action, – but all *wove* into *one*, with a one *Heroine* shining conspicuous through the Group, & that in what Mr Twining so flat-teringly calls *the prose Epic Style*, for so far is the Work from consisting of detached stories, that there is not, literally, one Episode in the whole plan'(*JL* 3:128–9). She made it both more 'multifarious' and more unified. Burney tells her readers in the opening statement that the subject of *Camilla* is 'the wilder wonders of the Heart of man'. These cannot really be defined. The heart 'lives its own surprise', and 'ere we can comprehend it we must be born again'. In this assemblage of strangeness, surprise, and weakness, 'one thing alone is steady – the perverseness of spirit which grafts desire on what is denied' (p. 7).

Everyone in this book longs for the thing that is not available. Sir Hugh wants to keep his eminently marriageable niece Camilla single, so that she can brighten his old age; he wants his nephew Clermont to marry the ugly Eugenia, quite ignoring their personalities; he plans that Edgar Mandlebert should link up with his niece Indiana, supplying her with a nearby estate. Eugenia wants to indulge her 'fearless credulity' (p. 341). Lionel seeks laughter without unforeseen consequences. Mr Tyrold wants women never to tell their love until they are engaged. Camilla wants to be able to follow her feelings – which assure her that she can trust Edgar. Edgar, tutored by Dr Marchmont, wants to be totally certain before he makes a marriage choice. Dr Marchmont wants a world without ambiguity. Indiana wants every superficial gewgaw she catches sight of. Her brother Clermont wants to yawn his way through life. The minor characters also aspire toward the impossible. The cultivated and generous Mrs Arlbery wants frankness and independence, with a soupçon of adulation. Dr Orkborne wants silence and uninterrupted time so that he can finish his irreparably fragmented book. Mrs Berlinton wants romance without loss of character. Her brother Melmond wants a marriage full of poetic swoons. The uncultured Mrs Mittin wants to be useful to people without making them despise her. Lord Valhurst, though old enough to be a grandfather, wants to be able to rape a pretty woman whenever the spirit moves. Mr Macdersey, an Ensign who thinks the 'law was made for poltroons', is with difficulty restrained from striking the master of some *'accomplished Monkies'*, because one of the animals seems to be wearing his colors (pp. 431, 430). Miss Fennel wants the independence of marriage without a demanding husband. Mr Dubster believes that simply by retiring from business he instantly metamorphoses into a gentleman. Mr Firl the linen-draper considers himself so canny that he can sniff out shoplifters merely by studying their demeanor. The diverse characters are too numerous to list.

This plan, although packed with humorous and even farcical scenes, creates a novel that is almost unremittingly excruciating, as painful throughout as Cecilia's briefer torment during her ride to London. The action that fulfills the plan is the marriage plot. But here, with an originality of conception typical of Burney, it is the man rather than the woman who is the orphan. Edgar is insecure about his entrance into the world and unduly influenced by his tutor, Dr Marchmont, who has been married twice and has allowed experience to triumph over hope. After being briefly lured by Indiana's beauty, Edgar realizes that he loves Camilla, but – abetted by Dr Marchmont – until he is absolutely certain that she is a proper object for his love, until he is sure that she loves *him*, he does not speak. Camilla herself is a remarkably appealing heroine, with bewitching characteristics that are perversely seen by her contemporaries as faults. She is beautiful, but not, like Indiana, perfectly beautiful. With characteristic attention to the body, Burney tells us that Camilla's uncle Sir Hugh finds her appealing because 'there's something in her little mouth that quite wins me; though she looks as if she was half laughing at me too' (p. 11). 'Her form and her mind were of equal elasticity', and Sir Hugh delights in 'her lightspringing figure' (p. 15). At a ball, she 'awakened an endless variety of remark' (p. 61). Burney clearly enjoys limning this character:

> Her disposition was ardent in sincerity, her mind untainted with evil. The reigning and radical defect of her character – an imagination that submitted to no control – proved not any antidote against her attractions; it caught, by its force and fire, the quick-kindling admiration of the lively; it possessed, by magnetic pervasion, the witchery to create sympathy in the most serious   (p. 84).

Indeed, Edgar is clearly drawn to Camilla because of her 'quick intelligence of soul' (p. 174).

All of the characters are squeezed by their unacceptable desires, but Camilla suffers the most, and she is the least at fault. The frustrations she endures are similar to those Burney had frequently experienced herself, at Court and at home. Edgar's silence forces Camilla into the passive, uncertain world that Burney inhabited when she hoped to be loved by George Cambridge. In Burney's world and in her novel, men's position is different from women's, and women's position is unnatural. Burney wrote to her sister Susanna, 'I am sometimes dreadfully afraid for myself, from the *very* different behaviour which Nature calls for on one side, & the World on the other' (Doody, p. 233). Camilla, attributing the differences to nature rather than the conduct-book rules, says to her sister Lavinia, 'They are not like us, Lavinia. They think themselves free, if they have made no verbal profession; though they may have pledged themselves by looks, by actions, by attentions, and by manners, a thousand, and a thousand times!' (p. 538) In the end, Camilla and Edgar marry, but only after she has been driven nearly into madness by the intolerable obstructions women suffer. Juliet McMaster calls Camilla 'a long and bitter consideration of the burden of silence imposed on the women'.[17] Frances Burney d'Arblay had at last herself escaped from this silence. She had attained in her own life the always rare condition of mutual love. In the confidence and joy of this experience, she gained the perspective to be able to write more clearly in her fiction about the perverseness of spirit that she saw everywhere around her and that she had often herself endured.

In *Camilla* Burney wrote about family life as an ideal, but also about how both within and without the family people manipulate one another unendurably. George Cambridge had pledged himself to her 'a thousand, and a thousand times', and in the character of Edgar Mandelbert, she wrote about George Cambridge. Another example of unbearable manipulation was even closer to home: her stepmother, Elizabeth Allen Burney. When Burney was considering where she would finish writing *Cecilia*, she dreaded going to her own home. There she could not escape the abrasive presence of her stepmother. She wanted to be with her sister Susanna, a place where she would not be clogged and obstructed. She described life with her stepmother obliquely, by envisioning life without her:

> If I find myself in good spirits, I shall not have the fear of wrath before my Eyes because I may happen to simper: if I am grave, & have had cause for gravity, I shall not conclude that you will be gayer than usual: if I ask you a common question, I shall not expect a stern look for an answer; if I make you a common reply, I shall not take it for granted you will pervert my words into an affront: if I talk of some favourite friend, I shall not prepare myself for hearing him or her instantly traduced; nor yet if I relate something that has made me happy, shall I know my conversation is the fore-runner of an Head-ache.[18]

This evocation of a perverse nature is chilling. It represents the personality of Elizabeth Allen Burney as always desiring what is denied, responding abrasively to every mood, destroying friendship, crippling every common pleasure. Then, having left this home for the Court, where George Cambridge and Mrs Burney paled before the unreasonable demands of Elizabeth Schwellenberg, 'Cerbera', Burney returned to write her third novel a decade after her second with a renewed sense of the stifling atmosphere most women inhabit.

In *Camilla*, Burney reproduced this choking restraint with such accuracy that her contemporary critics did not see that she was simultaneously undermining it. One case in point is the conduct-book Burney included in her novel, Mr Tyrold's advice to his daughter Camilla. This piece gathered considerable attention, and was reprinted separately in portmanteau form with other advice books.

William Gregory (1759–1816) visited Burney on 23 May 1813, a year or so before the publication of her last novel *The Wanderer*, and presented her with a copy of Mr Tyrold's advice printed together with his grandfather Dr John Gregory's *A Father's Legacy to his Daughters* and Bishop George Horne's 'A Picture of the Female Character' (*JL* 7:131, n. 17). Upon such occasions Burney was exceedingly gracious, but the position of Mr Tyrold's advice in its original setting is decidedly complicated. In her previous sets of strictures Burney was obviously satiric. In her 20s she had enjoyed her spoof '*Treatise upon politeness*' which suggested that no one should cough or blow the nose (*EJL* 2:48–52). In her 30s, at court, she advised that a woman whose hat pin has stabbed her should let her blood 'gush' in spite of her 'blurred appearance' (*DL* 2:353). Burney was quite aware of the bodily suffering caused by these kinds of rules. Mr Tyrold's 'Sermon' for his daughter – though well meant – is, within the context of the rest of the novel, clearly wrong-headed and destructive. It unthinkingly reproduces the requirement for passivity enforced by the eighteenth-century marriage market. Mr Tyrold notes that a woman's education 'can only prove to her a good or an evil, according to the humour of the husband into whose hands she may fall' (p. 357). Essentially, Mr Tyrold tells his daughter never to reveal her affections until a man chooses her. Since Edgar Mandlebert wants to be sure that Camilla cares for him before he declares himself, this creates a paradoxical situation whose only outcome can be unendurable misunderstanding.

Of the manifold scenes in *Camilla*, three will have to stand here as emblematic of the novel as a whole: the amateur production of *Othello*, the prank by which Lionel leaves his sister stranded in an unfinished summerhouse, and the iron pen. In *Cecilia* Burney used the works of Shakespeare as one of her chief templates. She returns to a similar frame of reference in *Camilla*. Whereas in *Cecilia* the chief pattern is *Romeo and Juliet*, in *Camilla* it is *Othello*. *Othello*, more than any other Shakespearean play, is about misunderstanding. Like Desdemona, Camilla is consistently misread by her lover, and though Burney eventually reaches a happy ending, the anguish her heroine experiences leaves readers like Juliet McMaster with a descriptive word no more positive than 'bitter' ('A Silent Angel', p. 242).

Though *Othello* is an important pattern for *Camilla*, and for the bitterness of *Camilla*, it also represents the extravagant comedy Burney invariably crushes together with her pity and fear. The chapter containing the play is called 'The disastrous Buskins', and it is a merry interlude.

Camilla, who believes that Mandlebert is planning to marry her cousin Indiana, is sadly in need of diversion when her animated friend Mrs Arlbery invites her to see *Othello* as played by a traveling troupe in a makeshift theater in Etherington, a performance that eventually became 'so truly ludicrous, that Camilla ... was excited to almost perpetual laughter' (p. 321). Though Burney's presentation of the play is unremittingly hilarious, a thoughtful reader continuously applies its content to the darker themes of the novel. This does not diminish the hilarity. All of the characters speak in different accents, so that their ability to communicate is exacerbated. Since the company is short on costumes, their *Othello* resounds with memories of other plays. Othello is dressed as Richard III, Iago as Lord Foppington from Vanbrugh's *The Relapse*, Brabantio as Hamlet's Ghost, Cassio as a Turk, Roderigo as Shylock, and Desdemona as the beleaguered novice Isabella from *Measure for Measure*. These other plays – with their switched identities, sexual betrayals, and cruel manipulations – resonate with similar themes in *Camilla*. Meanwhile, as Othello's wig catches fire and Desdemona jumps off the bed revealing that her proper costume ceases at her waist, Camilla laughs, although she must also worry that Mandlebert will wonder why she has no proper conveyance home. Sir Sedley Clarindel, who vaguely pursues Camilla and cannot let his fundamentally decent character replace his foppish surface, voices the hope that Desdemona will die promptly. In his case, the judgment is aesthetic – he can barely tolerate her nasal voice and its Worcestershire accent. Mr Macdersey, an ensign who is seeing the play for the first time, reaches the same conclusion by a different route. He adheres unswervingly to the double standard, and his sympathy lies entirely with the man. He comments chillingly that Othello is 'the finest fellow upon the face of the earth ... ; the instant he suspects his wife, he cuts her off without ceremony'. When a companion suggests that perhaps Othello could have 'made some little enquiry', Macdersey counters that a possibly injured husband can set all to rights afterwards, when no one will suspect him of weakness. It is no matter that his innocent wife is dead, hence somewhat past repair. Macdersey considers this fact beneath even mentioning: 'a man's honour is dearest to him of all things. A wife's a bauble to it – not worth a thought' (p. 323). Burney immediately follows this unyielding sentiment with another event that links Desdemona's suffering with Camilla's.

> The suffocating was now beginning but just as Desdemona begged to be spared –
> But alf han our –

the door-keeper forced his way into the pit, and called out –
'Pray, is one Miss Tyrold here in the play-house?'   (p. 323)

Neither Camilla nor her sister Lavinia dares to reply. They too are
being suffocated, though less obviously and less completely. It turns
out that Camilla's uncle is thought to be dying. In the distress of the
moment Mandlebert's judgmentalism briefly vanishes. But Burney
has already alerted us to the comparison – that female difficulties are
dire, and universal.

The *Othello* sequence is a set piece, orchestrating the discordant,
hilarious, frightening attitudes of Camilla's motley acquaintances.
The escapades of Lionel Tyrold provide more actively the intermingling of comedy and pain so characteristic of Burney's protean style.
In *Cecilia*, the action was often extraordinary and violent. In *Camilla*
the simplest exchange will veer nearly to madness. Mrs Arlbery expa-
tiates for paragraphs on the difficulty of obtaining a satisfactory cup
of tea. Lionel plagues everyone, pouncing whenever he sees someone
vulnerable. He is affectionate, charming, even generous, but he is also
a tease, a rampant tease, and an unrelenting one. When his uncle Sir
Hugh endeavors to learn Latin, Lionel mercilessly undermines these
pitiful attempts. Most importantly, Lionel aggravates and entangles
the rules of modesty and deportment by which his sisters must live. At
a ball, Lionel informs one group of men that Lavinia is the family
heiress, insists to others that Eugenia is the designated choice, and
points out Camilla to a third group. This machination of course bewil-
ders everyone. Solely to divert himself, Lionel persistently links
Camilla with a foolish and crass former wig-maker named Dubster,
whom Margaret Doody compares to Lewis Carroll's white rabbit (both
of them fret over their lost white gloves). Dubster has married two
fortunes, and has been lucky enough to have both of the women die,
though one 'cost me a mort of money to the potecary before she went
off' (p. 279). With truly sublime nonchalance, Lionel inveigles his
sisters and Mr Dubster up a ladder to the second floor of Dubster's
unfinished summerhouse, and then abandons them in this compromising position to be viewed by passers-by from the highway. When
the passers-by do not materialize, the sisters' mood veers from embarrassment to dismay. The only people to notice their plight are two
market women who refuse to deliver the ladder they have fetched,
because the penurious Dubster fails to offer them a sufficient reward.
They jeer at Dubster and deride the maimed Eugenia for her ruined
face and body. Eventually the ubiquitous Edgar Mandlebert arrives

and rescues them, only to misunderstand yet once again Camilla's attempts to show that she is independent of him.

Camilla really enjoys Lionel; her own imagination, after all, 'admits of no control'. And Lionel is pictured as not wholly responsible for his actions. He attributes his character and his difficulties to the fact that he has merely imitated his fellows, the 'merry boys' at Oxford, but he spirals badly out of control, extorting money from his Uncle Relvil by threatening in anonymous letters to blow his brains out. Eventually, still following his uncurbed desires, Lionel forces Camilla to accept a compromising £200 from Sir Sedley Clarindel, acquires a married mistress whose servants need 'hush-money' (p. 731), and ultimately spends so much money that his father is arrested and thrown into Winchester Prison. Indeed, Lionel's crimes are so extreme that commentators have surmised that they might be based on the escapades of the Burney black sheep Richard Thomas Burney. Richard Thomas Burney was banished to Bengal at the age of 19 and though he seems to have behaved commendably in his new environs, he was expunged so successfully from the family records that we know almost nothing about him. What is most remarkable here is that Camilla loves Lionel, even though he makes her suffer. Burney characteristically delineated characters with clear-sighted precision, in all their variety, with all their faults upon them. Then she allowed other characters to laugh with them and to forgive them. The reader, however, remains unforgiving.

Although Camilla shares some characteristics with her brother, she knows how to stop before she destroys. She is as strong and fearless as a woman can be in her squeezed situation. But in ordinary life, Burney insistently reminds us, men have the power for good or ill. 'I would cut off my left arm for Lavinia and Eugenia', says Lionel, 'and for thee, Camilla, I would lop off my right! – But yet, when some frolic or gambol comes into my way, I forget you all! clear out of my memory you all walk, as if I had never beheld you!' (p. 739) The imagery of self-disfigurement in the service of love, along with the moral amnesia, is as violent and unforgiving as a *Monty Python* skit – affectionate, outrageous, cruel, and absurd.

Although at the end Burney wrote *Camilla 'en verf'*, the beginning had not been quite so easy. The original *Camilla*, where the heroine had a different name – at times Ariella, at times Clarinda – was a Gothic sexual drama, though written before Gothic was actually in vogue. In the ur-*Camilla* version, the heroine had contracted such enormous debts that in order to save her family from disgrace she was going to marry a man who nauseated her. In a painful dream-sequence this ur-Camilla believed on her wedding eve that the man she really loved had entered her bedroom and was about to touch her. The maelstrom of feelings this sequence evokes – eroticism, shame, and dread – is an exceptionally vivid evocation of how terrifying marriage was for eighteenth-century women. Burney's friend Mrs Delany had been driven to marry a man who repelled her, and she was not shy about recounting her ordeal. Her rather difficult friend Georgiana Waddington never was able to adjust to the fact that she married a man she found unattractive. Burney herself in the case of Mr Barlow had experienced the kind of revulsion that felt like death.

In the published novel, this particular experience metamorphosed into the moment when the heroine dreams that she is writing with an iron pen.[19] This is the episode that most fascinates modern readers of *Camilla*. The foundation for this scene is the family, the nuclear family, that fraught, new phenomenon in eighteenth-century life. Gender and money combine here with the family to create an explosive mixture. Mainly through Camilla's brother Lionel's fault, Camilla's father has been imprisoned for debt, and Camilla too has been careless with her finances. Being female, she accepts more blame than is really her due. With her father out of reach, her recently returned mother is her sole resource. She is stranded at an inn where she is unable to pay the bill, and her ability even to send letters for help is gradually cut off. Her mother, instead of forgiving her, blames her for her father's situation and refuses to communicate directly, sending a message through Camilla's sister Lavinia. When Camilla sends a letter in reply, indicating that she is very weak and probably dying, she forgets to ask the messenger to bring an answer. She herself is just about to write again when she sees a 'silent though numerous' crowd carrying a dead body (p. 868). She later recognizes this body as her sister Eugenia's brutal husband.

Family, a sense of connection, is more important to Camilla than anything else. Self-murder or near self-murder[20] occur in all of Burney's novels, but in the other three the suicidal character is not the heroine. Camilla, rejected by her mother, rejected by her lover, simply wants to die. Here, uniquely, Burney attends closely to the psychology of suicide. Wanting to die, Camilla is nonetheless frightened by the sight of death, and feels immediately guilty at her wish, at the self-neglect which is hardly distinguishable from suicide. She falls into a feverish dream, where Death reaches out for her with the assurance of a lover, 'and with its hand, sharp and forked, struck abruptly upon her breast' (p. 874). The chilling sensuality of this experience remains from the early draft of *Camilla*, where the heroine is about to rescue the family from debt by marrying the rich man who disgusts her. There is no place in *Camilla* for the fearful moment when the ur-Camilla dreams that the man she loves has come into her bedroom and is touching her. Burney's new plot did not allow for this particular fearful moment, when the man a woman longs for is actually standing next to her bed, and her desire for him has embodied him and placed him destructively within reach. In the published *Camilla*, the nearly indulged sensuality is displaced onto the desire for death. 'O, Earth', she cries out, 'with all thy sorrows, take, take me once again'. There is no return from the loss of virginity, and there is no return from death. Richardson made this connection in *Clarissa*, and in *Camilla* so does Burney. The dream assaults her senses with a glacial chill, ear-destroying voices, and an atmosphere so heavy that every breath is toil. Suddenly she is holding an iron pen and writing in the book of Eternity: 'I have desired annihilation', she writes, a guilty desire she describes as 'pitiless, selfish, unnatural' (p. 875). She imagines her parents weeping out their eyes. The dream-forces demand that Camilla write her reasons for deserving mercy:

> She wrote with difficulty … but saw that her pen made no mark! She looked upon the page, when she thought she had finished, … but the paper was blank!   (pp. 875–6, Burney's ellipses).

For Burney, the written word was the key to life, the connection to reality, the way to find love. The most terrible isolation, then, would be the inability to write. This is a writer's special nightmare, the excruciating inability so often blandly referred to as 'writer's block'.

When Camilla first grasps the iron pen, she is able to write, but only in order to deny herself. She writes that she desires death, but though she can write out her desires, she cannot write her defense. She is guilty, and she cannot relieve her guilt. As before, her hearing is assaulted, when voices 'by hundreds, by thousands, by millions' (p. 876) from every direction call out to her that she must read her fate – and she wakes up.

Unlike Cecilia, Camilla even in such an extremity does not lose her reason. Family is what saves her. Even though she has trammeled her parents in debt, and their rejection has been severe, they exist, and the three of them, even in their mutual pain, are all confident of mutual love. Camilla acts sensibly. Convinced that she is dying, she calls for a clergyman. Here Burney's later version of the plot reflects the canceled one, because the presumed clergyman is her beloved tormentor Edgar Mandlebert, not here a threat, but a savior. This is not Othello, come to kill her, but Edgar, desperate to save her. Soon her mother arrives, and her father. The terrors of the iron pen are by degrees neutralized by romantic and filial love.

By all rights this unbearable plot should end, like *Cecilia*, in an uneasy resolution, but it does not. At the end of the novel all three of the Tyrold sisters – Eugenia, Lavinia, and Camilla herself – are happily married. In the spirit of the earlier novel, Burney did allow herself one final irony. With a last contemptuous fling, Burney married Camilla's cold and beautiful cousin Indiana to the Othello-loving Ensign Macdersey. For the heroine, *Cecilia* had ended more doubtfully, but by the end of *Camilla* the happily-married Burney allowed herself an optimism she had for many years lost. The suspicious Edgar simply changes at the end, unexpectedly and uncharacteristically displaying 'generous confidence'. With no hint that such a change might be short-lived, Burney stresses that Edgar now allows Camilla to be herself, 'and her friends read her exquisite lot in a gaiety no longer to be feared' (p. 913). Against all reason, Burney implies that Edgar will persist in this personality change, and that the marriage will be happy. Readers might doubt, but this time Burney does not feed their doubt.

From the strength of her position in a separate family she and her husband wrote on 15 July 1795 to her brother Charles that they wanted him to assume all the negotiations for *Camilla*. In capital letters they offered him 'CARTE BLANCHE!' Enthusiastically, they supported 'dear, good, bold, kind, generous Carlos!' (*JL* 3:135). Charles himself promised to fight all the dragons left over from the *Cecilia* negotiations: 'I have openly offered to take all the odium on myself; & I will do it, my dear D arblays [sic], in the face of my father, my Brother, & all the Booksellers in the world.'(*JL* 3:135, n. 1) Even the d'Arblays' baby, Charles's nephew and godson, whom his parents had dubbed the 'Idol of the World', was imagined as concurring. The Idol's need for present and future support was for Charles a good extra excuse for hard bargaining.

Burney took it upon herself to handle her father. Writing to him the same day, she used her son Alexander as a wedge, and spoke in her brother's voice:

'What Evelina, he says, does now for the Son of Lowndes, & what Cecilia does for the Son of payne [sic], let your third work do for the

Son of its Authour. – ' –
   Can we resist such a call? Is it in Nature? –
   You, he says, are too delicate, & James too ignorant of *this* sort of
business, to be able to act with the intrepidity he will do himself.
                                                                    (*JL* 3:140).

Her letter is long and expansively mollifying. She is concerned mainly
that her father and James should understand why she has turned to
her brother Charles as negotiator. She argues the case from every
possible angle, her completeness showing her concern, the felt need
to soothe. Since she had always tried at least to consider her father's
advice – asked or unasked – she evidently felt she needed to placate
him at length for neglecting that advice. This took persistence, if not
courage, but she was able to summon ample stamina for the task.

As soon as she had decided not to try to publish her tragedy *Edwy
and Elgiva*, she turned to the business of how to publish *Camilla*. For
Camilla, she and d'Arblay had decided to try to float a subscription.
Although this method of publication could be somewhat humiliating,
it could also be extremely lucrative. Despite the need to dun all one's
friends, a long subscription list showed that you knew all the best
people, those with money, position, and power. On 10 June 1795
Burney wrote her brother Charles a self-assured letter outlining this
scheme, at this point also including her father and her brother James
in the negotiating team. All the letters to Charles, to whom she writes
confidently as her equal, reveal a striking mixture of playfulness and
detailed business acumen. In the 10 June letter, she begins with verses
about the demise of *Edwy and Elgiva*, references to advice about how
to revise and publish the play, and a firm decision to leave it behind
her: 'So Much for That'. The remainder of the letter needs to be quoted
at length:

Now – to *The* business.
   All things considered, – & weighty are some of them! – – have just
come to a resolution to print my Grand Work, of which you have
never yet heard, – by subscription.
   But
   As in some points it is very disagreeable to us both to take such a
measure – And as in all points, it is a thing to be done but ONCE in
a Life, we wish to do it to MOST advantage.
   It is not finished.
   And I don't know how long it will be.

But I fancy in 6 Volumes such as Cecilia, or in 4 Oct^{vo}
Now what ought to be the subscription?
Pray give me your idea.
And know you in the least what the expence of the printing will
be? Good paper & Letter, though not the *superlative*
We think to have Subscriptions received by Messrs Payne, Cadell,
& Robinson. Advise upon this subject, I pray.
Must we have *proposals* printed?
or will newspaper *advertisements* suffice?
We mean to open with all the speed we can arrange.
Give us your Counsel, my dear & ever kind Brother & Agent.

JL 3:110–12.

Burney sounds very positive here, as if having d'Arblay to consult has
buoyed her up. Since she is no longer negotiating alone with her
father, she writes to her brother lightheartedly, even vivaciously. 'We
wish to do it to MOST advantage', she says. Charles, whom she can
banter with and be direct with, will be her 'Agent'. She and d'Arblay
are studying all the details. Her subsequent letters to both her father
and Charles bristle with detail about advertising, the amount to be
charged for the subscription, and the type of paper to be used. Thus
in a passage in a letter to her father, later excised, Burney discusses
paper and the percentage of the booksellers' profits. She has found
out some of the particular details about paper, and realizes that it is
the most expensive item. She was 'against wire paper & Hot presses'.
Wire paper, also known as wove paper, was especially smooth,
because it was made in a mold with a very fine wire mesh instead of
the more widely spaced wire mold which had been in use for
centuries.[21] The hot pressing would have made the paper glossy. She
did not, however, really know exact prices. Her next sentence shows
that she was searching for a general effect rather than a specific price:
'Yet surely paper & type should be good & clear & *respectable*.' (JL
3:118) Later, she and Charles reconsidered the expensive paper, and
a charge of two guineas per copy to cover it, but after mediating a
dispute over a guinea and a half versus a guinea, with Charles daring
the higher sum and her father and James arguing otherwise, the one-
guinea crowd prevailed. In the end, it seemed to Burney and d'Arblay
that the 'times will not allow it'. They should charge only one guinea,
printing the proposals quickly because 'every body says the Town is
even *Hourly* emptying' (JL 3:122). To accommodate this lower fee,
Burney limited herself to five volumes, though she would have

preferred six.[22] Besides the booksellers, three of her women friends collected subscriptions.

At first, she wanted her proposals to call *Camilla* a 'work' rather than a novel, not because she truly despised novels, but because they were so often reduced to the idea of a mere romance, and because the Queen had not at first allowed *Cecilia* to be read in her circle because it was a 'novel'.[23] To achieve sales among the audience she desired, she needed the good opinion of the royal family. The three friends who hawked the book worked tirelessly and successfully. Mrs Boscawen, for instance, was urged on by Mrs Montagu, who bought only one copy, but paid ten guineas for it.[24] Mrs Locke gathered the Duchess of Leinster, her husband Mr Ogilvie, and various other members of the powerful and rich FitzGerald family. Mrs Crewe collected £20 from Burke, who remembered how much his dead son and brother had loved Burney's other books, and bought two of his four copies in their memory. He paid £5 per copy, because one of Burney's books, as he wrote to Crewe, 'is certainly as good as a thousand others' (*Memoirs* 3:211). Whenever possible, her solicitors collected the money on the spot. Mrs Locke kept one end of her '*morocco* memorandum Book' for the paid subscriptions and the other for the unpaid ones (*JL* 3:128). One of the most uncertain aspects of subscriptions was collecting money that was merely promised. The whole process was somewhat unnerving, since the cost of printing *Camilla* eventually came to £183 6s, nearly twice the d'Arblay annual income of £100.[25] However, with *Evelina* and *Cecilia* behind her, Burney was confident that her book would sell enough to defray its printing costs. What was most important was to bring more of the profits home.

The subscription system worked. For the first time, Burney made a substantial amount of money. Her portly but active brother Charles had negotiated persistently and with flair, weighing the offers of at least six different publishers. James and Dr Burney were held at bay, with Burney's sister Susan testing the home waters, her brother Charles using his *carte blanche* to negotiate. It was common knowledge, Burney wrote, that Payne cleared £1500 with the first edition of *Cecilia*. She was wrong, but this was the story. She vowed not to be a dupe again. Besides the official bookkeepers – Mrs Crewe, Mrs Boscawen, and Mrs Locke – other friends rallied to the cause and scoured their acquaintance for subscribers. They and Burney's friends gathered a 37–page list containing 1060 subscribers, many of whom ordered multiple copies. This list is a cross-section of the reading public of the period: circulating libraries, authors, actors, powerful political and Church figures, old friends, a generous mass of strangers, and a flaunted number of titled dignitaries. Lords, ladies, dukes, duchesses, countesses, and on down the social scale even to esquires – all are listed with their titles. Dedicated to the Queen with her permission, the book was safe for the Court to buy, and Miss Goldsworthy, the sub-governess to the princesses, subscribed and is listed as such. Even Burney's old nemesis Elizabeth Juliana Schwellenberg ordered a copy. Women authors subscribed in force. Besides Elizabeth Montagu, Miss Jane Austen, Elizabeth Carter, Maria Edgeworth, Harriet Lee, and Burney's estranged friend Mrs Piozzi (as well as her daughters) bought copies. The Piozzi-Thrale contingent bought 12 sets among them. And the men were not far behind, though the male authors who subscribed tended themselves to write non-fiction. People of all intellectual stripes joined the crowd, from Hume to Dr Thomas Gisborne, popular writer of conduct-books.[26] Godwin is missing, but his disciple Thomas Holcroft is there. Although the important men of the day appear abundantly on this list, it is heavily female, with approximately two women for each man. The presence of women shows their desire to own their own copies and to indicate their support. Often, when a husband buys a copy, his wife and daughters sign up for their own separate sets. Burney could hardly have asked for a finer list.

The subscription method for *Camilla* brought in nearly seven times the money Burney had received for *Cecilia*. Not everyone paid up for the subscriptions, but on this part of the contract she probably cleared nearly £1000. Reluctantly, Charles had also sold the copyright to Payne, Cadell and Davies, chiefly as a hedge against piracy, but he negotiated the not inconsiderable sum of £1000, as opposed to £250 (plus £50) for *Cecilia*. This amount was considered so unusual that before the deal was finished no one had dared name the sum in a letter. Even after publication the publishers wanted to continue to keep it quiet, claiming, Burney said, that 'a similar price has never yet been given, & fearing to offend cotemporaries [sic]' (*JL* 3:227). Burney's letter to her brother about the final negotiations varies from confidence to apprehension: '25 setts I shall demand, beyond subscriptions, if I part with the Copy right', she says, and then admits, 'I am in a prodigious twitter at all this!' Yet Burney had been very strong throughout this entire procedure, a strength difficult for any writer to muster (*JL* 3:126–7).

Prefaced with its star-studded subscription list, *Camilla* appeared on 12 July 1796. In August, the reviews began to strike. Burney had finished the book in such a state of euphoria that although the reviews were significantly less supportive than they had been for her previous two books, she weathered their attacks particularly well.[27] Without her knowledge, her father tried to control the process somewhat by suggesting to his friends at the *Monthly Review* that his son Charles review the book, a manoeuvre he thought fair because he was convinced of 'the peculiar intrinsic merit of the work' (*JL* 3: Appendix B, p. 368). The *Monthly Review* editor Ralph Griffiths chose instead William Enfield, author of books on elocution, and himself contributed the last paragraphs. As a result, in August, Burney received three reviews that were calculated to shake the confidence of even a strong-hearted author. The review signed 'M' in the *Analytical Review*, likely written by Mary Wollstonecraft, stressed that *Camilla* 'contains parts superiour to anything she has yet produced' (p. 142), but pronounced the book as a whole inferior to her previous novels. The *Monthly Mirror* entirely failed to perceive Burney's plan, and accused her of writing just the sort of episodical book she had distinctly not written. 'Prolixity' was their chief complaint, and the fact that 'the picture is deficient of harmony' (p. 227). Enfield, dividing novels into the 'romantic, pathetic, and humourous' places Burney in the last category. He avoids invidious comparisons, and though he thinks the reader 'somewhat harassed', he sees that one central theme in the novel is 'innocence suffering through its own misapprehensions' (pp. 156–7). He enjoys most Burney's unusual characterizations, including the bumbling Sir Hugh Tyrold and the 'sprightly and eccentric Mrs Arlbery' (p. 160). The review ends positively by commending the book to young readers, who will learn how to live by it. Along the way, though, there is a long section listing many of the 'verbal and grammatical inaccuracies', such as 'scarce' for 'scarsely', mistakes with 'lie' and 'lay', and so on, and so on (p. 162). This infuriated Dr Burney and sent his daughter into a panic (*JL* 3:229). Burney insisted that the mistakes were printer's errors, but they were not. Most likely Alexandre d'Arblay, who was so new to English, had introduced errors, and his wife lacked the time to reread the manuscript carefully. The remaining reviews contained fewer strictures and extended quotations, as was the habit of the day, but none was ecstatic as those of *Cecilia*. Meanwhile, her brother Charles neutralized the reviews with a rhyme mimicking Swift's doggerel:

> Now heed no more what Critics thought 'em
> Since this you know – All People bought 'em   (*JL* 3:206)[28]

Writing to her father in November, Burney noted that her public had always bypassed the reviews, and that they were doing so again. She wanted *Camilla* to be perfect, nonetheless, and she continued to work on it, cutting it down substantially for a new edition that did not actually appear until 1802, and then expanding it again for a proposed third edition that never was to appear. Later, she returned once more to the manuscript, weeding it and taking out the Gallicisms. When her son died, she lost her will for this effort, and she never finished the revision. The Blooms reproduce many of these changes at the back of their edition of *Camilla*, commenting on Burney's undiminished intellectual power, and her 'sensitive determination' (p. xxv). At some point Burney also went back to the Gothic early draft, which was so different from the published book that she saw possibilities in it for a separate novel, but eventually she left this plot behind. Her family novel was written, panoramic and excruciating. It showed how women can suffer from men whose wild hearts contain 'the perverseness of spirit which grafts desire on what is denied'. In the early 1800s she did not need to return to an earlier Gothic idea. The most Gothic of her novels was forming in her mind.

7

Independence, Marriage, and Comedies Without Fetters (1792–1802)

> My imagination is not at my own controll, or I would always have continued in the walk you approuved. The combinations for another long work did not occur to me. Incidents & effects for a Dramma [sic] did. I thought the field more than open – inviting to me. The chance held out golden dreams. . . . I hope, therefore, my dearest Father, in thinking this over, you will cease to nourish such terrors & disgust at an essay so natural, & rather say to yourself with an internal smile, 'After all – 'tis but *like Father like Child* – for to what walk do I confine myself? – She took my example in writing – She takes it in ranging'.
>
> Frances Burney to Dr Charles Burney
> [10] February 1800 (*JL* 4:395)

The first few years after Burney's marriage were her most idyllic, and she remembered them always with joy. The d'Arblays immediately put the *Camilla* money to work. On the property of their old friends the Lockes at Norbury Park, they rented what her father called a 'slice' of land and built themselves a house Dr Burney designated as Camilla Cottage, a name that stuck. D'Arblay, who designed and helped to build it, filled it with 'closets, cupboards, and adroit recesses' and saw to it that every window fronted on a 'freshly beautiful view' (*Memoirs* 3:260). There, in the house whose name memorialized its professional connections and its unpretentiousness, they were to spend four happy years, cultivating cabbages, and with delight and unceasing attentiveness raising their charming son. Looking back on this period when she was nearly 73, in a comment at the top of her father's letter questioning the wisdom of her marriage, Burney wrote, 'Memorandum. –

This 7th. May, 1825. ... – – And NEVER – NEVER was Union more exquisitely blest & felicitous – though, after the first 8 years of unmingled happiness, it was assailed by many calamities – chiefly of separation or illness – Yet still MENTALLY unbroken'(*JL* 2:170). Alexandre d'Arblay had been dead for seven years and four days.

In the near family in the late 1790s happiness was as yet 'unmingled', but in the Burney family at large, breakage lay everywhere. Frances Burney was known to all her siblings as being stable, kind, and wise. They turned to her in their times of trouble, and she raised their spirits. They might not take her advice, but they nonetheless put themselves in the way of listening to it. At this moment, the Burney family had need of advice. Three months after the publication of *Camilla*, Burney's stepmother died. Burney expected that her 'so long-enduring Father' (*JL* 3:217) would actually be somewhat relieved, but the interrupted habit of intimacy, even with a termagant, leaves a void. Only by cajoling her father to write a poem on astronomy could she pull him out of his depression. Maria Allen Rishton, who when Burney had married wondered about the tumult in a vestal's veins, had long been writing to Burney about the woe in her own marriage. She was now negotiating for a public separation. It did not help matters that on 1 March 1798 Burney's widowed sister Charlotte Francis insisted on marrying Ralph Broome, who as it turned out was just as angry and arrogant as everyone had feared. Five months later, Burney's brother James abandoned his family and set up housekeeping with his half-sister Sarah Harriet, who was herself desperate to flee her miserable life as companion to her difficult father. Although this seemingly incestuous flight eventually proved to be merely an act of mutual assistance, it sent Dr Burney into a rage, chiefly because the couple lured away one of his favorite servants. When angry, Dr Burney habitually cut off communications. He did not attend Charlotte's wedding, and he would not see James and Sarah. Burney was the conduit, especially to James and Sarah. Sarah needed support. Although like all Burneys Sarah Harriet loved to write, and had already published her novel *Clarentine*, she suffered from the usual Burney poverty.[1] After she and James had spent five years together, he found the separation from his children unbearable, and he went back to his family. Left without support, Sarah found a position as governess, eventually returning in 1807, when Burney was abroad, to care for her father, a position her sister Esther termed 'more creditable to the family'.[2] Burney was rather severe at times about her character, writing to Susanna in 1798 that 'Sarah is capricious, & only loves, or likes, where & while she is served or amused' (*JL* 4:112). Sarah Harriet seems never to have idealized her father as Burney intermittently did, and her relationship with Dr Burney was conspicuously rocky.

The most terrible blow for Burney was the death of her sister Susanna. Susanna's husband Molesworth Phillips had moved the family to Ireland in 1796, to protect their property against political unrest. Susanna became ill, and Phillips was not helpful. He flirted flagrantly with another woman and actually appeared to be intercepting Susanna's letters to her son Norbury at school. The Burney family wanted her to return to England so that they could care for her. At last, after exhaustive tactful exchanges, with Burney offering in 1799 to go to Ireland herself to fetch her sister, the Phillips family began the arduous winter trip. Charles rode to meet Susanna and found her after egregious weather and many false stops at the White Lion Inn in Chester, but it was too late. On 6 January 1800, Susanna died. Charles did not dare to write to his sister; he asked their friends the Lockes to tell her, news Burney found so 'harrowing' it 'made me wish to be mad' (*JL* 4:386). Burney had not seen her sister for four years. Impassable roads – combined perhaps with Phillips's haste to prevent the Burney family from controlling the situation – kept her and d'Arblay from even attending the funeral.

Susanna had always been at the center of Burney's literary life. She was her first audience, the person she always imagined herself as writing for. Burney's original journals were for 'nobody', because Susanna was in the house, but whenever they were separated the journals were for Susanna. When Burney was at court, her sister's incessant journal-letters sustained her. Susanna's descriptions of young Norbury reminded Burney that there was an ordinary life, a sweet life outside her killing routine. Norbury told stories about countries where everyone had an extra arm, and the guns did not kill people. It was Susanna who thought the Chevalier d'Arblay was worth meeting, and it was always Susanna whom Burney ran to with every novel and every play. Though in 1791 'a little afraid of the *Moroseness* of the Tragedies', Susanna provided mostly a sensitive, detailed reading, and support.[3] Burney's brother Charles became her liaison with the commercial world, but Susanna was her other half. She was the sort of doppelganger every writer longs for. Her loss was insupportable. Burney had to send Alex away for a few days, for fear her paroxysms of grief would frighten him. '*We wanted nothing but each other... She was the soul of my soul.*' (*JL* 4:386) She could not speak about her sister. No words, no memories would console her. Years later, when d'Arblay was dying, he begged her to speak about him, to remember him with Alexander, not to recede as she had receded over Susanna. With her doppelganger gone, where would she find her inspiration? 'I must pray to God for new lights!' (*JL* 4:360)

In their idyllic life at Camilla Cottage, the d'Arblays struggled with two great imponderables. How could Burney recover from her sister's death, and how might d'Arblay regain his position as breadwinner? This couple who had courted one another in journals, now communicated on paper about these quandaries, in this case not their own words, but in excerpts from others. When Susanna died, Burney created a tiny commonplace book, just two inches by two-and-a-half, to fit into her pocket. With quotations from Dugald Stewart and Catherine Talbot, she memorialized mainly the anger she felt at her own deprivation and at others' inability to understand how bereft the world was without Susanna.[4] Not to have friendship, said one of the quotations she carefully copied, is 'a wretched destitution!' (p. 36). The words bewail as well those whose manners are not supported by 'native benevolence' (p. 37). In the midst of these excerpts showing how unique and unappeasable her sorrow is, there is a French passage in d'Arblay's hand from Montfort showing that men have a secret ambition, a need to flex their moral faculties. Women should indulge men in this ambition. After d'Arblay's segment, Burney resumes, seemingly in her own words, with an uncharacteristic wobbliness one can only compare to stuttering. Writing here, in agony herself, yet evidently trying to understand d'Arblay's secret needs, she cannot finish a satisfactory sentence. The prose is labored, the content self-critical. After some pages of this blackened and blotted effort to reconstitute herself, Burney returns once again to Talbot's cheerful, pleasant advice: 'Instead of always sighing for leisure, we should learn how to live sometimes without it. It is not trifling to be gay with our Friends; to enliven the circle of social good humour; to improve all our talents, small as well as great, to refresh ourselves with needful relaxation; & to indulge, at fit times, the innocent sportings of Fancy – .' (p. 53) After this, she leaves some pages blank, as if hoping to be able to follow the cheer with more cheer. Cheer she does not find, but there are more quotations claiming that true love is not a morbid sensibility, but something more positive. Duty is an important part of love, and it is more stable than sensibility.

Just before Susanna's death, there were plans afoot to stage a Burney comedy. Thomas Harris, manager of Covent Garden, offered £400 for *Love and Fashion*, to be produced in the 1800 season. To protect herself from unreasonable expectations, Burney planned to remain anonymous. But when Susanna died, Burney had no stomach for a comedy, and her father immediately insisted that *Love and Fashion* be withdrawn. This was the play that elicited the letter Burney wrote to her father one month after Susanna's death, telling him that it was normal for her to want to write a comedy, that her imagination was not at her own 'controll' and that he should 'cease to nourish such terrors & disgust at an essay so natural' (*JL* 4:395). The letter is very firm, but even so *Love and Fashion* was not produced. For unknown reasons, it did not even go into production during the 1801 season. Perhaps Burney thought the play was not good enough. Balanced on the simple opposition between passion and money, this is the weakest of Burney's comedies. When she tinkered with it in the 1820s and 1830s, her comments were unusually harsh: 'forced', 'Pretentious sickening to nullity', 'The Ghost stale and Innis insufferably stupid'.[5] The fate of *Love and Fashion* did not slow Burney down. She had some extra time for work, because d'Arblay went to France in November 1801 to reassume his career. He was about to go to San Domingo, to help quell (reluctantly) Toussaint L'Ouverture's insurrection, but when he stated that he would not fight against his wife's nation, Napoleon canceled the orders.

In d'Arblay's absence, Burney seems to have started work immediately on two other comedies, *A Busy Day*, and *The Woman-Hater*.[6] Burney had performance clearly in mind for both plays, listing specific casts for each. *A Busy Day* was intended for Covent Garden and *The Woman-Hater* for Drury Lane. *A Busy Day; or, An Arrival from India* is one of the few Burney plays reprinted separately before Sabor's complete edition. Tara Ghoshal Wallace edited it in 1984.[7] A director named Alan Coveney happened upon a copy, and mounted a production at the Hen and Chicken pub theater in Bristol, in 1993. The responses were overwhelmingly positive, with one reviewer hyperbolically claiming that Burney's 'true metier was the stage'.[8] The production was revived the next year for a month in London. One reason why a twentieth-century audience can appreciate this play is that the crux of *A Busy Day* is class. Eliza Watts' guardian has intended her to marry Cleveland, but his relatives object to her vulgar family. Burney has combined the situation in *Evelina* with that in *Camilla*, enjoying the opportunity this situation offers to show how money corrupts people, how few people who care about fashion have room in their hearts even for noticing other people, much less loving them. Eliza's sister thinks 'they'd been all savages' in Calcutta, 'nasty black things!' (1.451, 461, *Plays* 1:309). The rich Miss Percival screams when she sees the Watts family. Savages as she defines them simply come from a different class and live in another part of town. When she sees the Watts family, she not only shrieks, but also runs away, 'one hand covering her face', crying out, 'O the Savages are bearing down upon us!' (3.528–9; *Plays* 1:349). Of Miss Percival and her ilk, Tibbs complains, 'They'll leave doors and windows open upon one, in the middle of a sneeze or a cough; and they'll let one speak half an hour, before they'll give an answer; and they'll clean their teeth full in one's face, as if one was nothing but a looking glass.'[9] Burney's experience at Court, where Mrs Schwellenberg insisted on leaving the carriage window open even when Burney had a cold, where every distinction of class expanded into a chasm, sensitized her to the outrageous ways people treated one another. It was lines like these, the way people use their bodies to insult one another, that delighted the audience in 1993, and will do so again.

In 1802, with Crisp nearly ten years dead, Burney wrote *The Woman-Hater*. At last she wrote an unfettered drama, one that a delicate woman might not dare to call her own. Able at last to ignore Crisp's advice, Burney wrote with all the 'Wildness & friskyness' that the exuberant hornpipe had awakened in her (*EJL* 3:239). The irrepressible Joyce Wilmot above all things loves dancing. Her addiction to dancing is a tribute to Nancy Dawson and hence to Burney's younger self. More than any of Burney's other plays, *The Woman-Hater* incorporates the medley of tones she included in her novels. Hemlow surmises that it would have succeeded better in the early 1800s than *Love and Fashion* or *A Busy Day*.[10] There are two main plots, shifting from laughter to high sensibility, as many plays of the period tended to do. Seventeen years before the action begins, Lady Smatter jilted Sir Roderick, and as a result he is a woman-hater. Now, however, she is a widow, again available. Also 17 years ago, Lady Smatter's brother Wilmot married Sir Roderick's sister Eleanora, but in a jealous fit a few years later Wilmot expelled Eleanora for unfaithfulness. The innocent Eleanora stole away her child Sophia, and the nurse replaced Sophia with her own child, Joyce. When the action begins, all of these characters converge on the same spot. In *Evelina*, in a similar situation, the false Miss Belmont is a lovely, repressed girl. In *The Woman-Hater*, Joyce's presumed father Wilmot has tried to make a lady out of her, but she is not a lady. She is a wild young woman, what her contemporaries would call a hoyden, a romp.

The serious plot dwells on Eleanora's suffering, and Wilmot's unreasonable rejection of her. He is a woman-hater of the Edgar Mandlebert

Camilla type, always ready to misunderstand, a figure resembling Othello. He does not deserve to get his wife back. Burney saw this unfair repression of a woman as verging on tragedy. She intended the part to go to John Philip Kemble, the actor who had played Edwy on its ill-fated single night. She wanted Sarah Siddons to act his wife. Sir Roderick is a comic figure, and Lady Smatter a more tenderly handled reincarnation of her namesake from *The Witlings*. This second Lady Smatter is aware that the quotations that punctuate her speech have somehow become unmoored from their origins, and we are made to feel slightly sorry for her. The aging Burney had become more understanding about weakening mental agility.

In Joyce, who is the most important character, Burney personifies what has been in her writing career an increasingly freer and stronger commentary on the irrationalities of class divisions. She also expresses through Joyce the need a woman feels to break free from a repressive father and unleash her natural sensibilities. 'For Joyce', as Darby puts it, 'being alive means being *original*' (p. 156). Joyce's song, 'Rule ye fair ones, – Ye fair ones rule – the Men!' is a parody of Thomson's 'Rule Britannia' (5.6.4; *Plays* 1:268). This song, which was performed with increasing frequency after the French King's execution, may represent the patriotic side of Joyce's mule-mixture character, the words crying out for liberty, the tune resounding with British conservatism.

Joyce retains the rebellious blood of her true working class ancestry.[11] The dual influences she feels create some of her best scenes. When her father is in the room, she is distinctly monosyllabic, and her body is very controlled. Evelina was similarly silent when she first encountered Lord Orville and when she met her father. But Joyce changes drastically when her father is out of the room. The woman she is speaking to – though she does not yet know it – is her mother:

MISS WILMOT (peeping over the shoulders of the NURSE). Is Papa gone?
NURSE. Yes, Miss.
MISS WILMOT. Are you sure?
NURSE. Yes, Miss, up stairs to his own room.
MISS WILMOT (*jumping up and singing*).
    Then hoity, toity, whiskey, friskey,
    These are the joys of our dancing days –
Come, now let's get rid of all this stupifying learning. so march off, Mr. Thompson! decamp, Mrs Chapone! away, Watts' improvement of the mind, and off! off! off! with a hop, skip, and a jump, ye

Ramblers, Spectators, and Adventurers! (*throwing about the Books, and dancing round them*)

So hoity, toity, whiskey, friskey,
These are the joys of our dancing days –

(2.4.28–39; *Plays* 1:214–15)

Joyce shows us, as Crisp said of Burney's Nancy Dawson dance, 'there is certainly a nameless Grace and Charm in giving a loose to that Wildness and friskiness sometimes'.[12] Joyce asks her nurse to alle-mande, so she has a statelier dance in mind than the hornpipe, but it is also a more social dance, involving a partner. Joyce's unbuttoned nature is generally sociable as well as uninhibited. She has been forced to read Hester Chapone's *Letters on the Improvement of the Mind*, and she has taken to heart Chapone's suggestion that she make her 'body strong and active by exercise', but she does not wish to keep her 'mind rational by reading'.[13] She also refuses to keep quiet in company, a stricture which Chapone emphasizes (p. 115). When Joyce meets Lady Smatter, instead of keeping quiet, she tries (unavailingly) to involve her in her enthusiasms: dancing, singing, swinging, walking, running, jumping – and eating. All of these are centered on the body. Lady Smatter lives in the mind, though vaguely so, punctuating nearly every remark with one of her mis-attributed quotations, smatterings she never gets quite right. The earthy Joyce is simply not a part of her way of life.

Besides basing Joyce on her frisky younger self dancing Nancy Dawson, Burney ascribed to her the attributes of Dorothy Jordan, the actress she had chosen for the part. Jordan was especially good at hoydenish parts. Joyce is a hoyden. 'Hoyden' was applied before the Restoration only to men, and then in Restoration comedy was trans-ferred to women, the name of a character in Wycherley and in Vanbrugh. It means primarily someone who is rude, ignorant, and boisterous. Although Jordan was over 40 she still played successfully her Hoyden parts, her coarsening voice suiting those roles even better than when she had been younger.[14] Jordan was Viola, Ophelia, Rosalind, Lady Teazle, Miss Hardcastle, and many others, but the ones most relevant here are the part of Miss Hoyden in Sheridan's remake of Vanbrugh's *The Relapse*, which he called *A Trip to Scarborough*, and an afterpiece T.A. Lloyd carved out of Isaac Bickerstaff's *Love in the City* called *The Romp*. A 'romp' was synonymous with a 'hoyden', and the romp–hoyden in *The Romp* is aptly named Priscilla Tomboy. What Burney borrows, or at any rate does not jettison, from Sheridan's Miss

Hoyden is Joyce's desire for freedom, and her attraction to men. In addition, she borrows from Priscilla Tomboy frankness and generosity and – though with changes – her addiction to song and to bodily freedom. Burney omits the Hoyden's materialism, the Tomboy's tendency to knock people down, and both women's desire to raise their rank and join the genteel classes. One of the most important new elements in Burney's Joyce is the fact that when she discovers that she is working class she is glad. She is also playful and affectionate. In addition – and this is something not often noted in Burney – she also possesses a frank sensuality which harks back to Vanbrugh's Hoyden, but is more ebullient and less jaded. She also hates to lie, which is surprising, given the fact that she has been brought up on conduct-books. Conduct-books almost universally endorse hypocrisy. Since Joyce has rejected conduct-books, she has not learned to lie.

Presenting these qualities largely through gesture, Burney is applying in Joyce's case some of the current theories of acting, using in a fresh setting one of the most standard tensions employed by the eighteenth-century actor. In Aaron Hill's popular mid-century guide, the emphasis in many of the passions listed is on the kind of suspension someone experiences when pulled by opposite emotions. Grief, for instance, requires a 'struggle between caution and despair',[15] and in joy all parts of the body are 'firmly connected, and boldly braced' (p. 5). Hence, when Burney's Joyce sees that her father has left the room, when she slowly lifts her eyes from her books, looks around the room, and over her mother's shoulder, and then turns into the kind of person the famous actress Mrs Jordan would have made of her, she embodies the tension between caution and joy.

Aaron Hill's tensions had to some degree been modified by Garrick's more naturalistic practice and John Hill's theories as outlined in *The Actor* in 1750. Hill argued that natural acting was important, that gestures should not be 'study'd, elaborate, and practis'd'.[16] Through Huncamunca, Fielding was satirizing the practice John Hill is trying to change. Besides discussing natural acting, John Hill also focused on Garrick's transitions from one mood to another, and the scene where Joyce unfolds her true nature is a splendid opportunity not only for a tension, but also for a transition through gesture. John Hill tells us that educated persons have more restrained gestures. Joyce is educated, but she has always resented the process, at least as it is imposed on women. Because she longs for freedom, she retains her unrestrained gestures. She is happy to act like the daughter of a nurse and a journeyman shoemaker.

Freedom is an important theme for the Sheridan Hoyden, who has been shut up for fear she will elope. Joyce says to the innkeeper's son, Bob Sapling, that she has been 'in such subjection' that 'I don't chuse to put up with it any longer, Bob. I'm all for Liberty! – Liberty, Liberty, Bob!' (4.7.29; *Plays* 1:248). The difference between Joyce and the Hoyden is that Joyce's liberty is not tied to a desire for a coach and six. She longs for the freedom to choose her profession (she thinks she would be a good ballad-singer) and to select her mate (she thinks Bob would be just right for her). She wants to indulge her five senses: smell (when she finds herself in Lady Smatter's dressing-room she disdains her books, and instead smells her Jessamine, rose, and lavender), taste (and eats her bonbons); hearing (whenever possible she sings), touch (she grabs people to dance with her), and sight (she notices in a second when her nurse puts on a crabbed face, and mentions that she used to cry at that sort of face when she was a baby). Is Burney satirizing Joyce? If a comedy must include a standard against which we can judge our laughter, where is that standard in *The Woman-Hater*? Joyce's nurse tries to quell her masquerading daughter, knowing that her behavior will shock her genteel 'father's' friends. But are they right to be shocked?

Joyce helps to unite her false father with his lost wife and his missing child. She is the Burney version of Lear's fool, a character always cut out of Shakespeare's play as produced in the eighteenth century, but in this instance inserted and made fully comic: 'Why, Nurse, you scold if I speak' she says, adding 'and you scold if I hold my tongue'.[17] In spite of this kind of fettering, Joyce, like the fool, hates a lie. In fact, bringing her rebellion against conduct-books to its logical completion, she will not tell a lie, will not hold her tongue, which is why she jeopardizes her own fortunes by insisting on withdrawing her claim to be Mr Wilmot's real child. As Fool, one of Joyce's main messages is that she has words of her own, without books, and that the body is important, the hoity toity whiskey friskey dancing body that shocks everyone and yet also represents freedom, the kind of freedom Burney felt when she was, as she put it, 'so much celebrated for *Dancing Nancy Dawson*' (*EJL* 3:34). When Sir Roderick the woman-hater decides he would like to marry the now-widowed Lady Smatter, even though she jilted him long ago, Burney lets Joyce have the important summary speech, a kind of embedded epilogue:

Well! I have lost two Papas; but I have learned one thing as perfect as if I had read all the Books and authors in the Universe! – and that is – what is meant by a Woman-Hater! It is, – to hate a woman – if she won't let you love her: to run away from her – if you can't run to her: to swear she is made up of faults – unless she allows you to be made up of perfections: and to vow she shall never cross your Threshold, – unless she'll come to be mistress of your whole house!

(5.23.103–9, *Plays* 1:284–5)

Dorothy Jordan as Joyce in this speech would with her frisky body have possessed the stage, acting out the four transitions she mentions, nominating the degrees of foolishness and wilful misunderstanding that gave rise to all these years of suffering.

Joyce is an independent woman who makes her own choices. She plans to have Bob Sapling. She is pleased with him because he uses his body: he can skate, swim, cudgel, and box (2.4.77–8; *Plays* 1:216). She has already – almost the moment she met him – taught him to play questions and commands. 'If you were placed at the tip top of a high precipice, with me, and Miss Henny [his sister], and Nurse – which would you throw down into the Sea? And which would you leave to have her Eyes pecked out by the crows? And which would you carry down in your arms?' He answered just as she wished, 'I know which I'd carry down in my arms!' (2.4.105–9; *Plays* 1:216). She is knowledgeable and, manlike, proud of her knowledge. Whenever someone does not know something she knows, she offers to teach them. She is optimistic, quite powerfully so. She will insist that Bob will carry her over a threshold, and soon. And since this is a comedy, Burney has seen to it that they will have a comfortable little income, not because they groveled for it, but because they deserve it.

Joyce chooses to be ignorant, and Burney would not of course in life support her there, but Joyce is in many ways the most intelligent person in the play, just as the fool is in Shakespeare. She has the wisdom of the body. A sudden focusing on the body occurs in many eighteenth-century novels. The body is as important in Burney as it is in Richardson (we think of Mrs Sinclair's huge frame disintegrating into her painful death); or Smollett (where Matthew Bramble describes bits of skin and other detritus floating on the surface of the waters at Bath); or Sterne (where the lubricious body always glides just beneath the surface of the prose, and noses are worth an essay). Similarly in Burney's novels and diaries there are many set pieces that focus on the body. But these are always of the suffering body: Madame Duval clutching her clothes in the mud, the tottering 80-year-old ladies forced to race, the monkey tearing Mr Lovel's ear, Mrs Delvile lying on the floor with blood lacing her neck, Cecilia in her madness snapping her head back and forth, the oppressed courtiers who must not cough. All of these bodies, written about before *The Woman-Hater*, are under stress. Even amorousness is depicted as stress. None of these characters frankly enjoy their bodies as much as Nancy Dawson did, as much as Frances Burney dancing Nancy Dawson did, as does the character Joyce Wilmot in the *The Woman-Hater*. It is a celebration of the body. In 1802, Burney creates a character who dances with no fetters on, who in gesture and words speaks truth and joy. In joy, in Joyce, the married, free, bereaved Burney dances.

8

The Wanderer: Financial Success, Commercial Failure, and the Untamed Spirit (1802–28)

> 'What a rare hand you are, Demoiselle', cried Riley, 'at hocus pocus work! ... you metamorphose yourself about so, one does not know which way to look for you. Ovid was a mere fool to you.' – Mr Riley , describing Juliet to her face, in *The Wanderer* (p. 771)

The adventure of negotiating a contract for a novel always poised Burney on the border between exhilaration and insecurity. Although with *Camilla* she had found a formula for publication that had worked brilliantly, she could not use that formula again. In 1813, 17 years later, she was now once more setting out for uncharted territory.[1] Her husband was still in France, and her father was slowly dying. The one steady and forceful adviser she could depend on was her brother Charles. In addition, not to neglect her volatile brother James, she annexed his more level-headed son Martin Charles Burney. These two aides guarded her from sharp practices as she developed her plans for negotiation. Because she soon intended to join d'Arblay in France, she could not publish by subscription. Besides, she would soon reach the age of 63, her grand climacteric, the year in which she would by tradition either change greatly or die. What would happen to a subscription list, she argued, if there was a 'death on their side or ours?' (*JL*7:152). She had recently had a brush with death, and she knew intimately that she could die at any time.

While in France, Burney had written one of her best-known works, the harrowing letter to her sister Esther about her mastectomy.[2] Burney herself valued this letter especially, annotating it: 'Respect this & beware not to injure it!!!'[3] Her metaphor makes the letter an analogue for her body, somehow become whole because she has written so completely about it. The letter is not to be injured, as the original body was. She started her letter about six months after the operation, and wrote these 12 pages of narrative over a period of four months. In Paris, on 30 September 1811, '7 men in black' gathered around a makeshift operating table in the d'Arblay's Paris apartments and removed Frances Burney's right breast (*JL* 6:610). The breast was hard and painful, and the diagnosis was cancer. Modern medical opinion disagrees with this analysis, since we do not associate pain with cancer of the breast that can be cured, but it is possible that the operation was nonetheless necessary. Burney clearly suffered from a persistent infection. With only a 'wine cordial' as anesthetic, the 20-minute operation was pure agony (*JL* 6:610). Her surgeon, Baron Dominique-Jean Larrey (1766-1842), was extremely skilful, an army doctor who had served on nearly 60 battlefields, once doing 200 amputations in an hour. He warned her that she must scream, to diminish the shock of the operation. 'When the dreadful steel was plunged into the breast – cutting through veins – arteries – flesh – nerves – I needed no injunctions not to restrain my cries. I began a scream that lasted unintermittingly during the whole time of the incision' (*JL* 6:612). Burney had never feared writing about the intolerable. She describes the operation in unnerving detail:

> When the wound was made, & the instrument was withdrawn, the pain seemed undiminished, for the air that suddenly rushed into those delicate parts felt like a mass of minute but sharp & forked poniards, that were tearing the edges of the wound – but when again I felt the instrument – describing a curve – cutting against the grain, if I may so say, while the flesh resisted in a manner so forcible as to oppose & tire the hand of the operator, who was forced to change from the right to the left – then, indeed, I thought I must have expired. I attempted no more to open my eyes, – they felt as if hermettically shut, & so firmly closed, that the Eyelids seemed indented into the Cheeks. The instrument this second time withdrawn, I concluded the operation over – Oh no! presently the terrible cutting was renewed – & worse than ever, to separate the bottom, the foundation of this dreadful gland from the parts to which it adhered – Again all description would be baffled – yet again all was not over, Dr Larry rested but his own hand, & – Oh Heaven! – I then felt the Knife <rack>ling against the breast bone – scraping it! – This performed, while I yet remained in utter speechless torture, I heard the Voice of Mr. Larry, – (all others guarded a

dead silence) in a tone nearly tragic, desire every one present to pronounce if any thing more remained to be done; The general voice was Yes, – but the finger of Mr. Dubois – which I literally *felt* elevated over the wound, though I saw nothing, & though he touched nothing, so indescribably sensitive was the spot – pointed to some further requisition – & again began the scraping! – and, after this, Dr. Moreau thought he discerned a peccant attom – and still, & still, M. Dubois demanded attom after attom – My dearest Esther, not for days, not for Weeks, but for Months I could not speak of this terrible business without nearly again going through it! I could not *think* of it with impunity! I was sick, I was disordered by a single question – even now, 9 months after it is over, I have a head ache from going on with the account! & this miserable account, which I began 3 Months ago, at least, I dare not revise, nor read, the recollection is still so painful.   (*JL* 6:612–13)

Unable actually to speak about her experience, Burney has written it out. As Julia Epstein has emphasized, this writing of the unspeakable is characteristic of Burney, and so is her thorough professionalism. 'The combination of surgical particularity and personal trauma', Epstein writes, 'gives this letter its energetic ambivalence' (p. 70). Just before the operation, Burney wrote notes to her husband and son in case she should die. If not for the pain in her arm, she would have written to her family and friends. Her instinct was always to write.

Burney's doctors treated her as eighteenth-century women were habitually treated, somewhat condescendingly and fearfully, not telling her the chosen time for the operation until a few hours before. Yet Burney as she depicted herself was the strongest person in the drama. She protected d'Arblay, sending him off on an errand so that he would not even know exactly when the operation was to take place. Larrey, she mentions, at the moment when the doctors were about to tell her the fearful news that an operation was necessary, 'hid himself nearly behind my Sofa', and wept when she accepted their verdict (*JL* 6:604). The operation was halted for three weeks because he had not told her that she needed to write him the eighteenth-century equivalent of a consent form. As the actual procedure begins, she is the calm one, the one who climbs 'unbidden' on the two mattresses that served as operating table, the one who holds her breast so that it can be inspected, and explains her symptoms (*JL* 6:611). Her doctors' assumptions about women's weaknesses are so extreme that if it had not been for her protest they would have deprived her of her one remaining female attendant. She realizes that in her attempt to protect everyone from suffering she has denied herself the presence of a woman she could rely on. Although she writes about the operation in fuller detail than any woman had ever done,[4] sending the letter to Esther and asking her to share it with the immediate family, she plans never to tell her father or Frederica Locke about her ordeal. The woman who writes this letter keeps negotiating throughout among diverse considerations: modesty, pride, courage, fear, pain, mutilation,[5] altruism, professional acumen, stylistic sensitivity, audience awareness, and probably many others. Victim, she was also witness. At the end of the operation, 'my strength was so totally annihilated, that I was obliged to be carried, & could not even sustain my hands & arms, which hung as if I had been lifeless' (*JL* 6:614). But she was strong enough to note that Larrey's face expressed 'grief, apprehension, & almost horrour' (*JL* 6:614). After such an operation, in an age without antiseptics, many women died of septicemia. This was one of the sources of Dr Larrey's apprehension. Toward the end of the letter, Burney said that d'Arblay should add his own account of how he felt, and d'Arblay added a paragraph, saying mainly that he could not write the unspeakable, as his wife had done: 'No language could convey what I felt in the deadly course of these seven hours.' (*JL* 6:614)

Now, in England, nearly a year after the operation, she was ill, not only because of what she called 'the oppression upon my breast'(*JL* 7:102), the stretched skin and damaged muscles remaining from the mastectomy, but also because she could not shake a persistent low-grade fever remaining from a bout of influenza caught from Alex. Writing was painful. Even talking was difficult. The manuscript she had barely saved from confiscation by the ranting officer at Dunkirk was three-fifths of the whole and it had crossed the ocean twice. Because of d'Arblay's absence, she missed not only her dearest adviser and most loyal supporter, but also her amanuensis. Almost without comment in her correspondence, she wrote the remaining two-fifths by working mornings between her arrival in England in August 1812 and a sudden chilling moment a year later, when she feared that the book might not succeed: 'tired I am of my Pen! Oh tired! tired! oh! should it tire others in the same proportion – alas for poor Messrs. Longman & Rees! – & alas for poorer ME! –' (*JL* 7:163). She had promised her brother to curb her prolixity, the tendency toward repetition she knew was her greatest fault, 'to cut & slash unmercifully' (*JL* 7:496). Soon, Charles had read enough of *The Wanderer* to write, 'your

WORK will do! No lack of incident.' (*JL* 7:237, n. 2) Now the slashed book was essentially finished, and except for occasional weak moments, Burney thought it her best. The jitters she always felt during the final re-copying when publication approached were exacerbated this time by the fact that she could not read the scrawls written in pain by a one-breasted woman.

The work relentlessly separated her from the company of her son and her siblings. How much time did she have left with her sick and depressed father? When not amused and aroused he simply stared apathetically out of the window. Depression and apathy, always a problem, were now intensified by age and illness. Her letters to him took on the (for us unnerving) simplicity of a child turned caretaker. The work on *The Wanderer* seemed endless. In October 1813 she was anxiously adding 'MORE & MORE last touches' (*JL* 7:195). At last she delivered the manuscript to Longman on 4 November – the opening day of Parliament, 'can anything be grander!' (*JL* 7:196). She collected her first £500.

Somewhere along the line, d'Arblay had made the interesting suggestion that they should publish the book first in French, translating it themselves (*JL* 7:556). No one, he argued seductively, could pirate a French edition. No one could presume to translate the book *back* into English when Burney's original lay ready for the press. It is not clear how she turned down this idea, but she decided on the more usual route. She worked eagerly with her agents in England, suggesting variously: an auction (a letter to two booksellers per day, gradually gathering bids from every reputable house in London), a series of payments *not* connected to editions, and a subsequent negotiation for the American copyright. She met with the Edgeworths and discussed the virtues and drawbacks of Maria's publisher Joseph Johnson. But she seems never to have seriously considered him, possibly because his list was too radical for someone who depended on the Queen's pleasure. Meanwhile, Byron's publisher James Cawthorn joined the crowd, but was outbid by Henry Colborn and the House of Longman. Charles decided that he did not want to choose Mr Colborn, and Burney insisted, in a burst of characteristic unbusinesslike altruism, that they not string him along. She drafted a letter for Charles to send to Colborn gracefully apologizing for his 'useless trouble' (*JL* 7:155). Perhaps it was partly in memory of this graciousness that Colborn in the 1840s became the publisher of Charlotte Barrett's seven-volume selection from her aunt's letters and journals.

Burney's chief altruistic enterprise, however, was her family, her husband and her son. She wanted to gain for them as much money as she could. Baby Alex had been the excuse in 1796 when she negotiated over *Camilla*. Now, in a more elegiac mood, she wanted to leave a legacy. The earliest draft of the contract included both Burney and d'Arblay, to cover the fact that legally d'Arblay owned Burney's assets, and set up a complicated network of trustees and heirs. These specific references vanish in a later draft. The fact that both d'Arblays own the copyright is now assumed, but mention is made of the fact that one of the parties might die, and the idea of heirs is not forgotten. Burney was looking far into the future.

Longman's representative Owen Rees was worried over some of the stipulations. Hesitations are penciled in the margin, together with a brief dialogue about whether or not Longman is sufficiently covered 'shd the work fail'.[6] To protect the copyright, Burney had secured the advice of Sharon Turner, an expert who insisted on including extra protection. If Longman dallied over reprinting the book, the copyright would revert to Burney. In addition, her brother Charles or another representative would be allowed to inspect the number of copies left, and when there were only fifty to demand a new edition. Part of the penciled Longman note is worth quoting to show what a hard bargain Burney and her supporters insisted on driving:

> This is very unusual – the objection to it is that it compels L&Co to ask an obligation which they will have to return – and cannot refuse – independy of it lowering the name of their House to have to ask such a thing at all Events there ought not to be both Security given – & also the forfeiture of the Copyright required – I offered the forfeiture as a substitute for the Security – not as an addition. One of these must be relinquished.

The writer is clearly feeling manipulated and wants to resist. But the manipulation was successful. When the agreement was signed three days later, both stipulations remained.

Between the inevitable last-minute apprehensions, Burney was quite confident that her book would sell. It would become a classic. Longman, too, in this eighteenth-century version of a bidding war, was confident that it would sell, though they were less secure in their belief that the book would go through many editions. Initially, they had offered a copyright fee of £2000. At that moment, uncharacteristically, Burney gambled. She revised this initial offer into a promise of £3000, with

£1500 as the initial copyright fee, and the remainder spread over the next five editions.[7] Longman acceded to this suggestion, and on 4 November 1813 when Parliament opened and the agreement was signed these were the terms. To gather early opinions, Longman distributed copies of the first volume without the preface, a practice that annoyed the author, who thought that this truncated version would actually diminish the book's chance of gaining the approbation of its most important readers: 'if this premature communication be not checked, all the interest of the narration will be broken; all illusion will be abolished; & the Work will be born old' (*JL* 7:238). Some of the early responses were extremely positive. L. Baugh Allen wrote to Mrs Waddington that 'the better Part of the Vol. is exquisite, & interesting to a degree, if the Heroine gets thro, as well as she promises, she will eclipse all others hollow'.[8] Sir James Mackintosh, a lawyer and philosopher who frequently published reviews in the *Monthly Review* and *The Edinburgh Review*, wrote a letter to Longman so admiring that Burney asked to keep it so that she could place it among her papers for her son Alex to find after her death.[9] Byron, attempting to snag a copy for a sick friend, declared, 'I would almost fall sick myself to get at Madame d'Arblay's writings.' According to Burney's later comment, Byron, Godwin, Mme de Staël and many others greeted the first volume 'with almost unbounded applause'.[10]

Meanwhile, the rest of life went on, interfering as it always does with a writer's professional commitments, but at this particular moment in Burney's life, interfering even more than ordinary. Separated from her husband, Burney worried constantly about his health and his fate. Of course, she and d'Arblay wrote faithfully to one another, but many of their letters miscarried. They feared that they might never meet again, and as a hedge against fate tried doggedly to keep track of the undelivered letters. There was good news among the bad. Burney marshalled all her forces – including Lord Keith, the son-in-law of her lost friend Mrs Piozzi – to secure a Tancred scholarship at Cambridge for Alex. But bad news predominated. One particularly nasty blow was that just before the publication of *The Wanderer*, d'Arblay's dear friend the Comte de Narbonne died on the field of battle. Both d'Arblays had been fond of the charming erstwhile lover of Mme de Staël. He was hard on women, but he was an excellent friend, and he had died helping the wounded. His death was a reminder of how precarious life was for military men – and especially middle-aged military men. As publication day approached, William Lowndes, a man like his father with an eye always on the main chance, published a new edition of *Evelina* with a biographical preface, to which news the author replied dryly in the third person, 'she must entirely decline correcting any mistakes in Memoirs which she so little wishes authenticated, or printed, as those which would bring her very obscure life before the public' (*JL* 7:239).

In the midst of the excitement over Burney's book, in spite of all her cheery efforts, her father increasingly wanted simply to be alone. While the family denied to itself that their patriarch was failing, sorrow erupted in unexpected quarters. In February 1814, Burney's favorite sister Susanna's brilliant son Norbury suddenly died at the age of 29, reinforcing all her undiminished pain over her sister's death. Her letter about Norbury to her 'dearest Charlottes' (her sister Charlotte and her niece Charlotte Barrett) is full of woe and worry, financial as well as otherwise (*JL* 7:247-50). She felt guilty that she had not sent Norbury any money, '*alone* in Ireland' as he had been.

Her own financial anxieties were real. D'Arblay found it difficult to live on an income as restricted as theirs. For her part, having been brought up in the always financially strapped Burney household she had habitually experienced scarcity, and knew the myriad ways of making do. Alex's education was very dear, and their financial resources were depleted – 'our running small revenue is utterly insufficient for Alexander & me!' (*JL* 7:328). In the early 1800s they had lost more than £400 by venturing in an omnium stock speculation with their friends the Lockes. Now, to top off their monetary woes, they were likely to lose Camilla Cottage, which they had built on William Locke's land at Norbury Park. When his heir decided to sell, it was discovered that the d'Arblays had not secured a legal right to the land. And young William Locke was not generous to his father's friends. Aside from the financial loss, the d'Arblays anguished over the thought of losing the home that they had so carefully planned, with its intricate closets and diverse views. It was in perfect condition. All their books and clothes were in place, just as they had left them, in a secret closet they had filled and papered over. Now they were likely to lose the haven where they had hoped to retire, the home they had planned to bequeath to their son. The final negotiations on Camilla Cottage took place after the publication of *The Wanderer*. On 26 October 1815, the son of their friend deposited the sale price of £700 in their account at Hoare's, £600 less than Camilla Cottage had cost to build.

In the midst of all this personal and financial upheaval, *The Wanderer* was published on 28 March 1814. The first edition had sold out so quickly that it was completely gone before publication. Longman immediately pressed Burney to make corrections for the second edition and began advertising it. They did not even allow her to read proof. Ironically, this meant that her fancy negotiations worked against her. She would not receive all of her initial fee until the end of the first year. If she had pegged the payments to sales, she would have received her next £1000 on the spot. Instead of noticing this miscalculation, she responded ecstatically to the success of the work: 'Astonishing! incredible! impossible!' Her co-negotiating nephew Martin was inconsolable. Why had they not held out for £4000? Burney did not indulge in regrets. She found in the gigantic sales reassurance that the book would support the six editions contracted for: 'I think it *secure*', she wrote to her brother Charles (*JL* 7:269, 271).

Burney had been particularly clear about what she wanted to do in *The Wanderer*. She had shown it to no one, and this secrecy whetted the fury she felt when she learned that Longman had been sending around the first volume for reactions – especially that they had sent it around without the preface. She had kept *Evelina* secret from everyone. With *Cecilia* and *Camilla*, although she did not ask for advice, she did ask for support. Though she and d'Arblay habitually sat scribbling at the same table, she had not shown him *The Wanderer*. She wanted to spring it on her relatives as well as on the public. She did not want it to be 'born old' (*JL* 7:238). And as with the secretively written *Evelina*, she wanted to introduce it in her own terms. The last piece she wrote was the preface. *Evelina* had briefly but triply introduced itself to the public with the teasing poem to the 'author of my being', the arch letter to the editors of the *Monthly* and the *Critical*, and the claim for originality. Burney had let *Cecilia* go before the public with only a short 'Advertisement' indicating the 'precariousness of any power to give pleasure', but emphasizing that *Evelina* had gone through four editions in one year. She had written a much longer and complicated preface, but her better judgment (or someone's) had quashed it at the last minute. *Camilla* carried only the dedication to the Queen and a brief 'Advertisement' thanking the keepers of the subscription books. But in *The Wanderer* Burney included a full-blown preface dedicating the book to her octogenarian father whose imminent death she was not acknowledging to herself. She explained why the book did not take place in France, and defined the genre of the novel as she practiced it. In this introduction the style is her most heightened, formal mode, with passive constructions flowing extensively in extended sentences. She abases herself before her father, defines the novel in terms that would please him as well as herself, argues that *The Wanderer* is a historical rather than a political novel, and emphasizes that Britain and France are friends as well as enemies. The last two points indicate Burney's recognition that her novel might offend some patriotic Englishmen and that misplaced expectations might affect the way her public read her book.

Burney knew that *The Wanderer* had to hit the public just right, because the book makes severe demands on its audience, an aesthetic choice she had already successfully hazarded in *Cecilia* and *Camilla*. Though some critics had complained, other readers had accepted this practice. In talking about the usefulness of *Cecilia* Burney's friend the conduct-book writer Hester Chapone said, 'Let us complain how we will of the torture she has given our nerves, we must all join in saying she has bettered us by every line.' (*DL* 2:201) Once again, in *The Wanderer* Burney chose to torture her readers. They needed always to remember that the torture was for their own betterment. Perhaps for male readers the torture in *The Wanderer* was less obvious than in the early books. William Taylor, who reviewed *The Wanderer* in 1815, did not complain that there were any 'intolerable' scenes, as had one of the chief objectors to *Cecilia*. Taylor applied to the book five adjectives that usefully describe it: 'interesting', 'intricate', 'varied', 'busy', and 'original'.[11] Perhaps Taylor's word 'original' includes the 'intolerable', which sometimes in its very intensity may feel original.

Written mainly when Burney herself was poised on the border between exile and belonging, *The Wanderer* is such a varied, intricate, and original book that it puzzled and still puzzles its readers. Not the least of those puzzles is how to begin to unpack a book that is so complicated and so long. Burney insisted on a book this size, even though she well knew that the reviewers had complained over the length of *Cecilia*, and she promised her brother Charles as she was finishing *The Wanderer* that she would 'cut & slash unmercifully' (*JL* 7:103, n. 1; 7:496). Why did Burney need so many pages? Although the heroine, the wanderer of the title, is certainly at the center, as were her predecessors Evelina, Cecilia, and Camilla, this heroine too is accompanied by a host of other characters. All these are part of the central plan, and if we want to understand that central plan and retain the comic elements in this many-sided novel, we cannot ignore these other characters. *The Wanderer* is more seamless than Burney's other novels, harder to analyze through chosen scenes. She heightened this effect by numbering her chapters consecutively and failing to include the kinds of chapter headings she had used in *Cecilia* and *Camilla*, a decision in which many of her women contemporaries joined her. Burney stated her chief organizing idea in her subtitle. *The Wanderer* is about 'female difficulties', including the balance of power between men and women, the invisible rules governing female delicacy, the ever-present danger of rape, the lack of opportunity for honest work, the weird intersections of sex and class, and the padlocks on open communication and frank speech.

Here, it is necessary to begin with the wanderer herself, and to tell her story, something Burney herself does not do until the last third of the novel. In this rich and strange book, this historical novel set in the years of Robespierre and the guillotine, the plot is a familiar one for Burney, though in this case, to use Taylor's word, especially intricate. Like Evelina, the heroine Juliet Granville is the daughter of a secret marriage between a lord and a poverty-stricken commoner. Eventually, we learn the history of this union. Unlike Evelina's father, Lord Granville remained loyal to his lower-class spouse. Unfortunately, she died soon after the marriage and her 'irresolute' husband did not publically admit his action (p. 869). When he was about to remarry, instead of telling his new wife about his earlier connection, he sent Juliet and her grand-mother Mrs Powel to France, to live under the care of his close friend, a kindly Bishop. Lord Granville gave Mrs Powel the certificate of his marriage to her daughter. He also included a 'codicil' (p. 643) to what-ever future will he might write explaining that his estate would be divided between Juliet and any subsequent half-siblings. When Lord Granville died in a riding accident, his new brother-in-law Lord Denmeath sought to ignore Juliet's claims, promoting instead her 16-year-old half-sister Lady Aurora and her 18-year-old half-brother, Lord Melbury. In addition, Juliet's father's father, 'sickly, but imperious', refused to acknowledge the 'unsuitable' connection (p. 645). Even when the Bishop threatened to sue, these unpleasant relatives responded with a counter-offer, sending a promissory note for £6000, payable if Juliet were to marry a French citizen. Unfortunately, during the Revolutionary upheavals, all the documents proving Juliet's claim were burned, except for the promissory note. An officious commissioner of the French Republic, rifling through Juliet's guardian's papers, found the promis-sory note and conceived a hideous plan. The Commissary threatened to send the Bishop to the Guillotine if Juliet would not marry him and sign over the promissory note. To save her beloved mentor, Juliet allowed the ceremony to be performed, though she never actually spoke her accep-tance, and cannot quite fully believe that the marriage was legal. Before the Commissary (whose name is never provided) could consummate the marriage or even collect Juliet's signature, he was called away to deal with an insurrection.

The novel begins when Juliet flees to England in the hope that she can escape her husband and find sympathetic relatives, a quest that will be frustrated by her half-siblings' greedy uncle. Because she believes that her husband will follow her, she remains incognito, afraid to tell her name, a condition in which she has no social character. A woman without a social character is terrifyingly defenseless. The situation is exacerbated by the fact that Juliet loses (or is relieved of) her purse. Although Juliet's chief desire is to support herself through honest labor, in her exposed position she is frequently mistaken for a slut or a thief, in spite of the fact that she is an extremely strong person – candid, level-headed, self-sufficient, passionate and courageous – whom 'neither order nor menace' can force to an action she considers unwise (p. 746).

Burney shows us that this forceful, beautiful wanderer is everyone's victim, disdained by rich and poor alike. The landscape an unprotected woman inhabits in England is as fearful as the Italian castles in Ann Radcliffe, the cruel Spanish nunneries in Matthew Gregory Lewis, and the dark English world of predator and prey in William Godwin's *Caleb Williams, or Things as They Are*. In three scenes of sexual aggressiveness particularly striking to a modern reader, Juliet fends off her brother Lord Melbury (she knows he is her brother; he does not), escapes from a rich roué who has abducted her, and saves herself from being raped by two farmer's sons. Though fearful, Juliet is always strong. She convinces Lord Melbury that she is too dignified to be dragged off to bed. She leaps out of Sir Lyell Sycamore's carriage. And she faces down the two young men, who are somewhat distracted by their contest over who will have her first. By making friends with their dog Dash, and asking them to show off his 'various accomplishments', she becomes their companion rather than their victim (p. 690). This strategy occurs rarely in fiction and often in women's real lives.

Eventually, Burney allows her wanderer a happy ending. She is married to Albert Harleigh, who has always responded to her as a person rather than as a mystery.[12] Like all Burney's heroes he is somewhat feminized. He is notably sensitive to her feelings and his own. He is inconsolable, for instance, when he realizes that she has burned a letter he sent her. Always alive to every nuance of her body and voice, ready to protect her from any danger and even from any embarrassment, he is much more understanding than Delvile or Mandelbert, as gentle as Lord Orville and less idealized. Since Burney was so alive to words, their sounds, their overtones, their interactions, she may have heard in Albert Harleigh's name an echo of her 'dearest At', Alexandre d'Arblay. Baby Alex, trying to say 'Alexandre', called his father 'At'. The name Albert would be reduced in the same way. In addition, any French person pronouncing 'd'Arblay' would produce a word that sounds like 'Harleigh'. Burney's fictional men's names tended to have 'ville' or villages in them, or simply 'man', as in Mandlebert or Herrington (with the 'ton' perhaps standing in for 'ville'). Perhaps in 'Harleigh' the 'har' represents the 'herr', but more importantly the name Harleigh besides rhyming with d'Arblay also has fictional sources. It must have been connected in Burney's mind with the two famous literary Harleys, Henry Mackenzie's excessively tender *Man of Feeling* (1771) and Mary Hays' desired hero in the *Memoirs of Emma Courtney* (1796). The first represents Harleigh's refined sensibilities, and the second reflects the fact that Juliet's rival Elinor declares openly to Harleigh that she loves him. As if to join the Mackenzie source to a more practical world, the married Harleigh and Juliet buy the dog Dash, so that he can 'fetch, carry, stand on his hinder legs, leap over their hats, caper, bark, point', and carry on for their mutual enjoyment his many other accomplishments (p. 690). The man of feeling loved his dogs in a more sickly way. But Harleigh's care, for instance, to show himself publicly so that people will not surmise that he has run off with Juliet, reminds us of no one so much as the passionate emigré who leapt quickly into Burney's coach so that nobody would notice.

Juliet is not the only one who must endure the strictures hampering women. Women of every class and character suffer from and are malformed by the female difficulties society constructs to impede them. The chief of these difficulties is that people judge by appearances, that we all live in a constructed world, where people play many parts, taking their cues from others, acting and reacting in a wilderness of veils and unsupported assumptions. A woman without a name will be aided or rejected simply on the basis of a few superficial assumptions over which she has no control. Thus the jealous Elinor says to the man who has noticed that behind all the mystery and disguise the wanderer is a paragon, 'Oh, Harleigh! how is it you thus can love all you were wont to scorn? double dealing, false appearances, and lurking disguise! without a family she dare claim, without a story she dare tell, without a name she dare avow!' (p. 181) The

fiercely conformist Mrs Howel, herself misshapen because of the strictures circumscribing women, tries to read the proper cues as to how
she must act toward the wanderer: 'With all her accomplishments, all
her elegance, was she, at last, but a dependant? [sic] Might she be
smiled or frowned upon at will?' (p. 121)

Since Juliet's father's name is Granville, his daughter is certainly a
descendant of Evelina Anville. The extra 'Gr' at the beginning of her
name indicates that she is 'grand' – larger in every sense than her
predecessor – older, more sophisticated, more fraught. Both are
outsiders, and both are maltreated. Evelina complained to Orville that
besides himself, 'all others treat me with impertinence or contempt!'
(p. 314). Similarly, Juliet says about Harleigh, 'He knows me to be indi-
gent ... yet does not conclude me open to corruption! He sees me
friendless and unprotected, – yet offers me no indignity.' (p. 140) But
The Wanderer is also a totally new departure for Burney. Here she
embraces the Gothic sensibilities she had herself helped to initiate
with Camilla's dream of the iron pen, and had lived in her four
tragedies. Now she openly depicts the ways women are severely
hampered in the world of the 1790s.

The book begins with a scene evoking the elements of the Burkean
sublime – silence, darkness, and vacuity. So eerie is the natural world
that Burney does not need the fourth element, death, though the
possibility of the Bishop's death by the guillotine lurks throughout
the novel, and death will be the means for erasing Juliet's husband,
the evil Commissary, and removing the poacher turned smuggler
whose frightened wife gave Juliet a haven in the New Forest when she
desperately needed one. The Wanderer begins in darkness, with the
sentence that the gendarme at Dunkirk luckily did not attempt to
read. Burney claimed as she left France in wartime that the suspi-
cious-looking manuscript papers in her portmanteau had nothing to
do with politics, but Doody and Rogers clearly show detailed political
connections throughout the novel.[13] Burney throws us mercilessly in
the middle of things and leaves us there, in the midst of terror and
mystery, unenlightened:

> During the dire reign of the terrific Robespierre, and in the dead of
> night, braving the cold, the darkness and the damps of December,
> some English passengers, in a small vessel, were preparing to glide
> silently from the coast of France, when a voice of keen distress
> resounded from the shore, imploring, in the French language, pity
> and admission.   (p. 11)

This is riveting. And it raises expectations that Burney teases us with, and refuses to satisfy. She keeps her readers in a kind of suspense that no other writer had ever attempted. Fresh from struggling with her tragedies Burney allows her characters simply to speak for themselves as if this were the opening of a play, but she fails even to give us the capsule introductions a playwright would provide. In the dark a young man jumps up, an elderly man warns, an old sea-officer finally prevails, and the owner of the voice is ultimately allowed aboard. After the French Coast is out of hearing, the characters can begin to speak, and from the darkness their voices take on special attributes. Most of them receive names. But Burney tells the reader nothing extra, and the heroine, who for reasons she does not explain fears to divulge her name, remains the 'Incognita' even for the reader. What other writer would have dared to tell her audience so little about her heroine? Who else has ever left till the last act the essential facts of the heroine's life? Even her name remains a mystery for nearly half the book.

The heroines' names provided the titles for Burney's other novels. *The Wanderer*'s title is different in being generic, reflecting the quality of the central character, the sort of title Burney had used for her play, *The Woman-Hater*. Because the wanderer, the 'Incognita', is nameless, she becomes Everywoman, experiencing the 'female difficulties' announced in the subtitle. Other characters call her Dulcinea, Don Quixote's impossible dream; Ariel, powerful androgynous sprite; and at times simply 'the stranger'. Even a foolish old man notices how varied she is: '"What a rare hand you are, Demoiselle", cried Riley, "at hocus pocus work! ... you metamorphose yourself about so, one does not know which way to look for you. Ovid was a mere fool to you".' (p. 771) He thinks of the heroine as a witch, a paragon of metamorphosis.[14]

The wanderer's significance becomes even more extensive, because Burney provides three other women who are linked to her: Juliet's French emigrée friend Gabriella, her half-sister Lady Aurora Granville, and the rebellious Elinor Joddrel. By pairing the Incognita with Elinor Joddrel, a woman approximately the same age and in love with the same man, Burney replicates and revamps an important earlier technique. In each of the previous novels, Burney had included a particularly strong, free-spirited woman – Mrs Selwyn, Mrs Delvile, and Mrs Arlbery – but they were much older than the heroine, mentors rather than doppelgangers. Except for Mrs Arlbery, nearly an anagram for d'Arblay, these characters' names contain the French word, 'elle'; they are women and also woman. In fact, in *The Wanderer* many of the women, including the less pleasant characters, also contain 'elle': Mrs Howel, Miss Bydel, Mrs Maple. The idea of woman contains harridans as well as paragons, and all are rent by female difficulties.

Although the outspoken, strong woman in each novel needs occasionally to be put in her place, she always carries considerable power and gets some of the best lines. In *Evelina*, *Cecilia*, and *Camilla*, however, she is a separate character, totally distinct from the heroine. Elinor Joddrel is different. By chance, the wandering Juliet obtains a temporary name that reverberates with Elinor's. When the class-conscious name-dropping Miss Bydel insists that the stranger must have a name (how else to drop it?), others mention that she has received a letter addressed to the initials 'L.S'. This Miss Bydel misconstrues as 'Elless', and Elinor elevates into 'Miss Ellis', a name which also contains 'elle'. Elinor's 'nor' signifies her rebelliousness, and Ellis's 'is' indicates her courageous acceptance of things as they are.[15] Miss Ellis has another alter ego as well, her sweet, lovely friend Gabriella, whose 'elle' tags along after her angelic namesake. Burney describes Gabriella as an ideal woman, 'generous, noble and dignified: exalted in her opinions, and full of sensibility' (p. 622). But Gabriella was married in France right out of the convent, to a man with such a frigid nature that he is totally unable to appreciate her. She is the perfect woman, but she has been simply unlucky.

Elinor is at the other end of the spectrum, a mixed figure, a revolutionary and a romantic. Influenced by the French ideal of égalité, Elinor considers herself free to declare her love: it is not fair that men, who already possess all the military authority and honor, should also have the unique power to choose the women they wish to adore. Eleanor, who by choice and habit has listened only to herself, loves Albert Harleigh with thrilling self-absorption: 'if the whole world were annihilated, and he remained ... I should think my existence divine!' Emily Brontë's Cathy was to love Heathcliff with similar intensity, and to express it in similar terms, with the differences that her love is requited, that it is reflected in the landscape of her home, and that it is less sexual than Elinor's.[16] Ellis sees how much 'strong conflict' this belief creates in Elinor's mind (p. 154), and how much 'her intellects are under the controul of her feelings' (p. 203). Yet she is like her true namesakes 'Julie' and 'Juliet', heroines in Rousseau and Shakespeare, a woman with powerful feelings. Ellis-Juliet is a quite different heroine from Evelina, Cecilia, or Camilla – much more experienced, more able to bear the trials of solitude. Although she does faint, she never loses her equanimity or her sense of humor. Although she is married, and hence must not encourage Harleigh to make a declaration to her, she wants to keep open the possibility of marriage with him, a line she treads – and one chooses the word advisedly – masterfully. Her powerful feelings occasionally do threaten to overwhelm her. Only with difficulty can she restrain herself from flinging herself into her lover's arms when she sees him at a distance and knows that he might needlessly go to France.

> She felt inclined to forfeit, by one dauntless stroke, the delicacy which, as yet, had, through life, been the prominent feature of her character, by darting on, openly to conjure him to return. But habits which have been formed upon principle, and embellished by self-approbation, withstand, upon the smallest reflection, every wish, and every feeling that would excite their violation. The idea, therefore, died at its birth; and she sought to compose her disordered spirits, by silent prayers for courage and resignation. (p. 854)

This is the constraint that Elinor has not accepted, but that Juliet has practiced, though the lure of the 'dauntless stroke' has always been there. The hesitation in the prose, the many commas, shows with what female difficulty this dignity has been achieved, and indicates Burney's own hesitations over the efficacy of silent prayer. Elinor speaks always with authority, nearly always with ringing, uncluttered rhetoric. Juliet's more acceptable exterior requires constant monitoring on her part, and her statements are more impeded. Does the Frances Burney who would later follow her husband across France support Juliet's resignation? When faced with a similar situation she did not settle for silent prayer.

Reviewing Burney, Hazlitt praises Fielding for the '*double-entendre*' character, who is always surprising you. Yet how does this differ from the mule characters Johnson thought were superior to Fielding's? In a notebook, Burney discussed the analogy of body parts and mental qualities, and attempted to account for the realistically presented inconstencies of character that are one of her hallmarks as a novelist. The intellect, she writes, consists 'not of one whole, but of sundry parts.' One of these parts may be stunted or overgrown:

> The basis of the Intellect may be well formed, the Branches luxuriant & flourishing; – but unequal in growth, & size, & one part oppressing & overpowering another, as where generosity, overwhelming prudence, runs into extravagance, – or where prudence outmeasuring

generosity, extends into Avarice; – where Dignity of mind, enlarging itself above Humility, spreads into Pride, or where Humility, chancing to have the upper place creeps on into meanness.[17]

This theory accounts in the early novels for characters like Mrs Selwyn, who does not always assess the consequences of her advice to Evelina; Sir Sedley Clarindel, who is a more civilized person than his lusts will allow him to be; Mr Harrel, who is a quite decent young man suffering from ungovernable extravagance; Mrs Delvile, a splendid woman whose pride has spread beyond her control; and the spend-thrift Lionel Tyrold, whose unleashed jocularity leads him to threaten anonymously to shoot his uncle if he does not receive money. In *The Wanderer* this theory supports the free-thinking revolutionary Elinor, the quixotic, inadvertently destructive Giles Arbe, and the Prospero-like Sir Jaspar Herrington.

Burney worked on *The Wanderer* longer than on any of her other novels, and she packed into it the whole range of her observations and ideas, the themes of her tragedies and comedies, the complexi-ties of her varied life. Having carried the beginnings of *The Wanderer* with her when she went over to France in 1802, she worked on it steadily while there. In Passy, four years later, she kept notes in her diary of her progress. She was writing the section on work, and making steady strides ahead. In January, she completed 'Introd: of Sir Jasper [so spelled] – Needle Work for Ladies', and in February 'Introd. of Gatty', which must mean Gabriella, Ellis-Juliet's friend. All the rest is clear – a month to the Milliner's shop, a month to Sir Lyell Sycamore's chase through the countryside, a month to the Mantua-maker, a month to the 'Junket' at the Gooch farm (in the end, she seems to have combined Sir Lyell's abduction and the junket); and then Juliet 'Gives up Self-Dependence for Protection', and moves on to 'Toad Eating' (*JL* 6:785-6).

All of the descriptions of the public work Juliet engages in include the word 'Humours', as in 'Humours of Working for Shops'.[18] It is quite clear that Burney is playing with the Renaissance psychology of the four humors, the basis for Shakespearean psychology. Each of these incidents includes the attendant manifestations of the four humors – blood, phlegm, yellow bile or choler, and black bile. She is also interested in the elements from which they spring – earth, air, fire, and water. One of the most important sources and keys to the use of humors in *The Wanderer* is Burney's tragedy *Hubert de Vere*. She had first begun this play at court in 1790, almost had it staged in 1793, revised it as a closet drama in 1797, and timed it probably as late as 1836 (*Plays* 2: 93–5). It must always have been close to her consciousness. As Juliet resigns Harleigh to Elinor in order to prevent Elinor's suicide, so in *Hubert de Vere* Geralda is willing to cede her place to Cerulia. The play's Gothic atmosphere and the heroine's complete isolation also link it to Burney's most Gothic novel.[19] When the three specters who appear to Cerulia lead her to the place that will be her grave, she walks in willing terror through the four elements, from fire and air through earth to water.

Besides blood, or love, the humor that Burney had most consistently described in her earlier work was black bile, or melancholy. Suicide was a recurrent theme. There were phlegmatic people as well, such as the unbudgeable Dr Orkborne in *Camilla*. The question of suicide receives perhaps its fullest philosophical treatment in *The Wanderer*, where Elinor and Harleigh discuss the subject at length. Phlegmatic characters are largely absent here, but Burney makes up for this neglect with yellow bile, or anger. Mrs Howel, Mrs Maple, and Mrs Ireton are so ferocious that Admiral Powel calls them 'the three Furies' and informs them at the end of the novel that he exiles them from his house (p. 872). Though *The Wanderer* begins on the water, its most persistent element is air, the place where sprites live and the mind works. As in the other novels, quotations from Shakespeare frequently appear, extending the humor psychology. Though the references are more scattered than those to *Romeo and Juliet* in *Cecilia* and *Othello* in *Camilla*, Burney has concentrated here chiefly on *The Tempest*. She creates in Juliet not only a woman in love who is star-crossed and misunderstood, but also a mixture of Ariel and Miranda. In Sir Jaspar Herrington's relationship with Juliet, Burney expresses the combination of power, idiosyncrasy, and fatherliness that Prospero displays toward all of his charges.

Sir Jaspar considers himself to be in touch with the spirits of the air, 'sylphs, fairies, and the destinies' (p. 871). Otherwise, as in Burney's metaphor of the luxurious tree with the deformed branch, he is fairly if not perfectly rational. In love with Juliet, he often helps her, his age a protection against impropriety. When she is fleeing from the Commissary, he takes her to Wilton, and then, improbably, to Stonehenge. If he wants to be sure of continuing in her company, he seats himself and carelessly leans his crutches across the door. He is so obsessed with Juliet that he has found out her story. With 'fantastic gallantry' he chivvies her with his knowledge, speaking in riddles, and teases her as Prospero did his sprite: 'How's this my dainty Ariel? Why so serious a brow? Have some of my nocturnal visitants whisked themselves through the key-hole of your chamber-door also? And have they tormented your fancy with waking visions of fearful omens? Spurn them all! sweet syren!' (p. 627). Enjoying his Shakespearean analogues, Sir Jaspar also picks up bits from Hamlet and Macbeth. Though his idiosyncrasies are copious, they amuse Juliet. No matter how desperate she feels, he always makes her laugh.

Not content with drawing on Shakespeare, Burney has also included Cervantes. The plot line of Burney's *The Wanderer* is much like Fielding's in *Tom Jones*, where Tom is restored to his birthright after many picaresque Cervantaean adventures among characters who are sometimes important to his life and sometimes merely chance acquaintances of the road. The main difference is that Burney's character is female and that Burney imitates Cervantes more loosely than Fielding does, or than the other imitators of Fielding do, folding this material into the novel so seamlessly that commentators have failed to discuss it. Although Elinor brands Harleigh as quixotic in the early pages, the most truly quixotic character in the book is Sir Giles Arbe, a kindly old bachelor who tells Juliet that she must always pay tradespeople before she pays anyone else, and lends money to her whenever he can persuade her to take it.

The endings of Burney's other novels were somewhat problematical. The monkey incident had undercut *Evelina*, Cecilia chafed at not having her own money and the independence it would have brought, Camilla joined hands with Mandelbert only after he had caused her intricate suffering. It was not at all clear that the finally married couples were going to live unproblematic lives. Part of the problem is that most men in Burney devalue women, and if they marry or fail to marry, they tend to do so for the wrong reasons. Sir Jaspar has always feared that he would tie himself to a fortune-hunter, and now that he is 70 years old and on crutches, he finally meets in the wanderer a woman he feels he can trust. When he offers to marry Juliet she gracefully parries this gesture, kind and sad as it is (p. 634). It is to his credit that he makes this offer when he knows nothing at all about her history. Admiral Powel, Juliet's uncle, although he is worthy and benevolent, turns down Jenny Barker, because she has lost her beauty. He rewards her handsomely, but his benevolence does not by any means cancel out for the author or the reader the fact that he thinks women are the weaker vessel and that good looks are central to a good marriage. Dr Burney had not been willing to marry the unattractive but sympathetic Dorothy Young, a decision his family certainly saw as a failing in him. Sir Lyell Sycamore also responds mainly to appearance, and though interested in Miss Brinville, changes his mind when he sees her in the daylight. Young Ireton cares only about dress. Men, then, do not choose wisely. Women are not allowed to choose. Elinor is very clear about this. 'Why', Elinor asks, 'for so many centuries, has man, alone, been supposed to possess, not only force and power for action and defense, but even all the rights of taste; all the fine sensibilities which impel our happiest sympathies, in the choice of our life's partners?' It is bad enough that woman cannot fight or vote: 'must even her heart be circumscribed by boundaries as narrow as her sphere of action in life?' (p. 177). And yet, Burney does not give a simple answer, because Elinor's way of telling Harleigh she loves and wants him simply chills him. As if to counter Elinor's character, the play Burney uses within the novel in this case is not Shakespearean, but rather *The Provok'd Husband*, Colley Cibber's revision of Vanbrugh's unfinished *A Journey to London*. Burney provides no real detail from the play, possibly because she had no copy nearby when she wrote this scene, so that this play about the taming of Lady Townly by her Lord is made chiefly to represent Ellis's ability to act, and Harleigh's near 'rapture' toward the end when he sees her 'serious, penitent, and pathetic' (p. 96). The ultimate effect of the presence of Cibber's play is to show how important it is that women should behave. Once the choice is made, the institution itself comes under suspicion. Elinor's sister Selina, only 14 years old, is just about to be married, and Elinor remarks, 'It is a rule, you know, to deny nothing to a bride elect; probably, poor wretch, because every one knows what a fair way she is in to be soon denied every thing!' (p. 53) One of Selina's chief reasons for wanting to marry is that she erroneously believes that marriage will enlarge her freedom of choice, that 'she should very soon have a house of her own, in which her Aunt Maple would have no sort of authority' (p. 60). The man whom Sir Jaspar calls 'that brawny caitiff' (p. 755), Juliet's French husband, obviously has no respect for the institution of marriage, and her friend Gabriella has also been married in French fashion to a 'haughty and austere' stranger (p. 622). Surely, Burney's sense of the ridiculous is at work when she has Harleigh declare himself to Juliet's guardian in a bathing-machine at Teignmouth (p. 864). Yet, perhaps out of loyalty to d'Arblay, the actual marriage to Harleigh is foreseen as perfect, not least because 'the dearest delight of Harleigh was seeking to assemble around his Juliet her first friends'(p. 871). Eighteenth-century husbands were notoriously known for separating their wives from their friends, but Mrs Delany had undoubtedly told her young friend about how her husband had come to England every year so that she could keep up with her peers, and d'Arblay had always made room in their lives for Burney's most intimate acquaintances.

In criticizing marriage, Burney does not evoke the eighteenth-century extremes, like the wives confined in attics whose stories figured in Maria Edgeworth's *Castle Rackrent* and Sarah Chapone's *Hardships*. In all her novels and many of her plays, Burney reproduces for us the small, harrowing, soul-destroying petty hatreds: the vulgar spouse whose expressions grate, the husband whose body disgusts, the poacher who inflicts his dangerous negotiations. In *The Wanderer* marriage seems to be a completely exhausted institution. Among Burney's middle-class characters what is most remarkable is how few are married. Her three furies – Mrs Howel, Mrs Maple, and Mrs Ireton – are either unmarried or widowed. Indeed, none of her upper-class women seems to be attached to a living husband, and the older men who act as facilitators and occasional chorus in the novel are bachelors: Admiral Powel, Sir Giles Arbe, Mr Riley, and Sir Jaspar Herrington.

In 1778, when the author of *Evelina* solicited for the kindness of the critics in her preface, the critics themselves had not been especially powerful. A quarter of a century later, the situation had entirely changed. In the first decades of the nineteenth century, and especially in the pages of the *Edinburgh Review*, the literary review began to reach and affect the thinking of a large and influential audience. The combined readership of the *Edinburgh* and *Quarterly* reviews reached 20 000 subscribers and up to 100 000 readers in the year when Burney published *The Wanderer*.[20] Writing in 1831, Thomas Carlyle, indulging in his bracing characteristic hyperbole, said 'that Reviewing spreads with strange vigour; that such a man as Byron reckons the Reviewer and the Poet equal ... By and by it will be found that all Literature has become one boundless self-devouring Review.'[21] The reviewers saw themselves – and were seen by their readers – as men of letters, not merely creating or destroying individual authors, but writing the history of English literature, and in the name of that history accepting or rejecting particular authors – in short, establishing the canon. As had always been the case, these reviewers wrote anonymously, so that their judgments carried the ring of objective truth. In practice, of course, each reviewer purveyed his own attitudes, collectively the spirit of the age. Francis Jeffrey, editor of the *Edinburgh Review* for nearly 30 years from its inception in 1802, took as his quarry writing that was 'silly', 'babyish', and 'puerile'.[22] Others were more angry. One particularly vituperative reviewer was John

Wilson Croker, Secretary to the Admiralty from 1810 to 1830, and editor of Boswell's *Life of Johnson* and Pope's poems. Over his lifetime Croker wrote up to 270 pieces – reviews and political commentaries – for the *Quarterly Review*.[23] His political and personal enemy Macaulay called him 'that impudent leering scoundrel Croker', adding, 'I detest him more than cold boiled veal'.[24] Croker liked realistic fiction, and certain kinds of what he called 'extravagance', as in Byron's *Manfred*.[25] He disliked anything that smacked of the Gothic, and anything that offended his Tory political views. In 1823 he was to publish a translation with commentary of memoirs on the French Revolution by the surviving royal family.

In this new climate, Burney was especially apprehensive, and with reason. Reviews of *The Wanderer* followed hard on publication, much faster than usual, four in April, unprecedented for a book just published at the end of March. All were written from the conservative side of the political spectrum. Though there was occasional positive commentary, all four gave unexpectedly harsh judgments of *The Wanderer*'s style and content.[26] The most destructive remarks appeared in John Croker's article in the *Quarterly Review*. Croker did not so much analyze *The Wanderer* as cripple it. His method was analogy and unsupported judgment. When writing this piece, though complaining to the editors that he was 'oppressed and weary with business' Croker had nonetheless requested Burney's three earlier novels, adding, 'I should like to keep them'. He included no extract from the book, he said, because his own remarks took up too much room. His article was long and in his own word 'severe'.[27]

Indeed, in the published review Croker was on the attack right from the first paragraph. Burney's novel is so bad, he argues, that it cannot be distinguished from the trivial fiction turned out by the Minerva Press. It is a pale self-imitation: Burney has always been a mannerist, but 'her last manner is the worst' (p. 124). Warming to his subject, Croker turns to analogy again. He links Burney's genius to her youth and her diminishing talent to the decay of her body:

> The Wanderer has the identical features of Evelina – but of Evelina grown old; the vivacity, the bloom, the elegance, 'the purple light of love' are vanished; the eyes are there, but they are dim; the cheek, but it is furrowed; the lips, but they are withered.   (pp. 125-6)

Since Burney's heroine is actually rather luscious, this analogy is oddly misplaced. To support his invented picture, Croker invokes some of

Burney's real qualities, while giving them negative connotations: 'And when to this description we add that Madame D'Arblay endeavours to make up for the want of originality in her characters by the most absurd mysteries, the most extravagant incidents, and the most violent events.' After this judgment, he immediately returns to finish off his analogy of the aging author, 'we have completed the portrait of an old coquette who endeavours, by the wild tawdriness and laborious gaiety of her attire, to compensate for the loss of the natural charms of freshness, novelty, and youth' (p. 126). This is not criticism; it is commonplace nineteenth-century misogyny. The misogyny was widespread. According to Croker Burney's lips were withered, but Thackeray's male and aging Fielding whose lips may or may not have been withered, nonetheless retained 'aspect and presence'.[28] Croker is more interested in his metaphor than the truth. He increases the contrast between young and old by adopting the rumor that Burney had written *Evelina* when she was seventeen.

His ensuing summary of *The Wanderer* indicates that he read it as written in the realistic mode, rejecting its mysteriousness and violence. He fails to mention Juliet's shifting name, for instance, or the three times she is nearly raped. He must have read these five volumes very quickly. He misspells characters' names, elides complications in the plot, and makes an egregious mistake when he states that the heroine divorces her French husband, who in fact is guillotined. The chief reason for Croker's outrage becomes apparent at the end of the review, where he attacks Burney for writing sympathetically about France and forbearing to criticize the 'tyger' Bonaparte (p. 130). The book is too radical for him, too wild and violent, too original.

Croker's ability to recognize certain kinds of originality was distinctly limited. Four years later, he reviewed Mary Shelley's *Frankenstein* as if it, too, ought to be a realistic novel. 'What a tissue of horrible and disgusting absurdity this work presents', he complained.[29] Scott thought otherwise. It was Croker who wrote the review of Keats' *Endymion*, a review so intemperate that Hazlitt wrote a vituperative article complaining about it. As Keats's friends were later to do, Burney's family and friends gathered round to support her and more temperately to assess the book. Her son Alex, after first finishing his mother's novel said that if he were to meet a Juliet she 'would completely enchain' his heart (*JL* 8:472). He also wrote down his appreciations and criticisms, teasing her gently about the occasionally full-blown style.[30] She had to prevent her friend Georgiana

Waddington from writing to Croker in protest. Her brother Charles sent her a sputtering letter. From France, d'Arblay forwarded to her his carefully considered comments, now that he had finally been able to read *The Wanderer*. He was direct, and he spoke with authority. He admitted that as he read he was tempted to think that Burney's previous novels were better, but he ultimately decided that *The Wanderer* was in conception just as good and in execution superior. She had mingled seriousness and humor, pleasure and instruction, better than anybody else could. He thought that the reading public would eventually understand this.[31] Meanwhile, sales had stalled in the middle of the second edition.

There were more positive reviews. The *Gentleman's Magazine*, while referring much more glowingly to the 'almost matchless "Cecilia"' (p. 579), was respectful, and predicted a large group of future readers for this historical piece. The *European Magazine*, while not really positive, at least allowed Burney skillful execution, if not modern subject matter. Unfortunately, the tide turned again when in February 1815 William Hazlitt published his piece in the influential *Edinburgh Review*. By now, Burney was in France, where she and d'Arblay were recovering from their trip. She had been so sea-sick that d'Arblay sat with her in the wind on the deck, clasping her to him for the whole voyage to prevent her falling off the seat. Then, when they arrived at Calais, a cart had struck him in the breast so forcefully that he was thought nearly dead and was 'copiously blooded – in a sallad bowl! –' (*JL* 8:14). While he recovered, d'Arblay was feeling his way professionally, trying to keep in balance his democratic (though constitutionalist) beliefs, his dignity, and his job. He was not like Alex's old playfellow Maxime de Maisonneuve, the son of a friend Burney adored ('How I love to love her!' Burney had written to her husband in 1804, (*JL* 6:510)). Maxime supported the King with such alacrity and thoroughness, quickly voting to execute Marshall Ney, that he later became Ambassador to London and Minister of War.[32] Meanwhile, d'Arblay was an artillery commander in the King's bodyguard, biding his time until he could retire, and he was sent off to Senlis to fit up the bodyguard. Burney, who was to be introduced at Court, planned to hide her unfashionable clothes under a shawl. In the distant complexities of France, she could not worry very much about the fate of *The Wanderer* in England, though she presented what had been her father's copy to the Duchesse d'Angoulême, Louis XVIII's niece, distressed that such an influential person was reading the inferior French translation.

Still, Hazlitt's review was impossible to ignore. Of all the reviews of *The Wanderer*, this was the most important. Hazlitt, who hated Croker as much as the next fellow, wielded a different sort of power. Born with *Evelina* in 1778, he had early shown an independent mind, writing to his father at the age of eight that he thought America 'would have been a great deal better if the white people had not found it out'.[33] Friend of Coleridge and Lamb, much admired by Keats, he had already written an important *Reply* to Malthus's *Essay on Population*, a grammar, a book on the eloquence of members of parliament, and in 1812 *Lectures on English Philosophy*. One of Hazlitt's greatest achievements was to be to write the first comprehensive history of English literature, a somewhat scattered and idiosyncratic history, but nonetheless the first. When Burney's *Wanderer* landed on his desk, he was thinking about writing the history of the English comic writers on whom he was to give his popular lectures four years later. The Burney review was a chance to take a first pass at the genre of the novel, to place it within his definition of comedy as laughter, as the difference between things as they are and what they ought to be.

Cervantes and Fielding were Hazlitt's favorite templates for the comic prose narrative. He thought of Fielding as a window on history, a way of finding out a kind of truth unmentioned in the factual accounts. He likes the fact that Fielding ranges down through the hierarchies of class and work, and enjoys Fielding's '*double entendre* of character', where the reader suddenly encounters fresh traits (p. 327). Smollett, Richardson, and Sterne are part of the canon, but they come in for more guarded praise. When Hazlitt reaches Burney, the ostensible subject of the review, his rhetoric suddenly ignites. Henry Crabb Robinson characterized this review as 'severe and almost contemptuous towards Miss Burney, whose Wanderer was the pretence for the article'.[34] Hazlitt's severity seems chiefly to do with the fact that Burney writes 'as a very woman'. 'She is unquestionably a quick, lively, and accurate observer of persons and things; but she always looks at them with a consciousness of her sex', he writes, 'and in that point of view in which it is the particular business and interest of women to observe them' (p. 336). Hazlitt assumes that the wider scope of Fielding actually includes women's point of view, though, as twentieth-century feminist criticism has clearly shown, it does not. One kind of narrowness pleases Hazlitt, and the other makes him 'almost contemptuous'. The aphorism that has most forcibly struck the readers of this review is: 'The difficulties in which she involves her heroines are indeed too much "Female Difficulties"; – they are diffi-culties created out of nothing'.[35] This is not Croker's angry misogyny, but rather the male self-absorption Virginia Woolf so memorably defines when she shows in *A Room of One's Own* how women habitu-ally mirror men at twice their size. Used to seeing themselves reflected at twice their size men are shocked when the mirror merely reflects their natural dimensions.

Crabb Robinson found the review 'almost contemptuous', and Burney's brother James responded in the same vein. Hazlitt was James's friend, and for ten years had been dropping in for whist and conversation. Three months after the review appeared, James Burney wrote an irate letter to Hazlitt, claiming that some of his 'remarks' were 'unjust'. He took as a personal attack the fact that Hazlitt had not shared his attitudes before printing them. 'Your publication of such a paper showed a total absence of regard towards me, and I must consider it as the termination of our acquaintance.'[36] Learning of this letter, Alex immediately wrote to his mother in France. From her mental distance there she claimed that regarding *The Wanderer* she was 'gifted, happily, with a most impenetrable apathy upon the subject of its criticisers.... I never expected it would have any imme-diate favour in the World; & I have not yet shut out from my spying Glass a distant prospect that it may share, in a few years, the partiality shewn to its Elder sisters' (*JL* 8:317). She was sure that part of the problem was false expectations: some had imagined that the book would depict Revolutionary France; others hoped the *The Wanderer* would be the author's own story. They all expected too much from a book that carried the 'astonishing *éclat*' of selling more than 3000 copies before publication. In addition, Longman charged an unreal-istic two guineas for the book, twice as much as the longer *Camilla*, and way out of line with current prices.[37] Burney and her brother had carefully kept *Camilla* more affordable and assumed that Payne, Cadell and Davies would print subsequent editions in an even cheaper format. Longman stubbornly persisted into the second edition with its outlandish price. Burney takes the long view, that the book will even-tually either recover its reputation or be finally damned. Though she claims apathy, she clearly hopes and expects that the book will ulti-mately come into its own, though possibly only after her death.

A couple of weeks before James sent his irate letter, Alex carefully folded some paper to look like a duodecimo pamphlet and wrote the title: 'Observations on the last work of The Author of Evelina, intitled "The Wanderer"'. Of all the family comments on any Burney book, her son Alex's spoof review is the most tender and charming. It is dated 1 May 1815, at Norbury Park. Alex begins by saying that Mme d'Arblay is a good enough writer so as to be able to accept these 'little *cavils*, respectfully submitted by one too *sincerely* her admirer to offer at her shrine his *unchequered admiration*; – and too well acquainted with her private character and honoured with her confidence, to think that a tribute of praise sans aucun mélange could ever be acceptable to Her'. He hits her style exactly, from the carefully honed polite phrases down to the underlinings and the lapse into French. With an irony that gives a remarkably intimate view of the Burney family's ability to laugh at itself, he notes that there will be an article that will 'repair in the Edinburgh Review the partial injustice of the Quarterly', certainly a stalwart way to laugh at the kind of 'repair' in Hazlitt. Alex's subsequent discussion of the novel blames it for being too succinct. He chooses for exegesis sentences like, 'Elinor stood aloof, and spoke not a word!' Referring by indirection to the fact that Burney was being accused of imitativeness, he footnotes one of his own transitions, 'that sudden transition is an imitation of Sterne, you see'.[38] Did he send this loving tribute to his mother in France? Perhaps so. It was he, as we have seen, who told her about Hazlitt's review.

Luckily for Burney's ego if not for her purse, the periodicals were not quite finished with *The Wanderer*. In December 1815, two months after the d'Arblays had returned to England and settled in Bath, the *Monthly Review*, which had always warmly supported Dr Burney, finally joined the crowd. The author, William Taylor, in his refreshingly positive review (besides referring approvingly to 'this truly varied, original, and interesting novel', this 'agreeably intricate and busy novel') attempted to reply indirectly to Hazlitt and even Croker. In the midst of this difficult task, Taylor's tone varies so substantially that the review has been read in the twentieth century, and undoubtedly was in the eighteenth, as 'diplomatically and subtly negative'.[39] In fact, Taylor's background was such that he was especially likely to appreciate *The Wanderer*. He was an expert in German literature, and had translated Lessing and Goethe, so that he was primed to be responsive to the sensibility of Burney's fourth novel. Knowing that the book had suddenly ceased to be popular, Taylor argued that it evoked the England of the 1790s, but argued in such a way as to criticize his own era. 'We are glad', he says, 'to see depicted again such society as our matrons remember; and to escape occasionally from the smooth insipidity of modern polish, by reverting to the more various singularities and broader humour of an age of social tolerance and comparative indiscipline.' (p. 412) Of the scene where the Commissary nearly apprehends Juliet, he comments: 'This scene is finely imagined, and as finely painted. The English language, in its most essential powers, has not deserted the pen of Madame D'Arblay; and the French, in its most expressive neatness, is become familiar to her.' As if to explain the novel's sudden drop in sales, he mentions that it is 'more adapted, we suspect, for permanence than for immediate popularity' (pp. 413, 415, 419, 416). Unfortunately, this admiring review had no effect whatsoever on sales.

After Burney resisted the Longman move to remainder the second edition in 1817, *The Wanderer* sold in numbers that were pitifully small – 23 copies in 1815, the year of Taylor's review, and thereafter approximately six books per year up to 1824. Burney wrote to Longman on 1 February 1826 asking how many books had sold in the last two years. Again, she resisted the Longman plan to remainder or 'waste' the edition and in fact demanded the copyright back, calling on the terms of the initial agreement. Though Burney was negotiating as fiercely as she could, now that her brother Charles was dead, these maneuvers came to nothing. Although Burney worked on a revised edition of *The Wanderer*, making changes throughout, it was not to be reprinted until the Pandora edition in 1988 (*Wanderer*, p. xxxix). Permanence took longer than Taylor – or Burney – surmised.

It is a boon for us that we can read *The Wanderer* as a historical novel that takes place in the 1790s without wishing that it were something else. This was not the case for contemporary readers. Just three days after *The Wanderer* was published in 1814, Napoleon lost Paris. In such dramatic times, a historical fiction on women's difficulties could not make its way. While the booksellers tried to hawk the overpriced novel in its second edition, Napoleon was being exiled to jewel-like, mountainous Elba. In the same issue where William Taylor published his more positive review, the *Quarterly Review* also began a massive, four-part life of Wellington. Napoleon was back in Paris, and all Europe was holding its breath. In October 1815, with sales of *The Wanderer* down to a handful, the *Quarterly Review* published more than 40 pages reviewing eight books on Bonaparte.

Meanwhile, in Paris, Burney had more to worry about than her unfashionable clothes. Many years later she would write about her experiences there. When Paris was about to fall to Bonaparte she fled, not even knowing how to get in touch with her husband, who was now in the King's forces, fearing that she might never see him or her son again. She had carefully paid all her bills and entrusted the key to their apartments to a reliable person. But when she was in Brussels, thinking that she might have to embark for England, she was devastated at the thought that she would lose her literary past. She had left all her manuscripts, all her possessions, behind in Paris: 'all my MSS! – My beloved Father's! my family papers! – my Letters of all my life! my Susan's Journals! – !!! –'(*JL* 8:83). She was now herself really a wanderer, traveling incognito because she was the wife of a military officer, owner of nothing but 'a small change of linen' and a couple of gowns (*JL* 8:83). She found d'Arblay, but his health was a worry. He continued to serve his King, though he had never fully recovered from the blow to his chest at Calais. Not long after Waterloo he was kicked by a wild horse he had bought to train, whose iron-shod hoof sliced his right leg through to the tibia, crumpling it, an ugly wound complicated by bad surgery and an abcess. He was never to walk freely again. Her own experiences were unforgettable. For more than a week after Wellington's glorious victory, she looked out of her window in Brussels 'to witness sights of wretchedness. Maimed, wounded, bleeding, mutilated, tortured victims of this exterminating contest, passed by every minute: – the fainting, the sick, the dying & the Dead, on Brancards, in Carts, in Waggons succeeded one another without intermission' (*JL* 8:447).

Unlike Burney's contemporaries, we are not bewildered by these events into wishing *The Wanderer* were something else. We can recognize that the violence and mystery in Burney's last novel, the 'female difficulties' that irritated Croker and Hazlitt, were endemic in what one twentieth-century critic has called the 'Gothic social space' of eighteenth-century women's ordinary lives.[40]

The chorus of opinion about *The Wanderer*, both contemporary and present-day, compares it to the novels of the 1790s, and claims that its setting in the 1792–93 reign of Robespierre was too old-fashioned to survive in 1814. Like Mary Hays' *Emma Courtney*, it features a free spirit who unabashedly declares her love. Like Amelia Opie's *Adeline Mowbray* it uses as a template the rights of women, and their inherent complexities and dangers. Like Charlotte Smith's *Desmond* and Elizabeth Hamilton's *Memoirs of Modern Philosophers*, it includes complex English responses to the French Revolution and the rights of men. People read the book with the wrong expectations, as Burney had feared they might.

These expectations do not sufficiently explain why, when all of Burney's other books were republished in the nineteenth century, *The Wanderer* never stirred out of oblivion. Besides Croker's reiteration of his strictures in 1832 and Macaulay's rigorous destruction in 1843, I would hazard two primary explanations. The preface, even as it attempts to explain the book's purpose and genre, becomes so personal and roundabout that it simply cuts out a reader. With d'Arblay across the channel and her father dying, Burney wrote an outmoded, self-abasing, and fulsome introduction to her book. In spite of the subtitle of 'Female Difficulties', a woman picking up the book would not feel invited into a novel prefaced with such a protracted paean to a father. Skipping the dedicatory poem in *Evelina* was a comparatively easy matter. But the high style Burney uses in this preface is her least appealing mode, especially when it combines with self-abasement. 'The earliest pride of my heart', her dedication begins:

> was to inscribe to my much-loved Father the first public effort of my pen; though the timid offering, unobtrusive and anonymous, was long unpresented; and, even at last, reached its destination through a zeal as secret as it was kind, by means which he would never reveal; and with which, till within these last few months, I have myself been unacquainted. (p. 3)

Wrapped in these groveling sentences, with their periphrastic expressions and negative forms, is so much personal reference that the public audience is quite excluded. Soon, Burney finds herself having to provide footnotes to explain some of the references. Instead of inviting her public into her novel, she is shutting them out. In this first paragraph, for instance, she refers obliquely to the fact that her sister Susanna told her father about the authorship of *Evelina*, but she does not actually mention this fact. At the end of this often hermetic piece, Burney directly addresses the audience: 'Will the public be offended, if here, as in private, I conclude my letter with a prayer for my dearest Father's benediction and preservation? No!' (p. 10). But what if the answer is yes? Already shaken, the reader would immediately encounter the scene where strangers are talking on a ship in the dark. Nobody tells us who they are. The heroine has no name. Burney simply took too many chances with her audience.

In a particularly vivid metaphor, George Orwell described the position of eighteenth-century women. 'Stratagems', he said, 'are inevitable in a society where technical chastity is highly valued and a woman has in effect no profession except marriage. In such a society there is an endless struggle between the sexes – a struggle which from the woman's point of view often resembles an egg-and-spoon race, and from the man's a game of ninepins.'[41] Choosing by chance a metaphor that Burney herself had played with in the old women's race in *Evelina*, Orwell is making three points here: the importance of technical chastity; the fact that women had no profession, no work, no way to make a living; and the fact that by default marriage was a profession rather than a chosen partnership. The three are related, but they can be separated, and Burney does separate them. *The Wanderer* never really questions chastity, but it unceasingly deplores the fact that a woman cannot support herself. The institution of marriage is questioned at every turn. When Hazlitt complained that Burney's female difficulties are created out of nothing, his was a typical response to an egg-and-spoon race by someone used to the game of ninepins.

9
Memoirs of Doctor Burney: Circumscribing the Power (1814–40)

An awful stillness thence pervaded the apartment, and so soft became his breathing, that I dropped my head by the side of his pillow, to be sure that he breathed at all! – Frances Burney writing about her father, 1814, *Memoirs* 3:432

When I first came into the world, it was thought but a poor compliment to say a person did a thing like a lady
– Sir Joshua Reynolds, as quoted in *Memoirs* 2:236

We were as merry, and laughed as bonnily as the Burneys always do when they get together, and open their hearts, and tell old stories, and have no fear of being quizzed by interlopers.
– Dr Burney, 1799, quoted in *Memoirs* 3:283

Madame d'Arblay ... conceals from her readers, and perhaps from herself, that it is her *own Memoirs*, and *not* those of her father that she has been writing.
– John Wilson Croker, review in the *Quarterly Review* 49 (April 1833) 106–7

Two weeks after the publication of *The Wanderer*, in April 1814, Burney had watched over her dying father in his residence at Chelsea College. Writing her *Memoirs of Doctor Burney* nearly 18 years later when she was nearly 80, she evoked this scene. The sky was illuminated with 'the brilliancy of mounting rockets and distant fire-works' celebrating Wellington's victories in France, and her mind was suspended between 'joy and sorrow' (*Memoirs* 3:429). Although her father was dying, she would soon see her husband again after a separation of a year and a half. Meanwhile her father was sinking fast. Dr Burney's death as she describes it was consistent with his life. He was even more in control of the situation than most of his contemporaries, schooled as they all were in the art of a proper death. But for her it was an agonizing mixture of inflexible rejection, theatrical gestures, and private tenderness. When, hearing from her son Alex that 'his grandfather had passed an alarming night' (3:424) and that her brothers had been sent for, Burney first hastened to her father's room, he sat 'immoveable; and not a muscle of his face gave any indication that I was either heard or perceived!' (3:425). This was so distressing that she rushed out of the room, but she was soon called back to see her father standing, straighter than he had stood for years, and staring out of his window, where he could see his second wife's grave. He raised his arms, extending them in a kind of double waving motion, and said to himself, 'distinctly, though in a low, but deeply-impressive voice, "All this will soon pass away as a dream!"' (3:426).

Although his daughter allows this scene its full magnitude, she was always alive to incongruities of gesture and feeling, and she provides them here. The others in the room seized the opportunity to pull his dressing gown off his extended arms, and he was soon 'put to bed' (3:427). He did not say another word, and would not. Those had been his last words, and either by chance or by design he would not diminish them by others. She wanted to tell him that Wellington had won the war, but at first she could not, knowing that he would no longer respond with the vivacity she loved in him, never again show 'the ecstatic enthusiasm that would have hailed it with songs of triumph' (3:428). When she did tell him, he turned toward her, and though his eyes remained closed, she thought (or at any rate she wrote) that he gave her 'a look of vivacious and kind surprise' (3:430), but then as she continued to inform him about the situation she realized that he did not really believe her. Finally, 'An awful stillness ... pervaded the apartment, and so soft became his breathing, that I dropped my head by the side of his pillow, to be sure that he breathed at all!' (*Memoirs* 3:432). His servant George cried out, but Burney did not move.

Her father had died so quietly that she would not believe that he was dead. She insisted on staying by his body, watching for an hour, hoping to see one last sign of life. This need to watch has seemed to her contemporaries and to twentieth-century commentators excessive, but the belief that someone's spirit lingers about the body after death has always been widespread. Those who would hurry the watchers away from a dead body are responding to cultural strictures Burney chose not to follow. At this period stories were frequent of cases where people who seemed dead had suddenly revived, and Dr Burney himself had heard of a woman who lived for three days after her heart had stopped (*Memoirs* 3:376). Burney stayed. Still, this was an unusual action. Burney's father had been master of the proper gesture, the social joy that so often oddly precludes true intimacy. This act of sitting next to the unadmittedly dead body mimics their lifelong relationship. The fact that Burney would listen at a dead man's side 'a full hour, or more', hoping for one last sign, is a sadly just metaphor for her relationship with this difficult parent (*Memoirs*, 3:433).

And yet she closes the memoir by stating that she chooses not to mention his faults, but rather to transmit only his perfections to posterity, as an example to be followed. The last page of this acknowledged hagiography contains the inscription she wrote for his plaque at Westminster Abbey. She at first suggested to Charles that he should write it in Latin, but Charles thought English would be more appropriate and turned the assignment over to the member of the family most literate in that language. She labored over this task for months, trying to write as simply as possible, 'in plain un-inflated prose' (*JL* 9:347). In keeping with her habit of always tinkering with her prose, the version she renders in the *Memoirs* is slightly different both from her first draft and from the actual inscription in the Abbey, although the differences in this version mainly represent a return to her first draft. This reflects another persistent habit, loving and even clinging to her own prose. The most important difference is that she restores the statement that his 'accomplishments' were 'self-acquired', an emphasis that under her brother Charles's influence had become 'intellectual attainments'.[1] It was self-acquired achievement that Burney admired most in her father, and admired most in life. She underscored this kind of self-reliance in *The Wanderer*, where Juliet's guardian the Bishop writes that those who wished to triumph over fortune must 'whether female or male, learn to suffice to themselves' (p. 220). The final statement in *The Wanderer* even more eloquently invokes 'untamed spirits superiour to failure' (p. 873). Her father, whatever his faults, had acquired his accomplishments through his own unremitting efforts.

After her father's death, Burney accompanied her husband to France, to the terrors of the Hundred Days and Waterloo. Her literary efforts there in 1815 were limited to letters and pocket-book diaries, though she later wrote out many of her experiences in narrative form.

In October 1815, the d'Arblays returned to England. Since Alex had decided to live in the country of his birth, d'Arblay agreed to abandon his native land. Even so, he had to go twice more to France to secure his pension, in spite of the fact that he was not well. Burney knew he was ill, and she worried so much when he did not arrive as scheduled that in a 'nervous seizure' she nearly lost her eyesight, and became so pale that Alex often called out, 'Plus de separations, maman! cela vous tue'. In her empty house, feeling homeless, she identified with her heroine Juliet. Her husband's absence, she wrote, 'makes me seem to have never a Home, to be *myself* always a *Wanderer*! (*JL* 9:284–6). When her husband returned, she felt happily complete.

But she was soon to be a wanderer again. She lost both her brother and d'Arblay, her two chief remaining inspirers and critics. On Christmas 1817, when Charles Burney suddenly had a stroke and died, her jotted note on his death shows one of her most direct and idiomatic styles:

> My dear – very dear Charles was struck this sad Day with a death stroke of Apoplexy – from which he never recovered speech – though consciousness I believe revived! – though he lingered on 3 days – terrible days! – of alternate insensibility of mind & violent bodily emotion – whether *suffering*, or the convulsions of the poor machine, who can tell?   (*JL* 10:950)

For Burney the mind always dwelled in the body, and this final disjunction in Charles was particularly terrible. Meanwhile, when d'Arblay arrived home at Bath in October, he was terribly thin, and often in pain. Burney convinced herself that the problem was curable, and set herself to nursing her husband back to health. But he was dying.

The Burney and d'Arblay method of dealing with an emotional situation, or with any situation, was to write about it, to make it part of their literary life. This, their last mutual experience, was no exception. Each kept a journal, and Burney occasionally jotted down conversations. This time, however, they did not exchange journals as they had traded French notebooks during their courtship or shared the commonplace book about Susanna's death. Ultimately, Burney seems to have destroyed her original journal and replaced it with her 'Narrative of the Last Illness and Death of General D'Arblay', written a year and a half after her husband died, and she includes the act of reading her husband's journal in her replacement 'Narrative'.[2] The important thing to notice is how radically Burney's husband's death differed from her father's. D'Arblay was 20 years younger, and he resisted death as Dr Burney did not, but the difference in age does not account for the striking contrast in tone. Dr Burney withdrew, closed his eyes, retreated into silence. When he made a gesture, it was grand – even grandiose – with its Papal stance and dread pronouncement that 'All this will soon pass away as a dream!'.

Although his daughter allowed this scene its full magnitude in her edition of her father's *Memoirs*, her description of her husband's death shows us that she married a man entirely unlike her father and that when she wrote about these two men whom she so variously loved, she consciously or unconsciously emphasized this difference. Her father had always tended to retreat into himself, and had to be teased into activity. Though Dr Burney had always been amiable he had never been obliging.

D'Arblay 'had always spirit & love of obliging awake to every call' (*JL* 10: 847). At Bath in 1817, when Queen Charlotte asked to meet him, he made his last foray into society in order to be presented to her in the Pump Room. He wore his medals, the Legion of Honor, the orders of St. Louis and La Fidelité. Burney remembers him as being particularly handsome, 'his fine brow so open! his noble Countenance so expressive!' (*JL* 10:848). The Queen was altogether charmed by d'Arblay, though Burney makes it clear throughout that he was in excruciating pain and collapsed immediately after the Queen left. This was just before Christmas; d'Arblay died less than five months later. The last words of this obliging, strong, and thoughtful man were personal, intended for his family and their afterlife together: 'Je ne sais si ce sera le dernier mot – mais, ce sera la derniere pensée – Notre Reunion!' (*JL* 10:907).

Dr Burney never spoke after his last pronouncement, but d'Arblay did, and his actual last words were more individual and more interesting, since they reflected the quality of the d'Arblay marriage and some of the assumptions on which it was based. Throughout her narrative, Burney and her husband freely and yet with dignity had spoken to one another as fully as they could. When d'Arblay suspected (wrongly) that his wife had lost hope, and that she was hiding this fact from him, 'in a voice tremulous with strong emotion, yet void of all anger, all resentment, he called out aloud "Oh Fanny, Fanny! – what is become of your veracity!"' (*JL* 10:893). Dr Burney was always half elsewhere. D'Arblay was fully present to those he loved.

One always feels a bodily awareness between the d'Arblays, the tangibility that was also an important quality in Burney's writing, and had been from the start. *She* had never written a poem on masturbation, but within the parameters of her genres she had written compellingly about the body. Their relationship had always carried strong sexual overtones, and even now in their 60s both were still handsome people. Perhaps this is why her face changed in the way Mary Berry commented on, becoming more radiant (*JL* 7:52, n. 10). Writing about her dying husband, she tells us how handsome he is and how compassionate he remains. Once, when Burney cries out with a brief pain, in spite of his condition d'Arblay is instantly at her side. She sleeps near him, and he insists that she lie where he can see her at all times, simply to look at her. She kisses his forehead, and when he demurs, knowing that he is so sweaty as to disgust, she kisses his hand. Alexander is their 'mutual darling', the union of their sexual selves. So, at the very end, when Burney and Alexander join forces to adjust d'Arblay's pillows, Burney tells us that Alex lifts his father up, while she rearranges the bolster. Meanwhile, d'Arblay teases them, telling them that they do it almost as well as his absent nurse: 'Vous le faites – presque – aussi bien qu'elle!' He smiles angelically, but at 'presque' his lips slip into a 'playful expression' (*JL* 10:907). Thoughtfulness, tenderness, playfulness – all these seem to epitomize d'Arblay's character and his relationship with his family. He was thinking about his wife and their boy who had nearly reached adulthood, when in his last moments he found these most personal, kind, and domestic words.

But in 1814, d'Arblay was still living, and the death Burney had to deal with was her father's. After Dr Burney's death, Burney had to set to work with her siblings to divide and sell his property. It was a task that required tact as well as energy, since she needed to satisfy them. Her brother James, in particular, felt that he had been neglected in the will, which left the bulk of Dr Burney's estate to Burney and her elder sister Esther. Perhaps the snub to James was the final cut for the escapade with Sarah Harriet. Though initially Burney thought this chore would take a year, she pared it down to eight months so that she could go abroad with her husband. On 10 November 1814, Burney and d'Arblay left for France, and their son Alex stayed behind at Cambridge. During this time, it seems likely that Burney returned to her tragedy *Elberta*, whose chief theme is separation from the family. When she had begun it during her last ten months at Court, she was sunk in perhaps the most desperately lonely period of her life. Susanna's journal-letters told her how after an absence when she returned home,'my heart began to palpitate, and I already felt the near approach to my children'.[3] Childless herself, surrounded by the royal children, separated as if forever from her sister, Burney began to write about a woman who was married but unable to own her husband, who was a mother, but unable to stay with her child. On the pages of her 1814 calender, her sister dead, her father gone, separated from her son, she returned once more to this tragedy of a broken, severed family. Somewhere along the line the fictional son who had previously been called Edwin became Eric, closer to the name Alex, and in one of the fragments from the 1814 calendar Elberta has one child rather than two. Elberta dreams of returning to her children, mainly so that she can 'embrace their gentle Limbs', but also because they are beginning to recognize her as their mother (1.12.33, *Plays* 2:250).

This period in France was so chaotic that it was not a time when Burney could concentrate on any work of art. It is no wonder that *Elberta* exists in such tiny fragments. At some point in a different conception of the play Burney had intended that the mother should go mad, but in the document as it eventually developed the mother is, like Juliet Granville, impressive for her courage and her unshakeable sanity. After watching King George lose his mind, Burney gradually herself recognized the strengths that protect people from madness. In her second novel, the heroine briefly loses her wits; Cerulia in *Hubert de Vere* falls in love with death; and in *Camilla* there is a brief vignette of a woman who is incredibly beautiful – and insane. But by the time of *The Wanderer* Burney's most resounding theme is mental courage, and this kind of forceful resistance requires sanity. At the end of *Elberta* when Elberta's husband Arnulph is dying and appeals to her that she must live to raise her children, at first she cannot face this prospect, but then the 'wondrous calm' descends, and she becomes unexpectedly strong (5.13.18, *Plays* 2:302). No wonder Burney returned to it in the indescribable loneliness of 1814. If *Elberta* had been finished, the heroine would have been a woman of unusual power.[4] But Burney never did finish this play; perhaps it was veering too close to her own life. In the preface to the *Memoirs*, Burney says that her afflictions made it impossible for her to write, but that the passage of time, which took away her happiness, also restored her 'mental calm' (p. vi).

Actually, Burney exaggerates when she claims that she could not write in the period between 1814 and the publication of the *Memoirs* in 1832. She did not publish during that period, but she never stopped writing. Between 1818 and 1826, along with her work on her father's papers, she fashioned five autobiographical journals, directed to her son as primary audience. For Alex she wrote her 'Narrative of the Last Illness and Death of General D'Arblay'; the 'Ilfracombe Journal', about the time she was stranded on a pinnacle of rock and thought she would drown; the 'Waterloo Journal'; and the account of her desperate journey to find d'Arblay at Trèves. In 1825, 13 years after the fact, she wrote up vividly and humorously the scenes with which I opened this literary life, the encounter at Dunkirk with the officer who suspected her of being a spy, and the moments when her manuscript of *The Wanderer* was nearly destroyed.

Seen in this context, the confident and amused tone of Burney's description of the official who threatened to confiscate *The Wanderer* is even more remarkable. When Burney wrote this sequence, she had heard that the publishers had finally remaindered *The Wanderer*. Posterity might reclaim it, but posterity lay in the unknowable future. In the sad and demeaning present, the book had ceased totally to sell. Yet she could write about it with pride and seeming light-heartedness.

Meanwhile, she had also been sifting through her father's manuscripts. She described them to her sister Esther in 1820: they were much too inclusive, 'countless, fathomless' (*JL* 11:184), the significant mixed bafflingly with the trivial. They were also oddly incomplete. Dr Burney had destroyed all his letters to and from his wife Elizabeth Allen immediately after her death nearly 25 years before, though Burney found one letter from her stepmother and carefully preserved it, annotating it coldly as 'in the style of a certain lady' (*EJL* 2:292), the style uncannily like that of Lady Smatter. Also missing was every letter having to do with Burney's half-brother the black sheep, 'Bengal Richard', whom his parents had exiled to India, and some of whose pleasant children were now living in London. All these grandchildren, Burney tells us, emphasizing the positive, were remembered in their grandfather's will.

What was present among Dr Burney's papers was almost as distressing as what was absent. The 12 notebooks of actual memoirs of her father's childhood she found 'trivial to poverty, & dull to sleepiness'.[5] They were also unexpectedly mean-spirited about his relatives, including his sisters Ann and Rebecca, whom Burney had always been quite fond of. He said nearly nothing about her mother, Esther Sleepe. When in the narrative he moved to London, instead of writing details about the famous people he met he simply listed them. It is difficult at this distance to assess Burney's attitudes and her motives. She was so disappointed – possibly so angry at being designated to do this monumental task – that she slashed and burned, leaving fragments.

Her editorial decisions about her father's papers have justly angered Dr Burney's biographers, Percy Scholes and Roger Lonsdale. They are initially understanding: she was old and the task massive. But when they discuss the self-promotion so apparent in the *Memoirs*, they unleash terms like 'shocking ... senile vanity' and 'senile egotism'.[6] Lonsdale also accuses her of plain dishonesty. Those who write from the Burney side of the story see a more complicated picture. Hemlow emphasizes the frustrations of the job, stressing that Burney had first intended simply to publish a collection of letters written to her father, only to discover in 1828 that a law had been passed in 1813 by which letters belonged to their senders and could not be published by their recipients. She had been away in France and had missed the news of this change. This meant that she had to scrap all her previous work and begin again, now under the lash of competition, the danger of: 'causing all the trash that can be trashed to be poured forth upon the Public, if I should take such an unwarrantable liberty as to die before my task was performed' (*JL* 12:704). Hemlow argues that, having burned the majority of her father's papers, Burney needed to fill in the gaps, and did so by including her own memories. Doody combines the views of Burney's father's biographers and her own, arguing that the book was indeed hagiography and also understandably egotistical. She emphasizes Burney's distress at the unpleasant, resentful way her father depicted his relatives in his memoirs, including the people she herself remembered. It seems that Burney did not want to replace her positive memories with his negative ones. She was unnerved by the fact that her father had revealed himself in his manuscript memoirs as rather petty, trivial, and unkind. In her quandary, Burney dropped altogether the idea of providing memoirs, pursuing her ill-fated plan of publishing only letters. When forced back to the original biographical scheme, she justified the fact that she destroyed many of the papers by arguing that she was the chosen executor, that she had observed the way her father had rigorously weeded the manuscripts they had considered together. She asserted that she was simply revising her father into the sort of man she thought he wanted the world to remember. In Doody's scenario, she included herself as his companion, an obedient but also extremely successful daughter (pp. 376–7). Though there may be explanations and excuses, there is certainly no defense for the rampant destruction that Burney, joined eventually by her older sister Esther, committed on her father's papers. As with much Burney criticism, however, the various accounts can be made to agree. Doody's argument successfully attends to both sides of the question. I would emphasize even more forcefully how much of Burney's own life and achievement became a part of this book, and how important it is that Burney wrote as Madame d'Arblay.

To fit the *Memoirs* into Burney's literary life, I must first assess as fully as possible her mental and emotional state when she undertook this task. Burney was one of the foremost writers of her age. She never had attained in public an articulateness which fully reflected her confidence in her achievement, but she hoped and possibly believed that by her writings she had changed the position of women. In *The Wanderer* Juliet Granville cries out to herself: 'How few, ... how circumscribed, are the attainments of women!' (p. 289). By writing about women's difficulties, showing how cruelly the social strictures in eighteenth-century Britain circumscribed them, she wanted to educate and inform her public, and perhaps by informing them to remake them. Her father's great friend Frances Crewe, trying to convince Burney to found a periodical, understood her purpose: 'Miss Burney never shone more than when she made her Cecilia burst from the shackles of common forms at Vauxhall, to save the life of Harrel' (*Memoirs* 3:186). She wanted women to burst their shackles and she wanted other women – and men – to admire them for doing so. Publishing one novel per decade for 40 years, showing how women lived in their shackles and how they burst out, Burney had in each case made greater demands on her audience, male and female. Not everyone could respond. Her father said that he thought *Evelina* was her best book, because 'There are none of those heart-rending scenes which tear one to pieces in the last volumes of Cecilia and Camilla. They always make me melancholy for a week.' (*Memoirs* 3:370) Dr Burney wanted his daughter to write comedy without consequences, and many of his contemporaries shared that desire. Indeed, many twentieth-century critics see Burney as simply a delightful writer. Although the majority and especially the most reputed of critics in the eighteenth and nineteenth centuries judged *Cecilia* to be her best novel, until very recently *Evelina* was the twentieth-century favorite. But Burney herself sought to regenerate her audience by making them suffer. As she eventually saw the situation, in *The Wanderer* she wrote for an audience unready to hear her. At this juncture, any male writer of the period would have written his autobiography. But no woman of Burney's class, or at any rate of the class the Burney family had with difficulty entered, ever published her memoirs during her lifetime.

As a dignified woman born in the mid eighteenth century Burney felt that she could not simply sit down and write her own separate story. Her friend Mrs Delany had never published her autobiography, nor had Hester Thrale – nor, for that matter, had James Boswell. The genre of women's autobiographies tended to fall into two categories, neither of them acceptable to her. There were what Felicity Nussbaum calls the 'scandalous memoirs', often defenses of one's own impeccable conduct, as for example Laetitia Pilkington and Mrs Pennington, both accused by their husbands of adultery. There were also murky and emotionally confused narratives, as in Charlotte Charke's attempt to win her father's respect. At the other end were spiritual autobiographies, dignified books like *Memoirs or Spiritual Exercises of Elizabeth West: written by her own Hand*.[7] But neither type was relevant to Burney. However, she did have one possible model, the autobiographical work published by Laetitia Matilda Hawkins.

Laetitia Hawkins's life remained curiously parallel to Burney's. Besides being daughters of historians of music, copiers of their father's manuscripts, and writers of anonymous and publicly acknowledged fiction, they both wrote a species of memoir.[8] Hawkins took this last step nearly ten years before Burney, publishing four volumes, two with F.C. and J. Rivington in 1822 and two with Longman's in 1824. In the first of these, *Anecdotes, Biographical Sketches, and Memoirs*, though explicitly denying that she had written a biography of her father, Hawkins filled her pages chiefly with descriptions of her father's circle. Despite her demur, one of her main purposes was to defend Hawkins' biography of Johnson, a task she accomplishes as well as she can, although she admits that Boswell is better. Hawkins did not idealize her father, however, though she minimizes his 'greatest faults' as 'some degree of prejudice and stiffness of opinion' (1:220). The second segment, *Memoirs, Anecdotes, Facts, and Opinions*, is as its title indicates an even looser assemblage of observations and experiences. Although claiming that she is ill and not able to write as well as usual, Hawkins occasionally hits a conversational style that rivals Burney's. She is especially deft at devastating portraits: Horace Walpole 'always entered a room ... knees bent, and foot on tiptoe, as if afraid of a wet floor'; Bennet Langton often sat 'with one leg twisted around the other, as if fearing to occupy more space than was equitable', and George Steevens 'was a frigid calculator, a sort of by-stander to his own actions; and in his neighbourhood, as his true character unfolded itself, his attentions to young women were considered not as in themselves seductive, but as a blasting mildew which would injure their estimation'.[9] She filled out some of her space with her brother Henry's works, promoting him as well as her father. Her own story, which appeared consistently but incompletely, was often relegated to footnotes. This hodge-podge, although called 'anecdotage' by Thomas De Quincey, in general achieved kindly notices. *The British Critic* quoted extracts and ended by 'earnestly recommending Miss Hawkins's volumes to the attention of our readers'.[10] If Laetitia Hawkins could publish such a book successfully, why should Burney hesitate? Burney's father had linked their careers, pushing her to publish *Cecilia* in tandem with his *History of Music*. She would now go through all his papers and her own and fashion both of their careers as she wished posterity to know them. She wrote to her sister Esther on 15 February 1828 that the booksellers wanted her to fill out the story from her own memory, so that it would be unique and irreplaceable (*JL* 12:705). She worked on the book so assiduously that her correspondence fell off almost completely for five years.

Burney called her book *Memoirs of Doctor Burney, arranged from his own manuscripts, from family papers, and from personal recollections*. She stipulated her right to this title by frankly signing the book as 'by his daughter, Madame d'Arblay'. She was writing, therefore, in three roles: not only as admiring child, but also as wife of a distinguished Frenchman, and as known author of four novels and a political pamphlet. Another alternative would have been to emphasize more fully her professional life, declaring herself as 'his daughter, author of *Evelina, Cecilia, Camilla*, and *The Wanderer*'. This listing of previous works is the locution she used for her earlier books. However, it is not only as a professional author that she writes these memoirs, but as Madame d'Arblay. The description of Dr Burney's death at the end is introduced as taken from a letter to d'Arblay, although this letter, if it ever existed, has not survived.[11] When Burney wrote her father's memoirs, her brothers and her sister Susanna were already dead. In February of 1832, Esther died. By the time the *Memoirs* were published in November, Charlotte and Frances were the only survivors of the five children born to Charles Burney and Esther Sleepe. The scene of mingled sadness and joy at the end of the *Memoirs* gains greater poignancy when we realize that Burney wrote it more than ten years after her husband, too, had died.

One central anecdote from the *Memoirs* best shows that this book is meant to promote the author, as well as the ostensible subject. In June 1782, just before the publication of *Cecilia*, at a gathering at Sir Joshua Reynolds's house on Richmond Hill, Burney met Edward Gibbon and Edmund Burke, the host and guests together representing three of the most important thinkers of the age. This account appears in her original journal, but here it is much funnier, more acerbic and more worldly-wise. To begin with, her portrait of the historian, just short of 45, is as gleefully unrestrained as the Hawkins descriptions quoted above. Gibbon had published half of his *Decline and Fall of the Roman Empire* by 1782, but when Burney wrote these *Memoirs* he was safely dead:

> Fat and ill-constructed, Mr. Gibbon has cheeks of such prodigious chubbyness, that they envelope [sic] his nose so completely, as to render it, in profile, absolutely invisible. His look and manner are placidly mild, but rather effeminate; his voice, for he was speaking to Sir Joshua at a little distance – is gentle, but of studied precision of accent. Yet, with these Brobdignatious cheeks, his neat little feet are of a miniature description; and with these, as soon as I turned around, he hastily described a quaint sort of circle, with small quick steps, and a dapper gait, as if to mark the alacrity of his approach, and then, stopping short when full face to me, he made so singularly profound a bow, that – though hardly able to keep my gravity – I felt myself blush deeply at its undue, but palpably intended obsequiousness.
> (*Memoirs* 2:224–5)

Although bowing obsequiousness, Gibbon 'spoke not a word' and, indeed, remained quite silent for the entire occasion. Reynolds explained comically that Gibbon was unusually taciturn because 'he's terribly afraid you'll snatch at him for a character in your next book!' (*Memoirs*, 2:239). Here it is perfectly clear that Burney has set the scene chiefly to aggrandize herself. She cuts Gibbon down to size by describing his bodily idiosyncrasies, and then shows that even his mind is curtailed in this company because he is afraid he will pale in the conversational competition with Burke. Perhaps also, by implication, he may fear Burney's talent. In a long, earlier segment on the publication of *Evelina* Burney had displayed the fact that Johnson was one of her greatest admirers. She now shows that these three other eminent intellectuals placed her in the first rank.

The final exchange at Richmond Hill confirms this impression. Burney rhapsodizes at Burke's conversational abilities: 'I felt I had never known before what it was to listen! ... I seemed suddenly organized to a new intellectual existence.' (*Memoirs* 2:231) Though feeling inadequate as a scribe, Burney gave in her 1782 account some instances of Burke's conversation, especially on Cardinal Ximenes (1436–1517), his erudition, authority, humility, openness, and 'enlargement of mind', a mixture of qualities Burke flatteringly claims 'that even the pen of Miss Burney' could not adequately render.[12] Now, 50 years later, she has accepted this challenge, and through the medium of setting down Burke's conversation tries to describe both Ximenes and Burke. Later, on a different subject, Burke delivers the accolade, praising Burney in terms that satisfy her greatest ambitions. Burke claims 'with an air of obsequious gallantry' that 'This is the age for women.' (Memoirs 2:236) Sir Joshua Reynolds asserts that 'when I first came into the world, it was thought but a poor compliment to say a person did a thing like a lady!'... 'But now', Burke interposes, clearly directing his comment to Burney, 'to talk of writing like a lady, is the greatest compliment that need be wished for by a man!' (Memoirs 2:236–7)

Even though Memoirs is ostensibly her father's biography, Burney discusses three of her novels at length, mentions her article on the 'Emigrant Clergy', and refers to a generic tragedy her father suggests she revise. She relegates 50 pages to the publication of Evelina, backing up the need for this account – 'a proud self-defence!' – by telling her readers that in 1826 Sir Walter Scott suggested that she should write the 'real history of Evelina's Entrance into the World' (Memoirs 2:121–2). She mitigates somewhat the effect of this interpolation by including at length her father's responses to the book. Her desire to aggrandize her father and herself, separately as well as together, clearly manifests itself in the fact that she actually separates Cecilia from the publication of her father's second volume of the history of music, even though in fact the two works were deliberately published in tandem. Camilla, published after her marriage, is difficult to insinuate into the narrative. Burney does so mainly by way of the fact that Mrs Crewe, one of her father's best friends, helped with the subscription and brought the book to Burke's attention. And it was Frances Crewe who was so impressed with the political acumen in the 'Emigrant Clergy' that she suggested that Burney found a periodical. Although the first three novels receive due attention, The Wanderer is conspicuously absent. Perhaps Burney felt that its publication just two weeks before her father's death did not sufficiently intertwine it with his life to allow her to mention it. She may not have dared hazard the responses of reviewers to her reviled and forgotten last novel.

Burney attempts throughout to make her own literary life relevant to her father's. When describing the first time she met Burke, she notes more than once that this was also the first time her father had been with Burke in a private house, so that in some sense it was also the first time Dr Burney met Burke. She emphasizes that she and her father took a mutual interest in one another's careers. Whenever she is about to launch on a discussion of her own experiences or literary successes, she takes care to make them as relevant as possible to her father's interests and concerns. She was clearly worried that she would be accused of writing too much about herself, but she could not resist the opportunity. Besides, as Hemlow points out, because she had decided earlier that she would not try to write her father's life, she had destroyed so many of his papers that she did not have enough material to support a book that contained only his story. Looking back over her own professional career, Burney felt confident about her writing abilities. Her ego was extremely strong. But she knew that women needed more outside support than men. Even now, we condone men's self-confidence as an acceptable and just self-estimation. Alexander Pope's way of revising his correspondence, even occasionally changing the addressee, is simply his right as a great author. His biographers may grumble, but they do not criticize. When, a century later, the 22-year-old Henry Adams writes that he 'would like to think that a century or two hence ... my letters might still be read', he piques a twentieth-century historian into saying only that 'He could afford such grandiosity.'[13] Burney knew that because of her sex she was more likely to be accused if not of 'senile vanity', at least of sneaking her own autobiography into a book ostensibly about her father.

Her fears were justified. The *Memoirs* were published on approximately 23 November 1832. Amid a welter of pleasant commentaries elsewhere, the relentless Croker accepted the 'task of reviewing this book' in the *Quarterly Review*, although he could find 'not a word to say in its favour'. Croker's review of *The Wanderer* had been based on an obviously cursory reading. In the case of the *Memoirs*, he turned his remarkable intelligence diligently to his task and combed the book carefully to support five main points. (1) One of Croker's chief objections is that 'Madame d'Arblay ... conceals from her readers, and perhaps from herself, that it is her own *Memoirs*, and *not* those of her father that she has been writing.'[14] Croker also argues that: (2) Dr Burney had intended that his twelve notebooks of memoirs be published without editing – or at any rate with light editing (Burney argues otherwise); (3) Burney's contention that her father's style had deteriorated was untrue (in fact, argues Croker, her own style had deteriorated); (4) Burney had imposed her own view of her stepmother instead of her father's; and she had (5) suppressed dates in order to make it seem that she had composed *Evelina* at the age of seventeen.[15] Croker's crucial over-all comment is that Burney had imported to biography the 'habit of *novel-writing*'. By applying its techniques to her 'anecdotes' she supplies 'sonorous epithets and factitious details, which, however, we venture to assure her, not only blunt their effect, but discredit their authority' (p. 125).

Croker was essentially right that *Memoirs of Doctor Burney* was not a good biography of the musicologist Croker had admired as 'this amiable man' (p. 99). Whenever Burney begins to discuss her father, she chooses her most exalted and periphrastic style, muffling Dr Burney in trailing clauses of glory. At times the tone is almost Biblical: 'And the whole of his generation in all its branches, children, grand-children, and great-grand-children, all studied, with proud affection, to cherish the much-loved trunk whence they sprang; and to which they, and all their successors, must ever look up as to the honoured chief of their race.' (*Memoirs* 3:411) Because she wants to show him in the company of the great, the book is continually deflected into descriptions of famous people. The form is like Laetitia Hawkins's, but in the context of Burney's book this kind of anecdotage diverts the purpose of the work.

A different organization was easily available. One of the most appealing passages in the book, for instance, is Dr Burney's description of intimate Burney life: 'We were as merry, and laughed as bonnily as the Burneys always do when they get together, and open their hearts, and tell old stories, and have no fear of being quizzed by interlopers.' (*Memoirs* 3:283) As quoted, however, this fragment simply stands by itself, out of context. Burney could have written about her father both within his family and in public life, moving back and forth between them, showing the merry, bonny side of Burney family life, and setting her father's achievements in a double matrix. As anyone who has written about the Burneys knows, however, this is a tall order. There are so many Burneys that to introduce them and keep them straight in the reader's mind is a daunting task. Instead, Burney barely mentions her siblings. Sarah Harriet, her half-sister who lived with her father during his last years, simply vanishes from the picture as a caring daughter, although Burney does mention her publications. Burney briefly summarizes the careers of her siblings, but with the exception of a thumbnail sketch of her mother, a moving and prolonged account of her sister Susanna's death, and a tender evocation of d'Arblay, she emphasizes only her father and herself.

I believe that the chief reason why Burney destroyed so many of her father's papers was her frustration at the need to cull them instead of attending to her own manuscripts. She lacked the eyesight and energy to read the undigested mass he gave her, and she feared that somewhere in the welter of documents there might be secrets they both would have preferred effaced. The need to hide secrets may also account for the absence of dates in the early years. When Burney and her elder sister Esther burned manuscripts together, their likely motive was to suppress the fact that Esther was born before their parents were married. One secret Burney refused to hide was her active dislike of her stepmother. She would whitewash her father, but at the 'Lady' she drew the line.

When Burney finished the *Memoirs* in 1832, she immediately wrote to her nephew Charles Parr Burney, addressing him in the tones she had once used for his father:

> My dear Carlos –
>   This instant
> Friday 2 o'clock, 27th July –
> I am liberated –

She wanted her nephew to take her 'in custody' by visiting, and to help her in her negotiations with her publisher, Edward Moxon (*JL* 12:758–9). But for some reason her brother Charles's son did not play this role. In the end, Burney's charming, well-connected, and obliging friend the Rev. Mr Harness apparently was an intermediary with Moxon. Burney was strong in her relationships with publishers, but evidently she was never able to do all the negotiating by herself. When Moxon asked if Burney would approve the price of £1 16s 0d, instead of £1 11s 6d (*JL* 12:765, n. 1), she went for the lower amount, perhaps fearing that the higher price would cut into her sales, as had been the case with *The Wanderer*. Except for this letter about price, all the other papers regarding the negotiations with Moxon have vanished (*JL* 12:755, n. 1). Unfortunately, like his predecessors, Moxon was slow about paying, but Burney by evidence of her increased investments may have made £1000 from the *Memoirs* over the three years from 1832 to 1835.[16] Though all of the reviews complained about the occasionally turgid style, most were positive. One review in particular praised the characterizations, saying that there is no description 'of greater vivacity & strength than those contained in these volumes' concerning Garrick, Johnson, James Bruce (who discovered the source of the Blue Nile), Mrs Thrale, Burke, Gibbon, and Reynolds (*JL* 12:765, n. 1).

Relieved at last from the burden of reliving her own life through her father's, one of Burney's first tasks was to mollify her close relatives. Her nephew the Rev. Richard Allen Burney, Esther's son, had never told his wife that his grandmother came from humble origins, and wanted this fact deleted from the book. Burney argued that truth is better than speculation. Writing to Richard's aunt Rebecca Sandford, who lived with Richard and who had once played Cleora to her Huncamunca, Burney said to tell him this decision and to '*offer no apology!*'. Yet she also made clear her own recognition that in publishing the book she was exposing the family and uncovering herself to a degree she thought dangerous. She had planned, she says, 'a posthumous production' (*JL* 12:764). But Alex and Charles Parr Burney insisted, along with practically all the other remaining men in the family, that she publish the book while she could answer for it. Only she knew the material well enough to clarify and parry. In 1833, she wrote to her step-brother Rev. Stephen Allen to elucidate details about the amount of money his mother had brought into the marriage with Dr Burney. In this letter she strains her tact to say that she has fairly presented her step-mother Elizabeth Allen Burney, whereas in fact her dislike is everywhere apparent. Her guilt speaks, though, because she offers to change one of her phrases for him in the second edition. But in spite of the positive reviews and the widespread interest, the book never reached a second edition. Perhaps Moxon, like some of his predecessors, had printed a large first edition.

Though Burney had successfully ignored Croker's article on *The Wanderer*, she was so distressed at his review of the *Memoirs*, especially his accusation of embellishment and factitiousness, that she hoped someone would reply. She feared that this attack would snowball, engulfing her reputation. Even more important, she wanted it to be shown that she had done what her father desired. Her son Alex shared her reaction. He was so incensed that she gathered for him 'all the documents in my Fathers letters'.[17] Alex, and Burney's nieces Frances Raper (Susanna's daughter) and Charlotte Barrett (Esther's daughter), drafted a 'Retort', but they never published it, perhaps fearing that they were not equal to a contest with Croker.

Croker also accuses Burney of embroidering her tale, of writing fiction.[18] In suggesting that Burney might frankly have written her auto-biography and that she uses the techniques of fiction in her biography, Croker is judging a woman born in 1752 by the laws of a man born nearly 30 years later. When Burney first began to publish, the lines between fact and invention or imagination were much less fixed than they were in the 1830s. In the 1730s, for more than two and a half years, Samuel Johnson had written the parliamentary debates and published them in *The Gentleman's Magazine*, though he had only once actually been in the gallery of the House of Commons.[19] No one in Parliament complained. This was not a unique case. The practice of intermingling the invented and the factual continued. Burney's friend Mary Delany gave Greek names to some of the characters in her autobiography, and her tale though unpublished appeared in veiled form in Sarah Scott's *Millenium Hall* (1762). In the eighteenth century, as Lennard Davis has made clear, the separation between news and novel, fact and fiction, was a permeable partition.[20] 'What Novel's this?' says Wisemore in Fielding's *Love in Several Masques* (1728), upon hearing the details of a complicated maneuver in letter-switching.[21] Lady Vane's actual memoirs appeared in the middle of Tobias Smollett's *Peregrine Pickle* (1751). In novel after novel, authors claimed simply to be editors of found autobiographical manuscripts. This fluidity of discourse is reflected in Burney's memoir of her father, especially in her way of heightening scenes with detail. By the time Croker was writing his review, the scientific method had permeated more of private life and the partition between fact and invention was stronger. Burney herself remained a palimpsest or a miscellany of these incompatible attitudes. In theory she was as concerned about her veracity as Croker was, but in practice she retained her eighteenth-century habits of heightening the picture. She was full of edges; she had herself become a medley.

Therefore, in a study of Frances Burney's literary life the most pertinent approach to the *Memoirs of Doctor Burney* is to see it both as autobiographical and as a species of fiction. Burney knew that she was writing her own life. This fact embarrassed her sufficiently so that she briefly fell into periphrasis whenever she felt that she had strayed too far from her father's concerns. Croker lists her many embarrassed 'circumlocutions', such as 'this memorialist', 'the present editor', 'the Doctor's second daughter', and even more complicated writhings (p. 107). On the other hand, most of her book is vivid and straightforward, especially the scenes where she is the central narrator.

Large sections of the *Memoirs* are wordy, circumlocutory, by turns egotistical and self-abasing. Yet the book contains some of Burney's best portraits, the oddly mixed characters she so enjoyed portraying, the mules. Gibbon is one of these mules. And there is, for instance, James Boswell.

The description of Boswell in the *Memoirs* is not the only word-portrait of Boswell written by a Burney. When Burney's younger sister

Charlotte was 20 and the still-young Boswell was twice her age, she remarked on first meeting him that he was a 'sweet creature', and that she enjoyed flirting with him, especially because she knew he was 'safely married'. Charlotte's Boswell 'idolizes Dr Johnson, and struts about, and puts himself into such ridiculous postures that he is as good as a comedy'.[22] Burney herself, who had refused to hand over to Boswell her letters from Dr Johnson, remarked in 1792 that she was angry at the way Boswell had indicated in his biography so many of Johnson's weaknesses and prejudices, diminishing 'the first and greatest good man of these times'. And yet Boswell, when she saw him at a breakfast party, 'soon insensibly conquered, though he did not soften me'. Boswell changed 'my resentment against his treachery into something like commiseration of his levity'. This encounter roused in Burney the ability we have seen to recognize complexity, to judge, yet also to respond. 'There is no resisting great good humour', she concludes, 'be what will in the opposite scale' (JL 1:181–2).

Both Burney opinions appear in Frank Brady's biography of Boswell, but he entirely ignores the *Memoirs*. This is unfortunate, because Burney's last recreation of Boswell is incisively sculpted, self-serving, winning, requiring a complex response similar to the one she outlined in 1792. She frames her Boswell segment by having Dr Johnson compliment herself – wishing that she would not go home with her father: 'Sir! I would have her Always come ... and Never go! –' (*Memoirs* 2:190, Burney's ellipsis) First, she describes Boswell's body. Her point is that his appearance imitates Johnson's, not in mockery, but from an overflux of reverence. Boswell affects a solemn air, slouches, wears a scatty wig and clothes too big for him – all in insouciant imitation of his idol. Like Johnson, but without Johnson's excuse of St Vitus' dance, he too is always in motion. Burney's father wonders that Johnson does not notice this mimicry. When their host insists that Burney sit next to Johnson, Boswell sits just behind and between them both. In this situation, when Johnson talked, Boswell's 'eyes goggled with eagerness; he leant his ear almost on the shoulder of the Doctor; and his mouth dropt open to catch every syllable that might be uttered: nay, he seemed not only to dread losing a word, but to be anxious not to miss a breathing; as if hoping from it, latently, or mystically, some information' (*Memoirs* 2:194). Johnson appreciates Boswell's affection, but in this case he makes fun of him. Startled to find Boswell seated within inches of his back, he commands him to the table, and then orders him not to leave the table – lest he be mistaken for a Branghton. Boswell's discomfiture is palpable. To top it all off, he has never heard of the Branghtons, Burney's vulgar family in *Evelina*. Someone takes him aside to tell him, and before he comes back Burney has glided upstairs. This has been seen as sheer envy, self-aggrandizement. It is certainly that, but it is also something else, a perfectly believable, somewhat acrid description of the assiduous hero-worship that made *The Life of Johnson* possible. This is Macaulay's Boswell, 'one of the smallest men that ever lived'.[23]

As Laetitia-Matilda Hawkins had done, Burney described people in memorable phrases, though Burney's differed from Hawkins's in their characteristic, irreducible complexity. Her father's friend, her godmother Frances Greville, long-suffering wife of Dr Burney's flamboyant patron Fulke Greville, was kind-hearted, but rather forbidding. In old age she unnerved people by 'lounging completely at her ease, in such curves as she found most commodious, with her head alone upright; and her eyes commonly fixed'.[24] Frances Brooke, the novelist and playwright who once asked Burney to join her in a periodical venture, 'had much to combat in order to receive the justice due to her from the world; for nature had not been more kind in her mental, than hard in her corporeal gifts. She was short, broad, crooked, ill-featured, and ill-favoured; and she had a cast of the eye that made it seem looking every way rather than that which she meant for its direction.' (*Memoirs* 1:334–5) Though in 1775 Burney had archly called this set of difficulties 'the art of shewing Agreeable Ugliness' (*EJL* 2:4), she had shifted 60 years later from the position as audience to an identification with the sufferer. Catherine Read (1732–78), the painter, 'who, in crayons, had a grace and a softness of colouring rarely surpassed', was in person 'awkward and full of mischances in every motion' (*Memoirs* 1:335). This portrait is more generous, though one might also say more genteel, than her 1775 description of Miss Read, which includes her dress, 'more soiled than if she had been Embraced by a chimney sweeper' (*EJL* 2:70–1). The word 'mischances' is a brilliant stroke, carrying a sense of her awkwardness with indications that her personal misfortunes in part account for her ungainly behavior.

Dr Burney himself, on the whole, is not granted the complexity of personality a mixed character requires. Rather, Burney treats him very gently and with unstinting admiration. He is unfailingly agreeable. When Reynolds' sister Frances wanted to paint his portrait, in spite of the fact that he was extremely busy, he 'had too natively the spirit of the old school, to suffer No! and a lady, to pair off together' (*Memoirs* 1:333). This unwavering esteem is a hindrance to analysis when Burney discusses the famous people her father knew. Although her vivid portrayal of Garrick has delighted most of his biographers, George Stone and George Kahrl complain that she had 'very little insight into the relations of the two men'. Even in her best vignette, they claim, she notes only that Garrick was entertaining. That vignette is certainly one of her best pieces of writing, tripled in size from the incident as first written in her journal at the age of 22.[25] Garrick tended to drop in on the Burneys, catching them sleeping late, or just in the midst of breakfast. On this early-morning occasion, after startling the house maid and resisting her attempts to announce him, the 58-year-old Garrick burst in on his friends. A hairdresser was in the midst of applying pomatum and powder to Dr Burney's thick curls, while his daughters read him the newspaper, made his tea, and straightened his books. Garrick made himself at ease in the clutter, and gradually transformed himself into an insignificant, envious blockhead, staring unremittingly at the 'scared and confounded' hairdresser. Just as this specialist was about to make his escape, Garrick took off his unsightly scratch wig and suddenly squeaked out, '"Pray now, Sir, do you think, Sir, you could touch me up this here old bob a little bit, Sir?"' (*Memoirs* 1:348). At this the hairdresser caught the joke and left the room bursting with laughter. As the conversation required, Garrick became by turns an auctioneer, Samuel Johnson, a trumpeter announcing the *History of Music*, and four or five other characters, seemingly growing larger and smaller as he shifted personalities.

Another occasion shows even more fully how closely Garrick knew the Burneys. This time, Dr Burney is about to introduce Garrick to his old friend and literary abettor Thomas Twining, when the footman suddenly announces their mutual enemy Sir Jeremy Hillsborough. When Sir Jeremy immediately slouches into the room, they realize that he has heard their shocked attempts to deny him. He is authoritatively silent, sitting 'in an armchair near the fire; filling it broadly, with an air of domineering authority'. The silence is so profound that they wonder if Sir Jeremy is in his right mind:

The pause that ensued was embarrassing, and not quite free from alarm; when the intruder, after an extraordinary nod or two, of a palpably threatening nature, suddenly started up, threw off his slouched hat and old rocolo, flung his red silk handkerchief into the ashes, and displayed to view, lustrous with vivacity, the gay features, the sparkling eyes, and laughing countenance of Garrick, – the inimitable imitator, David Garrick.   (*Memoirs* 1:356–7)

The whole family claps, as if at the theater, and Garrick remarks that introductions are always difficult, and that he had adopted this 'method of skipping at once, by some sleight of hand, into abrupt cordiality'. Stone and Kahrl omit this incident, but it indicates that Burney was more aware of the relationship between Garrick and her father than they allow. Daughters in their 20s as a rule do not fully understand their parents' intimacies, and even when children are in their 70s, they are notoriously opaque about their parents. But this is a significant encounter, as Burney was aware, because she masked the true facts. Lonsdale has pointed out that the initials of Sir Jeremy are J.H., and that there is a scrap left in the Berg collection that says in Dr Burney's handwriting: 'Garrick sending in the Name of Sr Jno Hawkins – when Twin^g & I were making remarks on his hist^y.' Burney has omitted in her *Memoirs* the rivalry over Sir John Hawkins's musical *History*, so persistent a conflict that it required a chapter in Lonsdale. Perhaps Burney regarded this rivalry as beneath her father. Besides, there was no reason to cause needless pain to Laetitia-Matilda Hawkins, who would be sure to read this book so like her own.

Memoirs of Doctor Burney does not enhance its author's reputation. In spite of its vivid scenes and its important sketches of Gibbon, Boswell, Garrick, and others, the book suffers from the author's guilt. She does not want to admit to her audience and even to herself how ambivalent she feels toward her father, how desperately she wants to explain her career. Looking back over her 80 years, she longs to set the record straight in a public forum, but custom forbids her. It is not decorous to tell the stories of the merry and not-so-merry Burneys, to let the interlopers know their secrets. Nor can she write a bildungsroman and keep her reputation for delicacy. The clang of motive and counter-motive resounds in this unusual and valuable book. Burney can still write with the same power and intricacy, but for the first time she is really afraid of the reviews. Her courage is not sufficient to the task, her frankness not adequate for the mixed genre she invents, her health and spirits too unpredictable. She had seven years left. In her last years, Burney did not neglect her literary life.

10
Fiction and Truth: All the Unpublished Words

> *scene* 'To tell you the truth' beginning –
> I hate the Truth of all things –
> – There's nothing so unpleasant ... It's only a way to take a liberty – Just a method to say something nobody can bear to hear.
> — Frances Burney, Berg, Fragments, Folder 3

Now that the *Memoirs* were at last published, Burney was able to return to her own papers. She had been sifting through them since her husband's death. Finished with fiction, she turned to fact. She was not the character she envisioned in a fragmentary note, who thought the truth was too unpleasant, 'a method to say something nobody can bear to hear'. But she did imagine this character, and she knew from her stepmother's hectoring that brandished truths can hurt. In an era when many people burned their personal papers, Burney destroyed some, but carefully organized others. A few of her editors and commentators – most notably Hemlow and George G. Falle – emphasize that she was putting together these papers for her son's 'Fire-Side Rectory'.[1] They stress the fact that much of this work was meant for her dream grandchildren. Burney was also sustained by the thought that by writing about d'Arblay she still kept in touch, re-lived their days together, their superb friendship. When d'Arblay died he asked her specifically to talk about him, to write about him, especially for Alex. 'Parles de moi – Parles!', he had said, ' – Parles à Alex – ! qu'il ne m'oubliè pas! – ' And she had replied, 'Je ne parlerai pas d'autre chose! – Helas! – *nous* ne parlerons pas d'autre chose! – mon ami! – mon ami! – je ne vivrai que pour cela!' (Egerton 3696, f. 97, n. 10). They would talk about nothing else. She would live for nothing else.

To this end she recreated their experiences in France, including the scenes on the seashore at Dunkirk when she was returning illegally to England at the age of 60, the encounter with the Spanish prisoners, the near disaster over the manuscript of *The Wanderer*. It was in the Dunkirk narrative that she referred to 'the Fire-Side Rectory'. But Burney's family was not her only audience. She also knew that her papers were important to her reputation, that her journals and letters were a work of art on the side of truth. This life-writing was in many ways a more limited medium than fiction, but a medium she had practiced all her life, with pleasure. Doody has called the relationship of the diaries and letters and the creative pieces 'the life in the works'; Katharine Rogers makes the distinction between 'the private self and the published self'.[2] Certainly Burney used her life in her works, as all authors must. We recognize Dr Burney in the passionate, idealized, and yet destructive fathers. We see Burney's sister Susanna in *The Wanderer*, divided between Juliet's idealized half-sister Lady Aurora Granville and her friend Gabriella. But much remains that never found its way into the fiction. Is this segment the private self, as Rogers calls it? Burney's family considered her particularly truthful, but there are certain kinds of truth she never talked about. Some of her contemporaries were more open, though perhaps not more truthful. Thrale left in her *Family Book* details that Burney would probably have erased, such as her husband's infatuation for Sophia Streatfield. Boswell seemed compelled to uncover all his weaknesses, and tried to erase only the section where he mistreated his dog Jachone, beating him, hanging him briefly from trees, and starving him to keep him from running away. Boswell's subject was himself. Burney's subject was also herself, but she was nearly always part of a dialogue, if not with family and friends, then with 'Nobody'. All three of these journal-writers loved to create a character and tell a story, and they did not hesitate to impose story on life. What is left is in multiple ways part of the literary life, though it must be called the unpublished, not the private, self. The private self remains always untouchable, too difficult to record, beyond words.

Now that Burney was in her 70s, a more strict editor than Thrale or Boswell, more cautious about hurting other people, she decided that she had to relinquish some of her favorite manuscripts. She had carried all of Susanna's papers everywhere, leaving them behind only when she fled Paris during Napoleon's hundred days. But rereading them in 1723, she wrote to her older sister, 'how few dare I keep from the flames! for the very charm of their unbounded their fearless openness, which gave them their principal delight, has cast around them dangers & risks that, should they fall into any hands not immediately our own, might make them parents to mischief, rancour, & ill will incalculable!' (*JL* 11:424). We can scarcely imagine what it must have cost her to lose these last remnants of her adored Susanna.

With an eye to family and posterity, she devised a system of marking her journals and letters. She made plus-signs, sometimes upright, sometimes tipped, and encrusted them with dots or encased them in circles. For these marks, she provided a key, indicating that the circled material was perhaps more private than the rest, and, conversely, that some of the papers had more general interest. She scrupulously preserved the materials she cherished. If the ink had faded, she sometimes retraced it. She also made a 'Register' of the letters in her archives, indicating how she had organized them. For what she called her 'Juvenile Journals', the roster she made of characters is frustrating, because many of those listed are missing from the surviving texts. In the letters and journals themselves, she overscored in heavy black ink passages she wanted to obliterate. Luckily, her modern editors have been able to recover the majority of this material, though there are many instances where pieces are simply cut away. When Burney reread a particular letter or journal, she would often comment at the top, as when she described her journal to Nobody as a 'strange medley of Thoughts & Facts'. On the outside of that notebook, many of whose leaves are obviously cut away, she wrote, 'Curtailed and erased of what might be mischievous, from Friendly or – Family considerations'.[3] The medley message is for posterity, to record Burney's own musings on herself, and put her journal in the proper perspective. The other is a mediating statement, also for posterity, explaining why so much is gone.

Burney's editors have emphasized that she organized her papers for her family, but besides the fireside rectory, she had many different agendas in mind. Often in her annotations the older Burney tries to fix the attitude of the reader and fill in a detail a biographer might need. For instance, an early letter is marked 'Mr Barlow and marriage', soon followed by 'Mr Barlow & rejection' (*EJL* 2:125, 15 May 1775; *EJL* 2:137, 2 June 1775). On top of a letter d'Arblay sent her dated 27 March 1815, she writes, 'This Letter was brought to me ... bearing me the first News of the safety – nay, existence, of the most beloved of Husbands, after Ten Days utter ignorance of his destiny.' (*JL* 8:62) She is also concerned about her own professional history, and she helps her biographer. In a box at the top of a letter to Thomas Lowndes, she writes 'No. 5', and in another box, 'N.B. This was the hand Writing in which F.B. copied all Evelina to have her own unseen' (*EJL* 2:217, and facsimile, p. 218).

Sometimes the directives are meant for a historian, summarizing information like 'Just before Waterloo' (*JL* 8:211). Or, at an earlier period, 'Delightful Early intercourse with Dr. Johnson and Mrs. Thrale. March 1779' (*EJL* 3:255, to Samuel Crisp). Her own reputation is occasionally at stake. She shows that she understands how naive she was when she first published *Evelina*: 'rapturous. & most innocent happiness during anonymous success' (Letter to Susanna, 5 July 1778, *EJL* 3:34), and 'a very *young* Letter of honest buoyancy of delight at wholly unthought of *Success*' (*EJL* 3:44, to Susanna 6–8 July 1778). Is this disingenuous? Probably not; there was no precedent for the success of *Evelina*, and no one could have predicted it. Sometimes the annotations are generally personal. She says at the top of a letter by d'Arblay, 'To be kept forever by my Family. F. d'Ay' (*JL* 8:55). At times, indeed, as Hemlow and Falle have stressed, the notes are purely personal, meant for the individual whom she imagines rummaging through her papers after her death. On the top of a letter from her half-sister Sarah Harriet written on d'Arblay's death, she writes, 'a most kindly appropriate Letter from my dear Sarah on my Heart's dechermont'. The letter itself expresses Sarah's worry that her attempt at consolation may pain her sister even more, and the message dispels that concern (*Letters*, p. 212). Thinking that Alexander will survive her, she addresses him at the beginning of a section of a journal written eight years after the fact, 'And Now, my dear Alexander will be glad, I should think, of a narrative of my residence at Brussels' (*JL* 8:392).

Again and again, as Burney re-read and arranged her papers, she thought of her readers, Alex and his family. But in spite of all this care and anticipation, Alex never did rummage through her papers, never did become a paterfamilias in his fireside rectory. He did not survive his mother. The history of the d'Arblays' child, and especially Burney's relationship to Alex, is an important segment of Burney's literary life, revealing in many ways how Burney closely intermingled writing and daily experience. Language and Alexander are inextricably mixed. Born to parents who married late, a winsome and intelligent child, Alexander d'Arblay instantly became in their grandiose and self-mocking phrase the 'Idol of the World' (*JL* 3:135). Even when very young, initiated by his parents, he obviously cared about language. Burney's niece Marianne Francis recalled that 'when he was quite a baby he called his nurse a *Fool* one day. "My dear," said his Mama, "you must never call your nurse a Fool". "Who may I call Fool, then?" "Nobody, my little boy". *"Why, then, what's the word made for?"* said Alex, sharp enough'.[4] A large part of Alex's early education was studying what words are made for. His mother taught him early – and we presume taught him often – the friction between truth and paradox. He began as soon as possible to write in notebooks, which his mother scrupulously saved and organized in her 87th year as 'My Alex's Sacred MSS'.[5]

In these sacred manuscripts, Alex's ambition is clear, but so too is his lassitude. The manuscripts are numerous, including a many-chaptered 'Voyage' to France; transcriptions of the letters Alex exchanged with his friend Adrienne de Chavagnac; a history of France; and a notebook of dramatic works. All this he wrote between the ages of eight and 13. But the voyage, written in a large and unformed hand, where the central issue is that he loves his parents, peters out on page six. His copy of the letters exchanged with Adrienne, where one word will frequently take up a whole line, breaks off in mid-sentence. His scrupulously neat and illustrated 'Abregé de l'histoire de la France', with nearly every paragraph in a different handwriting, ends in a scrawl around the year 825. His tragedy and comedy never got beyond the preface and a statement about how long they would be. His history he says was his parents' idea. In the midst of an account of Charlemagne's son, Louis le Débonaire, he writes his own name, and adds in the third person about himself, 'J'avoue quil es indigne de ses chers et excellens parens' – he is unworthy of his dear and excellent parents. The pressure must have been overwhelming (Egerton MS 3701D, 3701E).

In his competition with his parents Alexander only rarely met their expectations. He studied intermittently, and when he did study he was clearly an outstanding student, but he could not stay the course. He was also unlucky. Though he loved mathematics, the subject was taught so differently in France and England that he foundered. When at last after a heroic bout of study he won a scholarship at Cambridge, he did momentarily feel the twang of ambition. But he instantly worried that his father would press him toward even higher ambition. When he was nearly sent down from Cambridge, his concerned father suggested to his mother an arranged marriage or a military career in France. Burney resisted the French alternative, and pushed successfully for England and academic perseverance. The dying d'Arblay warned Burney that she must help her son through his 20s. She thought he was charming and could make his own way: 'Il n'a pas besoin – il plait beaucoup'. She must watch him, d'Arblay replied – 'il faut le *voir* dans le merde, pour savoir par où il a besoin d'une amie' – she had to see him in the shit in order to know where he needed a friend. (Egerton MS 3696, f. 92) The aged Mme d'Arblay left the word 'merde' for posterity to find, though her English rendering of this exchange is of course more tepid.

She did watch over Alex, treating him to an expensive bookcase as late as 1820. Eventually, without much enthusiasm on his part, he was ordained. He found a living, lost it, found another. Because he still cared about language and trusted in its power, he published two of his sermons. One, on the death of William IV, incidentally attacks Court toadies, a breed Alex must have met often in his mother's conversation. The other is a eulogy of William Wilberforce, whose triumph in the anti-slavery movement he celebrates. It was thinking about what words were for that led him, when writing about Wilberforce, to end with a peroration evoking 'that glorious day when England, foremost in arts and arms, shall be foremost also in sending through the world the bright lesson of humanity, and shall say to the bondsman and to the slave, *Thou art free to depart in peace!*'.[6] Like his mother, like all the Burneys, Alexander d'Arblay believed that words can change people.

Like his mother, he also occasionally succumbed to the vice of over-writing, and this was sometimes a difficulty with his congregation. When in 1815 he saw Camilla Cottage, about to be lost forever, he wrote so fulsomely to his parents that Burney criticized his prose, telling him in no uncertain terms that his 'expressions upon its view lose much of their effect by being over strained, *recherchée* & *designing* to be pathetic'. Quite unsparing, she generalized her comment to ensure its effect: 'I remember you once wrote me a Letter so very fine from Cambridge, that if it had not made me laugh, it would certainly have made me sick.' (*JL* 8:114) How often, we wonder, did the loved Alexander, knowing that writing is the most important thing, have to wince under criticism as harsh as this?

Occasionally as an adult Alex would vanish for days at a time. Burney worried frantically. On 20 October 1834 she cautioned her nearly 40-year-old son: 'O be careful for *watch* is the word! Let nothing *strange occur.*' (*JL* 12:842) In desperation at not hearing from him, she would write to his verger to find out if he had returned. Alex's 'greatest defect', she wrote to her nephew Charles Parr Burney, was 'an absence of mind that nearly amounts to impassivity' (*JL* 12:894). But Alex's depression was more profound than 'impassivity', and in a wild undated letter he himself wrote of his 'deep, deep gloom', how difficult it was to leave his bed, how he almost wished to die. His mother, he continues, is both his critic and his savior:

> O my dear dear Mammy how – beautiful your patience your forbearance has been – How unworthy I feel of it – how it cuts me to the Soul
>   Why have I fled from you who alone can even attempt to console me – O it is a madness – a delirium without a name – (*JL* 12:885, n. 2)

When in the darkness of January 1837 he lay dying of influenza, by his 'express wish' she did not go to his bedside (*JL* 12:912, n. 1).

Why did Alexander d'Arblay not allow his mother to see him when he was dying? Doody speculates that 'perhaps he feared that his officious "Flapper" would work too successfully at keeping him alive' (p. 380). Perhaps remembering his father's and grandfather's deaths he felt he was not equal to the occasion. Just 42, he was possibly too young to realize that, no matter what the torment, those who love you must have the chance to say goodbye. For Burney, of course, this lack of closure meant even greater agony. Yet she remembered Alex only with tenderness. She had not known he was dying: 'I had no premonition – nor even a *thought* had crossed my mind that he would go first!' (*JL* 12:948). She found out about his last days from her servant Rowena Mills, who had attended Alex. He had prepared himself for death, but appeared also to pray for recovery, and his 'every *agitation*' was for his mother; he wept every time he mentioned her. If the mere thought of his mother brought Alex to tears, it is understandable that he felt he could not endure her physical presence. Burney's sister Charlotte attempted to reconcile her to his loss by arguing that he was such an innocent, so incapable of coping with the world, that it was better that he had died before her. Without her 'he was no match for the world' (*JL* 12:921, n. 1). Burney found comfort in this thought. Although it is doubtful that Alex could have supported the dailiness of marriage, his fiancée Mary Anne Smith remained loyal. She moved in with the bereft woman who would have been her mother-in-law, and in November 1838 Burney was declaring, 'My very amiable Miss S *keeps me alive!*' (*JL* 12:959).

Burney used one of Alex's scantily filled yearbooks as her own diary, the better to dwell on her memory of him. Though a cataract cloaked one of her eyes, and the other was peripatetic at best, she went through all his papers. She found that he had often acted on her behalf, and at times protected her. When her sister Esther's son, the

Reverend Richard Allen Burney, had written from Brightwell urging that Alex should influence his mother to destroy the memoirs of Dr Burney, he never showed his mother his reply justifying her work. When she found the letter on 5 May 1838, more than a year after Alex's death, she annotated it top and bottom, as a 'noble & tender though concealed & unshewn Defence of his mother'.[7] She rediscovered poignantly the plan to reply to Croker. As a mother Burney undoubtedly loved too much. But her son, although trying at times to escape the weight of his parents' expectations for him, always returned their love, massively and variously. Enthusiastically, in the Burney mode, he saved all his own manuscripts and every scrap of memory that might be important to the family.

As she continued to sift through her own collection of papers, Burney almost lost heart. She was old and tired. She could barely see. Burning manuscripts was so much easier than evaluating them! She wrote for help to the two Charlottes, her sister and niece. Her sister Charlotte herself had complained that even though she had never been a 'woman of letters', she had nonetheless become a 'woman of litters', her old manuscripts mixing disastrously with her current bills.[8] Burney could not maintain her sister's lightheartedness:

> Were *they* disposed of – those myriads of hoards of MSS. I might enjoy a more tranquil resignation I might think of my Alex without that perturbation that makes the *thought* of Him so tragic! because it is with abrupt recollection, that brings him with some affecting incident to my sight – AND – from his living with me his whole life, every paper – every chattel I possess speaks of him. I would fain make him my theme – yet without this agony. Make it with a serenity that should only brighten remnant life by its prospect – not its inflexible regret – ! – (JL 12:954)

By losing Alex, she had lost her joy in the past. She wanted only to dwell with death and the impossible dream of reunion.

The younger Charlotte replied first, fearing that if Burney were to destroy her manuscripts, regret would immediately supplant relief. She suggested that Burney seal up the manuscripts and designate them for some trustworthy person to go through after her death, to publish or not to publish, as this trustworthy person might decide. Nearly three weeks later, Burney's sister answered in a different vein. The elder Charlotte argued that Burney could not simply burn all or burn none. 'So celebrated as your name is', Charlotte Broome wrote, 'it strikes me, that, *sooner*, or *later*' after everyone has died, someone will simply send all the manuscripts to a publisher. The only safe course was to burn any letter that Burney really did not want posterity to see (*JL* 12:954, n. 3). This reaffirmed Burney's sense of the worth of the enterprise, and she continued to sort her manuscripts, burning some, until 'My eyes will work at them no more!' (Berg, Memorandum Books, in Hemlow, p. 486). Her sister visited her one last time, and then in September 1838 Charlotte Broome died, 'that last original tie to native original affections', leaving Burney yet again bereft, with her amiable Miss Smith just barely keeping her alive (*JL* 12:963).

In her last 16 months of life, amid the shards of her family, Burney prepared for death. Her sight failing, her health random, she continued to try to set the record straight, to monitor her own reputation as a writer and a person. She asked the remaining Charlotte, her niece, if she would '*like*' to be her 'Executrix' (*JL* 12:960). She wanted to be sure that she was leaving her manuscripts to someone who would enjoy having them. Always helpful to other writers in the family, she advised Sarah Harriet Burney to look for the epigraphs for her novel *The Romance of Private Life* in Johnson's *Dictionary*, and Sarah Harriet acted on her advice. Once more, Burney rewrote her will. Now, her life began to replicate her fiction, her great nightmare of the iron pen of death. In March 1839, when she turned over a sheet of a letter she was writing to Charlotte Barrett, she was suddenly unable to continue – 'an incapable unwillingness seized my pen' (*JL* 12:964). Because of what Barrett was to call 'Spectral illusions', she could not sleep (*DL* 6:416). Still, some words needed to be said. She forced herself to write a few more letters. She explained that she had abandoned her black mourning clothes, because she did not want anyone to 'suppose a moment I mourned for my Second Alex more than for my first' (*JL* 12:966). D'Arblay alone 'stood as equal Companion' (*JL* 12:966). For reasons that are unclear, she moved to new apartments, though she was stunned with regret at losing the rooms where Alex had been such a frequent presence.

Her last letter, written six months before her death, her niece docketed as a 'defence of her veracity' (*JL* 12:966). Barrett had roused her by sending her praising words about the *Memoirs* from a Dr Jones, and she re-read a letter she had received from the Bishop of Limerick, which said that he had gained graphic knowledge of 'the last age', and that even 'its occasional defects of style are valuable, as additional evidences of its genuineness and truth to nature' (*DL* 6: 412). In four pages written over three weeks, she went back again to Croker's article on the *Memoirs*, wishing that she or Alex had answered it. Among her papers she left a note requesting that Macaulay reply for her. She had obviously read with pleasure Macaulay's withering review of Croker's edition of Boswell's *Life of Johnson*: 'Tell McCaulay I honour him for his manly & upright way of speaking of D^r J ... I w^d have gladly accepted my vindication from his hand' (*JL* 12:976). Charlotte Barrett passed on this request to Macaulay, who sensibly replied that 'the article in the Quarterly Review has long been utterly forgotten while Evelina and Camilla are just as much read as ever' (Berg, in Hemlow, p. 460). In her last letter, then, Burney was still trying to adjust her career so that posterity would view it in the proper fashion.[9]

During the last three months of Burney's life, everything seemed to fall away. She could barely see. She could no longer concentrate on reading and writing. The spectral illusions haunted her at night, and her fever seemed permanent. Nonetheless, she was a kindly patient, and Alex's fiancée Mary Anne Smith amiably watched over her. Unlike her father and her husband, she did not fashion an exit-line. Or, if she did, no one captured it. There is no grandiose statement like Dr Burney's, nor a tender one like d'Arblay's. Perhaps the chief problem here was that Burney had lost her audience. Her most beloved hearers were all dead. When, one day, Charlotte Barrett said to her that she needed sleep, she replied, 'I shall have it soon, my dear', and this stands as her final, representative statement in Barrett's account. Its honesty emphasizes that enduring and important quality in Burney's life. As often as she could, she forced herself to face reality. Without self-delusion she coped as best she could with the adverse criticism of her work she encountered late in life, and she valiantly endured the implacable series of losses – her siblings, her husband, and her son – that now left her quite alone. With no one to protect but herself, she was able to indicate clearly that she knew she was dying. She hung on until the month of January, when Alex had died. She did not last till his death-day, but she expired on another day that had haunted her for 40 years. This was 6 January, when her adored sister Susanna had perished far away in a Chester inn. Burney was buried near her son and husband in Bath, in the graveyard of Walcot Church.[10]

When Burney died, her niece immediately set to work editing the manuscripts bequeathed to her. Publication of the *Diary and Letters* commenced two years later. Focusing on Burney the professional author, Charlotte Barrett opened her edition with the publication of *Evelina*: 'This year was ushered in by a grand and most important event ... whence chronologers will date the zenith of the polite arts in this island!'[11] Once again, Croker reviewed Burney's work, the first three volumes of Barrett's seven-volume edition, this time lambasting Burney for 'extravagant egotism' and triviality. Diminishing her by calling her 'Fanny', he claims that she never mentions any books but her own, and that all speakers are reduced to 'what flattering things they said about *Fanny Burney*'. At the end he puts Burney's diary in a unique category of inferiority: 'we do not remember in all our experience to have laid down an unfinished work with less desire for its continuation'.[12] Croker's reviews of Burney were so implacable that the Burney family surmised that Croker was angry because Burney had refused to share her writings about Johnson with him. Charlotte Barrett claimed to her daughter Juliet that 'Croker has a personal pique against my Aunt – *I know*'.[13] Actually, Barrett had emphasized the egotism by beginning her edition with Burney's most extravagant claims for *Evelina*, 'the first publication of the ingenious, learned, and most profound Fanny Burney!'[14] The ironies in this passage are muted in Barrett's edition because it stands alone at the start of the volume. Anyone reading the same passage in the Troide edition easily sees it as part of an ironic continuum. This is not to say that Burney was not egotistical, but only that the egotism was unduly magnified by Barrett's editorial decision. Other reviewers were also struck by the egotism, but they argued nonetheless that Burney's work was interesting and valuable. The *Athenaeum* found it 'entertaining'; the *New Monthly Magazine* asserted that it was second only to Boswell; by the fifth volume the *Monthly Review* actually seemed won over, claiming 'That the interest of this series does not become exhausted, and, not even diminished, must be owing to some rare qualities in the diarist and letter writer'. Thackeray was approving, if condescending, writing of volume six that it is 'the pleasantest of this very pleasant and useful work'.[15]

At last, in the *Edinburgh Review* of January 1843, Macaulay weighed in, reviewing the first five volumes of the *Diary and Letters*. Macaulay pronounced on Burney so eloquently that his opinion reigned well into the twentieth century. He took the occasion to write a brief biography of Burney, in the manner of Johnson's *Lives of the Poets*, a life followed by criticism. He evokes Burney eloquently, with an abundance of detail that shows how thoroughly he had read the first five volumes of the diaries, which he characterized as 'written in her earliest and best manner, in true woman's English, clear, natural, and lively'.[16] He attacks Croker, 'a bad writer of our own time', for the 'truly chivalrous exploit' of studying 'the parish register of Lynn' in order to show that Burney was not seventeen when she wrote *Evelina*. Unlike Croker and others he finds no egotism in the diary, but simply Burney's desire to share with her family the experience of phenomenal success: 'Nothing can be more unjust than to confound these outpourings of a kind heart, sure of perfect sympathy, with the egotism of a blue-stocking, who prates to all who come near her about her own novel or her own volume of sonnets.' (1:563) But on the subject of Burney's writing, his opinion is mixed. 'She lived to be a classic', Macaulay intones, immediately diminishing his statement by a comedic comparison: 'Like Sir Condy Rackrent in the tale, she survived her own wake, and overheard the judgement of posterity' (1:546). Macaulay insists that, after *Camilla*, 'everything which she published during the forty-three years which preceded her death, lowered her reputation'. *The Wanderer* and *Memoirs*, Macaulay says, 'are very bad; but they are so, as it seems to us, not from a decay of power, but from a total perversion of power' (1:592–3). Once he gets hold of this theme, Macaulay waxes eloquent. From France, Mme d'Arblay 'brought back a style which we are really at a loss to describe. It is a sort of broken Johnsonese, a barbarous *patois*, bearing the same relation to the language of Rasselas, which the gibberish of the negroes of Jamaica bears to the English of the House of Lords. ... It matters not what ideas are clothed in such a style' (1:594–5).

It is unfortunate that Macaulay emphasized so memorably this negative view of *The Wanderer*. The image of 'broken Johnsonese', slavish imitation gone wrong, persisted and affected posterity's views not only of *The Wanderer*, but of *Cecilia* and *Camilla* as well. Macaulay was so struck with Burney's use of ruling passions, as he calls her application of Renaissance humor psychology to her characters, that he failed to notice the propensity that Johnson had stressed, the mixed and deliberately inconsistent traits that complicated these characters seemingly governed by a single passion. He did not realize that Burney was creating mules. Macaulay found some faults in Burney's second and third novels, but he also praised them and stressed how popular they had been when first published. Besides characterization and style, Macaulay's criteria appear to require chiefly that if women are to write novels, they had better be sure to retain as well their reputations as decent, moral women. In *Evelina* Macaulay praises the 'great force' and 'broad comic humour', but he commends even more highly the fact that it does 'not contain a single line inconsistent with rigid morality, or even with virgin delicacy' (1:599). The effect of Burney's ability to produce novels in which different classes appear with 'great force, and with broad comic humour',

Macaulay argues, was that 'She vindicated the right of her sex to an equal share in a fair and noble province of letters' (1:599–600). This judgment is similar to the one Burke gives in Burney's *Memoirs*, that because of Burney a man is complimented when someone tells him he writes like a woman.

Macaulay delighted in the variety and freshness of Charlotte Barrett's selections from Burney's *Diaries and Letters*, but he did not say they were her most outstanding achievement.[17] Many subsequent critics have insisted that Burney's autobiographical materials are more valuable than all of her work in other genres. Among current scholars, perhaps the most forceful supporter of this view is Katharine Rogers.

> Burney's own life supplied her with more genuine challenges than she allowed her heroines; she met them with more convincing courage and described them with more moving, because more authentic, language. Her journals show her developing from a sharply observant but timid girl, shrinking from self-assertion and fearful of deviating from propriety, into a mature woman of impressive strength and resolution, one who could get what was important to her and deal with situations that would test a liberated contemporary woman. (Rogers, *World*, p. 180)

What is most striking about Rogers' statement is that it depicts a Burney who changes. She is neither perpetual 'Fanny', nor is she bifurcated into warring dualities. At a period when, according to Macaulay, Burney is writing 'broken Johnsonese' (1:595), indulging in a 'perversion of power' (1:593), Rogers depicts her as 'a mature woman of impressive strength and resolution', meeting more 'genuine challenges' than in her novels, and depicting them in prose that is poignant and strong.

In place of the decayed woman Macaulay portrayed and the changing woman Rogers depicts, I would put a Burney who could never be divided in two, who certainly evolved over the years, as she gathered experience, but who always combined her sharpness of observation with an unusual blend of comedy and tragedy. She inveterately mixed humor, timidity, wildness, propriety, boisterousness, and delicacy. She embraced inconsistencies, a love of hats with a hatred of sewing and a penchant for bare feet, an altruistic reflex with an ebullient impulse and a wicked tongue, an apparently shy and retiring personality with a gift at cajoling people, all supported by a bravery apparently summonable at will.

The diaries are not better than Burney's other work. They are simply different. When Burney wrote a novel or a play, she had an organizing plan. She wanted to show, for instance, that different kinds of men can hate women, and for different reasons; or that firm and upstanding people can torment others, whether by holding them too rigorously to a theory of morals, by teasing them mercilessly, or by prying too insistently into their private thoughts. 'I have other purposes for Imaginary Characters than filling Letters with them', she wrote to Crisp rather early in her career, emphasizing that in letters she tried to recreate people as they are in life, saving her invention for her fictions (*EJL* 4, forthcoming). Those fictions are too various for many twentieth-century tastes. With difficulty, we have had to exhume the serious content of *Evelina*, rediscover the power of *Cecilia*, accept the agonies of *Camilla*, and overcome Macaulay's fierce judgment by simply reading *The Wanderer* and discovering its excitements.

But we also misunderstand the diaries and letters if we see them only as what Peter Quennell calls a 'transparent' medium.[18] In the diaries Burney did occasionally assemble the camera obscura images that Hester Thrale disparaged in *Cecilia*. Sometimes, in fact, these truths are so pointed, so unpleasant and hurtful, that Burney subsequently erased them. Christopher Smart did not know if the '<horr>id *old Cat* – as he once politely called his wife, <be> dead yet or not' (*EJL* 1:91). Others, less unpleasant, also seem to be breathtakingly exact. They bring us back to those moments more than 200 years ago when Burney persistently observed and described. The Tahitian Omai, who accompanied Captain Cook's expedition back to England in 1774, was so intelligent and polite that 'you would have thought he came from some foreign Court'. He sympathized with Burney, who was somewhat indisposed, '& looking at me with an expression of pity, said "very well to *morrow-morrow*?"' (*EJL* 2:60). Her Samuel Johnson is much more relaxed and tender than Boswell's, and yet also quite believable. He tries, for instance, to inveigle Burney into eating a large supper and includes the lowly word 'rasher' when speaking of bacon. The next day, Johnson apologizes for this caper: 'So you must not mind me, Madam, – I say strange things, but I mean no harm.' (*EJL* 3:89) This does not mean that she avoided fierceness when the occasion called, and that she always left the fierceness unerased. At Court, when someone offered to read a book to the oppressive Mrs Schwellenberg, Burney's unpleasant companion answered in her bastardized, Germanic-style English: 'I won't have nothing what you call novels, what you call romances, what you call histories – I might not read such what you call stuff, – not I.' (*DL* 3:184) This was the woman with whom Burney had to spend every evening. For revenge, Burney saw to it that Schwellenberg's fractured English and stupid literary prejudices graphically reached posterity. Women in particular interested Burney, and she noted their achievements. In 1786 she went out of her way to look through a telescope at Caroline Herschel's comet, which was undistinguished. 'But', Burney writes, 'it is the first lady's comet, and I was very desirous to see it.' (*DL* 3:18) Burney convincingly caught King George as he talked incessantly in delirium: '"I am nervous", he cried; "I am not ill, but I am nervous: if you would know what is the matter with me, I am nervous"' (*DL* 4:136). Her later portraits were often more political: besides Warren Hastings and Burke, there were Fox and Pitt. Fox 'looked all good humour and Negligent ease the instant before he began a speech of uninterrupted passion and vehemence, and he wore the same careless and disengaged air the very instant he had finished' (*DL* 3:473). Napoleon, amidst 'all the delusive seduction of the martial music' had 'far more the air of a Student than of a Warrior' (*JL* 5:314). Sometimes the observations were cultural. Burney was especially observant of cultural details. French women, she slowly learned, never kissed other women. They indulged only in an elaborate pretense. They would present a mouth or a cheek 'for the sole purpose of drawing it hastily away' (*JL* 5: 345). The variety of tone is apparent in this smattering of examples. French women amuse and puzzle Burney. Personalities are complex: Fox is a medley; Napoleon is a mixture of incongruities; Schwellenberg is powerful and ridiculous. No one whom Burney writes about is simple; she always digs beneath the skin.

She tended to idealize those who were really close to her, though she cared about truth well enough, so that some of the complexity broke through. When her brother James died, she wrote of him to her sister Esther that 'his promotion had softened his Heart and his Temper. ... All his prejudices of every sort were shading off, & his generous Nature was struggling to find vent for its pleased feelings.' (*JL* 11:300) At times, however, she cut the complexity out, and twentieth-century readers have recovered it only by arduous efforts, gradually deciphering her letters under bright lights, dim lights, and ultra-violet lights. At the end of d'Arblay's letter proposing matrimony, for instance, he had added a paragraph complaining that some passing British soldiers had refused Juniper Hall's offer of a convivial drink of beer, for fear that the French emigrés would poison them. They made him feel like leaving England, although his reasons for staying easily overcame his angry desire to flee. This flare of anger, together with the second message that Burney's charms had overset d'Arblay's annoyance, was probably typical of his habit of thought, but Burney chose to obliterate this equivocal and human touch. With the twentieth-century's unslakeable thirst for detail, we have uncovered these darkened lines. Like Mr Morrice in *Cecilia*, we have denied Burney the privacy she desired, with the important result that we have restored to her much of her characteristic complexity.

The characters who people the diaries and letters are often personalities who did not find their way into the novels or plays. Besides Mr Barlow, Mrs Thrale, the French gendarmes, Miss White, Johnson, Gibbon, and Boswell, there are countless others. Burney could never have described her mastectomy in a genre like the eighteenth-century novel, and there was no way sufficiently to mask autobiography in plots that would have contained her experiences as a successful woman writer or as the child of a famous musicologist. The story of her courtship could not be rendered sufficiently anonymous for fiction, and it slipped into *The Wanderer* only in the character of Harleigh and his rhyming name. In the novels, when Burney told the truth, she always told it slant, just as in the diaries she told it so straight that she often had to erase it.

Examples of Burney's most mature style in the diaries and letters include her mastectomy letter, the encounters with the gendarmerie at Dunkirk, the flight from Paris to Brussels, and the time on the north Devon coast at the mouth of the Bristol channel when she was stranded by a sudden tide. Of these four accounts the last contains the purest emotions. Here the source of fear is not man, but nature. Burney had gone to Ilfracombe in 1817 to accompany Alex while he was being tutored for his degree examination at Cambridge. The Ilfracombe account mixes apprehension, pain, humor, gaiety, and tenderness. As the waters rise, Burney's little dog Diane escapes through a cave that is too small to accommodate her mistress, and would catch her head as if 'standing in the pillory' (*JL* 10: 695). Impeded by her female clothing, Burney clambers up a small pinnacle of rock, and Diane with difficulty returns and joins her. Burney forces herself and her readers to relive this harrowing experience with an unsparing exactness. In order to help Diane up the last rock, Burney hooks her collar with her umbrella. To stop Diane's trembling she wraps her shawl around her and makes a cushion out of her 'bag of Curiosities' (*JL* 10:705).

Eventually, Alex and a friend found her on her perch, though there was no way to rescue her until the tide had fallen further. Alex's companion was John George Shaw-Lefevre, who was the first to see Burney clinging to her pinnacle. Lefevre's son later claimed that Burney had wrought up the details, that she was actually sitting on the sand, totally out of danger. This opinion, if true, is an extravagant tribute to Burney's inventive faculties. More interesting to us is the fact that Macaulay, at breakfast with Lefevre senior, 'spoke strongly in favour of her literary style' and chose to read this incident, asking his guest if he was the Lefevre mentioned (*JL* 10:714, n. 20). It is ironic that Macaulay, who represented Burney as in perpetual decline after *Cecilia*, should have chosen this post-*Wanderer* piece to represent her. He had not read it when he wrote his review, which covered only the first five volumes. Perhaps if Macaulay had read the last two volumes he would have softened his condemnation. Besides admiring the Ilfracombe journal, he would certainly have recognized the power of Burney's description of d'Arblay's death, even in the shortened Barrett version.

One of the most moving and compellingly written accounts in all of these diaries is Burney's five-day journey from Brussels to Trèves (Trier) in July 1815. Macaulay never read this piece in its entirety. Although it, too, was published in the last volume of Barrett, it was drastically cut, and by this truncation lost most of its complexity and power. When Burney fled Paris just before it fell to Bonaparte, d'Arblay left her in Brussels while he went on duty at Trèves. Hearing that he was dangerously ill after his horse kicked him in the leg, with gangrene a strong possibility, Burney set off immediately with minimal luggage and very little money. Having just missed the weekly diligence that went direct to nearby Luxembourg, she was forced to take a circuitous route through Liège, Aix La Chapelle (Aachen), Juliers (Jülich), Cologne, Bonn, Koblenz, and at last west again to Trèves. D'Arblay was fascinated by her account of her trip and urged her to write it up as soon as possible. Her first intention was to work with d'Arblay on this narrative, so that his writing and his experience could mingle with hers, but he died before she had the chance. He had already procured the paper for this task, and it lay ready when she began the work nearly ten years later. For him and for Alexander she wrote this account, folded the quarto sheets, pinned them together, and paginated the 176 pages.

There is less room in here for the humor that laced the memory of Ilfracombe, no place for a friendly little dog, a useful umbrella, or the recalcitrant shoes that kept getting caught in crevices. Yet the variety of emotions in Burney's wild journey of 1815 does not exclude laughter. Incongruously, for instance, as she runs home after planning her journey, she is forced to hide so as to avoid the Princesse d'Henin, whose forceful volubility will compel her to defend her desire to leave immediately, and might make her miss her coach.[19] Mainly, though, the journey from Brussels to Trèves is a search, full of anguish, as if Burney had decided to combine Cecilia's drive to London and her desperate final chase after the vanishing Delvile. The emotions she evoked in this fiction dreadfully foretold her life. Torment is the subject here. A loving heart struggles toward reunion with the beloved, and every hindrance is agony.

The beginning stutters, with the first segment ending in a dash and another attempt two years later breaking off in mid-sentence. Here, Burney presents to d'Arblay the plan that they will both write themes, and then simply trails off:

> et ce livre, que vous m'avez donné pour le consacrer à mes souvenirs, deviendra
> So, in 1818! – had I begun a little Narration
> So had I begun a little Narration in happier days! – days never to return, days such as few have known – & none – oh NONE have more penetratingly, more gratefully appreciated – ... I begin with what He most wished, my hazardous Journey to join him at Treves.
>
> (*JL* 8: 475–6)

Although we know the happy ending of this story, Burney keeps us in suspense throughout. One method she uses to accomplish this difficult literary feat is to invoke the fearful Burney, the frightened and retiring person who was always a part of her personality: 'How dread was the impulse of impatient emotion that could raise a courage so little natural in a character that natively is so retiring & so fearful.' (*JL* 8:490) It seems impossible that this timorous and yet courageous woman will convince a dour, sleepy official to renew her passport, but she accomplishes this more than once, in an inspired moment invoking the powerful name of General Kleist, 'a Prussian Commander in Chief at Treves, who had distinguished M. d'Arblay in a manner the most flattering & even cordial.' (*JL* 8:488) Kleist's name is miraculously effective. Brutal officers suddenly smile and sign their names. Each encounter is a hazard and a triumph. Another source of suspense is that Burney has very little money; the bank was closed the day she left, and she planned to borrow from a friend who unfortunately departed in a slightly earlier coach. She describes the gradual depletion of this money, mentioning that in the end she may have to sell her gold repeater watch, the watch which so faithfully measures out the increments of this journey, helping her to wake at 4:00 a.m., which seems to be the hour the coaches usually leave. When at last the time comes when the watch and ten francs (that is, approximately eight shillings) are all she has left, the bookkeeper's amazing response is to allow her to take the coach on credit. He even sends ahead so that she will not have to pay at the inn where she must sleep on the way. Throughout, there is additional anxiety in the fact that Burney never can be sure about the politics of the people she meets, whether to say she is English or French. People's responses are as fierce as they are unpredictable. In an observation that is part of the playfulness that accompanies the torment in this piece, she notes that one German couple speaks English in order to keep their conversation private. 'This at some other time might have amused me; but I was not then amusable.' (*JL* 8:489) Danger, both obvious and masked, is everywhere. She almost accepts help from a 'sarcastic, severe, & sneering' German, who suddenly turns kind and offers to protect her if she can 'procure a vehicle', but his dual personality concerns her. Suddenly realizing that to let him accompany her is to put herself in his power, she rejects his offer (*JL* 8:491).

The most agonizing passage in this narrative occurs when Burney loses her way in Bonn and nearly misses her coach. Forced by her poverty to separate herself from her traveling companions, she walks to a market, fixing in her mind as landmark for her return a 'hideous little Statue ... meant for a young Jesus'.[20] Walking further to look at some ruins, fortifications blasted by the war, she suddenly realizes that she cannot locate the way back. No one she sees speaks anything but German, and she is totally ignorant of the language, even though, long ago, the Queen had encouraged her to study it. When Burney was a Keeper of the Robes, German seemed part of her servitude. Now, locked in gibberish, she can only dart back and forth, hoping to find the inn where the diligence will soon depart. The agony of this memory, for both author and reader, is nearly unbearable:

If I should be late for the Diligence, I too well knew not another would pass for a Week: & even if I could here meet with a separate conveyance, the tales now hourly recounted of marauders, straggling Pillagers, & military Banditti, with the immense Forests, & unknown roads through which I must pass, made me tremble – – as I now do, even now, 9 years after – at looking back to my position at this fearful moment.

Oh! this was, indeed, nearly, the most tortured crisis of misery I ever experienced! one only has been yet more terrible! – nay, a thousand & ten thousand – ten million of times more terrible, because – Alas! irretrievable! This, however, was a herald to my affrighted soul of what the other inflicted – To know my Heart's Partner wounded – ill – confined – attended only by strangers; – to know, also, that if here detained, I could receive no news of him; for the Diligence in which I travelled was the Mail: – to know the dread anxiety, & astonishment that would consume his peace, & corrode all means of recovery, when Day succeeding Day neither brought me to his side, nor yet produced any tidings why I was absent – Oh gracious Heaven! in what a distracting state was my Soul! – In a strange Country – without Money, without a Servant – without a Friend – & without Language! Oh never – never shall I forget my almost frantic agony! Neither can I ever lose the remembrance of the sudden transport by which it was succeeded when, in pacing wildly to & fro', I was suddenly struck by the sight I have already described of the Unhappy Divinity stuck in a Nic[he.][21]

Here, Burney's prose rises passionately, filled with interjections, extra adjectives, clauses building on clauses, all joining to recreate in language the time when language would not serve her. In her beloved English, she tells us about the 'almost frantic agony' she felt, and now feels again as she sits in her small, graceful rooms at 11 Bolton Street[22] and reproduces in memory an anguish worse than the original experience. Now, as she forces her chosen reader Alexander and her other readers, all the rest of us, to remember, d'Arblay is no longer waiting in a different town. He is buried in the Walcot churchyard. For seven years, Burney has lived without him.

But Burney does not give us merely the torture. Once again the ugly many-colored Jesus appears, a moment of humor amid the desperation. She catches the mail coach seconds before it leaves, with all the other passengers already aboard, the coachman just cracking his whip. Once she is settled, her distress turns to rapture. She describes the hills, the Rhine, war-ruined castles and fortresses, and white houses 'covered with blue slate' shining in the crystalline air (*JL* 8:505). Finally reunited with d'Arblay, she addresses her son: 'Dreadfully suffering, but always mentally occupied by the duties of his Profession, I found Your noble Father my dear Alex.' (*JL* 8:518) When they return to England, she stops by to see her brother Charles, and her last mood in this narrative is elegiac: 'Oh my dear Charles! how little – I thank Heaven! – did I then conceive I saw your affectionate Face for the last Time on Earth!' (*JL* 8:541).

One of the reasons why Burney procrastinated over writing these narratives must have been the felt need to include so much detail. So far as we know, her notes were minimal. In the case of the Trèves journal, for instance, all that remains is a torn scrap of paper about eight inches by three inches listing the places where she went, with a record of where she slept. To remember the particulars must have taken prodigious energy, especially for a 72-year-old woman. Yet she tells us how many people sat in each diligence, what they looked like, what the towns looked like, what the officials said, who accompanied her to sue for her passport, what colors glaringly adorned the 'short, thick, squabby little' Jesus, and innumerable other facts (*JL* 8:500). She leaves blank only two place-names; in all other cases she supplies the names and detailed descriptions, with the effect that she vividly recreates the experience for Alex and for us. She lets the past collide with the present, allows desperation to vie with rapture, misery, humor, tenderness, and intelligent reportage. Concerned to make her experience as lifelike as possible she mixes the important, the remarkable, the everyday, and the plain. We trust her, even though she seems to catch each coach seconds before it leaves, even when she rises to hyperbole. We believe that d'Arblay is a superb husband and an unmatchable friend, worth Burney's courageous and hazardous trip.

Charlotte Barrett, in spite of pieces like this, emphasized Burney's 'Fear of doing Wrong'. But she also asked Susanna's daughter and Burney's namesake Frances Raper to write down some thoughts about her aunt. She did not include Raper's answer in her edition, but luckily she left it among her papers:

> a passion for writing ... innate conscientiousness, strength of mind, self denial, rectitude of principles, precision of judgment, keenness of apprehension, depth of feeling and warmth of heart formed the basis of her character; to which was added generous appreciation of the merit and character of others; discriminate selection, humorous clear-sightedness, every power of heart and intellect.   (Egerton MS, in Hemlow, p. 489)

The writer of this passage was the daughter of Burney's favorite sister Susanna, three years older than the brilliant Norbury. She was nearing 60 when her famous aunt died. Born in 1782, when her aunt was 30, she was most familiar with the woman who had already written

Evelina and *Cecilia*. Frances Raper's portrait is of the mature Burney, unalloyed by the earlier self so many people take for the total self. The niece knew a woman who possessed rectitude of character combined with generosity, discrimination, and humor. Twentieth-century readers have recovered only with difficulty what Burney's niece saw in her: 'every power of heart and intellect'.

Notes and References

1 Writing as compulsion and the redefined audience

1   *JL* 6:721.
2   I will call her 'Burney' throughout. A full explanation appears below.
3   This passport was obtained with the collusion of M. de Saulnier of the Paris Police Office. Burney bribed M. de Saulnier with a signed copy of *Evelina* for his daughter (*JL* 6:709). At Dunkirk, of course, the fiction needed to be maintained.
4   I stress this point here because Hemlow and others argue so prominently that Burney was heavily influenced by conduct books. One example from Hemlow will suffice: 'It was not Fanny Burney's policy to write about politics – a sphere allotted to men by the plan of creation and the advice of the courtesy-book' (p. 225). Burney did read conduct books; she was influenced by them. She included a conduct book in *Camilla*, but she also wrote a satiric conduct book in her diaries (I will discuss both of these below). The point is that to see Burney as a conduct-book woman is by no means the whole story.
5   One powerful example will make this point clear: for nearly a century Burney has been condescended to as 'Fanny Burney', the perpetual child. Beginning with the first decade of the twentieth century, all of Frances Burney's novels and all her diaries have been published under the name of 'Fanny Burney' (although Stewart J. Cooke's and Kristina Straub's recent editions of *Evelina* break this tradition). When Frances Burney was alive, her name never appeared on the title pages of her novels. After the anonymous *Evelina*, the books were designated as 'by the author of *Evelina*', and the like, and everyone who bought the books knew exactly who had written them, though the name did not appear. When Burney published her last book, *Memoirs of Doctor Burney*, she signed it as 'by his daughter, Madame d'Arblay', and frequently referred to herself therein as 'Frances'. The first editors of Burney's journals, soon after her death in the 1840s, called her either Frances Burney or Madame d'Arblay. However, in 1903, when the indefatigable popularizer of eighteenth-century figures Austin Dobson called his life in the *English Men of Letters* series *Fanny Burney* and referred to her in 1904 as 'Fanny' in his preface to his edition of Charlotte Barrett's *Diary and Letters of Madame d'Arblay* (p. vii), the diminutive name seemed appealing, became popular, and eventually stuck, gaining currency through sheer repetition. Is there any other author whose name has sunk to a diminutive? In one comparable case, when James L. Clifford published his biography *Young Sam Johnson* in 1955 (New York: McGraw-Hill), he called his subject 'Sam' in order to counteract the formal, stereotypical Johnson, who was seen primarily as a man who demolished all comers with his powers of conversation. Of course, Clifford did not mean for the name to be adopted, and of course it was not. When I first

began seriously to read Burney's work, in the 1980s, I became convinced that the chummy name was peculiarly unfair, and especially inapt for a writer who stood on her dignity as Frances Burney d'Arblay did on that nightmarish day in Dunkirk. Hence, whenever I included Burney in a conference paper, I began to stress the point that Burney scholars needed to stop using in public the diminutive private name that appeared so frequently in Burney's private journals, to counteract the vision of Burney as a little girl who lisped appealing fictions. (The conference papers were: 'Frances Burney and Circumscribed Power' at the Northeast MLA (NEMLA), University of Hartford, March 1985, and 'Frances Burney and Intimate Death' at the Eighteenth-Century Women Writers' International Conference: 'Eighteenth-Century Women and the Arts', Hofstra University, October 1985).

In 1988 Margaret Doody seemingly settled the matter beyond dispute in her definitive and boisterous biography, *Frances Burney: The Life in the Works*. The subject of her biography and of this literary life is not 'Fanny', but Frances Burney, referred to here as Burney. The dispute over Burney's name is not won. Kate Chisholm, for instance, in her wonderfully evocative biography, *Fanny Burney: Her Life* (London: Chatto, 1998), retains the diminutive and the slightly condescending attitude throughout. Burney would have been horrified to see herself known only as 'Fanny'. When her niece Frances wrote her section of a book she and her siblings assembled in 1793, she mentioned that she was called 'Fanny' because she was 'so little' (The Pierpont Morgan Library, New York. MA 4160 R-V).

Burney's sensibilities would have been slightly unsettled at the thought of losing her designation as Madame d'Arblay, but in this latter case her professionalism would have prevailed. I am sure that she would have been pleased to join her colleagues as Frances Burney.

6   Peter Sabor credits Austin Dobson and Annie Raine Ellis for giving Burney her first serious attention as a novelist. Ellis edited *Evelina* (1881), *Cecilia* (1882), and *The Early Diary of Frances Burney, 1768–1778* (1889). Her work is extensive and exact, her footnotes copious. Austin Dobson re-edited the *Early Diary* (1904–5), and (lightly) edited *Evelina* (1903). In his biography he argued that the diaries were more important than the fiction. Sabor shows that the powerful image of Burney created by these two scholars dominated Burney criticism for over half a century. *The Burney Journal* 1 (1998) 25–45.

7   George Sherburn, 'The Restoration and Eighteenth Century (1660–1789)', in *A Literary History of England*, ed. Albert C. Baugh (New York: Appleton-Century Crofts, 1948) p. 1034.

8   Rose Marie Cutting, 'Defiant Women: The Growth of Feminism in Fanny Burney's Novels', *Studies in English Literature* 17 (summer 1977) 519–30.

9   (*DL* 6:418); Barrett also deftly flipped another statement out of its context and reapplied it. From Macaulay she borrowed without attribution the statement that 'she lived to be a classic', a comment Macaulay seriously qualified by later referring to 'Madame D'Arblay's [sic] later style, the worst style that has ever been known among men' (Barrett, p. 419; Macaulay, *Literary and Historical Essays Contributed to the Edinburgh Review*, 2 vols. (Oxford: Oxford University Press, 1923) 1:546.

10 See Spacks, *The Female Imagination* (New York: Knopf, 1975) p. 3, and *Imagining a Self: Autobiography and Novel in Eighteenth-Century England* (Cambridge: Harvard University Press, 1976) ch. 6; p. 191. Janet Todd also emphasizes the 'fear of doing wrong' in *The Sign of Angellica: Women, Writing, and Fiction 1660–1800* (New York: Columbia University Press, 1989) pp. 275 ff., as does Katharine M. Rogers, 'Fanny Burney: The Private Self and the Published Self', *International Journal of Women's Studies* 7 (1984), who refers to 'excesses of timidity', and quotes Spacks, p. 111. Judy Simons applies the fear of doing wrong argument in *Fanny Burney* (London: Macmillan, 1987), generalizing it to the women in the novels, p. 35, ff., and uses it as the capstone in her life-summary in *Cecilia* (New York: Penguin, 1986).

11 Julia Epstein, *The Iron Pen: Frances Burney and the Politics of Women's Writing* (Madison: University of Wisconsin Press, 1989) p. 83; Kristina Straub, *Divided Fictions: Fanny Burney and Feminine Strategy* (Lexington, Kentucky: University Press of Kentucky, 1987) p. 22.

12 Doody, p. 3.

13 Claudia L. Johnson, *Equivocal Beings: Politics, Gender, and Sentimentality in the 1790s; Wollstonecraft, Radcliffe, Burney, Austen* (Chicago: University of Chicago Press, 1995), especially pp. 1–19, 141–88.

14 *Familiar Violence: Gender and Social Upheaval in the Novels of Frances Burney* (Newark: University of Delaware Press, 1997) p. 15.

15 Burney is an excellent example of Bakhtin's 'heteroglossia', or multiple voices. Bakhtin emphasizes that in the novel the language of the characters, competing with one another and with the author, constitutes its full meaning. Mikhail Mikhailovich Bakhtin, *The Dialogic Imagination*, ed. Michael Holquist, trans. Caryl Emerson and Michael Holquist (Austin: University of Texas Press, 1981), 'Discourse in the Novel', pp. 259–422.

16 The chief books and articles I have drawn on are (besides those already noted): Juliet McMaster, 'The Silent Angel: Impediments to Female Expression in Burney's Novels', *Studies in the Novel* 21 (1989) 235–52; Katharine M. Rogers, *Frances Burney: The World of 'Female Difficulties'* (New York: Harvester Wheatsheaf, 1990); Joanne Cutting-Gray, *Woman as 'Nobody' and the Novels of Fanny Burney* (Gainesville: University Press of Florida, 1992); Betty Rizzo, *Companions Without Vows: Relationships Among Eighteenth-Century British Women* (Athens and London: University of Georgia Press, 1994); Catherine Gallagher, *Nobody's Story: The Vanishing Acts of Women Writers in the Marketplace, 1670–1820* (Berkeley: University of California Press, 1994) pp. 203–56.

17 All the quotations in these paragraphs are from *EJL* 1:1–2.

18 One paragraph has been recovered from the end of this excised section, where Burney mentions that her half-sister Maria Allen plans to visit one of her father's wealthy patrons and 'look about her for conquest' before subsiding into marriage – as she eventually did – with Martin Folkes Rishton (*EJL* 1:3 n. 4).

19 Sir Walter Scott's great aunt asked him to lend her Aphra Behn's novels, but when he sent them to her, she returned them 'properly wrappd up, with nearly these [words] "Take back your bonny Mrs Behn and if you will take my advice put her in the fire for I found it impossible to get through

the very first of the novels – But is it not she said a very odd thing that I an old woman of eighty and upwards sitting alone feel myself ashamd to read a book which sixty years ago I have heard read aloud for the amusement of large circles consisting of the first and most creditable society in London?"' Letter to Lady Louisa Stuart, c. 6 September 1826, *The Letters of Sir Walter Scott*, ed. H.J.C. Grierson, 12 vols (London: Constable, 1932–7) 10:96.

20 See Neil McKendrick, John Brewer, J.H. Plumb, eds, *The Birth of a Consumer Society: The Commercialization of Eighteenth-Century England* (Bloomington: Indiana University Press, 1982), and the Clark Library Series: John Brewer and Roy Porter, eds, *Consumption and the World of Goods* (London: Routledge, 1993); John Brewer and Susan Staves, eds, *Early Modern Conceptions of Property* (London: Routledge, 1994); and John Brewer and Anne Bermingham, eds, *The Consumption of Culture 1600–1800: Image, Object, Text* (London: Routledge, 1995).

21 See Donald Grant Campbell, 'Errors of Profusion: Cash, Credit, and Consumption in the Novels of Frances Burney', Ph.D. Dissertation, Queen's University at Kingston, Ontario, Canada, 1989.

22 Lady Augusta Llanover, *The Autobiography and Correspondence of Mary Granville, Mrs. Delany*, 6 vols (London: Richard Bentley, 3 vols 1861, 3 vols 1862) 3:171.

23 Judith Phillips Stanton, 'Statistical Profile of Women Writing in English from 1660–1800', in Frederick M. Keener and Susan E. Lorsch, eds, *Eighteenth-Century Women and the Arts* (Westport, Conn.: Greenwood Press, 1988) p. 248.

24 Judith Phillips Stanton, 'Charlotte Smith's "Literary Business": Income, Patronage, and Indigence', in Paul J. Korshin, ed. *The Age of Johnson* 1 (1987) 375.

25 Stanton, 'Statistical Profile', p. 252.

26 See Lawrence Stone, *The Family, Sex and Marriage in England 1500–1800* (New York: Harper, 1977), passim. See also: Janice Farrar Thaddeus, 'Hoards of Sorrow: Hester Lynch Piozzi, Frances Burney D'Arblay, and Intimate Death', *Eighteenth-Century Life* 14:3 (November 1990) 108–29.

27 In *Fanny Burney: Selected Letters and Journals*, ed. Joyce Hemlow (Oxford: Clarendon Press, 1986) p. xv.

28 Lonsdale, p. 3.

29 See *EJL*, 3: Appendix 1.

30 Lonsdale, p. 79. Lonsdale gives in Dr Burney's own words an anecdote about his assumption of his title that encapsulates the humor and charm that delighted everyone who met him: "'I did not for some time after the honour that was conferred on me at Oxford display my title on the plate of my door; when Mr Steel, author of 'An Essay on the melody of Speech', says, 'Burney, why don't you tip us the Doctor?' When I replied in provincial dialect, 'I wants dayecity, I'm ashayum'd' – 'Poh, poh, (says he) you must *brazen* it"' (*Frag. Mem.* (Osborn), reprinted in *Memoirs of Dr. Charles Burney, 1726–1769*, edited from autograph fragments by Slava Klima, Garry Bowers, and Kerry S. Grant (Lincoln: University of Nebraska Press, 1988) as Fragment 115, p. 178. This is one of the stories by which Dr Burney charmed Mrs Thrale. She gives it in *Thraliana*, 1:137.) Burney

herself copied it with slight changes into the *Memoirs*, 1:214.

31 This was Dr Burney's description of the man he also called 'half mad & unfeeling' (Hemlow, *Selected Letters*, p. 40). A note in *EJL* 4: forthcoming shows that Phillips' claims about killing Cook's murderer are almost certainly false.

32 See Egerton 3697, where Rishton writes to Burney that when she found out about her husband's affair she considered publicly breaking her relationship with Mrs Hogg (Dorothy Tayler had married George Hogg in 1769). Her brother convinced her that this was an unnecessarily cruel and useless gesture, since she was by this point quite emotionally detached from Rishton. Rishton's child by this affair was his residuary legatee. There is only one recovered reference to Dorothy Tayler in all of Burney's manuscripts (*EJL* 1:9, n. 28).

33 Arthur Young (1741–1820) was married to Martha Allen (1741–1815), sister of Dr Burney's second wife.

34 *Memoirs* 1:143–4.

35 *Memoirs* 2:123.

36 'A 70–Year Follow-up of a Childhood Learning Disability: The Case of Fanny Burney', *The Psychoanalytic Study of the Child*, eds Albert J. Solnit, Ruth S. Eissler, Peter B. Neubauer, p. 38 (1983). Kris calls Burney's condition 'severe childhood dyslexia', implying by her use of the word that it was a life-long condition. Some of her further arguments, especially that Burney's childhood disability may be associated with a 'lifelong propensity for shame and cognitive disorganization' (p. 638), I would quarrel with. There is no evidence for 'cognitive disorganization', and the question of shame is extremely complicated. I would agree, however, that Burney did carry with her the free-floating anxiety she must have felt at not being able to read and write, when everyone around her placed such a high value on these accomplishments. Although there is a 'low correlation' between 'optical distortions of the eye' and reading problems when young, Burney's difficulties do seem to have been optical rather than perceptual (Irving J. Peiser, 'Vision and Learning Disabilities', in Robert M. Wold, ed., *Vision: Its Impact on Learning* (Seattle: Special Child Publications, Bernie Straub Publishing Co., 1978) p. 410). Whatever they were, they suddenly resolved themselves between the ages of eight and ten.

2   Publishing Anonymously

1 *Memoirs* 2:128–9; the *Memoirs* say he delivered two volumes, but the original letters make clear that she sent them one at a time (*EJL* 3:216). In the account that follows I have drawn promiscuously on the two chief versions of this event in Burney's own accounts: letters and journals as they appear in Troide's edition and her later re-telling in her edition of her father's *Memoirs* (there are some discrepancies, which I will note when necessary).

2 Egerton MS 3695, f. 5; reprinted in *EJL* 2:214, with slight changes.

3 *DL* 1:9, quoted in Barrett's introduction.

4 By Burney's cousin Edward Francesco. Reproduced as the frontispiece to

JL 2; now in the Brooklyn Museum.

5   *A Biographical Dictionary of Actors, Actresses, Musicians, Dancers, Managers and Other Stage Personnel in London, 1660–1800*, eds Philip H. Highfill, Jr., Kalman A. Burnim, and Edward A. Langhans, 16 vols. (Carbondale, Illinois: Southern Illinois University Press, 1973–93) 4:240.

6   Burney's sister Charlotte is the source here, Egerton 3700B, in Doody, p. 28.

7   *EJL* 1:319. Burney later erased this phrase, which may seem ungenerous, but perhaps merely reflected her later, more sober judgment of Crisp's letters compared with her own.

8   *EJL* 1:280–1;313, and *passim*.

9   Burney first wrote 'His mouth is in perpetual motion', but changed it later. In this instance I left the change, because it is clearly only an attempt not to repeat that phrase in the description, and has no other apparent motive that would be interesting to a scholar (*EJL* 2:225).

10 See, for instance, *EJL* 2:51.

11 Swift is often on her mind; she enjoys his deadpan way of describing the ridiculous. In this case she uses a Lilliputian-style description of what they do at Chessington, beginning 'Imprimis; – *We Walk*' and proceeding through the other activities of the day, describing the process of eating, for instance, as if she were writing a technical manual about an unknown subject (*EJL* 2:220).

12 See Cheryl Turner, *Living by the Pen* (London: Routledge: 1992), ch. 6, pp. 102–26. Turner notes that 'the bulk of popular novels, including those by women, were probably sold to the publishers for around the five guineas received by Phoebe Gibbes from T. Lowndes on 14 April 1763 'for the novel called "The Life of Mr. Francis Clive"'; in 1770 Lowndes had paid twenty guineas for Anne Dawe's *Younger Sister*, and in 1772 the same amount for Sophia Briscoe's *Fine Lady* (*Gentleman's Magazine* 1824: Vol. 94, 136), in Turner, p. 114. In *Memoirs*, Burney amends the sum she received for *Evelina* to a mere £20 (*passim*).

13 *Evelina*, pp. xxxiv–v, gives an accurate listing of the various editions, approximately 27 of them during Burney's lifetime, including German, French, and Dutch translations. Burney later recalled that Lowndes had printed 800 copies as the first edition. This seems unlikely for an unknown, anonymous author, especially since – as Burney mentions – Lowndes' letter to Charles Burney in 1779 indicates that for the second and third edition he is printing 1500 copies, of which 500 are a second edition and 1000 the illustrated third edition. In any case, editions were printed in multiples of 250, so if Lowndes had printed more than 500, he would have printed 750. See *DL* 2:481–2; Egerton MS 1695, f. 12. On 19 August 1782, Burney wrote to her sister Susanna that Lowndes' first edition had been 500 copies. From every angle, then, the 800 copies seems to be a mistake. Lowndes himself says so. In the appendix to *DL* 2, Dobson prints a bristling, envious letter from Lowndes dated 5 September 1782, two months after the publication of *Cecilia*, in which Lowndes says he printed two editions of 500 copies, and that upon the second edition he sent an extra 'Bank Note' (p. 481; Burney says in the *Memoirs* that Lowndes sent this money after the third edition (p. 2:151)), and that on

the illustrations for the third edition he spent £73. His aim in writing this letter was to find out why he had not been given *Cecilia*.

14 The surviving Hookham and Carpenter records (1791–98) are in the Chancery Masters' Lists in the Public Record Office, C104/75/1–3. This information is listed in Ledger G137a. I would like to thank Ruthe Battestin for bringing these records to the attention of Jan Fergus, and to thank Jan Fergus for sharing them with me.

15 The fact that an inflationary period began during the 1790s may skew these figures somewhat, but there is no way precisely to account for this factor. Paper varied in price also, so that it is possible that Lowndes was able to keep his prices down by buying cheap paper.

16 Commission was a system by which the publisher took a percentage on the sale price of the book, but the author was ultimately responsible for the printing costs if the book's sales failed to meet them. The modern system of offering royalties – a commission to the author on the sale price of the book – was not yet practiced. A fifth method – the author shouldering the entire financial burden and allowing interest to the bookseller, a version of present-day so-called vanity publishing – may not have been as common as is supposed by modern scholars. Authors who were going to have to assume the debt in commission publishing may have confounded this assumption of debt with language that seems to imply that they needed to supply the money up front. The Hookham and Carpenter ledgers show that the firm never required that the author initially supply the funds for printing. See Jan Fergus and Janice Thaddeus, 'Women, Publishers, and Money, 1790–1820', *Studies in Eighteenth-Century Culture* 17 (1987) pp. 191–207.

17 Regarding the eighteenth-century double view of an author as an immaterial self as compared to a personality reflected in the text, see Mark Rose's discussion of Francis Hargrave's *Argument in Defence of Literary Property* (1774), *The Invention of Copyright* (Cambridge: Harvard University Press, 1993), pp. 124–9. Rose connects the separation of the author and the text with the advent of paper money. Dr Burney had sold the joint copyright of his two musical tours for £300 after they had sold out their first editions (Lonsdale, pp. 130–1).

18 For Dr Burney's rivalry with Hawkins, see Lonsdale, pp. 189–225. Burney had expected Hawkins to publish long before him, and found the competition increasingly unnerving. Lonsdale makes clear that Burney did not relish sharing his glory, much less his paying clientele.

19 Quoted in *The Letters of Sarah Harriet Burney*, ed. Lorna J. Clark (Athens: University of Georgia Press, 1997), pp. 175, 157.

20 Laetitia-Matilda Hawkins, *Anecdotes, Biographical Sketches and Memoirs* 2 vols (London: F.C. and J. Rivington, 1882) 1:156n. Hawkins' *Memoirs* were originally published as a separate volume in 1824. Hawkins published her first novel 'some few years previous' to Samuel Johnson's death in 1784. See Jan Fergus, *Jane Austen: A Literary Life* (Basingstoke: Macmillan, 1991), who compares Hawkins' and Burney's 'parallel stories' as comparable publishing endeavors, pp. 10–11, and Janice Thaddeus, biographical article in Janet Todd, *A Dictionary of British and American Women Writers, 1660–1800* (Totowa, N.J.: Rowman and Allanheld, 1985), pp. 154–6.

21   Anonymity even in the twentieth century has its uses, and they are much the same uses. Joe Klein, American author of *Primary Colors*, a *roman-à-clef* about Bill Clinton's 1992 campaign, says that he chose to be anonymous not merely to give the book a particular cachet, but from 'a combination of cowardice and whimsy. ... I'd never written fiction before. ... I didn't know if it was any good.' Quoted in *The Boston Globe*, 18 July 1996, p. A24.

22   *The London Review of English and Foreign Literature* 7 (February 1778) 151.

23   Troide surmises that 'there may be a dry irony intended here; Kenrick was notorious for his scurrilous attacks on writers and personalities' (*EJL* 3:15, n. 31). The other reviews are so different in tone, that even if irony is intended here, Burney has come off very well.

24   *London Review* 7 (May 1777) 373; (March 1778) 219; (September 1777) 230.

25   Lonsdale emphasizes Dr Burney's 'acute awareness of the social status of the musician in the eighteenth century, the escape from which was to lie at the heart of his own ambitions and achievement.' (pp. 7–8)

26   Here, Lord Orville is markedly close to Burney's conception of Nobody in her early journal. Of Nobody she says: 'In your Breast my errors may create pity without exciting contempt; may raise your compassion, without eradicating your love.' (*EJL* 1:2)

27   Perhaps the strongest passage to vanish was this one: 'Richard absolutely *made* me hold by his arm [sic] all the morning, & whisked me about with him, up & down the College, as if I had become a part of his own person, & neither of us could move but by mutual consent' [and then there is an illegible line] (*EJL* 2:267).

28   1741–1821, after 1784 Piozzi. For consistency, I will call her 'Thrale' throughout; *EJL* 3:35.

29   In *The Family Book*, published as *The Thrales of Streatham Park*, ed. Mary Hyde (Cambridge: Harvard University Press, 1978), 1 April 1778, p. 201.

30   In 1791, Thrale described Burney as both appealing and vain: 'no one possesses more powers of pleasing than She does, no one *can* be more self interested, & of course more willing to employ those Powers for her own, and her Family's Benefit' (*Thraliana*, p. 821).

3   *Evelina*

1   Thrale quotes Montagu in a letter to Burney on 13 February 1781, printed in *EJL* 4, forthcoming.

2   Critics who see *Evelina* as a comedy of manners also tend to downgrade Burney's later work. The number of articles on *Evelina* has burgeoned in the last few years, and it is impossible to list them all. The most useful collection is *Fanny Burney's Evelina*, ed. Harold Bloom (New York: Chelsea House, 1988). Bloom's introduction is an interesting study in refractoriness. Although he has put into his book articles by Susan Staves, Patricia Meyer Spacks, Judith Lowder Newton, Mary Poovey, Jennifer A. Wagner and Julia Epstein, he resists them. He cannot see the book as a 'chronicle of assault' (Newton) nor does he sympathize with the 'trauma of growing up female' (Poovey). 'Delicacy under assault', he says, 'is very difficult to represent except in a comic mode, since more of our imaginative

sympathy is given to rambunctiousness than to virtue' (p. 2). He also adds that 'Evelina (and Fanny Burney) are ... less dismayed by female difficulties, than many among us', a statement that by the evidence of Burney's last novel, *The Wanderer or Female Difficulties*, is plain wrong. Still, he seems to have felt that the feminist work is the best, since Ronald Paulson is the only other man represented in this anthology. Other articles include: Toby A. Olshin, '"To Whom I Most Belong": The Role of Family in *Evelina*', *Eighteenth-Century Life* 6, n.s. 1 (October 1980) 29–42; Catherine Parke, 'Vision and Revision: A Model for Reading the Eighteenth-Century Novel of Education' *Eighteenth-Century Studies* 16,2 (winter 1982/83) 162–74; Kristina Straub, 'Women's Pastimes and the Ambiguity of Female Self-Identification in Fanny Burney's *Evelina*', *Eighteenth-Century Life* 10, n.s. 2 (May 1986) 58–72; Gina Campbell, 'How to Read like a Gentleman: Burney's Instructions to Her Critics in *Evelina*', *English Literary History* 57 (1990) 557–84; Margaret Anne Doody, 'Beyond *Evelina*: The Individual Novel and the Community of Literature', *Eighteenth-Century Fiction* 3 (July 1991) 359–73 (this complete issue is devoted to *Evelina*); William C. Dowling '*Evelina* and the Genealogy of Literary Shame', *Eighteenth-Century Life* 16, n.s. 3 (November 1992) 208–20; Julia Epstein, 'Marginality in Frances Burney's Novels', in John Richetti, ed. *The Cambridge Companion to the Eighteenth-Century Novel* (Cambridge: Cambridge University Press, 1996), pp. 198–211; John Zomchick, 'Satire and the Bourgeois Subject in Frances Burney's *Evelina*', in James E. Gill, ed. *Cutting Edges: Postmodern Critical Essays on Eighteenth-Century Satire, Tennessee Studies in Literature* 37 (Knoxville: University of Tennessee Press, 1995), pp. 347–66; Emily Allen, 'Staging Identity: Frances Burney's Allegory of Genre' *Eighteenth-Century Studies* 31, 4 (1988) 433–51. Other critics have pointed out important facets of the book, such as its relationship to the new commercial world and to religion: Edward W. Copeland, 'Money in the Novels of Fanny Burney', in *Eighteenth-Century British Fiction*, ed. Harold Bloom (New York: Chelsea House, 1988), 257–68; Irene Tucker, 'Writing Home: *Evelina*, the Epistolary Novel and the Paradox of Property', *English Literary History* 60, 2 (summer 1993) 419–50; James Thompson, 'Burney and Debt', *Models of Value: Eighteenth-Century Political Economy and the Novel* (Durham, N.C.: Duke University Press, 1996), pp. 156–83; Sharon Long Damoff, 'The Unaverted Eye: Dangerous Charity in Burney's *Evelina* and *The Wanderer*', *Studies in Eighteenth-Century Culture* 26 (1998) 231–46. There are two excellent new editions of *Evelina*: ed. Kristina Straub (Boston: Bedford, 1997), and ed. Stewart J. Cooke (New York: Norton, 1998). Both contain substantial extracts of background material. See also the individual chapters in the books mentioned in Chapter 1.

3 *The Middling Sort: Commerce, Gender, and the Family in England 1680–1780* (Berkeley and Los Angeles: University of California Press, 1996).
4 *The Politics and Poetics of Transgression* (Ithaca: Cornell University Press, 1986), p. 115. One should note here that Stallybrass and White admit that this kind of mixing had occurred before the eighteenth century, but that it had exponentially increased in the 1700s, especially in the work of Alexander Pope.

5 Catherine Gallagher, *Nobody's Story: The Vanishing Acts of Women Writers in the Marketplace, 1670–1820* (Berkeley: University of California Press, 1994), p. xvi. Gallagher defines this wild space as female, but in *Evelina* the situation is more complicated.

6 *Gulliver's Travels*, ed. Robert A. Greenberg, Bk. 4, Ch. 6 (New York: Norton, 1970), p. 219.

7 See Joyce Appleby, 'Consumption in Early Modern Social Thought', in *Consumption and the World of Goods*, pp. 168–9.

8 Burney says in her journal for 1778: 'Perhaps this may seem a rather bold attempt & Title, for a Female whose knowledge of the World is very confined, & whose inclinations, as well as situations, incline her to a private & domestic Life. – all I can urge, is that I have only presumed to trace the accidents & adventures to which a "*young woman*" is liable, I have not pretended to shew the World what it actually *is*, but what it *appears* to a Girl of 17.' (*EJL* 3:1)

9 Irene Tucker argues that this process is interleaved with epistolarity, and that in *Evelina* the letter-writing activity of an ignored heiress becomes involved with issues of property and identity in such a way that the specific audience for the letters and the book's actual audience become interinvolved.

10 On this evidence Catherine Coussmaker surmised that the novel was by a woman, even though the majority of readers attributed it to a man (*EJL* 3:28).

11 September 1778, 48:425.

12 Gina Campbell, p. 582. Campbell also stresses that in order to please these critics Burney disguises the sexual feelings in the novel.

13 12 mo. 12 s. Hookham. *Critical Review* (June 1784) 473–4.

14 This is the time estimated by Hemlow, p. 47.

15 Charles Burney, *A General History of Music from the Earliest Ages to the Present Period*, ed. Frank Mercer (1935; New York: Dover Editions, 1957), 1:13.

16 Zonitch summarizes this poem as ambivalent. These lines 'suggest both a desire for and an anxiety of her father's notice' (p. 57).

17 30 August 1773, CB*Letters*, p. 139.

18 Twining to CB, 22 June 1775, in Lonsdale, p. 162.

19 Charlotte Charke, *A Narrative of the Life of Mrs. Charlotte Charke*, written by herself (1755; London: Hunt and Clarke, 1827), p. 11.

20 Charke, pp. 14, 15.

21 To Susanna, 7 September 1778, Egerton MS, in Hemlow, p. 90.

22 Katharine Rogers in *Frances Burney* refers to this passage, but she argues that the scene touched Coussmaker only lightly, that she was 'delightfully distressed' (p. 177); yet Rogers also makes the general point that 'more vividly than any of her contemporaries, Burney expressed the feelings of these trammeled women and analyzed the internal as well as the external restraints upon them' (p. 188).

23 The best article on this subject is Susan Staves' '*Evelina*: or, Female Difficulties', in Bloom, pp. 13–30.

24 See pp. 11, 15, 42, 57, 66, 76, 77, 81, 86, 88 (three times), 120, 127 (twice), 140, 141, 147 (twice), 152, 167 (twice), 169, 174, 181, 183, 184, 199, 208,

211, 240, and 252. I wish to thank Patricia Brückmann for pointing out the frequency of this word.

25   See Katherine Anne Ackley, 'Violence Against Women in the Novels of Early British Women Writers', in *Living By the Pen: Early British Women Writers*, ed. Dale Spender (New York, Teachers College Press, 1992), pp. 212–24. Ackley argues that the violence in Burney pales by comparison to that in Mary Brunton's *Self-Control*, and Eliza Haywood's *Betsy Thoughtless* (the squirrel being thrown against the fire-screen by Betsy's husband, for instance). To my mind, the comparison emphasizes the violence in Burney, who was very probably familiar with the other books.

26   Sherburn, *Restoration and Eighteenth Century*, p. 1032. Cf. Michael E. Adelstein, *Fanny Burney* (New York: Twayne, 1968), who mentions 'variety' (p. 30), but consistently sees the work as a 'novel of manners' (p. 39 ff.). Recent criticism has restored a more complex view of the eighteenth-century concept of manners. Natalie Rose, in particular, plays the two views against one another in an as-yet-unpublished article, '"Civility" and "Decorum" versus the "Vulgar" and the "Violent": The Female Body in Frances Burney's *Evelina*'.

27   Critics of *Evelina* have noted that in the recognition scene Sir John Belmont feels such an overwhelming surge of guilt and desire that he rejects his daughter even as she feels the force of his love, a pattern that reflects Burney's relationship with her father. See Gina Campbell, 'Bringing Belmont to Justice: Burney's Quest for Paternal Recognition in *Evelina*' *Eighteenth-Century Fiction* 3, 4 (July 1991) 321–40; Irene Fizer, 'The Name of the Daughter: Identity and Incest in *Evelina*', in *Refiguring the Father: New Feminist Readings of Patriarchy*, eds Patricia Yaeger and Beth Kowaleski-Wallace (Carbondale: Southern Illinois University Press, 1989), pp. 78–107.

28   Susan Staves, 'Fielding and the Comedy of Attempted Rape', in Beth Fowkes Tobin, ed., *History, Gender, and Eighteenth-Century Literature* (Athens: University of Georgia Press, 1994), pp. 86–112.

29   Margaret Doody notes this masculine resemblance, and though she does not compare Mme Duval to a rape victim, she connects her name with the 'valley' into which she has fallen, and emphasizes Captain Mirvan's misogyny (pp. 52–3).

30   Earl R. Anderson, 'Footnotes More Pedestrian Than Sublime: A Historical Background for the Foot-Races in *Evelina* and *Humphry Clinker*', *Eighteenth-Century Studies* 14, 1 (autumn 1980) 56. Anderson suggests as a source the foot-race between Melford and Birkin in *Humphry Clinker*, but the comparison is rather far-fetched. Arthur Sherbo, in a follow-up 'Forum' entitled 'Addenda to "Footnotes More Pedestrian than Sublime"', suggests a number of other sources culled from the *Gentleman's Magazine*, showing clearly that callousness and racing were often allied in eighteenth-century practice. However, none of the sources either man has unearthed appears to be Burney's primary source, if such an item exists. *Eighteenth-Century Studies* 14:3 (spring 1981) 313–16.

31   Frederick W. Hilles, *Portraits by Sir Joshua Reynolds* (New York: McGraw-Hill, 1952), pp. 92–3, mentioned by Sherbo.

32   Burney could not resist improving on the prose somewhat here; Susan had

written, 'there's a something disgusting' (*EJL* 3:28–9 and n. 78).

33   The phrase 'the radical unruliness of things' is used by Claude Rawson to characterize the satire of Jonathan Swift (*Gulliver and the Gentle Reader* (London: Routledge, 1973), p. 99). I have reapplied part of Rawson's phrase here, because Burney and Swift – though differing in their views of the body, the need for brevity, and a number of other issues – share this sense of the 'unruliness of things'.

34   'Serial publication gave novelists an opportunity to study the public's response to their work while it was being created ... But with George Eliot morbid diffidence deprived her of what might often have been helpful criticism. Knowing their disastrous effect, Lewes rarely let her see unfavourable comments' (Gordon S. Haight, *George Eliot: A Biography* (Oxford: Oxford University Press, 1968, p. 366)); cf. Frederick R. Karl: 'Unable to handle criticism, she made sure her companion, George Henry Lewes, screened all comments on her work, and she conditioned her publisher, Blackwood's, to suppress anything that might not prove entirely positive', *George Eliot: Voice of a Century* (New York: W.W. Norton, 1995, pp. xii-xiii).

35   Burney to Susanna, 3 February 1781, in Doody, p. 109; *EJL* 4, forthcoming. Burney despondently recalls this scheme to Susanna at the moment when her sister is considering marrying Molesworth Phillips, controlling her emotion by expressing herself in the third person.

4   Open authorship

1   These quotations sound dead accurate – and may well have been so – since Burney claimed that she could memorize a part in a play by reading it through once, an aptitude she may also have extended to remembering and recording conversations.

2   There are many such lists among the Burney manuscripts. Most of these names appear on a two- by twenty-inch fragment now in the Berg, in Folder I of Misc. Holographs, which in all includes 417 pieces.

3   I wish to thank Betty Rizzo for this figure.

4   Charles Beecher Hogan, ed., *The London Stage: 1660–1800*, Part 5: 1776–1800, 3 vols (Carbondale: Southern Illinois University Press, 1968) 1:cxc-cxciv. Hogan points out that managers wanted their plays to be fresh, and a published play was never as novel as an unpublished one, available only in the theater. On this principle, for instance, Sheridan never published his perennially successful play, *The School for Scandal*.

5   The definitive critical book on Burney's plays is Barbara Darby, *Frances Burney Dramatist: Gender, Performance, and the Late-Eighteenth-Century Stage* (Lexington: University Press of Kentucky, 1997). See also Joyce Hemlow, 'Fanny Burney: Playwright', *University of Toronto Quarterly*, 19 (1949–50) 170–89; Peter Sabor, 'The Rediscovery of Frances Burney's Plays' *Lumen*, 13 (1994) 145–54; Sabor, '"Altered, improved, copied, abridged": Alexandre d'Arblay's Revisions to *Edwy and Elgiva*', *Lumen*, 14 (1995) 127–37; Introduction to Sabor and Geoffrey Sill, eds, *The Witlings and The Woman-Hater* (London: Pickering and Chatto, 1997); Doody, especially chapters 3,

5, and 8; for background, see Nancy Cotton, *Women Playwrights in England c. 1363–1750* (Lewisburg: Bucknell University Press, 1980); for a fruitful new line of analysis, showing that Burney uses the 'emergent industrial discourse in which time, production, and money are imbricated, and a leisure class which appropriates this discourse but produces nothing', see Sandra Sherman, '"Does Your Ladyship Mean an Extempore?": Wit, Leisure, and the Mode of Production in Frances Burney's *The Witlings*', *Centennial Review*, 40,2 (spring 1996) 401.

6　This opinion appears in a letter Burney wrote to her father just before telling Mrs Thrale that she was author of *Evelina*. Part of her motive is to explain to her father her discomfort with the fact that she has included vulgar characters. Still, she sees herself in a strong and important tradition, signing herself Francesca Scriblerus (*EJL* 3:47–51).

7　For a superb discussion of the toadeater, see Betty Rizzo's *Companions Without Vows*.

8　*EJL* 3:346, n. 74. Though equally apportioning influence, Sabor attributes the final responsibility to Crisp (Plays 1:4). Katharine M. Rogers argues of Burney that 'with strange perversity she chose to focus her ridicule on Bluestockings', implying strongly that in this case Burney's instinct to rebel was stronger than her instinct to succeed. Dividing the influence equally between Crisp and Burney's father, Rogers judges Burney's 'regrets' on having to abandon her play 'pathetic' (*The Meridian Anthology of Restoration and Eighteenth-Century Plays by Women* (New York, Penguin, 1994) pp. 290–1).

9　It is not clear whether the fourth act that remains in manuscript is the original or the revised version.

10　Cotton, *Women Playwrights in England, c. 1363–1750*, p. 138; Chisholm mentions that Thomas Harris, proprietor of Covent Garden, actually assaulted Elizabeth Inchbald (1753–1821), having lured her to his house on the pretense of discussing a new play. She saved herself by pulling his hair (p. 86). About five years after the *Witlings* disaster, Inchbald was to appear in her first play, and she was to write 19 more. Inchbald had begun as an actress, so she was both more vulnerable and less class-hampered than Burney. Frances Burney, like it or not, was a member of the aspiring Burney family.

11　(*EJL* 3:205); Doody points out that in a second published poem an anonymous author repeated the phrase that had bothered Burney so much, and that this anonymous author was Burney's father.

12　Michel Foucault, *The History of Sexuality* (New York: Vantage, 1980) 1:87–9.

13　The author of *The Sylph* is usually given as Georgiana Cavendish, Duchess of Devonshire (1757–1806), but Antonia Forster has found evidence that it might be by Sophia Briscoe (Antonia Forster and James Raven, *English Novels 1770–1829: A Bibliographical Survey of Prose Fiction Published in the British Isles 1 (1770–99)*), forthcoming. I would like to thank Antonia Forster for her generosity in sharing this information and much else.

14　*CBLetters*, 267–8.

15　Hemlow and others have depicted the writing of *Cecilia* as driven, whipped along by Burney's father, subservient to his schedule, with no time for revision, hardly any time to think (Hemlow, pp. 142–9). Burney made more than 300 alterations of words and phrases in the page proofs, but the significance of this number is not clear, since these are the only Burney proofs that appear to have survived. These proofs, for volumes 2–5 of *Cecilia*, are in the Houghton Library at Harvard University, Lowell *EC8 Ar173 782ca. To my knowledge, no Burney scholar has referred to them. It is clear that Burney meticulously counted letters so as to require minimal extra typesetting, in one instance amending her insertion of 'through' to 'thro'' so that it would fit into its line (5:169). For the second edition of *Cecilia*, Burney made only 100 more 'alterations' (World's Classics Edition, p. xl). This small number of revisions does not indicate an author who is suffering from massive dissatisfaction.

16   *Madness and Civilization: The Carnivalesque in Eighteenth-Century English Culture and Fiction* (Stanford: Stanford University Press, 1986) p. 269.

17   *Works of Samuel Johnson*, 15: *Rasselas and Other Tales* (New Haven: Yale University Press, 1990) p. 18.

18   Cecilia's namesake in *The Witlings*, also seen as unworthy of her suitor, is similarly isolated, 'unprotected, unassured, and uncomforted' (*Plays* 1:92). Her solution is to hire herself out as a companion.

19   This information is in Jan Fergus's soon-to-be finished book, *Readers and Fictions*, on readership in the Midlands, 1740–1800.

20   Many critics noticed virtues in *Cecilia*. Austin Dobson both condescended and praised: 'though the book has less freshness than its predecessor, it has more constructive power and greater certainty of hand' (*Fanny Burney* (New York: Macmillan, 1903) p. 203). Sherburn was grudging, but he too saw the book's emotional power: 'The story is more melodramatic than *Evelina*, more sentimental, less comic, but equally thrilling' (p. 1034).

21   In my account of the publication of *Cecilia* I am deeply indebted to Stewart J. Cooke's article, 'How Much was Frances Burney Paid for *Cecilia*?', in *Notes and Queries* 39 (December 1992) 484–6, which draws on material not merely consulted in the Berg Collection, but with effort recovered from the manuscripts there. The material he covers will be published in *EJL* 5.

22   This letter, and the reply, are printed in *DL* 2, Appendix 1, pp. 481–2. Dobson says that he saw 'a printed copy in the possession of Archdeacon Burney'.

23   Charlotte Barrett did not make clear in the *Diary and Letters* how much Burney received. Macaulay assumes that the copyright for *Cecilia* was £2000.

24   At this point, in her letter of 19 August 1782 (Berg), Burney is clear about the fact that the first edition of *Evelina* was 500 copies, reprinted in Cooke, p. 485.

25   This figure actually consorts rather well with the one I calculated for Lowndes in Chapter 2 above, where he would have cleared about £52 for each 500–copy increment. To make the £700 necessary to gain this profit and pay Burney her £200, Payne and Cadell would have had to clear £175 for each 500 copies. Their first move was to charge 15s for the five-volume edition, sewed. This meant that for the 2000 copies they would have cleared £250 on the extra 2s 6d alone. (This calculation assumes that they sold all the volumes at full price.) Since the edition was five volumes instead of three, they would have gained two fifths more per copy, or £138

for the whole edition. So far, this calculation adds up to £600. How did they procure the other £100? Payne and Cadell had turned out a large edition quickly. The printing is unevenly inked and the paper extremely thin. Cheap paper was certainly one way to save money; paper was the primary expense. The paper for the two-volume *Ianthé* cost £53 4s 0d. If Payne and Cadell had managed to halve the amount for paper they would have saved £60, and possibly the other £40 could have been saved on the large print-order – or possibly Johnson had rounded his figure up slightly.

26   In *Burford Papers*, ed. William Holden Hutton (London: Archibald Constable, 1905) p. 81.
27   Joseph A. Grau, *Fanny Burney: An Annotated Bibliography* (New York: Garland, 1981) pp. 7–9.
28   Quoted in Constance Hill, *Juniper Hall* (London & New York: J. Lane, 1904) p. 244, a lovely book which contains drawings of various houses and rooms connected to Burney, many of which are no longer extant.
29   Examples include: 'had by the Dean been entrusted', which becomes 'had been entrusted by the Dean', (p. 6, p. 958, n.6); 'and, obsequiously bending to your divine attractions, conjure' becomes simply 'and conjure' (p. 109, p. 967, n.109); 'felicity unmixed' becomes 'unmixed felicity' (p. 240, p. 978, n.240), and so on.
30   See Margaret Doody's conjecture, pp. 392–3, n. 9. Lonsdale shows that Dr Burney was very careful to control the reviewing process as best he could (pp. 108–10, 121–2).
31   *Memoirs*, 2:213–16, 220, 240. Lonsdale points out that she also misstates the publication date of Charles Burney's *Memoirs of Metastasio*, placing it a year earlier so that it does not compete with *Camilla*, p. 446 (*Memoirs*, 3:212–14).
32   46 (September 1778) 204.
33   Egerton MS 3696, ff. 1–3, reprinted with notes in the Oxford edition of *Cecilia* as Appendix I, pp. 943–6.
34   52 (January 1783) 40.
35   15 (1783) 99.
36   Doody, p. 257. Doody is talking about *Camilla*, but the point holds true for *Cecilia* and *The Wanderer* as well.
37   *Thraliana*, p. 536; Cutting-Gray reads Thrale's remark as responding to some degree to the loss of the epistolary novel, and its replacement by 'patriarchal "authoring"', p. 33.
38   For *Cecilia*, besides Margaret Doody's discussion, see the following. Alvaro Ribeiro, 'The Publication Date of Fanny Burney's *Cecilia*', *Notes and Queries* 225 (1980) 415–16, straightened out the date of publication. As mentioned above, Stewart Cooke's 'How Much was Frances Burney Paid for *Cecilia*'?, depicts the publication history. Terry Castle, *Madness and Civilization*, pp. 253–89, discusses the masquerade scene chiefly as a literary presentation, and as part of the economic theme, where the masquerade 'has become almost exclusively an emblem of luxury and the improper use of riches' (p. 260); she briefly discusses the influence of *Romeo and Juliet*; Joanne Cutting-Gray, *Woman as Nobody*, uses Foucault to analyze 'The Madness of Reason' in *Cecilia*; Julia Epstein's chapter on *Cecilia* in *The Iron Pen* deals with all of the most violent scenes; Jan Fergus,

Jane Austen and the Didactic Novel: Northanger Abbey, Sense and Sensibility and Pride and Prejudice (Totowa, New Jersey: Barnes and Noble, 1983) pp. 62–72, discusses in detail Burney's influence on Jane Austen, especially the phrase 'pride and prejudice', which Austen found in Burney's novel, and their comparable attempts to 'educate their readers' responses' (p. 72); Catherine Gallagher interprets the 'suspended identity' (p. 247) in *Cecilia* in her chapter on Burney in *Nobody's Story*; Juliet McMaster's 'The Silent Angel', though it chiefly concentrates on *Camilla* and *The Wanderer*, is also helpful for an understanding of language in *Cecilia* (*Studies in the Novel*) 21:3 (autumn 1989) 235–52; Kristina Straub in *Divided Fictions* discusses love and work in *Cecilia*.

39   Christie McDonald is at present working on an extended study of current literary works that rephrase for the contemporary audience the characters and events of the French eighteenth century.

40   For more details about the influence of other women dramatists, see Doody's Introduction to the Oxford *Cecilia*, p. xv.

41   So Sir Robert Floyer dates his letter on p. 312: May 11th, 1779.

42   By choosing the name of Lydia Languish's fictitious Ensign lover in Sheridan's *The Rivals*, Burney chooses a particularly demeaning name. This connection is not mentioned in the book, but many readers would have it in mind, and so might the Delviles.

43   Romeo says this at 2.2.1 of *Romeo and Juliet*, although Burney has changed the original 'that' to 'who', which is simply more contemporary grammar, with the effect of making Delvile seem less stuffy than he would be if he insisted on quoting the line exactly. It is also of course possible that Burney simply mis-remembered the line, and had not thought that she needed to check it (p. 510).

44   *The London Stage*, Part 5, pp. 8, 12, 106, 108, 113, 197, 275, 277, 282, 363.

45   Thomas Wilkes, *A General View of the Stage* (London, 1759) p. 251, in George Winchester Stone, Jr. and George M. Kahrl, *David Garrick: A Critical Biography* (Carbondale: Southern Illinois Univ. Press, 1979) pp. 571; 739, n. 108.

46   Syndy McMillen Conger, *Mary Wollstonecraft and the Language of Sensibility.* (Cranbury, N.J.: Fairleigh Dickinson Univ. Press, 1994), *passim.*

47   On pp. 112–13, 602, and 614.

48   Choderlos de Laclos, 'Cecilia ou les Mémoires d'une héritière' *Oeuvres Complètes* (Paris: Gallimard, 1979) p. 463: 'Cette scène de fâcheux n'aurait peut-être pas été désavouée par Molière.'

49   *Masquerade and Gender: Disguise and Female Identity in Eighteenth-Century Fictions by Women* (University Park: Pennsylvania State University Press, 1993) p. 14.

50   Richard D. Altick, *The Shows of London* (Harvard: Harvard University Press, 1978) p. 85.

51   At the masquerade, for most of the evening, Cecilia thinks that Belville is the white domino; it is only after Don Quixote is unmasked that she realizes that the white domino is really a stranger, which of course makes him even more interesting and desirable. She almost goes to the Pantheon, which she usually would consider frivolous, expensive, and dull, just because she has had such a good time talking to the white domino.

52 Innumerable critics have pointed out that Jane Austen probably derived her title from this segment of *Cecilia*. The best discussion of the similarities and differences in Burney's and Austen's conceptions of the meanings of pride and prejudice appears in Fergus's *Jane Austen and The Didactic Novel*, pp. 62–72.

53 William Godwin, *The Herald of Literature; or, A Review of the most Considerable Publications that will be made in the Course of the Ensuing Winter: with Extracts* (London: John Murray, 1784), 'Article IV. Louisa, or Memoirs of a Lady of Quality. By the Author of Evelina and Cecilia. 3 vols. 12 mo.', reprinted in William Godwin, *Four Early Pamphlets (1783–1784)*, Facsimile Reproductions with an introduction by Burton R. Pollin (Gainesville, Florida: Scholars' Facsimiles and Reprints, 1966). In an early draft of *Caleb Williams* the narrator goes mad. Godwin had reread *Cecilia* before writing his novel.

5   Sufferer, tragedian, and witness (1784–92)

1 Grau, *Annotated Bibliography*, pp. 7–8.

2 (London: George Faulkner, 1735) p. 10. Chapone is definitely the author of this pamphlet. She refers to it obliquely by quoting it in her correspondence, but there is also one direct reference to her authorship. Writing to Ballard, Anna Hopkins says about Chapone, who will probably lend Ballard her copy of Astell's *Proposal to the Ladies*: 'Tho' I knew that she was the Author of Hardships of English Laws &c: I did not mention it to you because I thought it was a Secret' (Evesham, 14 December 1741, in *The Ballard and Forster Collections*, Harvester-Wheatsheaf Microfilm, #43, f. 106).

3 Doody emphasizes Dr Burney's desire to keep his daughter-amanuensis at home, downplaying his later urgings that she seriously consider Barlow. She credits this experience with showing Burney 'the artificiality of the language with which men address women', and generally helping her to hone her ironies for Evelina's adventures in the marriage market (*Frances Burney*, p. 43); Newton argues that *Evelina* was 'a mode of coming to terms with this experience' – with Burney's sudden sense that everyone wanted her to provide for herself, the painful night when she felt already married, the loss of 'status and power', this 'species of assault' (*Women, Power, and Subversion*, p. 26). Doody dismisses Newton's argument, citing *The History of Carolyn Evelyn*, Burney's comedic treatment of Barlow, and the fact that she 'felt herself essentially safe' (p. 42). However Burney's diary version and *Evelina* are such complex works that both Doody and Newton are right. There is no reason to exclude either interpretation.

4 Judith Lowder Newton sees this experience as underlying the aggressive suitor Mr Smith in *Evelina*, and reinforcing Burney's presentation of Evelina as 'treasure rather than merchandise' in the book, in Bloom, *Fanny Burney's Evelina*, p. 67.

5 The fullest account of this relationship appears in Doody's *Frances Burney*, pp. 150–8. Hemlow provides a briefer version, chiefly on pp. 187–93, as does Kate Chisolm. Chisolm emphasizes that there were actually a series

of admirers, none of whom, it seems, wanted to marry a portionless woman. Charlotte Barrett suppressed the George Cambridge ordeal, which will finally be published in the requisite volumes of *EJL*.

6   Hester Chapone was daughter-in-law to Sarah Chapone, the author of *Hardships*. Her character and views were markedly different from her mother-in-law's.

7   Burney to Susanna, 25 November 1783, Berg MS Diary and Letters, in Doody, p. 154.

8   Berg, Folder 8. I would like to thank Mary Nash for giving me this reference.

9   Berg MS Diary and Letters, from Burney to her sister Susanna, 15 March 1789, in Hemlow, p. 190; Susanna is saying that even at this late date Cambridge may have this power, and that Burney might suffer.

10   George Cambridge married a beautiful and rich young woman named Cornelia Mierop in 1795, two years after Burney herself had married General Alexandre d'Arblay. He continued to be Burney's friend, and was especially helpful as a surrogate father to Alex after d'Arblay's death. When Burney herself was dying, George Cambridge was at the door. He was not admitted. That right he had lost by his silence in the 1780s.

11   Letter to Thrale, January 1783, in Doody, p. 162.

12   In the end, Burney was right that Thrale would lose control over her children, and that she would never regain the majority of her friends. She kept her country and her religion, and to some degree she regained her character, but only by unremitting effort. Her entire circle condemned her for her match. This sense of distastefulness was remarkably persistent. Henry William Fitzmaurice, Lord Lansdowne, who edited the letters about this affair, is withering in his condemnation, saying that she suffered from a '"sex complex"' (*The Queeney Letters* (New York: Farrar and Rinehart, 1934) p. 57).

13   Egerton MS 3695, 20 February 1781.

14   Berg, Susanna's MS Diary, 1786–92, p. 15.

15   See A. Mervyn Davies, *Strange Destiny: A Biography of Warren Hastings* (New York: Putnam, 1935) pp. 390, 433, and 414–5. Davies notes that Reynolds, Johnson, Boswell, Elizabeth Montagu, and Hannah More also became 'ardent friends and admirers' (p. 390). In 1813, after giving evidence about the East India Company to the House of Commons, Hastings received an ovation. See also T.O. Lloyd, *The British Empire, 1588–1983* (Oxford: Oxford University Press, 1984) pp. 102–5, and Geoffrey Carnall and Colin Nicholson, eds, *The Impeachment of Warren Hastings* (Edinburgh: Edinburgh University Press, 1989).

16   Unpublished excerpt from June 1787, in Hemlow, p. 36; Doody, p. 177.

17   Berg, MS Diary and Letters, p. 3295.

18   Berg, MS Diary and Letters, p. 3298; *DL* 4:119.

19   Darby remarks that 'the plays she wrote while in the Queen's service focus on the uneasy and often enforced mingling of the personal, the filial, and the socio-political' (p. 44).

20   *Observations and Reflections made in the Course of a Journey through France, Italy, and Germany*, 2 vols (London: A. Strahan and T. Cadell, 1789).

21   1.8.15, *Plays* 2:244;1.11.19, *Plays* 2:24;2.382–3, *Plays* 2:119

22   Darby points out that 'Confinement and manipulation are shown to be pervasively emotional, intellectual, and especially physical. Burney uses the stage as an effective vehicle for her depiction of these myriad types of containment.' (pp. 45–6)

23   Darby discusses as possible sources five other histories, by Robert Henry, Tobias Smollett, Rapin de Thoyras, and Edmund Burke. Hume is the primary source, but Burney had read the others and included details – atmospheric or exact – from them as well.

24   5.3.1, *Plays* 2:70, and n.

25   Doody connects de Mowbray's behavior with Dr Burney's callous treatment of his daughter while she was at Court and the chill she felt when she realized that George Cambridge would never marry her (pp. 190–1). Darby's description of this play could well be a description of Burney's life at the time: 'This is a tale of the insistence that a woman do as she is told, at any cost to herself.' (p. 87)

26   Hemlow gives an unpublished passage from Burney's diary: 'Three works which I have now in hand seize me capriciously; but I never reprove them; I give the play into their own direction, & am sufficiently thankful, in this wearing waste of existence, for so being seized at all', ('Fanny Burney, Playwright', p. 180, n. 34).

27   Sabor has established this fact (*Plays* 2:167).

28   In my account of Burney's tragedies I have emphasized the interfaces between the plays and the life. Darby argues that these Gothic plays need to be considered as 'stageable' dramas. She emphasizes their originality and force (p. 106).

29   *Plays* 2:306. Before Stewart Cooke proved otherwise, Burney scholars thought that this passage was central to the plot of *Elberta*.

30   'Lapis Lazuli', *The Collected Poems of W.B. Yeats* (London: Macmillan, 1955) p. 338.

6   *Camilla* and the family

1   Metz: la Veuve Antoine et fils, 1787, pp. 142–50. D'Arblay's name is never written out completely, but the book is ascribed to him in the *Dictionnaire de Biographie Française*, s.v. d'Arblay, and the Bibliothèque Nationale catalogues it under his name. On 26 January 1797, Burney wrote to her father that d'Arblay had seen a 'lady formerly very high in his good graces' and had asked her for some of his 'juvenile pieces' which she had brought with her in her flight from France (*JL* 3:256); in a note glossing this statement the editors mention the anonymous D'*** or Danceny volume of poems (n. 3), but do not discuss its contents.

2   (Lausanne, 1760). See Theodore Tarczylo, 'Moral Values in "La Suite de l'Entretien"', *Unauthorized Sexual Behavior during the Enlightenment*, ed. Robert P. Maccubbin, *Eighteenth-Century Life* 9. n.s. 3 (May 1985): 43–60.

3   *Forbidden Best-sellers of Pre-Revolutionary France* (New York: Norton, 1996) p. 96. The author is usually assumed to be Jean-Baptiste de Boyer, Marquis d'Argens, ca. 1748.

4   14 August 1793, to Susanna (Hemlow, p. 239); Pope, 'Eloisa to Abelard',

'What means this tumult in a Vestal's veins'? (*The Poems of Alexander Pope*
ed. John Butt (New Haven: Yale University Press, 1963) p. 252). I would
like to thank Patricia Brückmann for pointing out the source of this line.

5   Later she added a note indicating that she had not realized that Mme de
Staël truly was the mistress of M. de Narbonne.

6   Susanna replied that she trusted d'Arblay's affections; once he had chosen,
she was sure, he would remain faithful, even if his wife were ten years
older. Besides, he looked older than his age. But Susanna was distinctly
worried about the income of £100 per year (*JL* 2:41–2 n. 4).

7   In assuming that d'Arblay might want a richer and younger wife, Burney
was reflecting not merely her own insecurities, but her well honed sense
of what her neighbors would think about her marriage. She herself had
criticized Hester Thrale's marriage to Piozzi, ironically a quite similar
marriage of passion by an older woman to a Catholic foreigner. Soon after
Burney's marriage, Sarah Scott was to write to her sister Elizabeth
Montagu, observing that d'Arblay, who lacked an income, 'wanted a much
richer Wife than Miss Burney, who has scarcely an independence for
herself' (16 December 1793, Huntington Library, San Marino, CA, MS MO
5497).

8   See Constance Hill, *Juniper Hall*, pp. 166–7.

9   2 (December 1793) 450. The *Monthly Review* gave it a one-sentence paean
(12 (December 1793) 475); the *Critical Review* relegated it a respectful four
pages, mainly in order to say at the end that the 'amiable author' should
'*Write on*' (10 (March 1794): 321).

10   Doody points out that 'Burney's sense of embarrassment and exposure, of
the power of pain, the force of the illicit lethal wish, is present in this
pamphlet, as in her other writings' (p. 204). She adds that Burney makes
the practical economic point that the money will not be carried off to
France, but will help support the English economy (p. 204). Other critics
have stressed the Gothic language which emphasizes the savageness and
suffering in France. See also Claudia Johnson's introduction to the
Augustan Reprint Society edition, no. 262 (Los Angeles: William Andrews
Clark Memorial Library, University of California, 1990).

11   See *Plays*, 2:8, for a description of this history.

12   *London Stage*, 5, 1: cxlix.

13   *Thraliana*, p. 916, n. 1.

14   Sabor has studied the revisions d'Arblay suggested for the play, trying to
harden his wife, as he put it, against the first thorns she had experienced
in the roses of her career. Sabor concludes, 'D'Arblay's belief that he would
be at best a mediocre collaborator in Burney's literary productions thus
proved to be true, and he never again attempted to revise her works in this
fashion. It would, of course, have been difficult for Burney to have turned
his prose directives in French into the formal English blank verse of her
play, and it is equally difficult to envisage a Burney tragedy with a
powerful resolute hero such as d'Arblay's Edwy and a strong, self-sacri-
ficing heroine such as his Elgiva' ('"Altered, improved, copied, abridged"',
p. 135).

15   The Blooms, editors of *Camilla*, surmise that Lionel 'is a composite of three
personalities significant in FB's life: her half-brother Richard Thomas; her

brother Charles, Jr.; and her friend Charles Locke' (p. 79, n. 1). Burney might also have had James in mind, remembering how she felt when he emphasized the fact that she couldn't read by putting books upside down in her hands.

16 Sir John Hawkins' 1787 *Life of Johnson* had included Johnson's remark that 'My old friend, Mrs Carter, could make a pudding as well as translate Epictetus', in James Boswell, *Boswell's Life of Johnson*, ed. George Birkbeck Hill, revised and enlarged edition by L.F. Powell, 6 vols (Oxford: Clarendon Press, 1934–64) p. 123, n. 4.

17 'The Silent Angel', p. 242; McMaster also writes about the body in *Camilla*, summarizing *Camilla* as 'a sustained meditation on the relation of mind to body, and the ways in which the one can be figured forth in the other. It is more especially a meditation on woman's body: its determining force, its value in the market, its status as a system of signs' *Burney Letter* 3,1 (spring 1997) 5. The best and fullest discussion of *Camilla* is Doody's, in *Frances Burney*, pp. 199–273.

18 Hemlow, p. 152; Berg, from Burney to Susanna, sometime between 14 July and 16 August 1782.

19 This scene provides the title of Julia Epstein's *Iron Pen* and she designates it as 'the harrowing climax of Burney's third novel' (p. 123); Doody discusses this scene as 'an author's complete idea of hell' (p. 265); she also discusses it at length in her article, 'Deserts, Ruins, and Troubled Waters: Female Dreams in Fiction and the Development of the Gothic Novel', *Genre* 10 (winter 1977) 548–52.

20 The case of *Evelina* is complicated, since Macartney appears to be attempting suicide with his pistols when Evelina rescues him, but later admits that he was planning a robbery. If the robbery goes awry, he plans to kill himself. Robbery, as Macartney sees it, is itself a destructive act.

21 D.C. Coleman, *The British Paper Industry 1495–1860* (Westport, Conn.: Greenwood Press, 1975; originally published by the Clarendon Press, Oxford, 1958) pp. 117–19.

22 Another plan was 'to make 4 *udolphoish* [meaning very thick octavo] volumes, & reprint the Edition that succeeds the subscription in 6 volumes duod^{mo} common, for a raised price' (*JL* 3:137).

23 She disputed this point with her father, who she assumed was resisting her argument: '*now don't fly Dr Burney!* – I own I do not like calling it a *Novel*: it gives so simply the notion of a mere love story, that I recoil a little from it. I mean it to be *sketches of Characters & morals, put in action*, not a Romance. I remember the Word *Novel* was long in the way of Cecilia, as I was told, at the Queen's House.' (*JL* 3:117)

24 See *JL* 3:119, n. 8.

25 See 'The Cash accompt [sic] books of William Strahan' (6 vols, 1777–1829, BL Add. MSS. 48, 828–33), under 28 December 1797 (Vol. 1), cited in *JL* 3:111 n. 4. This was the price charged by the publishers for five volumes.

26 Gisborne did not approve of novels, suggesting in his *Enquiry into the Duties of the Female Sex* that women should read poetry instead.

27 The reviews included: *English Review* 28 (August 1796) 178–80; *Analytical Review* 24 (August 1796) 142–8; *Monthly Mirror* 2 (August 1796) 226–7; *Critical Review* 18 (September 1796) 26–40; *Monthly Review* n.s 21 (October

1796) 156–63; *Scots Magazine* 58 (October 1796) 691–7; *British Critic* 8 (November 1796) 527–36; *Monthly Magazine & British Register* 3 (January 1797) 47. See the discussion of the reviews in Edward A. and Lillian D. Bloom's introduction to the Oxford World's Classics edition, pp. xix–xxi, and Epstein, *Iron Pen*, pp. 205–7.

28   The source is the 'Verses on the Death of Dr Swift, 1731', 'Nor, can I tell what Criticks thought 'em; / But, this I know, all People bought 'em', in Jonathan Swift, *The Poems of Jonathan Swift*, ed. Harold Williams, 2nd edn (Oxford: Clarendon Press, 1958) 2:565, ll. 311–12.

7   Independence, marriage, and comedies without fetters

1   Sarah Harriet Burney and Frances Burney needed to be generous with one another. They had to overcome experiences like the fact that Mary Wollstonecraft reviewed *Clarentine*, damning it as 'exactly proper, according to established rules... an imitation of Evelina in water-colours' (*Analytical Review* 24 (November 1796) 404).

2   Lorna J. Clark, *The Letters of Sarah Harriet Burney*, p. 87, n. 1. Hemlow and many subsequent biographers have assumed that James and Harriet had an incestuous relationship. Clark argues convincingly that this was not the case (pp. xxxvi–xli).

3   Berg, Susanna Burney, Holograph Diary, 1786–92.

4   Doody has pointed out that anger pervades this little commonplace book, an observation as just as it is subtle, p. 288. HM 293 'Consolatory extracts ... c 1800', The Huntington Library, San Marino, CA.

5   Berg. For the best succinct discussion, see *Plays*, 1:105–7. Darby finds in all the late comedies, however, that 'the heroines' responses to the competing forces of finance, the family, and class are more psychologically complex' than in *The Witlings*, p. 109.

6   Darby stresses that these plays 'focus primarily on the coercive potential the institution of the family has in confining female choice and evaluating daughterly and wifely behavior according to very strict notions of obliga-tion, loyalty, and obedience', p. 130. This is true, but as Darby also points out, questions of class dominate *A Busy Day*, and in *The Woman-Hater* the irrepressible Joyce Wilmot breaks through the strictures that bind her.

7   New Brunswick: Rutgers University Press. The Wallace edition was published both in hardback and paperback. The hardback edition contains a description of the manuscript, an analysis of Wallace's editorial changes, and notes that are omitted in the paperback edition.

8   Jeremy Brian, *The Stage and Television Today*, 11 November 1993, in *Plays*, 1:291.

9   3.49–52, *Plays*, 1:349. Sabor notes that 'Toothpicks were often of expensive materials, such as tortoiseshell, affording an opportunity for fashionable display.'

10   Hemlow adds that *A Busy Day* 'with its original scenes and its realistic and satiric comedy will now afford more amusement'. 'Fanny Burney: Playwright', p. 189.

11   This plot where blood tells might seem over-used to a twentieth-century

reader, but it remained popular, resurfacing alive and well in George Eliot's *Felix Holt* (1866), where the heroine Esther seems too refined to be a minister's daughter, and it finally appears that in fact she is much more highly born.

12 EJL *3:239*. Unfortunately, this statement is followed by four obliterated lines.

13 1773 (Chiswick: C. Whittingham, 1822) p. 97. Chapone advises reading exactly those periodicals that Joyce is tossing away.

14 See Hogan, *The London Stage*, Lamb's comments on Jordan, 1:cxxi.

15 The quotations here are from an 1821 compendium of Hill's materials, *The Actor; or a Guide to the Stage* (London: Lowndes, 1821), a 're-arrangement-of Hills' celebrated Essay upon the Histrionic Art', p. 6.

16 John Hill, *The Actor: A Treatise on the Art of Playing* (London: R. Griffiths, 1750) p. 178.

17 3.10.78–9; *Plays* 1:239. In *King Lear* the comparable passage is: 'they'll have me whipp'd for speaking true, thou'lt have me whipp'd for lying; and sometimes I am whipp'd for holding my peace' (1.4.190–3).

8   *The Wanderer*

1 The materials for this discussion are scattered throughout *JL* 7. I have given page numbers only when I have quoted.

2 The mastectomy letter is reprinted, for instance, in the anthology *Eyewitness to History*, ed. John Carey ((1987) New York: Avon, 1990) pp. 272–7; Richard Selzer, a doctor, opens his book *Raising the Dead* by referring to the fact that Burney's surgeon has tears in his eyes (New York: Whittle Books in association with Viking, 1994); Penelope Fitzgerald used it as the basis for her fictional description of an operation without anesthetic in *The Blue Flower* (Boston: Houghton Mifflin, 1995) pp. 190–4; Marilyn Yalom summarizes Burney in *A History of the Breast*, noting that 'Burney's description of the surgery itself remains one of the landmark moments in the literature of breast cancer. Her story is told with such lucidity that one marvels at the author's courage, both during the harrowing procedure and afterward, when she forced herself to relive it in writing' (New York: Knopf, 1997) p. 224.

3 *JL* 6:597. This injunction covers a fair copy of the original manuscript. Both copies are at the Berg. All of the quotations about this operation are drawn from *JL* 6:596–616.

4 Julia Epstein, in her excellent, exhaustive discussion of this text, mentions that Mary Astell, 'who died of breast cancer in 1731, is reputed to have reported of her mastectomy only that she "prayed to God and ... didn't cry out"'. Lady Delacour in Maria Edgeworth's novel *Belinda* (1801) refuses to have her injured breast treated, fearing the mutilation (*Iron Pen*, pp. 77–8).

5 Epstein points out that mutilation, though implicit everywhere in the narrative, is never made explicit.

6 There are four drafts of the agreement at the Berg; the final draft is in the Osborn Collection at Yale University. The House of Longman at this junc-

ture consisted of Thomas Norton Longman, son of the founder, Owen Rees, Cosmo Orme, Thomas Hurst, and Thomas Brown. Rees undertook much of the negotiating. At the back of one of the drafts there is a summary in his handwriting. At least two people took part in the penciled exchange.

7   Burney's terms were: £1500 for a first edition not to exceed 3000 copies, £500 for a second edition of a thousand copies, and £250 apiece for the next four editions, with inspections to force the printing of these subsequent editions, also no more than a thousand copies apiece. Hence, she would not gain the full £3000 until the printing of the sixth edition. The initial £1500 would be paid much earlier in the process than was usual, and at a stated period unrelated to sales: £500 on delivery of the manuscript, £500 six months after publication, and £500 one year after publication. These terms show how confident Burney was in the quality of *The Wanderer*. She believed that it would sell 8000 copies, a huge and unusual number.

8   Egerton MS 3700A, f. 208. Allen's response to the first pages may have been less enthusiastic – they are illegible.

9   Unfortunately, this letter has vanished (*JL* 7:240, n. 2).

10 This, at any rate, is the way Burney remembers it in July 1815, just after Hazlitt's review (*JL* 8:317). The comment by Byron was noted by J.T.W. Angerstein on a scrap of paper, now in the Egerton MS (Hemlow, p. 338).

11 *Monthly Review 76 (April 1815) 415, 416.*

12 Craft-Fairchild, *Masquerade and Gender: Disguise and Female Identity in Eighteenth-Century Fictions by Women* (University Park: Pennsylvania University Press, 1993), emphasizes that Harleigh idealizes Juliet, and intrudes on her (pp. 140–41). Like the many characters that Burney makes deliberately inconsistent, Harleigh is both a typical and an exceptional man.

13 Doody writes, 'The kind of insults made to Madame Duval and M. Dubois in *Evelina* are now political issues and central topics in *The Wanderer*.' (p. 326) See also, *The Wanderer*, Appendix I, 'The French Revolution in *The Wanderer*', pp. 875–883. Rogers, *Frances Burney: The World of 'Female Difficulties'*, calls her chapter on *The Wanderer* 'A Political Analysis of the World'.

14 For a brilliant discussion of the theme of metamorphosis in this book, see Craft-Fairchild, pp. 123–62. Craft-Fairchild emphasizes the way women are hampered by their need to appear acceptable; she discusses Juliet mainly in relation to her alter ego, Elinor.

15 Doody discusses inventively and exhaustively the names in all of the novels, passim. Of 'Ellis', she mentions the conection to 'l.s.d.' and the reverberation 'elle' among Ellis, Elinor, and Gabri*ella*, noting the importance of 'Elle is' (pp. 329, 331).

16 *The Wanderer*, p. 162, Burney's ellipsis; Rogers points out this passage and makes the Brontë connection, p. 158.

17 Berg, Miscellaneous Notebook 87, pp. 11–12.

18 In the case of 'humours of a milliner's shop', this phrase found its way into the final copy (p. 426). The editors' note emphasizes that 'humours' indicate 'modes of characteristic behaviour ... also freaks, vagaries of the

place. The phrase hints at Ben Jonson's influence on Burney's ideas of characterization' (p. 936). Jonson's satiric portraits undoubtedly affected Burney. He too had written a play about a woman-hater, for instance. But the deeper sources of this psychology were certainly influencing Burney as well, and she quotes Shakespeare much more often than Jonson.

19 Juliet's isolation ultimately proves her strength. Cerulia needs to die, but Juliet, like a 'female Robinson Crusoe' has drawn on her independent resources to rescue herself (p. 873).

20 John Gross, *The Rise and Fall of the Man of Letters* (London: Weidenfeld and Nicolson, 1969) p. 2.

21 Gross, p. 1. Gross says categorically that 'it was only at the beginning of the nineteenth century that the review emerged as a really powerful institution, a major social force ... no one has ever doubted that essentially the revolution which Carlyle describes dates from the launching of the *Edinburgh Review* in 1802' (p. 2).

22 Gross, p. 5.

23 Myron F. Brightfield, *John Wilson Croker* (Berkeley: University of California Press, 1940) p. 317.

24 Macaulay was writing to his sister Hannah, quoted in John Clive, *Macaulay: The Shaping of the Historian* (New York: Knopf, 1973) p. 194.

25 Brightfield, p. 274.

26 The reviews of *The Wanderer* included, in roughly the order they appeared: *Anti-Jacobin Review* 46 (Apr. 1814) 347–54; *British Critic*, n.s. 1 (April 1814) 374–86; *Quarterly Review* 11 (April 1814) 123–30, by John Wilson Croker; *Theatrical Inquisitor and Monthly Mirror* 4 (April 1814) 234–7; *Gentlemen's Magazine* 84 (June 1814) 579-81; *European Magazine and London Review* 66 (November 1814); *Edinburgh Review* 24 (February 1815) 320-8, by William Hazlitt; *Monthly Review* 76 (April 1815) 412–19, by William Taylor. There is not enough room in the main text to quote from all of these reviews, but I will include a few details here: The *Anti-Jacobin Review* allowed the novel 'sound and judicious reflections'(p. 349), and other qualities that constituted 'the merit which it unquestionably possesses' (p. 340), but it also accused *The Wanderer* of excessive length, occasionally tedious incidents, and sporadic caricature. From the start, it fairly oozed disappointment. The *British Critic* stressed the fact that Burney could not publish a novel critical of France, given her sensitive personal position, and praised the book, except for its intermittently bloated style. Though not up to Mme d'Arblay's standard, this novel was better than most. The *Theatrical Inquisitor and Monthly Mirror* bristled with disappointment.

27 Croker requested *Evelina*, *Cecilia*, and *Camilla* on 9 [March], and had finished his review by the 28th (Brightfield, p. 339, quoting from the BL Murray archives. Brightfield dates Croker's letters in May, but since the review was published in April, I surmise that this is a misreading for March).

28 One aspect of nineteenth-century misogyny was simply to ignore women. Thackeray's *English Humorists of the Eighteenth Century* (1851), contains no women, only Swift, Congreve, Addison, Steele, Prior, Gay, Pope, Hogarth, Smollett, Fielding, Sterne, and Goldsmith. Of Fielding, Thackeray reports enthusiastically: 'He is himself the hero of his books, he is wild Tom Jones,

he is wild Captain Booth. ... When Fielding first came upon the town in
1727 ... His figure was tall and stalwart; his face handsome, manly, and
noble looking; to the very last days of his life he retained a grandeur of air,
and although worn down by disease, his aspect and presence imposed
respect upon the people round about him' (New York: Crowell, n.d.) pp.
128–9. Croker's vituperation encapsulates an attitude about old women
that Burney had always been aware of. 'I don't know what the devil a
woman lives for after thirty' Lord Merton said in *Evelina*, 'she is only in
other folks way' (p. 275). Daddy Crisp had warned Burney even in her 20s
that an old woman could not command respect the way a young one
could, that 'years and wrinkles' would 'succeed' (*EJL* 4, forthcoming). As
for the metaphor's references to dress, in fact 'laborious gaiety of ... attire'
had always been problematical for Burney, who could never afford to be
truly fashionable, and during her years at court had frequently lamented
the time she spent applying her needle to her inadequate wardrobe. In
France, where the Revolution had propagated a bewildering succession of
styles, Burney tried to figure out how to modify her wardrobe, and finally,
'gave over the attempt, & ventured to come forth as a Gothic *anglaise*, who
had never heard of, or never heeded, the reigning metamorphoses' (*JL*
6:290), appearing as if in costume. Croker's description of Burney is particularly ironic, because her appearance was anything but withered and had
actually improved during the ten years she had spent in France; Horace
Walpole's friend Mary Berry wrote, 'She is wonderfully improved in good
looks in ten years, which have usually a very different effect at an age
when people begin to fall off. Her face has acquired expression and a
charm which it never had before. She has gained an *embonpoint* very
advantageous to her face' (*JL* 7:52, n. 10.)

29 *Quarterly Review* 18 (1817-18) 379.
30 These comments are in the Berg Collection.
31 On 3 July 1814, from Paris, d'Arblay wrote: 'J'ai lu ton ouvrage, et je
    t'avoue que plus d'une fois j'ai été tenté de le trouver moins attachant que
    ses ainés: mais je dois – à la verité d'ajouter que le plus souvent j'ai
    reconnu mon tort, et qu'après l'avoir achevé, mon idée predominante a
    été que tu y as deployé autant de talent que dans tout ce qui l'a precedé;
    que ton plan bien conçu est superieurement executé, et que cette nouvelle
    production peut etre de la plus grande utilité. Personne ce me semble, ne
    suit mieux que toi le precepte d'Horace de mêler *l'agreable à – l'utile*; et je
    suis bien certain que tôt ou tard le Public sortira de l'espace d'apathie où
    il reste concernant *the Wand*' (*JL* 7:389).
32 *JL* 8:24–5, n. 23.
33 P.P. Howe, *The Life of William Hazlitt* (1922; Harmondsworth: Penguin,
    1949) p. 30.
34 Crabb Robinson's memoirs, 24 April 1815, in Howe, *Hazlitt*, p. 193.
35 P. 337; the later comment, that 'we perceive no decay of talent, but a
    perversion of it' (p. 338) vanishes from the later, published lectures.
36 Howe, *Hazlitt*, pp. 193–5; *JL* 8:317, n. 1.
37 According to the *Quarterly Review* 'List of New Publications' for 1814 and
    1815, no other novel cost as much as Burney's. The well-known women
    did command the highest prices. Maria Edgeworth's *Patronage*, 4 vols, sold

for £1 8s. Laetitia-Matilda Hawkins' *Rosanne, or a Father's Labour Lost* was three volumes and cost £1 7s, but her publishers F.C. and J. Rivington had decided on octavo volumes, whereas nearly every other work was duodecimo, so that her novel was probably as long as Burney's. There is one novel listed at exactly the same size: Ann of Swansea's *Conviction; or, She is Innocent: a Novel*, whose 5 vols were £1 7s 6d; Sir Walter Scott's *Waverley*, also published by Longman, was 3 vols and cost a guinea (Scott had been offered a £700 copyright fee, but had turned it down for profit sharing, which paid off (Butler, *Edgeworth*, p. 490, n. 1)); Jane Austen's *Mansfield Park*, also 3 vols, sold for 18s.

38   These comments are filed under Holographs A-M in the Berg Collection.
39   Epstein, *Iron Pen*, p. 209.
40   Erin Isikoff, 'The Dilemma of the Woman of Understanding in the Gothic Social Space of the Eighteenth Century, as Depicted in the Four Novels of Frances Burney', Harvard University thesis, 1990.
41   *The Collected Essays, Journalism, and Letters of George Orwell*, eds Sonia Orwell and Ian Angus, Vol. 3: *As I Please, 1943–5* (New York: Harcourt, Brace, 1968) p. 270.

9   *Memoirs of Doctor Burney*

1   *Memoirs* 3:436. The phrase 'self-acquired accomplishments' is a theme that Lonsdale stresses as perhaps the most important facet of Dr Burney's personality, pp. 477–84.
2   The 'Narrative' is printed in *JL* 10:842–910.
3   R. Brimley Johnson, *Fanny Burney and the Burneys* (New York: Frederick A. Stokes, 1926) pp. 152–3.
4   See Darby, 'the heroine's maternal imperative legitimates her activity and permits her, unlike Burney's other dramatic heroines, to be almost entirely self-directing' (p. 67).
5   *JL* 11:188; cf. Virginia Woolf's opinion: 'When he died at the age of eighty-eight, there was nothing to be done by the most devoted of daughters but to burn the whole accumulation entire. Even Fanny's love of language was suffocated.' (*Second Common Reader*, p. 100)
6   Scholes, 2:280; Lonsdale, p. 451.
7   Cited in Nussbaum, *The Autobiographical Subject: Gender and Ideology in Eighteenth-Century England* (Baltimore: The Johns Hopkins University Press, 1989) p. 172.
8   Hawkins never wrote a tract supporting a political cause, as Burney did in her pamphlet on the *Emigrant Clergy*. She did, however, publish a separate conduct book, *Letters on the Female Mind*, whereas Burney's only published attempt along those lines was Mr Tyrold's letter in *Camilla*. Hawkins' advice book is more wide-ranging, since it takes the form of a reply to Helen Maria Williams's supportive writings on the French Revolution. Hawkins advises women to avoid politics, because 'they are a study inapplicable to female powers by nature, and withheld from us by education' (2 vols (London: Hookham and Carpenter, 1793) 1:25)). She interposes herself frequently in the book, drawing from her own experience, chiefly

arguing that 'virtuous cultivation of the mind is the only source of enjoyment to be depended on' (1:51).

9   *Anecdotes* 1:106; *Memoirs* 1:288–9; *Memoirs* 1:261.

10 De Quincey wrote in *The London Magazine* for March 1823, reprinted in *Collected Writings* 1889–90 ed. Masson 5:146; *The British Critic*, New Series, 22 (July–December 1824) 173.

11 One of the letters to d'Arblay mentions 'the joy and sadness that mix', but there is no detailed description of Dr Burney's death (*JL* 7:291).

12 (*Memoirs* 2:232); Burke refers to the man now called Francisco Jiménez de Cisneros, whose various life included political as well as religious posts. Among other things, he led the 1509 expedition which captured the African town of Oran.

13 *'The real war will never get in the books': Selections from Writers During the Civil War*, ed. Louis P. Masur (New York: Oxford University Press, 1993) p. 3.

14 *Quarterly Review* 49 (April 1833) 97, 106–7. Lonsdale argues that Croker's review is essentially correct. He goes through the review and ably supports each of its five points, concluding that Burney was writing fiction rather than biography (pp. 445–8).

15 Croker, who actually checked the records at King's Lynn to ascertain Burney's christening date, emphasized as if new the fact that she was 26 when *Evelina* was published. Macaulay, whose gift for verbal destruction rivaled Croker's, may have had this incident in mind when he said that his political opponent would go 'a hundred miles through sleet and snow, on top of a coach, in a December night, to search a parish register, for the sake of showing that a man is illegitimate, or a woman older than she says she is' (in Walter Jackson Bate, *John Keats* (Cambridge: Harvard University Press, 1963) p. 369).

16 (*JL* 12:785, n. 1); the heirs of her sister Esther presumably also received £1000, since by Dr Burney's will she and her sister were to share the income from the publication of his papers.

17 *JL* 12:976. From an early age, Burney thought 'that falsehood & (calumny) s^d never go with[ou]t being stopped & taken up or they w^d surely increase like a snow ball' (*JL* 12:976).

18 This accusation was repeated by Mrs Delany's housekeeper, who did not like the portrait of her employer in the *Memoirs*. See Lonsdale, p. 447.

19 Walter Jackson Bate, *Samuel Johnson* (New York: Harcourt Brace, 1977) pp. 202–5.

20 See Lennard Davis, *Factual Fictions* (New York: Columbia University Press, 1983).

21 Henry Fielding, *Love in Several Masques* (London: John Watts, 1728) 4.4, p. 54.

22 7 April 1781; Egerton MS 3700.

23 Macaulay, *Literary and Historical Essays*, 1:222. This essay was published in 1831, too late for Burney to have read it as a source for this opinion. She and Macaulay simply agreed about Boswell. This review, which was of Croker's edition, must have been immensely gratifying to Burney, since it blasts Croker nearly as fiercely as it does Boswell.

24 *Memoirs* 1:57; Frances Greville wrote the 'Ode to Indifference', one of

Burney's favorite poems, and one of the most widely known poems of the
era. Its point was that the only way to survive love's pain was indifference:
'Nor peace nor ease the heart can know / That, like the needle true, /Turns
at the touch of joy and woe – / But, turning – trembles too'! *Memoirs*
1:115). Burney often read this poem when she needed solace.

25 Stone and Kahrl, *David Garrick: A Critical Biography* (Carbondale: Southern
Illinois University Press, 1979) p. 383; *EJL* 2:95–7; *Memoirs* 1:344–60;
Lonsdale, pp. 224–5.

10 Fiction and truth

1 *JL* 6:730; in the introduction to *Journals and Letters* Hemlow mentions
that Burney's 'immediate end' was to gather materials for Alex and his as-
yet-unborn family, 'dream readers in a dream rectory, that is, for
Alexander and his children' (*JL* 1:xxxv–vi); Falle's remarks are similar
(*JL* 5:xxxv).

2 These phrases appear in the title of Doody's biography and the title of one
of Rogers' articles.

3 *EJL* 1:1; the introductions to *EJL* and *JL* discuss these activities in detail.

4 Egerton MS, Eng. MS. 589.53.

5 Berg, notebook for January–June, 1839, p. 32.

6 Egerton MS 3701L, f. 74r, p. 35.

7 Berg, Scrapbook: Fanny d'Arblay and family. 1653–1890.

8 Egerton MS 3693, ff. 217–18b, in *JL* 12:953, n. 1.

9 The records of the Burney family's distress over Croker's allegations
remain widely scattered through the manuscripts both at the Berg and in
the British Library's Egerton MSS.

10 See *JL* 12:982–9 for the story of these graves, how Burney was by her direction buried *in* her son Alexander's grave, how d'Arblay's simple black
headstone was somehow lost and Frances and Alexander's monument was
moved. It is a confused and lamentable story. Perhaps the d'Arblay graves
will be rediscovered one day, so that all three can have a memorial erected
at the actual gravesites.

11 *DL* 1:21. In the original Burney mentions in a previous, here omitted,
paragraph that she has written nothing in her diary before March. Barrett
does include as a kind of preface a few paragraphs from the initial invo-
cation to 'Nobody', calling it 'THE AUTHOR'S INTRODUCTION', but
omits all intervening material, saying in a footnote that the material
before 1778 is too personal, and the decision to address Nobody 'rather
embarrassing' (*DL* 1:19–20). Annie Raine Ellis filled this gap by publishing
her excellent *ED*. Familiar with all the papers available to her, Ellis
included relevant materials written by other family members, such as
Susanna and Charlotte Burney, and Maria Allen. A complete list of the
writers drawn on appears on pp. xci–ii. The Troide edition replaces this
work, but Ellis is still worth reading for the other manuscripts excerpted
and for the excellent notes.

12 *Quarterly Review* 70 (June 1842) 135; 136; 157.

13 Egerton MS 3702A, f. 90; Macaulay also assumed that Croker had asked for

Johnsonian materials and had been refused (See Brightfield, *Croker*, pp. 359–63).

14 *DL* 1:21–2. Burney's half-sister Sarah Harriet said in 1842 of the early volumes of the diaries that 'After wading with pain and sorrow through the tautology and vanity of the first volume, I began to be amused by the second, and every succeeding volume has, to my thinking, increased in power to interest and entertain. That there is still considerable vanity I cannot deny. In her life, she bottled it all up, & looked and generally spoke with the most refined modesty, & seemed ready to drop if ever her works were alluded to. But what was kept back, and scarcely suspected in society, wanting a safety valve, found its way to her private journal'. Sarah Harriet thinks that Barrett should have omitted more than she did. She abhorred Croker's review, however, calling it 'coarsely & ill-temperedly done' (*Letters*, p. 463).

15 Grau, pp. 32, 36. In *English Humorists of the Eighteenth Century* (1851), Thackeray mentioned no woman novelist, but he quoted at length (and with occasional condescension) in *The Four Georges* from the 'capital "Burney Diary and Letters"',and, as Doody points out, his post-Waterloo scenes in Brussels in *Vanity Fair* owe much to Burney. *The Complete Works of William M. Thackeray, Roundabout Papers, The English Humorists, Miscellaneous* (New York: Crowell, n.d.) p. 319; Doody, p. 372.

16 1:546; if this is 'woman's English', one wonders what Macaulay would require of men's English.

17 Beginning with Austin Dobson's edition of Barrett's selections, there has been a persistent strain of criticism which argues that Burney's diaries and letters are better than her efforts in other genres. Dobson himself had already written in his biography that he could not fathom 'why Macaulay, who praised the *Diary* so much, did not praise it more, – did not, in fact, place it high above Mme D'Arblay's efforts as a novelist' (p. 205). Reviews in both the *Spectator* and *The Nation* claimed in 1905 that the diary is her 'masterpiece', her 'most permanent contribution to literature'. Peter Quennell, reviewing a selection by Lewis Gibbs in 1940, notes that though the *Diary* is her 'masterpiece', it also 'is a record of an exceedingly limited mind – of a spirit circumscribed by upbringing and taste and temperament' (Grau, *Annotated Bibliography*, pp. 39, 40, 43). George Sherburn, who places Burney's novels in the courtesy-book tradition, does not quite commit himself; 'perhaps', he writes, her *Diary* is 'her greatest work after all' (p. 1033).

18 Grau, p. 43.

19 This detail is not in Barrett.

20 *JL* 8:500. This was not in fact a representation of Jesus, 'but rather a crude allegorical representation of the rainbow' (n. 30).

21 *JL* 8:504; the entire Bonn stopover is missing from Barrett.

22 There is a blue plaque on this small, lovely building commemorating the time when Burney lived there.

Index

With the exception of FB, authors' works are listed at the end of their respective entries.